Magheen

Louise Gherasim

E.M. Press, Inc.
Manassas, VA

This is an original work of fiction. Except for actual historic characters, events, and places, all characters in this book have no existence outside the imagination of the author.

First Edition

ISBN: 1-880664-24-0
Library of Congress Catalog Card Number: 97-6765

E.M. Press, Inc.
P.O. Box 4057
Manassas, VA 20108

To my beloved husband, Teodor.

Doru

I know that God
Designed your heart.
He made it pure
A place apart.
A garden filled with love.

Louise

FOREWORD

While the historical facts are accurate to the best of my knowledge, as are the movements of historical characters, license has been taken with regard to the names and actions attributed to fictional family members of the principal historical characters.

ACKNOWLEDGMENTS

I wish to thank Jane Bly for her help in typing this book. Patient at all times, she was available at a moment's notice. Fast, efficient, and accurate, she made the work so much easier.

A very special thank you to John K. Payne of Payne Literary Agency, Inc., New York, who as far back as 1984 encouraged me with the words: You're a born writer, and you have that kind of drive that can result in success so don't give up before the miracle, please.

And to my editor, Ms. Ellen Beck, *go raibh mile maith agut* (a thousand thanks) for the faith and confidence placed in my abilities. For your encouragement and patience, and for making it so easy to reach you at all hours, day or night, a most grateful thank you. You are, indeed, someone very special.

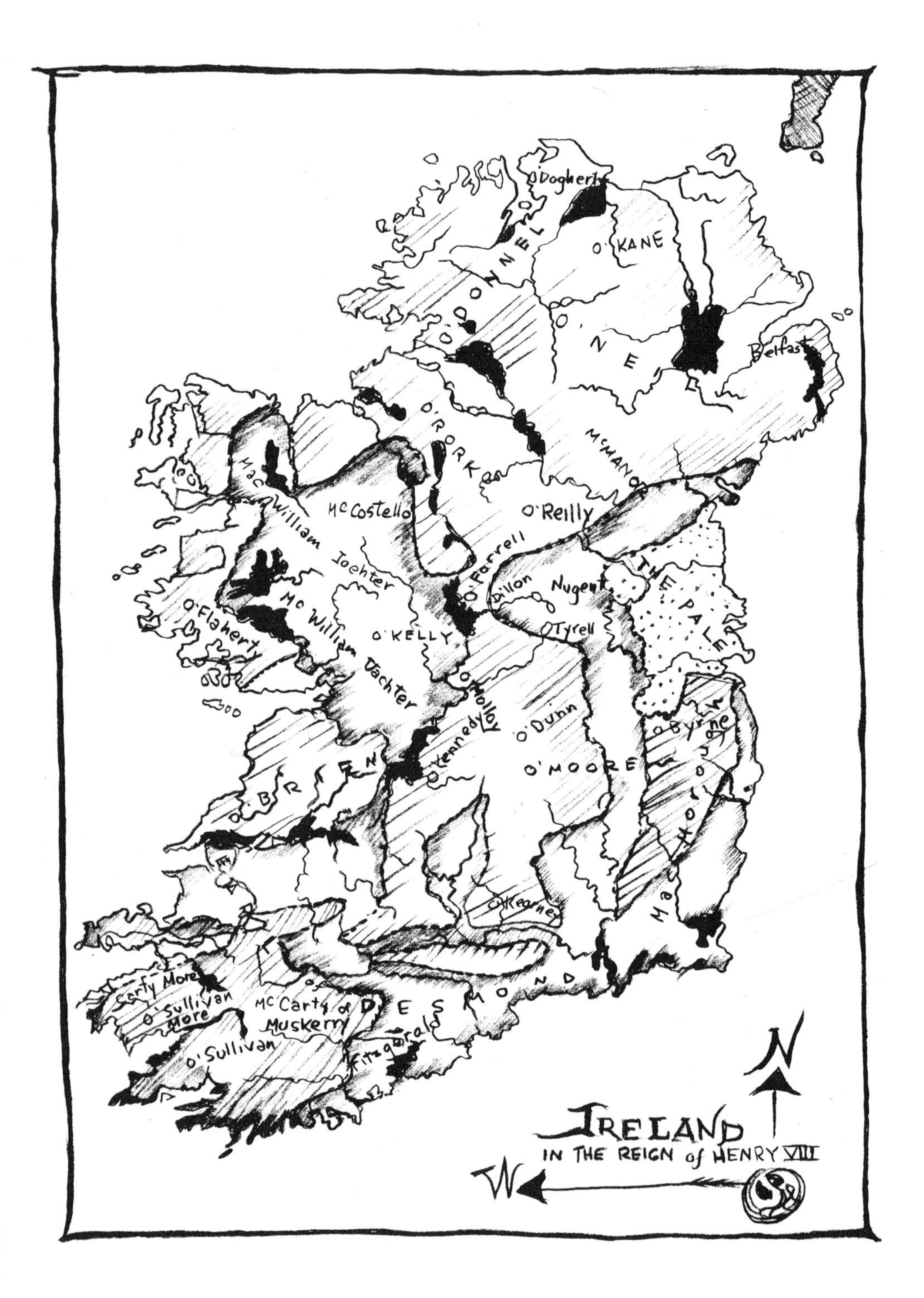
IRELAND
IN THE REIGN of HENRY VIII
O'Dogherty
O'DONNEL
O'KANE
O'NEIL
Belfast
O'RORKE
McMANON
Mac William Iochter
McCostello
O'Reilly
O'Farrell
Dillon
Nugent
THE PALE
Tyrell
O'Flaherty
McWilliam Dachter
O'KELLY
O'Molloy
O'Kennedy
O'Dunn
O'Byrne
O'MOORE
O'BRIEN
Mac Morrogh
O'Kearney
DESMOND
Carty More
O'Sullivan More
McCarty of Muskerry
Fitzgerald
O'Sullivan
N
W

Prologue

"So ye're Margaret!" Con O'Neill's great bass voice boomed to the oak rafters and echoed around the stone columns in the ancient hall of his castle home.

"No, no!.... Magheen...Sir." The small voice was clear and determined. No one knew that the little girl's knees felt weak under her green silken gown, the full skirt of which covered her right down to the tips of her soft leather slippers, for looking up at the enormous figure seated before her, the large brown eyes did not flicker. This great hulk of a man, they told her, was her grandfather. He looked cross and Magheen, at five, knew fear for the third time in her young life. But this time, she was determined to be brave.

She remembered when her mama had died some six weeks before, how she had cried until she thought she'd shrivel up like a dried plum. She cried because her lovely mama had gone to heaven and would not come back ever again; cried because she was all alone and there was no one to love her. She was so afraid in the sad, lonely days that followed, when all by herself in a big house with only the servants, she awaited her father's homecoming. The servants had little time to spend with her, though they felt sorry for her and tried to express their feelings. Magheen, unaccustomed to words of comfort or expressions of sympathy from any save her mother, became more confused.

Magheen shivered even as she sat beside the blazing turf fire in the kitchen. Silent, wide-eyed and pale-faced, she had again started to suck her thumb, a habit long forsaken, and she had acquired the completely new habit of biting her nails. It was all so strange, so different now. There was a great empty space inside her like a hollow reed, and she knew that the emptiness would never again be filled. Only the soft, warm arms of her lovely mother about her, only the happy singing laugh and the love in her brown eyes could make that great deep empty place full again.

One day, she overheard some of the servants talking. "Poor child, what is to become of her?"

"Expect she'll be going to live with her grandfather."

"No, I won't!" she screamed. "Who'll look after Papa if I'm not here?"

"There, there, a leana. Didn't mean to upset you none."

"You'll see! When Papa comes home, everything will be all right. He won't let them take me away."

"Yes, yes, of course," the servant reassured her.

"When will Papa be home?" she demanded.

"Soon, very soon."

Magheen knew that her father was with the fighting men in her grandfather's army and that they were trying to drive the Sasanach, those bad men who didn't belong in her country, out of Ireland.

"They have a land of their own called England and that's where they should stay," she had heard her father say.

One cold evening, after what seemed like a very long time indeed, her father did come home, but Magheen saw little of him. He spent many hours talking to the priest, Father Dwyer, to the servants in the house, and to the workmen. Finally, he took her by the hand and led her to her mother's room. At the bedside, he lifted her up so that she could kiss her mama's cold grey cheek. A shiver ran through her body, and she wanted to cry out, but the servants had gathered around the bed. They were all wearing their best clothes. Some cried, others prayed with mumbled words and bowed heads, and she knew she must be silent. The priest, in flowing robes and low tones, sang sad Latin songs while he sprinkled the bed with holy water. The big candles sputtered, and a river of hot wax ran down the bronze candlesticks to the base, forming little lumps that kept getting bigger and bigger. The room was damp and cold, and the air was heavy with the odors of burning tapers and incense.

Magheen, standing beside the bed, began to feel dizzy and

faint; then the room was spinning. She gripped the bed clothes to steady herself as she drifted into a hazy world of sadness and loneliness. She didn't hear the rest of the prayers, the Litany for the Dead, or the Extreme Unction Rites. She woke up sitting in a chair as they put the lid on the great wooden box into which they had placed her mama. When they nailed it shut, it felt like they were hammering at her small heart.

She started to cry. It was then that her papa took her in his strong arms and told her how important it was for her to be brave. Yes, she remembered the words: "Mo stoirin, come now. You must be a brave little girl; show your brave face." She tried because she wanted to please her father. But why was it so important for her to show a brave face? She couldn't answer at the time; only somehow, she knew it was expected of her because she was different. She knew she was different from the other people who moved about her, the servants who kept the house running in an orderly manner, the workers on her father's lands, the people in the small houses beyond the woods, but she didn't know why at that moment. Then, as she pondered, it occurred to her that everyone expected her father to be brave because he was a great soldier, and her mama had told her often how brave he was. Perhaps, she thought, it was because she was a soldier's little girl that she must also be brave. That must be it, she decided. Yes, of course, and that must be why she was different, too.

So Magheen stopped crying. She put on a brave face and pretended that the hurt wasn't there, deep down in her small heart. The baby innocence left the large vibrant eyes, and from that day her naturally happy, confident disposition also left her. She withdrew into herself, becoming defensive and suspicious of the many adults who now, it seemed, had taken control of her life.

Then word came of her father's death. They told her that he had been killed by the Sasanach, and that he had gone to live with her mama, leaving her all alone in the world. At that time, she remembered her father's words, and she put on a brave face. Nor did she forget, a few days later, when the carriage came and she knew she would never see her home again for she must go and live with strange people in her grandfather's castle far away in County Tyrone.

But despite the brave face, Magheen could not help being afraid inside; now as she stood before the old man with the black beard and the dark eyes, she felt a great fear grip her stomach and drag at her legs. Her mouth was dry. She wanted to cry out, but her tongue wouldn't move. She wanted to run from the spot to which she felt rooted, to run and run and run and never stop until she reached the place where her mama and papa lived. But her little legs refused to budge.

"Well, now." O'Neill studied the child before him. Too thin, but well formed; intelligent, aye, that was obvious. Eyes beautiful, but too sad. Pluck, by God! She certainly had that. There was no doubt about it, this lass had the O'Neill blood.

"So ye're Magheen, eh?" The old man was amused. He threw back his blackbearded face and laughed aloud.

"Ha, ha, ha. Ye have no mind to be English then? It's Magheen ye'll be called and nothing else! Ha, ha, ha."

Magheen watched him intently. She hadn't said anything funny, so why was he laughing? At her? Surely, not in front of all these strange people. All grown-ups, too. She became angry.

"Sir," the treble voice with its commanding inflection silenced O'Neill. "I'm Magheen! Magheen Ni Neill. Are you my grandfather?"

O'Neill again focused on the small figure boldly standing before him. The serious, determined little face, the poised proud head, and the large pleading eyes touched his heart.

"By all the saints of Ireland," he cried, "ye're an O'Neill an' no mistaking it. Aye, Lass, that ye are. Come give yer old grandpa a wee kiss."

During the conversation that followed, Magheen learned that she was to be sent to a far off place in the west called Ballindee, to her mother's only brother, Tom O'Connor.

"There's no fighting over there, Lass. An' what's more, the Sasanach won't find ye. They'd like nothing better now than to get their filthy hands on ye and haul ye off to England."

Magheen shivered. "Oh, no! I don't want to go to England."

"Nor shall ye, a gra."

"But why would the Sasanach want me, Grandpa?"

"Because ye're an O'Neill. Ye see, love, they aim to have all the children of Irish lords brought up in England. That way they hope to make us all English one day."

"No, no, Grandpa, I don't want to be English. I'm Irish! Papa always said I must not forget that."

"Yes, yer papa was right. So to yer Uncle Tom ye'll be goin', Lass, and that as soon as possible."

"Yes, Grand...pa." Magheen yawned.

"This child is tired," O'Neill spoke to the women in waiting. "We'll speak some more tomorrow, child."

"Grandpa, I'm...I'm glad...I came," she said as she was led from the room.

The Lord of Tyrone smiled. There's a wise head on those baby shoulders, he thought.

The following day Magheen saw her grandfather for only a few brief moments before setting out in the company of trusted friends for the little village of Ballindee. But, before she bade him farewell, Magheen learned more about herself and the part she was expected to play in her country's future.

"Yer father told ye never to forget that ye're Irish; now I'm telling ye, never forget that ye're an O'Neill. 'Tis a proud name. Hold yer head high, bow to no one, an' when ye're of age to marry, choose a husband from a noble Gaelic house."

"Oh, Grandpa, that's a long way off. My head can't think that far."

"Ha, I'm not asking ye to think of it now, child. Only remember yers is a lofty destiny. Keep that chin up." The Lord of Tyrone tilted Magheen's head as he said the words. Then he bent down and placed a kiss on her creamy forehead. "Go with God, child. Be a true O'Neill."

Magheen was hustled away before she had time to say anything; but in her heart, she felt that an enormous burden had been laid upon her. She would be great, as great as her father and even as great as her grandfather, The O'Neill.

PART I

One

Magheen left the house in a hurry. The morning light cast a ruddy glow over the distant hills as she reached the stables. She glanced over her shoulder and paused a moment, a warm feeling rising within. Glistening sunbeams danced on the granite facade of the O'Connor ancestral home, Inis Fail. One day it would all be hers, so beautiful, how she loved it. Then she reflected, it hadn't always been so. For ten years before, when she came to Ballindee as a little girl of five, things were very different. She hated everything and everyone. She remembered the day that Moll, the housekeeper, had tried to comfort her. Thinking that she needed a playmate, Moll had sent to the village to invite Eileen O'Reilly to come to Inis Fail. But when the two were introduced, the proud Magheen, according to Moll, looked the village child up and down, raised her head, and clenched her teeth. "I won't play with her." She shouted and stomped out of the kitchen and ran to her room where she threw herself on her bed.

"Oh, Mama, Papa—why did you leave me? I want to go home."

The loud sobs drew Moll to her bedside a short time later and picking her up, the housekeeper pressed the tear-stained face to her ample bosom. She could not bring herself to deliver the well-earned scolding; instead she caressed the yellow curls.

"Come now, let old Moll love you," she whispered. "I don't have a little girl to love. Like you, I've nobody in the whole wide world."

Her great sad eyes looking even sadder, Magheen lifted her head. "I don't want to love anyone. I'm supposed to be brave, Papa said."

"Praise be to God! Sure you're only a wee girl. You're not supposed to be anything."

Magheen opened her mouth to protest, but nothing came out.

"Now dry those eyes; you've cried enough for one day."

It felt strange, she remembered, to be in the strong arms of the servant woman. She had a nice clean smell; a mixture of lavender, herbs, and turf, and Magheen felt comforted for the first time in many weeks.

Magheen, or little Margaret, had an impish face. A tousled head of golden curls, that no amount of brushing could control, was a legacy from her paternal grandmother. But it was her large, melancholy, brown eyes that were her most attractive feature. She had but to turn those eyes in Moll Flynn's direction and that good woman was completely under her spell.

"No more stray kittens in this house. We scarce have enough milk to feed ourselves, an' you keep abringing in every scrawny creature from here to Donegal." Moll took hold of the ends of her long coarse apron as if to shoo from her spotless kitchen the tiny, shivering, half-starved animal that followed Magheen.

"Oh, Moll, you can't! You can't turn the poor little creature out! She hasn't a home. I found her down on the strand today."

"Aye, indeed you did. An' do you know how she got there? Well, I'll tell you," said Moll, gathering up the bedraggled kitten. "Someone tried to get rid of her, but in spite of them she survived. The crafty wee thing."

Moll looked at the frightened animal, its wet coat clinging to a boney frame. "Reminds me of yourself the night they brought you home from far off County Tyrone."

Magheen's eyes opened wide. "Heavens! I hope I didn't look like that."

"Not much better, I can tell you. Sure, 'twas one of them horrible winter evenings with the rain pelting down in such fury that you'd a' thought 'twas the Deluge all over again. Like this wee drowned kitten you were when they carried you in. An' shivering! Sure, I thought you weren't long for this world." Moll stopped to catch her breath. "But no sooner had your little feet touched the floor than you let it be known to all that you intended to stay only till you married a Gaelic lord. Aye, with your pert, wee chin held high, you announced that you were Magheen Ni Neill. Such a great speech I never before heard in all my life from a wee lass. 'I'm Magheen,' says you, 'Magheen Ni Neill, an' soon I'll marry an Irish lord, grandpa said. An' I'm not going away with the Sasanach.'"

"Oh, Moll, I don't believe a word of it."

"Believe it or not, it's all true. Now, would your Ladyship kindly take this wretched creature out of my kitchen. I've no time to fuss with her."

Magheen paid no attention to the servant for she knew Moll hadn't the slightest intention of turning away the stray animal. The old lady made a lot of noise and appeared hard, but her heart was as soft as the yellow butter she so skillfully rolled into little balls for "his Lordship's" breakfast.

Magheen mounted Leprachaun, her sorrel mare. The years had slipped away and now she was no longer a little girl but a young woman eager for adventure.

The O'Connor estate, though modest in dimensions, was to the village folk a fortress rising from the rocky soil. The family owned all the land west of the town of Ballindee, down to the treacherous rocks that stoutly defended the delicate blooms of spring and summer from the pounding Atlantic. The house stood facing the sea and exposed to the elements; the massive stone exterior glistened in the changing light. Because of its remote position, it had remained in O'Connor hands through the centuries.

Magheen had been given complete freedom to come and go as she pleased on the hundred acres that surrounded Inis Fail. In her uncle's eyes she could do no wrong, and Mrs. Flynn regarded her as her "own child".

It was a brisk morning and a strong westerly brought the tang of the kelp to Magheen's nostrils. She dug her heels into the mare, and as she approached the village, she decided to go by way of the glen to the strand. There was no use telling the whole world her business.

Ballindee, meaning God's town, had been named or renamed in the early decades of Christian Ireland. No records existed to confirm or deny the fact, but tradition was strong. It was a typical fishing village, one which had known its heyday in the early centuries of Christianity and had been declining ever since. This was due, in part, to the destruction of the local monastery by the Norsemen in the 12th century and, in more recent times, to attacking English forces, which plundered on land and sea. The once thriving fishing industry carried on with Spain and Portugal was almost a thing of the past.

Emerging from a clump of trees, Magheen was within sight of the beach. She scanned the coves. No, he wasn't there. Had he gone to the fishing then, she asked herself, knowing Padraig was an early riser. She dismounted and walked Leprachaun closer to the edge of the cliff.

She heard him before she saw him. His melodious voice sent a thrill through her body. She felt her heartbeat quicken with a certain tremulous excitement. What was it about him these last months that made her feel so? She had known him all her life, for he lived with his mother in a small cabin overlooking the sea not far from Inis Fail. Yet, until recently, she had hardly paid him any mind. Now it seemed, she had only to hear his name spoken and she became alive with a fierce longing, an ache that would not be eased, with feelings so hungry, so restive, so impelling that she wondered what was happening to her. Was she losing her senses? Where was her self-control?

Padraig O'Toole was a young man in his early twenties. A strong, ruddy, weather-beaten face, topped by a red mass of tight curls, he stood over six feet tall with broad shoulders and long limbs. "A giant of a man," they called him. Padraig was a fisherman, the son of a fisherman who was the son of a fisherman before him, and so it was for generations.

Magheen hesitated. Padraig, although a real friend, was only a fisherman, not one of her kind. Moll had told her that it was time for her to be more circumspect; she must keep her distance. "It just isn't fitting for a lady to be spending time with the fisherlads, good lads an' all though they be. You're almost a woman and..." Moll wasn't ready yet to spell out the reasons. "Besides, the village folk expect you to be different. Remember your station in life." Moll's words rang in her ears.

Magheen didn't need to be told she was different; she always knew that. But what did that have to do with Padraig? He was different too. Didn't he spend time with her uncle? Long hours in fact.

No one else, with the exception of Father Donald, spent so much time talking and discussing with him, and she knew Moll exaggerated at times. What did she expect? She had to speak to...to someone besides the housekeeper and her uncle, for pity sakes.

In spite of herself, she was propelled in the direction of the singing. Reason and judgment kept tugging in opposite directions. Why was she, Magheen Ni Neill, seeking the company of a lowly fisherman? But her thoughts kept suggesting that Padriag was no ordinary fisherman. "He's a man of letters like my uncle, isn't he?" she addressed Leprachaun. The mare paid no attention; the dew-laden grasses were too sweet. How many evenings had he spent in the company of her Uncle Tom, the older man imparting the riches of his life-long interest in the classics. Yes, Padraig was different. He's got a keen mind and a gentle nature, a man of culture and refinement, albeit a fisherman, she concluded.

The singing stopped. Magheen watched him as he stitched his nets, intent on his work. His red curls tossed about in the breeze and his tanned features portrayed inner peace and contentment. Let him alone, she heard an inner voice say, but a wild surge drowned the plea. She felt the blood course through her veins and rise to her throat. Her lips burned, her heart quickened. She couldn't withdraw now. Turbulent, tortuous, and compelling, the urge to be near him, to find herself somehow in his arms, was overpowering.

As if he sensed her presence, Padraig lifted his head and a broad smile lit up his ruddy face. He raised his hand and waved.

Magheen, all other thoughts banished, scrambled down the cliff. A little out of breath, she called as she made her way over the rocks, "I was hoping to find you here," but her voice was inaudible above the pounding breakers.

He disentangled himself from his nets and, wiping his hands on his trews, went to her assistance. As he drew near, Magheen saw the glint in his pale blue eyes and her heart started pounding again. Her mouth was dry and her tongue seemed stuck to her palate. Her knees were weak and she was trembling.

"Give me your hand, Magheen, 'tis slippery those rocks can be." His well modulated voice resonating like the breakers in the nearby caves was pure music and sent a shaft of fire through her breasts.

She felt the strength of his rough hands as he guided her over the kelp strewn rocks and a little foolish, as she knew perfectly well that she had no need of his help whatsoever. She was trembling, not from fear, these rocks were no strangers to her. Her breath came in small shallow gulps and a rivulet of perspiration ran in the cleft formed by her maiden breasts. When she reached the sand, she looked up into his smiling face, his straight nose and full lips were not all she had remembered, but his smile was captivating. She was aware, as if for the first time, of his pearly white teeth and the fascinating dimple in his left cheek which appeared and disappeared, coaxing her to stretch out her hand to caress the spot. The twinkle in those pale blue eyes was a charm common of many in the Emerald Isle, but with Padraig the sparkle was livelier, more intense.

"You're out early, Magheen."

Why didn't he say he was glad to see me? she asked herself. Then addressing him, "No fishing today?"

"Yes, the fishing's good, but my nets need mending. No nets, no fish. It's that simple. But you didn't come here to ask me about the fishing, now did you?"

She couldn't tell him she had sought his company for...for some strange impulse, nor could she share with him the sensations and unfamiliar stirrings in her maturing body when in his presence. "No, not really. I've heard rumors about the French," she lied. There were always rumors about the French so it was a safe statement.

"Rumors!" He lifted his flaxen eyebrows in his own inimitable way.

Magheen hesitated. Why didn't he take her in his arms? "Oh, you know the usual, that the French are sending help."

Padraig didn't answer immediately. He looked more closely at Magheen. "And where did you hear that?" His voice had an urgency in it.

"Oh, I have ways of finding out things," she answered offhandedly.

"Have you, now?" He smiled. Padraig was not unmindful of the beauty that was unfolding before his eyes day by day. "Darlin' Magheen, you shouldn't be troubling your pretty head with such stories."

Magheen stomped her foot and the blood robbed the cream from her slender throat. "You men, you think women mere ornaments! Have you forgotten our warrior ancestors? Celtic women fought side by side with their menfolk since the dawn of time." She turned to go, he obviously considered her a mere child.

"Wait darlin', I didn't mean to offend you. Rumors like these are dangerous, and my only thought is for your safety. There are spies...."

"There you go again...protection...I don't need any man's protection. I can manage very well all by myself, thank you." She turned and took a step, but as she did she caught her boot on a rock and was propelled sideways.

In a flash, Padraig's strong arms encircled her waist. "Careful now."

Magheen felt the sinewy leg muscles stiffen as she fell against his body and a thrill of excitement ran through her slender frame. She could feel his warm breath on her neck, a ripple, a quiver in her breast, a warm flush mounting with ever stronger impulses to the very roots of her hair.

"That was a near one, young lady." He was looking into her beautiful smoldering brown eyes and for a moment was caught in their sensuous depths.

As he spoke, she realized her compromising position. Quickly, she pulled away. "Thank you for breaking my fall," and to hide her embarrassment, "Must watch that Spanish wine—too early in the day for this sort of thing."

They both laughed and the tension between them released.

He took her hand in his. "You're right, Magheen darlin', perfectly right and a truer Celt than yourself they'll not find, of that I'm sure. And...and yes," he studied her, "there is news from France."

But she didn't hear the last phrase, she saw only the sincere admiration and deep devotion in his honest eyes. "Aren't you a descendant of the great Queen Maeve?"

For a moment Padraig was puzzled, then, as if choosing his words carefully, "Aye, that I am...but you know she lived so long ago that I doubt there's much 'blue blood' left in my poor veins." Before Magheen could say anything, Padraig continued, "You've grown into a very beautiful young woman, Magheen, and I'm honored that you should think so well of me, Lass. But I must remind you, that yours is a destiny not given to many. I may have the honor to play a part in it, who knows, but a minor role 'twill surely be."

Magheen hung her head and the fire in her cheeks was full of pain. She had made a fool of herself; she dare not look at him again. She must get away as quickly as possible.

Knowing her thoughts and to save her further embarrassment, Padraig turned towards the sea. "You know, Magheen, the real reason I'm not out with the men is because I'm here to keep watch."

"Watch, you mean it?" She knew his intention, her voice had lost vitality and interest.

"Sure, we got word three days ago that a boat has left France."

Magheen's eyes opened wide, so he wasn't just placating her. "Then it should be here by now!"

"Aye, depending on the weather."

"Do you think they'll land off this coast?"

"Nothing's certain. I'll tell your uncle you know; we've a meeting tonight. Time you join the discussions, be prepared... you're growing up fast." The almost imperceptible assessment of her womanly figure didn't escape Magheen. "Forewarned is forearmed. A young woman in your position should not be ignorant of the intrigues of ambitious chieftains and local princes, or the scheming of timorous, avaricious bishops and archbishops, and power hungry monarchs abroad."

So their talk was not always of Plato and Aristotle, the *Iliad* and *Odyssey*, or of the ancient Celtic tales *Oisin* and *Fiann*, *Dierdre* and *Maeve*, but of present day scoundrels and traitors and fawning royal parasites, the scum who held sway and wielded the real power in Ireland. She would be more than happy to join in these discussions and debates, attend these meetings, and parley with the influential and intellectual. She agreed with Padraig, it was high time she took an active part in the political affairs of her country, and prepare herself for the day when...

"You agree then, Magheen, with my suggestion?"

"Most certainly." She had forgotten, for the moment, the tantalizing sensations, the aching raw yearnings of her young body, and was now afire with emotions of a more altruistic nature.

"Till tonight then," he said and again turned his attention to the sea. She saw his eyes narrow and glisten like cold marble. His face muscles tightened, his long jaw bone protruded over clenched teeth, and she knew a side of Padraig that she never before thought existed.

The news from France was of a serious nature then; from whence had it come? she wondered. To be privy to such information; and to be acknowledged, accounted mature, responsible, intelligent, and discerning by her uncle and those whom he considered reliable, trustworthy, and dedicated men, was no small honor.

A sense of her own importance and power, a deepening realization of her identity and heritage, that she was destined for positions of distinction, to live for all time in the Annuls of the great, caused her to refocus and redirect her energies and thoughts. The words of her grandfather, The O'Neill, resounded in her mind, "One day you'll marry a Celtic prince."

The feeling that she would be great and achieve fame and fortune, that she would play a leading role in the tragic yet dramatic political and social arenas of her time and country—a vital role—was paramount and dominated her thoughts. Yes, Padraig was right. She must prepare for the future…the not so distant future.

"I must be off; see you tonight," she said as she set her head high and, with deliberation evident in her slight frame, retraced her steps up the rugged path.

He watched her go, a slip of a girl, he thought, but one with a will to conquer worlds. A brooding melancholia descended on him, enveloping him like a thick cloud, a mesmerizing experience reminiscent of his Celtic past, and he saw her youthful beauty enshrouded in cruel, agonizing pain, her golden head bent in poignant sorrow, and great tears spilling from her luminous brown eyes. Then, all at once, he felt cold with a coldness that entered to the very marrow of his bones, and his body trembled and shook in a convulsive spasm. As she reached the top, she waved for a moment. Then she was a warrior maid, spear drawn, riding against the wind on a great black stallion, golden hair billowing, clad in a mantle of shimmering silver. Her maiden form was silhouetted against the gold and crimsons of the evening sky, and he knew she was Ireland and that she rode to victory, freedom, and honor.

Two

"Come on, Finn. I'll race ye to the top o' the hill."

In sunny serenity lay the little town of Ballindee on that Autumn morning of the year 1542. September had been glorious; its burnished sun continued to bring warmth to the earth and fullness to the table. Now, as the month drew to a close, there was an air of contentment, security, and quietness. Lazy animals, fat and heavy, moved about slowly or simply lay in the pastures, their thickened coats absorbing what heat was left in the slanting rays of a waning sun.

The village folk went about their everyday chores as usual; the men, busy with the fishing, had been out since early morning. Noon would see them back if the catch were good, but they would surely stay a few hours longer if the biting were slow. The women were occupied with cooking; little puffs of purple smoke arose from white chimneys, and the air was heavy with smells of fresh baked bread, boiled mutton, and fish. The children had left their play and gone indoors to satisfy healthy appetites.

Brian, a lad of ten, had spent the morning hunting rabbits with his dog, Finn. He had managed to catch two, not a bad morning's work, when he decided to return home by way of the Tower. As he gained the rise that overlooked the whole area, his rabbits slung over his shoulder and his faithful Irish terrier close on his heels, his attention was caught by a glitter, a flash of silver, far away near Murphy's swamp. He raised his hand to protect his eyes from the glare of the midday sun. It looked like a moving column of sparks. He squinted. His little dog barked. "What is it, Finn? Do you see it, too?"

The dog answered his master's question with a sharp woof and a wag of his tail.

"Oh boy! 'Tis the Sasanach; soldiers, Finn, soldiers!"

A long line of men, armed with pikes and swords, were coming over the dusty road, the only one that led to the village of Ballindee.

"Come on, let's go, Finn. We've got to get home fast. We've got to reach the village afore the Sasanach."

The boy and his dog bolted forward, fear and anxiety gripping his heart. As he raced through the quiet lane that divided the rows of whitewashed cottages, he could scarcely speak. "They're comin'...the Sas - an - ach, soldiers...com - ing!"

Mrs. O'Reilly rushed to her open door but Brian was already halfway down the lane. "What's up, Brian?"

"Sas - an - ach. There." He pointed toward the hill as he turned to answer her.

"Mother o' God protect us." She blessed herself and hastily withdrew, bolting the door.

Brian sped on until he reached his own home down near the beach. He burst into the house, his face drained of its natural glow, and collapsed on the stone floor before he was able to gasp, "Mother...they're...com...in'."

"Who's comin'? What ails you, Son?" his mother, confused and terrified, asked.

"Oh, Mother...the...Sas...Sasanach...they're comin'." By now he was shaking and his violet-blue eyes protruded under heavy auburn lashes.

"Are you sure? Where did you see 'em?"

"Over in the...direction o' Murphy's swamp." He was regaining control of his breath but he was deadly pale and still trembling.

"Are ye sure they're soldiers, lad?" Brian's grandfather stood up from his place by the fire, put his hand on the boy's shoulder, and squeezed hard.

"Aye, Grandad, I'm sure," said Brian.

"Then Tom O'Connor at the Big House must be warned." The old man looked at the frightened child, then made for his walking cane, a black thorn cut the spring before and daily polished with beeswax. "I'll be off then," he said.

"No, no Grandad, I'll go by...the beach...cut across the shallows...I think the tide's out," Brian crawled then stumbled to the front door.

"Better go by the back door, Son. Keep low against the wall in the cow field till you reach the strand," cautioned his mother, a fresh complexioned, stout woman with a soft voice.

"I'll do that. If I don't come back with Tom O'Connor, I'll stay beyond at the Big House. So don't ye be frettin' about me, Mother."

"All right, Son." She watched him go, an ache in her heart. A wee bit of a lad, silky auburn hair falling on slender shoulders, thin white legs, and small feet scarcely touching the ground as he sped across the yard to the pasture beyond.

Mrs. O'Roark, like the other women, secured the doors of her home, then she sat down by the fire, the smaller children about her, and waited.

These people, fisherfolk for the most part, were of kindly, gentle, simple stock, innocent as children; they lived in that isolated region in comparative peace and security. They had learned to adapt, as generation succeeded generation, to the harsher elements of that remote corner of western civilization and, though poor in worldly goods, they were, true to traditional Irish hospitality, ever willing and ready to share their meager fare with those less fortunate than themselves.

The soldiers filed two abreast into the village. At the head of the column strutted the sergeant named James Fletcher, a burly little man with blue-grey eyes; thick, bushy black brows; a bulbous nose with a wart on the end; a florid, pox-scarred complexion, and a double chin. To the rear, a few paces behind the common foot soldier, Captain Hawks rode on a black stallion. He was a tall man and sat his horse well. A man who was conscious of his rank, self-possessed, and self-confident, his steel-grey eyes betrayed no emotion as he surveyed the seemingly deserted hamlet, but they had caught the almost imperceptible movement behind the O'Reilly curtain. He drew closer to the house.

"Sergeant, give the order."

"Yes, Sir." Sergeant Fletcher stepped to the door. He pounded three times with the butt of his lance. "Open up, in the name of His Majesty, King Henry VIII!"

Not a sound escaped from the interior of the house.

"Break down the door," Captain Hawkes ordered.

The Sergeant repeated the command and immediately three soldiers near him rammed the wooden door. It groaned. A sound of splintered wood was heard from inside, but the door held firm. A moment of silence ensued. Again Hawkes spoke, and this time his tight pale lips betrayed determination and anger, and his cold eyes cruelty.

"Repeat your command, Sergeant."

Once more, the gruff voice of the sergeant broke the awful stillness. "Open up in the name of the King."

An eerie hush gripped the village. A lone dog whined and slunk away with its tail between its legs to the cover of a nearby bush, and in the distance the call of the sea gulls grew fainter, while the constant rhythmic pounding of the eternal breakers on the rocky beach emphasized the stillness.

"Perhaps there's no one here, Sir?" Sergeant Fletcher waited for his commanding officer to reply. His swollen fatty jowls thrust forward, he was sweating profusely.

The Captain sat motionless a moment, eyes fixed. He did not look at the man whose appearance disgusted him. "Fool." He urged his horse past the sergeant and shouted at the soldiers. "Break down that door and bring the vermin out." A faint cynical glint flashed across his cold slate eyes, and his knuckles showed white as he tightened his grip on the reins.

The soldiers soon had the door torn asunder, casting the bits and pieces in careless abandon to left and right. Several men entered the dark interior and dragged the terrified Ellen O'Reilly and her six screaming children into the sunlight. Little Una, a baby of only two, stumbled and fell as she tried to scramble over the debris. "Mama, Mama," she called, stretching out her small plump arms. Above her frightened dark blue eyes, red stains had already soiled the gold in her tumbling curls.

Ellen instinctively turned to snatch up her baby, wrenching herself free of the soldier. A cry of horror escaped her purple lips when she saw the blood, but for her trouble she suffered the butt of a lance in her ribs. Undaunted, seemingly unaware of the blow, she picked the child up and clutched her to her heart. "Mo stoirin," she mumbled. The child, too terrified to cry, clung to her mother and hid her face against her breast.

"Line them up," shouted Captain Hawkes. "And now we'll show these lice what happens to those who do not obey the orders of His Majesty's officers. Cut them down." The order was given sharp and swift as the swords that pierced the hearts of four innocent children. Ellen, still clutching her baby, her golden hair flying, ran to protect her oldest child, thirteen-year-old Eileen. She stood firmly in front of the girl and defied the monster to come any closer. Like a tortured animal, she took a stance ready to fight to the bitter end.

"Move aside," ordered Captain Hawks sneering.

Ellen looked at the man, her mouth open, her teeth bared. A froth had gathered on her bloodless lips. Vicious as a snarling, mad dog, she would strike to kill.

"You, yes, you, move aside," he repeated and this time used his sword to drive home his words. The blood flowed from the wound in Ellen's arm. She was unaware of it, but the thrust caused her to lose balance. She stumbled; the baby whimpered.

"Seize the girl. A virgin would pleasure me," shouted the Captain.

"No, in God's name!" cried Ellen, realizing the intention. "I'd rather see her...."

The Gaelic words meant nothing to Hawkes, but the frantic gestures and wild cries of the mother only fanned the flames of his lust. "Shut her mouth," he shouted to a soldier, who immediately knocked her unconscious.

"Jenkins." Hawks motioned toward the terrified girl.

The young Lieutenant stepped in front of Eileen, grabbed a handful of her coarse dress and ripped it to the waist, exposing creamy skin, rounded full breasts, and slender hips. His actions drew guffaws from the soldiery who enjoyed the spectacle of tortured innocence and suffering.

"God's teeth, ain't she a beauty," remarked a soldier standing close by.

"Finish the job," ordered the Captain, beads of perspiration heavy on his lined forehead.

Eileen kicked and scratched and screamed in desperation as

Lieutenant Jenkins reached out and tore at the sagging tunic. It ripped easily, uncovering a chestnut triangle and long slender legs. The girl trembled, her green eyes riveted on the Captain no longer saw him; vainly she tried to cover her nakedness with her delicate white hands.

"This one's mine." Hawks dismounted. With one savage movement, he tore away the rest of her clothes, then stood back to better appreciate the natural perfection, for he was a man of refinement and taste—an exquisitely curvaceous body. His eyes devoured the trembling form. Then, taking a step forward, he grabbed her flaming hair and pulled her to him. Holding her tight with one arm, he used the other to explore her body. He squeezed the soft breasts and roughly ran his hand over her stomach and hips and into the hair between her legs. He prodded her with brutal force until she screamed with pain and terror. His manhood was about to explode. Clenching his teeth and fighting to control himself, he flung her on the ground. Lifting his outer coat, he loosened his venetians showing her his stiffness.

The horror in her eyes confirmed his suspicion. "All the better!" he rasped as he fell on her. She struggled, kicking and beating with her arms, no longer screaming. This one would have to be tamed, he thought, and his ardor increased. He lashed out at her and, as her cheeks turned to an angrier red, he pushed himself inside, once, twice, three times with savage brutality. Eileen shrieked, a fierce, agonizing scream that pierced the air and echoed through the village, then her fragile body went limp. With a triumphant howl, he emptied his seed and a spontaneous applause erupted from the onlookers as heated loins anticipated their turns would come ere they quit the village. For a moment longer, he lay on the unconscious girl, then slowly got to his feet. He brushed the dust of the road from his doublet and hose and glanced at his conquest. A scarlet stain on the bruised thighs, he was exultant and kicked the limp form as he buttoned his venetians.

The bloodied bodies of the other children lay strewn on the dusty lane where, only an hour before, they had played. Their mother lay a bleeding heap a short distance away, her arms clenched around the blue contorted body of her baby, Una.

"You there." The Captain spoke to a soldier standing near the body. "Take that runt and show these swine how quickly we can dispose of their litters."

The soldier lowered his pike and impaled the lifeless body of the baby girl. A dark red stain slowly spread over the plain white pinafore as the limp form dangled in the air.

"Raise it on high. Carry it to the end of the lane. Let them see, let them all see! We will show no mercy to the enemies of the King."

* * * *

Young Brian ran into the O'Connor kitchen where Moll was busy making bread, his blue eyes straining in their sockets, his face drawn and drained of all color. He was again gasping for breath.

"Glory be to God!" Moll stared at the boy as her hands dug into the dough. "What's up?"

"The...Sass...Sass...anach...." He tried to point but the effort to regain his breath was too great. "In...the...village."

"What are you saying, Lad?"

"'Tis true...tell...O'Connor." Again he pointed, this time in the general direction of the master's room.

"Great God in heaven!" Moll took her hands out of the bowl, and without waiting to wipe off the dough, she led the boy to O'Connor's room.

A man of action, Tom didn't hesitate. His first concern was for Magheen, who had taken Leprachaun for an early ride and hadn't yet returned.

"Brian, Laddie, you have been a brave boy this day. Now, I want you to do one more thing. Find Magheen and warn her, then come back here, Son. You'll be safer."

"Aye, Sir." The child turned and in a flash was out the door and heading for the cliffs where he knew Magheen liked to go.

Tom O'Connor, accompanied by Sean, the yardman, rode in haste towards the village, but as they drew near, Tom ordered Sean to remain where he could be seen on the brow of the hill.

"I'll need you to gather up what men you can if trouble breaks out."

"Aye, Sir. I understand."

Concern changed to outrage and then to anger when Tom beheld the carnage. He confronted the Captain.

"Great God Almighty! What is the meaning of this? In the name of God, have you lost all regard for innocent lives?" Tom O'Connor was livid. A tall man, imposing, commanding respect, he had no fear as he confronted the English soldiery at that moment. His pale face and clear blue eyes showed only his fierce anger and utter contempt for the animals that surrounded him.

The Captain scrutinized him and there was a moment of pregnant silence. "Well, I see there's one civilized person here, someone who can speak the English tongue. All I got from this lot was open defiance," he sneered as he indicated with a toss of his head the bloodied, lifeless bodies strewn about the dusty lane.

"What do you mean open defiance?" He was about to continue but the Captain interrupted.

"I mean they deliberately refused to obey my command, to open in the name of His Majesty."

"Good God, Man! Do you realize that these people didn't understand a word you said? I'm responsible here. I'll have no more of this butchery. Tom O'Connor is the name, and I'll have you know that I could wipe every last man of you from the face of this earth. I have only to signal my man yonder."

The Captain never flinched. "We need food and lodging for a few days," he spat as if ordering a subordinate.

"You're an insolent cur." Tom gave vent to his rage in Gaelic. "You'll not be welcome in this village, that I can assure you. Nor will I vouch for your safety or for the lives of any of your men." His clear eyes never leaving the Captain's face, he continued, "I'm warning you for the last time."

A sneer spread across Hawks' countenance. He was enjoying this fellow and admired his pluck.

"You have the effrontery to ask for food and lodging. What guarantee do I have that you'll not repeat this barbarism?" Tom demanded.

"For the time being, you have my word, the word of an officer and a gentleman in His Majesty's army." The Captain pulled himself up to his full height. Then realizing he was not O'Connor's equal, he mounted his horse.

Tom wanted to tell him what he thought of His Majesty and his army, but he refrained. Instead, he decided to play for time. "I demand upon your word of honor then that there will be no more bloodshed, looting, or raping in this village."

There was a moment of tense silence before the Captain spoke. With an expression of utter contempt, he stared down at O'Connor. Who was this upstart? he asked himself. "I give the orders," he snarled. "What accommodations are there in this wasteland for myself and...."

Tom turned his back on Hawks and was about to raise his hand to signal.

"Wait! Perhaps we can come to some agreement?" The Captain's voice had lost its edge. He moved in his saddle, perhaps in this situation discretion would be the better part of valor, he thought.

Tom turned around slowly to face the enemy. His bluff had almost been called. He waited to steady his nerve as he, in turn, stared at his opponent with steel blue eyes. "You have acted wisely, Sir. Now, have I your word of honor regarding the treatment of my people?"

Hawks grunted. He was mortified—and before his men. He glanced about, looked with practiced eye in the direction of hills, and examined the contour of the land. He scanned the empty village lane, then out to sea. Where were the men? How many had this contemptuous parvenu to command? Were they well armed? Then a sly, knowing look appeared in his cruel, calculating eyes. The French, the supply ships, they had landed! "You have my word."

Tom was quick to respond, "Then you and your officers may share the shelter of my home. Your men can bed down in a small grove nearby. Now, if you'll follow me." Tom walked away from the village, his head held high. A surly Captain Hawks and his men tagged along behind.

As soon as the soldiers were out of sight and Tom was sure that Captain Hawks was safely lodged, he returned to the village. He went from house to house trying to reassure the terrified women and children. He inquired about Magheen. Had anyone seen her? Then before he left, he asked the women to have their menfolk meet him at the Tower at nine that night.

The Round Tower, one of the many built in Ireland during the Danish raids as a lookout, also was used to shelter and protect the inhabitants in time of danger. A single door about twenty feet above the ground was entered by a rope ladder which could be pulled up when all were safely inside.

Tom O'Connor thought it would be better for all if they did not see the extent of the slaughter. He arranged with Father Donald to have the bodies buried immediately in the little graveyard on the south side of the church.

Magheen returned home accompanied by Brian and his dog, Finn, just before dinner. It had taken Brian several hours to finally find her in a little cove a few miles away, where she was gathering kelp, the special kind Moll liked.

That evening Captain Hawks and Lieutenant Jenkins were billeted in Inis Fail. Moll grudgingly fed the unwelcomed guests, but she refused to dine with them. "I'll not sit at the table with them barbarians. I'm trying, in my heart, to forgive, but the Lord Himself wouldn't eat with the likes of them."

"Well, I can't forgive and never will," said Magheen bitterly. "I want to fight with every fiber of my being. Why, why such wanton slaughter?" She couldn't understand.

Tom and Magheen tried to be civil at dinner, but as soon as they had finished, Tom excused himself, saying he had business to attend to.

The Captain did not like Tom O'Connor. The man, without trying, made him feel inferior.

Tom called Magheen to his room before he left the house. "Magheen, my dear, I want you to keep an eye on that pair for an hour or two. I don't trust either of them."

"I've been trying to talk to you all evening."

"I'm sorry, my dear, it's been...."

"I heard what happened. What senseless brutality."

"I know, Magheen, but there's nothing we can do at the moment." Her uncle's mind was on other things.

"You don't think so?" Magheen wanted to say that if she had the making of decisions things would be done differently. "Can you tell me why these soldiers are here? What can they want in a place like this?"

"I really don't know, Magheen. Now I must go, my dear."

Her uncle didn't know! Magheen's mind was racing ahead. "Be careful, Uncle," she called after him.

Magheen returned to the reception hall. The Captain was dozing in front of the dying fire, and the Lieutenant seemed lost in thought as she entered.

"I've been detained."

The Lieutenant arose, but the Captain didn't move. The effects of the fine wine and good food of the O'Connor household, no doubt, thought Magheen.

"Seems the Captain has dropped off." Jenkins nodded in speaking.

"Aye, it looks like it." For a moment the conversation was strained.

"Well, Miss, I'd best get some sleep too."

Magheen ignored the remark. "Where do you come from?"

"Kent. Southern England. My folks have a small farm there."

"Have you been in Ireland long?"

"Goin' on a year now. But...."

"But you would prefer to be home."

"Aye!"

"I've been told your men did their share of killing today. Surely a man like you can't condone such behavior?"

"'Tweren't me, Miss. Believe, me, I don't hold with killin' women an' children." The Lieutenant glanced at the Captain.

Magheen was silent.

Should she venture the question uppermost in her mind? No, better not. He might become suspicious. She walked to the window. A half moon was barely visible behind a bank of clouds; she pretended to be interested.

"We've had some really good weather here for the past few days. How has it been elsewhere?" Magheen asked.

"Fairly good. Can't say it's been too bad. Although, we did have some rain near Galway."

"Oh, you've come a long way!"

"Come further than that."

"From Cork?"

"Aye, come up the whole coast."

"The coast!" Magheen looked directly at the young man. She perceived a slight hesitation, so she smiled and continued to appear unconcerned. "It must be beautiful to travel by the coast when the weather is good."

"Aye," he relaxed. "Especially when there are some good lookin' colleens around." The Lieutenant grinned sheepishly.

Magheen ignored his remark.

"Not intendin' to be bold, but you're one of the prettiest colleens I've seen."

"Oh! Thank you, Lieutenant." Magheen heard the front door close. "That must be my uncle. It's time I retired. I'll have Mrs. O'Flynn show you to your room. Good night."

"Good night, Miss."

Magheen informed the housekeeper Moll that the "murdering bastards" in the hall were ready to retire. She rarely used the word, but she couldn't find another better suited to describe them at that moment. She then went to join her uncle.

"Was your evening successful?"

"Yes, everything is quiet in the village."

"Do you know how long these soldiers will be here?" she asked.

"Not really, but I imagine a day or two. Why they are here is what I'm more interested in. I have a hunch it has something to do with the Butler family in the south."

"What do you mean, Uncle?"

"Well, my dear, you are too young to remember, but about nine or ten years ago, the Earl of Kildare was governor of Ireland. Because of his alliance with Gaelic families, he was denounced as a traitor and spent six long years in the Tower of London. While he was in prison, his cousin, the Earl of Desmond, entered into an alliance with Francis I, King of France, to drive the English forever out of Ireland. Meantime, the Earl of Kildare died and his son, Thomas, infuriated, rose in rebellion. He fought courageously for some time, but eventually was forced to surrender when he saw the brave Irish lads dying all around him. He was captured and also sent to the Tower of London, where he was cruelly tortured and finally hung, drawn, and quartered. With him also died his five uncles, despite the fact that three of these noble, scholarly men didn't even take part in the rebellion. Six heads were placed on spikes and displayed on Tyburn for all to see."

"I do remember you telling me that only Gerald, the youngest who was about twelve at the time, escaped. I remember, too, about the horrible massacre which followed here, in Ireland. The English were not satisfied with those six deaths, but set about to methodically destroy all that belonged to the Fitzgerald family."

"The final blow came when all the land that once was theirs was given to the Butler family, the Earl of Ormand. That's why the Butler House has become the most prominent Sean Ghall family in the country. The Crown thought it was just reward for their long years of loyalty."

"But I still don't see what the Butler family has to do with the coming of the English soldiers to Ballindee?"

"Well, the rumor is that the Butler family has broken with England and has allied with the Desmond family, a very important political move. The present Earl is the first Butler to show openly that he is proud of his Irish heritage. Could be, Magheen, that the English, also, have heard these rumors and are sending out their spies and soldiers to ascertain the truth and to see if the country is preparing to rise in revolt again."

"Perhaps you're right, Uncle. War and killing, when will it end?" With these thoughts, Magheen left her uncle. It had been a day of terror and death. Why had the Sasanach come to Ballindee? Why was such suffering, pain, and sorrow visited on this peaceful little village? Magheen was determined to find the answer to these questions. She had a mission to accomplish. Her whole world had been changed in a single day!

Three

Magheen awoke early the next morning with a throbbing headache, a headache she had taken to bed the night before. She rarely had headaches. Why should this one persist so long? Then she remembered, still not her usual self, the happenings of the day before. She sat up, rubbed her eyes, and took up her train of thought where she had left off the previous evening. Again, she vowed to herself to find out the information.

She stepped to the window. All was silent now. The village, in the distance, looked deserted and black, but as she watched, the sun rose slowly over the sleeping land. Down on the lawn below her window, the lowest form of human life lay sprawled in careless abandon. They had drunk well the night before of her uncle's ale and mead and now were oblivious of the crimes they had so easily committed only a few short hours ago.

Were I in charge, Magheen thought, I would surely have slain the vermin as they slept. As she watched, a young soldier stirred, stretched, yawned, sat up, and looked around. She had better not be seen. She withdrew behind the heavy drape but continued to watch as he got up, walked a few paces away from his sleeping companions, looked around again, and relieved himself on the soft grass.

Why had they come? What was there in Ballindee for so many soldiers to do? Surely, they were not going to murder the entire village in cold blood. She just had to find out what was going on. In the meantime, she would put everything else aside and would not think of herself or her own feelings; her utter contempt for these Sasanach lice, her aversion to speaking their language, her revulsion at the acrid odor of their unwashed bodies, and their disgustingly uncivil manners. That she could deal with the natural fear she felt for her own personal safety, she did not doubt. She would take every precaution by arming herself and staying close to home. But did she lack confidence in her physical strength were she challenged to defend herself?

Her uncle was fearful, she knew, yet he did not allow his feelings to interfere with his duty. She had heard of his courage, had seen his composure, and had admired the way he had organized the men of the area right under the very nose of the enemy.

Could she do less? She was convinced that her life had taken a new direction, a path that would ultimately lead to the recognition of her abilities, her true worth. For even at fifteen, Magheen was well aware that she was talented, capable, intelligent, aggressive, and courageous. Yesterday she bade her childhood farewell. Today she was a grown woman with a woman's strengths, resolved to shoulder responsibilities. She would go forward with determination, courage, and fortitude, ready for whatever challenge this new day and all the days to come brought.

"Good morning, my dear," said her uncle as she entered the dining room, dressed in a light green flowing skirt with a blue silk bodice trimmed in lace. Her golden hair, drawn back from her face by a blue satin ribbon, fell in whimsical curls on her slender shoulders.

"Mornin', Miss." The Lieutenant cast a shy glance as she floated to her place, like green seaweed on the surface of gentle lapping wavelets, he thought.

The Captain inclined his head slightly but remained silent. His eyes alone spoke and from them Magheen and her uncle read his salacious thoughts.

The blood rushed to Tom's face, his muscles tensed; this insolent cur, this bloody bastard, how dare he. It took every last ounce of the control of his innate gentility to restrain his impulse to lash out at the swine. He grabbed the back of his chair, grating it on the wooden floor and set it down vehemently.

Betrayed by his own lust and momentarily caught off guard, the Captain withdrew a red pocket handkerchief and blew his thin nose loudly before seating himself.

Magheen regarded him with contempt, revulsion, and hate. A sickening feeling burned in the pit of her stomach. She no longer wanted to eat. She picked at her poached egg with the point of a wooden skewer. It bled and as she watched the yoke spread over the white porcelain plate, she thought of Eileen and knew she would avenge her death.

Tom ate in silence, automatically, without knowing or tasting what he ate. He wouldn't allow this "boyo" out of his sight; he'd personally stalk him day and night.

The Captain had buried his head in his plate again, gulping down the food in front of him. It wasn't pleasant eating with the enemy, but the fare was good, the best he'd had in weeks, he grudgingly acknowledged.

The Lieutenant too had fallen on his food with the intention of putting away as much as possible in the shortest possible time.

Magheen broke the silence. "Looks like it's going to be a beautiful day. Did you take your walk, Uncle?"

"Yes, of course, my dear." Then addressing Hawks, "You seem to like an early morning hike also. Saw you on the cliffs, a magnificent sight on a clear day." Tom detected a slight tensing of jaw muscles as the Captain's eyes met his.

"Huh," he said and chose to ignore the last remark. "Yes. I like a walk early in the morning." He looked down at his plate. "It's invigorating," he added, then continued to hack at the pork sausages.

"Helps give one a healthy appetite," Tom could no longer hold back the remark as he glanced at Magheen, then bent his head.

Surly, filthy scum, she thought. If I were a man, I'd kill you. She stared at the congealing mess on her own plate but didn't see it any longer; her thoughts were elsewhere. She had to get away as quickly as possible.

Tom decided he'd waste no more time with pleasantries. Blunt talk, no beating about the bush, might better suit his purpose. "Captain Hawks, I'd like to know how long you intend to remain in Ballindee?"

With clenched teeth and eyes which had instantly become mere slits, dark reflections of his cynical mind, slowly, deliberately, Hawks growled, "We will leave when we will leave." Then rising,

"Now, if you will excuse me." He then addressed the Lieutenant. "Come."

"One minute, Sir." Tom's anger was aroused. "You will see that your men are continually supervised and kept busy. I hold you personally responsible for any misconduct."

Hawks had not bothered to turn as his host addressed him, he waited for Tom to finish, then without comment left the room, followed by Jenkins.

Magheen had to work fast to accomplish what she had set her mind to do. She entered the hall. The Captain had gone upstairs. Lieutenant Jenkins was awaiting his commanding officer near the front door.

"Meet me at the Tower at noon," she whispered as she flung the great door open and tripped down the steps to the gravel beyond.

The young man smiled. These Irish girls are easy, he said to himself. Then the thought occurred to him. Animals! Mere animals! Of course, that's all they are! Some are very beautiful, like this one, but they are no more than animals, so they had been told before departing English soil.

Well, he'd have a little fun, some relaxation with this beautiful creature, but he wouldn't get involved in any other way. No, Sir. He was a loyal subject of His Majesty, and he was here in this wretched country to do a job for his King.

The morning was spent in a series of maneuvers, and as the troops moved over the landscape, the broken voice of a sergeant issuing orders rose and fell.

The village was deathly silent when Magheen rode through on her way to the beach. A sinister stillness had descended on the entire area, she noted. Few women were seen and then only briefly from behind the half-doors. No children were in sight, nor did they make a sound. Only the men appeared now and again outside the shelter of their homes. They acknowledged Magheen by nodding but did not speak as she passed. There was stubborn determination and defiance stamped on their rugged faces.

Even the animals had sensed the tremendous depression that had fallen on their world: the brute beast, it seemed, divined that an unnatural deed had been done and in its own way grieved. Dogs lay listless beside cabin doors or slunk by close to the stone walls with bent heads and drooping tails; horses and cattle stood in pathetic little groups close to home, silently eyeing the slightest activity with suspicion; chickens kept to the coop.

Down by the water's edge, Magheen pretended to be digging for shells among the white coral sands. From her vantage point, she kept a close eye on the Captain's movements; he was again on the cliffs and had stood a long time gazing out to sea, a solitary figure on the bleak headland. At length he mounted his horse and rode towards the village, his head held high. He was arrogance and disdain personified, Magheen concluded.

God forgive me! she said to herself. How she hated that man and all he represented. She thought of him as a monstrous, diabolical adversary, a ruthless monarch who sought power and wealth at the expense of a people and a culture he did not understand. She watched his receding figure with growing resentment. Atrocities such as he committed had to be avenged and it was up to the chieftains, or those who were in positions of authority, to take the initiative. She sucked in her breath, clenched her teeth in determination, and then made her way to the Tower. The young Lieutenant awaited her, and as she approached she knew his innocent, smiling, sunny blue eyes were deceiving. He had removed his hat, allowing his sand-colored hair to blow freely in the sea breeze, while he fumbled nervously with the edges as he turned it round and round in his hands.

Magheen dismounted and looped the reins around a willow bough, then stood a moment. A cold shiver ran through her as she asked herself what madness had possessed her. Should she mount and ride as fast as she could from the spot? Then, recollecting her resolve and her previous commitment, she stoutly rallied her weakening willpower.

"No," she mumbled, "I'm Magheen Ni Neill. I've made up my mind; I've set my heart to this task. I'll not look back." She would sooner die than be a coward. She turned and faced the Lieutenant and then sallied up to him. "Been waiting long?" she asked casually.

"No, not too long." He was clearly not at ease, still fumbling with his hat. He blushed when she addressed him, and the freckles on his boyish face seemed to be more prominent. He had a sheepish grin, which from time to time forced his thin lips to part, revealing discolored and uneven teeth. Although she was still three feet from him, she was nauseated by the stench of his unwashed body.

"Shall we walk?" Magheen suggested.

"Why not? 'Tis a nice day."

They did not speak again but strode in the direction of the cliffs. When they reached the edge, Magheen broke the silence.

"There's something I'd like to ask you." She didn't look at him but out to sea, to the far horizon.

"Oh, what is it?"

"Tell me, why have you soldiers come to these parts? Why Ballindee?" She could restrain herself no longer and she suddenly turned to face him and searched his small blue eyes.

"Now, Miss, you didn't bring me out here just to ask me that, did you?" he seemed baffled, hurt.

"No, of course not, Lieutenant Bill, but I would like to know. Wisha, there can't be any harm in telling me, now can there?" She appeared amiable, familiar. Bill Jenkins thought a moment but didn't answer. He wanted to please, but he was no traitor.

Magheen realized his dilemma. "Well, let's sit down here anyway." She sat on the edge of the cliff with her legs swinging over the rocky ledge.

"You're in a terribly dangerous position," he said, looking down to the churning breakers far below.

Magheen laughed. "I've been hanging from these rocks since I was a child. Come sit down near me; it's not so bad." She patted the ground beside her and looked at him coaxingly.

The Lieutenant laid his sword aside, then sat close to her, somewhat embarrassed. There was something about this girl, this young woman. "Miss...why did you ask me to meet you here?"

"I often come here alone. I thought it would be nice to have company for a change." She smiled at him and thanked God for the Atlantic breezes and the strong odor from the kelp strewn beach in the nearby cove.

Her eyes! Bill Jenkins' heart was touched by the beauty of Magheen's lustrous large eyes. "I...I think ye're beautiful." He drew a little closer.

Magheen could feel his breath warm against her cheek. She

shuddered, was repulsed, her stomach heaved, and she wanted to vomit. Yet despite her natural revulsion, she felt a certain pity for the youth. He was an ignorant lad. What did he know, one of the herd, doing as he was bid, following orders to kill, destroy, loot, steal, pillage, and rape. Oh, God, give me the strength necessary to do what I have to do, she prayed in her heart. Then she turned to face him. In that moment he drew her to himself. She raised her hand to her breast as he placed a kiss on her cheek. Magheen pulled away.

"Lieutenant Jenkins!" She waited, feigning surprise, playing for time to regain her composure and allow some fresh air to enter her lungs. Then, as if nothing were amiss, she completely ignored his obvious advance.

"Why does the Captain spend so much time alone, looking out to sea? He's not a happy man, that I can tell. Has he perhaps lost a...a loved one at sea?"

"Oh no, Miss, nothing like that." The young man smiled, he tried to be playful, teasing. "Give me a kiss an' I'll tell ye." He gazed longingly at Magheen's shapely red lips.

Before he knew what was happening, Magheen, a mischievous twinkle in her great sad eyes, bent toward him and quickly placed a kiss on his damp brow. "Ye're the crafty one," he said with a light happy laugh, like a small boy.

"Well...Lieutenant? You promised!" Magheen's large innocent eyes were full upon him and he noticed the gentle heaving of her shapely bosom.

"Ha! I can see I won't get anywhere with you until I do." He picked up a stone and threw it into the sea below.

"Well...well, it seems that some Earl or other in these parts has been plotting, trying to get help from France, they say. Bloody traitor, that's what I call 'im, plotting with the enemies o' the King." He interrupted himself, seeing the anger in Magheen's eyes. "I shouldn't be talkin' like this. They're your countrymen, but you wanted to know."

"So you've been sent to patrol the coast?" Magheen insisted.

"Aye, there are men in all the major ports. Them bloody Frenchies won't set foot on this soil, that I can tell you."

Magheen's blood shot through her veins like red hot arrows.

Then just as quickly a cold, clammy feeling took hold of her. She grew furious.

"My God!" She turned again to face the Lieutenant. "You mean to tell me that...that Eileen Reilly and her whole family had to be slaughtered just because there's a rumor that the French are...are coming? It's...you English bastards! Savages!"

She started to rise, determined to quit the spot immediately. The Lieutenant wasn't to blame. It was that accursed Captain... yes....

"Oh, no ye don't. Ye got what ye wanted out o' me. Now it's my turn." At that moment, he caught Magheen by the arm and pulled her to himself with all his strength.

Taken by surprise, she fell over on her side. She was at his mercy, and within seconds he was astride her. Looking up into his eyes, she saw the Englishman in a different light. His eyes were mere slits. They had lost whatever innocence and sympathy they had held previously. He became as one possessed; lust and a cruel determination to have his way with her had taken command.

"Let me go. Let me go, you swine!" Astride her, Magheen was unable to free herself or move. All she could do was pound on his chest with her clenched fists. Ignoring her futile efforts, Bill Jenkins grabbed at her bodice with both hands and tore it open down to the waist. In that same instance, Magheen withdrew the knife she had concealed over her breast and struck with all her might, plunging the sharp blade into the unsuspecting chest. Incredulously, the young soldier looked at her for a brief moment, then, with his right hand, he tried frantically to stop the flow of blood as he sought to dislodge the blade with the other.

"Slut, Irish bitch, you'll die for this," he groaned and the blood gushed from his mouth as Bill Jenkins fell forward on top of her.

"Aaa....h! My God!" For a moment Magheen froze, then realizing her predicament, and that at any moment she might be discovered, she pushed the body to one side. She got up and looked at the dying youth who now lay face upward, the knife still protruding from his breast. Her face showed only revulsion; no pity, no regret, no remorse. In her mind, it had been a life and death struggle; she was the victor.

"Scum! You think you can come here and rape and kill and

plunder at will. Well, know this, there'll always be those of us who will fight back. It's our land, our people. In the end, we'll prevail!"

A moment longer Magheen watched the crimson drops stain the chalky shale, then calmly she stooped down and retrieved the knife before she pushed the corpse over the cliff. After she heard it splash into the boiling waters below, she moved to the edge and dropped his sword into the same watery grave.

The ground was splattered and sullied with dark splotches. A little rain, she concluded, would rid the spot of all the evidence. She scanned the horizon. It wasn't going to rain, at least not in the next few hours, so she hacked at the sparse grass and mosses with her knife. That should do it. The wind and the spray would do the rest. She cleaned the evidence from the knife and concealed it once more in her torn bodice, pulled the tattered pieces together over shapely breasts, and set out for home.

Upon entering her room an hour later, Magheen felt her knees buckle. She had skirted the village to the south, circled back, and came home by the north side. She had planned everything well, she told herself, and she had succeeded in her mission, in accomplishing what she had set out to do. In some small way, she felt she had avenged the death of the O'Reilly family by inflicting a blow against the enemy. Her only regret at that moment was that the enemy had to have been the young Lieutenant, Bill Jenkins, and not Captain Hawks, the murderer.

She changed her dress. Her white inner skirt was spattered with red. A vision of the bloodied corpse flashed before her eyes. She swayed, a dizzy, reeling sensation; her stomach heaved and a cold sweat broke over her body. Her hands and feet were ice cold and clammy.

"I'm not the intrepid Celt I thought I was," she confronted her image in the burnished mirror. "You'll have to do better than this girl, if you intend to make a difference in the affairs of the country."

Who could tell what the future would bring. If the past were any indication, she would have her fill of dangers, risks, intrigues, and betrayals. She might even find herself in the Tower of London. She shuddered as she thought of the Fitzgerald family—Kildare annihilated, wiped off the face of the earth. But she had only to think of the atrocities of the previous day in her own village. What could she expect as granddaughter of The O'Neill when the innocent children of a simple fisherman were hacked to death in broad daylight. She was living in perilous times, and if she were to survive, she must use any method within her control to do so.

Before descending for dinner, she decided not to tell her uncle anything until later in the evening, thus, she would ensure his complete ignorance of the matter. She considered herself beyond suspicion. However, the topic did not come up. The Captain evidently thought the Lieutenant was detained and did not question his absence.

It was difficult to break the news to her uncle, but it was something that had to be done. She really didn't know how he would react. He was a scholar, an intellectual. Violence and destruction were not in his nature.

"My God, Magheen, you could have been killed!"

"Yes, Uncle, I'm aware of that, but I, at least, had a choice. Poor Eileen O'Reilly had none. She was younger than I by a full year, yet she went to the slaughter like an innocent lamb. What harm had any of those little children ever done? What good can come of this slaughter?"

"My dear girl, to these questions only God has the answer. We must believe that out of all our pain and suffering a greater good will surely come, if not in our lifetime, then perhaps for future generations. I'm not a pious man, Magheen, but I do believe that Christ had a message for us."

"I want to believe, but I can't." Her uncle chose to ignore her remark.

"Magheen, we have to be rid of this Captain Hawks as soon as possible. What will we do if the body is found?" His blue eyes were troubled as he tried to answer his own question.

"It won't ever be found, Uncle." She was surprised at how confident and calm she sounded.

"Why do you say that?"

"Because it went over the Dunmore Cliffs."

"I see," Tom said. "Maybe you're right. But just the same, the Captain will be furious and may retaliate when he finds out his Lieutenant is missing."

"True, but I think the best course for us is ignorance. He has no reason to link us with Bill Jenkins," answered Magheen.

"You're perfectly sure?" Again she noted the fear on his gentle face and in his kindly eyes.

"Yes, Uncle. The important thing now is that we do know the real reason why the Sasanach are here. The English not only believe that the Fitzgeralds of Desmond are 'traitors' but that now the Butlers also have joined us, the Gaelic Irish, in our fight for freedom, and that the French are sending aid which may arrive at any moment."

* * * *

To say that Captain Hawks would be furious was a far cry from the reality. He was livid, in a mad frenzy for two whole days, ranting, raving, threatening to kill every living thing. He stomped and stormed, swore he'd burn every last house in the village with its despicable occupants. He fumed and cursed over the time lost in the futile search for the body. In the end, the strength shown by Tom O'Connor and his persuasive arguments convinced Captain Hawks that the young man must have met with an accident.

Magheen, as she had surmised, was not suspected of having anything to do with the disappearance of Bill Jenkins. She now found herself, as a consequence, propelled far sooner than she had expected into the political life of her country. She had proved to herself and her uncle that extreme danger would not prevent her from doing whatever she thought was her duty or was necessary for the general good. She was willing to sacrifice her life and to inflict death to further the cause of freedom.

Four

"That's better," said Magheen as she closed the broad oak doors behind her, hesitating a few moments to relish the coolness of the large entrance hall. The black marble beneath her bare feet was invigorating, and a surge of new vitality swept through her. She spread her arms wide and twirled in a burst of exuberance.

She had been out with Leprechaun and her peregrine falcon, Maeve, named for the ancient warrior queen of Connaught. Now that the Sasanach had left, the village had, with the exception of Magheen, her uncle, Padraig, Seamus O'Reilly, and the local priest, Father Donald, settled somewhat uneasily back into its normal, sleepy, easy-going existence.

Inis Fail had now become the center of local resistance. Meetings took place regularly, and it quickly became evident to all that Magheen was someone to be taken seriously. Her opinions were considered, her suggestions evaluated, and although no one except her uncle knew the part she had played in the withdrawal of Captain Hawks and his men, they were aware of a new vitality and strength, a maturity beyond her years. As a result, each man, in his own unique way, grew to respect and admire her and did not deem it beneath his dignity to consult with her on varied and sundry matters. In this way, she gained valuable experience and practice in dealing with problems great and small and of a diverse nature.

On this particular afternoon, she was unusually lighthearted and happy. She had enjoyed the canter on the cliffs, where she had released the hawk on the most westerly promontory and did not retrieve her for more than an hour. It had been a very pleasant forenoon; a brisk breeze from the sea, collecting various perfumes in its wake: seaweed, gorse, heather, and wild woodbine, had generously scented the air. The sea, a greenish color, sparked with flecks of silver and gold under an almost cloudless sky. Cattle and sheep roamed the pastures, content to munch on coarse Autumn grasses, and as far as the eyes could see, the land was untroubled. Magheen exulted; if only it were so throughout the length and breadth of Ireland, she thought.

"That you, Magheen?" Moll's voice called from the kitchen.

"Not now, for heaven's sake," Magheen murmured. "Who's the servant around here, anyway?" Then in an audible tone, "Yes, what do you want?" She waited a moment, then receiving no answer, she dismissed the notion of attending the housekeeper.

Goodness gracious, she was old enough now to be mistress in this house. Why should she have to run errands like a common housemaid. She tilted her head showing her defiance. Moll could wait. Like the house itself, Moll would go on forever. Magheen wanted it so...but deep in her heart she knew things and times were changing. Even as she thought, she realized that Moll Flynn herself had changed with the years. A few faded red strands were all that was left of her youthful coloring. She still had quick, alert grey-blue eyes, but her rather prominent straight nose had grown larger. Her mouth had always been small, her lips thin, and often it seemed they disappeared altogether, leaving only a line to mark the place. At such times, Magheen knew she'd best keep out of her way.

Moll had come as a young woman to the O'Connor household. Having lost her husband, as so many others did to the sword of the enemy, she was forced to go into service to keep body and soul together. She was a good plain cook when she arrived at Inis Fail, but soon learned to serve as fancy a meal as was concocted in the best establishments. A religious woman, she was honest, hardworking, and devoted to her duty. She was clean in body and mind, and scrupulously clean about her household chores.

When Magheen arrived, Moll was the only house servant left on the O'Connor estate, so she ruled the roost. She even took it upon herself to handle the yardmen, delegating responsibilities and ordering all from "her" spotless kitchen. Even the master of the house, Tom O'Connor, did not intrude or presume to step uninvited into that wholly feminine and totally incomprehensible world.

Magheen looked around, taking in the vastness of the entry hall with its stuffed deer heads and extravagant array of peacock feathers. How she loved this house. Then her eyes came to rest on what was once a very fine canvas portrait of the first lord and ruler of the O'Connor clan. A tall, striking man of fair complexion, he commanded respect even from his golden frame. This was her grandfather.

She opened the carved doors on her right; the Connemara marble fireplace seemed to beckon to her. She entered. The old harp stood silent now and the stool, an antique, endured a lonely existence. Then Magheen cast her eyes upon the velvet covered chairs and couches. The exquisite carvings on legs and arms would always look elegant, but the velvet upholstery, faded and worn, was a relic of days long past. The same wine-colored material dressed the casements, but happily, they had weathered the passage of time with less wear, even though the golden trimmings and tassels were tarnished. She stroked the polished surface of the sideboard, rearranged a Venetian vase to her liking, and glanced at the fine tapestries that adorned the walls before she finally seated herself and mused aloud.

"Madam, won't you partake of a little light refreshment?" Then turning, "Sir, allow me." She offered her imaginary guest a plate. "Oh, I quite agree with you, the weather has been excessively warm. Why, it's been at least two weeks since we've had a drop of rain!"

One could easily envision the evenings spent in this room, the lively conversation, the music, poetry, the songs that echoed and re-echoed to those proud rafters, and the grace, elegance, and refinement of the occupants.

The scriptorium, as Magheen called it, stood on the left of the entry. This was her uncle's domain and boasted of many priceless manuscripts, several of which had been handed over for safe keeping by monks and clerics fleeing from attacking invaders who pillaged and plundered the coastal towns. These treasures, masterpieces of literature and art preserved for countless generations, were, by those men of letters, prized even above their lives.

Tom O'Conner's most valuable possession was a section of

The Senchus Mor, a manuscript of monumental proportions dealing with civil law and forming part of the greater book of ancient Irish laws. These laws, which governed every aspect of Irish life in and before the Christian era, the Fourth Century, were now forbidden by the foreign sovereign. Second only to this manuscript, Tom prized a gold torque said to belong to the great King Cormac MacArt who ruled Ireland in the Third Century A.D.

Magheen loved her uncle dearly. Often she would stand before his portrait in the dining hall, a picture painted while he was still a student in the French capital. He had been a handsome youth with regular features, fair complexion, and smooth skin. His clear blue eyes showed the world the sweet serenity of his soul, while their intentness mirrored generations of learned Celts. His hair, golden with the faintest tint of red, and his beard were neatly trimmed; in later years he wore a mustache. Perhaps he did so because by then he could no longer claim a great abundance of hair where it was most becoming. His bearing was manly; he stood a good five feet ten in his stocking feet. A man of gentle manner, he was a prince among men and was treated accordingly. Secretly, Magheen wished that she would find such a man when it came her time to marry and, if the whole truth were known, it might reveal that she was herself in love with the handsome youth in the elegant frame.

She opened the door. Her uncle was out for his daily stroll on the beach. A solid oak writing desk adorned the center of the room. The wooden floor was covered with well worn rugs and although the edges were frayed, the Celtic design was still visible in a multitude of faded hues. How often she had traced her finger over the circles and the odd shaped figures as she sat listening at her uncle's feet. This room was so special and it had a smell so different from the rest of the house, a strange blend of the present and the past, her uncle's smell mixed with the tang of leather, the piquant odor of old parchment, and the sweet pervasive scent of the turf fire. It was a man's room; it spoke of her uncle: the heavy leather chairs, the dark solid furniture, and the great stone fireplace flanked on either side by sturdy oak shelves stocked with manuscripts from every part of Europe. Tom O'Connor spent a large portion of his day and even larger portions of his night pouring over volumes and scrolls, deep in thought. Ever since Magheen could remember, she had been encouraged by him to read and, occasionally, he would even leave his own studies to read to her. On these rare occasions, she would sit enraptured as the deep resonant voice rose and fell in the musical lilt of their native tongue. The wonders he painted, the magical world he created, the glories of the olden days when noble knights and lovely ladies abounded. She so loved those precious moments and wished that they would never end.

"Why wasn't I born a boy?" Magheen asked. "It must be wonderful to go to school in France or Italy. I'd sure love to be as clever as my uncle; he knows so much!"

O'Connor had never married. He did not lack charm where the ladies were concerned, but, as he said himself, when asked the inevitable question, "Well, let's say that I've not had the good fortune to find the right lady."

Everyone liked him; he was kind and gracious. The fishermen bowed and called him "Sir" and the womenfolk curtsied. He was known by important people all over the land and they called him a learned man. Some even said he would have made a good and wise king, but Tom O'Connor wanted none of that. A peace-loving man, he had lived on the ancestral lands all of his life, except for a brief period in his youth when he went to study in France.

"Magheen, I'd sure like some help!" Moll sounded desperate.

"Ach, wisha," Magheen's scowl betrayed her thoughts. "Coming!" She closed the door and hurried off to the kitchen.

Magheen was growing into a high-spirited young girl who was interested in everything and everybody. Tall and slender, she had gained her full height of five feet five inches in her fourteenth year. Her independent nature, so perilously close to defiance, was a constant concern to the solicitous housekeeper. Her long sojourns on the moors and her dallying in the lonely coves gave the old woman many anxious hours. Moll Flynn's maternal instinct prevented her from making known these wild escapades to her uncle, so she had no one to blame but herself when Magheen defied her.

The small service rendered, Magheen raced up the spiral stairs to her own room to dress for dinner. She fastened a rose to her tight fitting bodice and then stood back to admire her image in the oak framed mirror. She was growing up, that was obvious. Her body was that of a woman. It was beautiful, how gently it curved. She placed her hands over her breasts and slowly, as if savoring the sensual pleasure of her young body for the first time, she traced the graceful lines. Then her eye caught the color of the bright red rose lying against her breast. It was a happy choice, complimenting the pale pink of her gown and contrasting with her pretty brown eyes.

"I'd sure like to be going to dine in one of the fine houses back in Dublin tonight," she said to the figure staring back at her. "You know, I think it's a pity not to let such a pretty girl be seen by the whole world, don't you?"

"Magheen," the housekeeper called. That meant that dinner was ready.

"Why doesn't Moll ring the bell? It's high time things were done in a more sophisticated manner around here. Perhaps I should talk to Uncle...mmm...yes, you're supposed to be preparing to take over a large household someday. Well, aren't you?" she asked the image in the mirror.

"Magheen, Magheen, dinner is served."

"Coming, coming," she said as she hurried to join her uncle who was already standing behind his chair when she entered the room.

"Good evening, Magheen. And how are you today, my dear?" his gentle blue eyes radiated peace and happiness.

"Really fine, Uncle, thank you."

"You look especially beautiful." He came to assist her with her chair and she admired his delicately shaped hands and manicured fingernails. On her twelfth birthday, her uncle had decided that she was no longer a child, but a young lady, and, as such, she should be accorded the little attentions due her position.

Moll always served the evening meal and then joined the family for dessert. This wasn't the time to bring up the question of her taking over the management of the house, but it was a very good opportunity to bring up the all important matter of her sixteenth birthday celebration. She and the housekeeper had been planning for months. It was so exciting. This would be the most spectacular event of her whole life.

"Uncle, I will be sixteen next month and would like to have a celebration. Do you think it could be arranged?" she asked in her forthright way, her glorious brown eyes eager with anticipation.

"Well, I don't see why not. I suppose it is a big event when a young lady reaches her sixteenth year." He smiled and Magheen couldn't doubt the love in his eyes. "Perhaps you should discuss this matter with Moll. She really knows so much more about these things than I do."

"May I invite anyone I wish?" Already she was counting the guests.

"Within limit. What kind of celebration were you considering?" he asked, thinking of his modest resources.

"Well, Moll was telling me that it's usual when a young lady gets to be of marriageable age, for her parents or guardian to hold a formal 'coming out' reception and ball so that she can be properly introduced to society." She folded her hands on her lap and assumed a pose calculated to show her uncle how grown-up she was.

"Oh, so Moll is already aware of the matter." He should have guessed.

"Well, sort of. We didn't really plan anything, we just talked." Magheen had learned from the housekeeper that the hand which rocked the cradle ruled the world and though the menfolk might consider themselves the lords and masters, if they so chose, as long as they were allowed to harbor this illusion and believe that their judgments and decisions were paramount, women knew they were free to carry on pretty much as they wanted.

Moll entered at this point, her face flushed from the exertion of carrying the heavy tray laden with a dish of steaming apple dumplings, a silver jug of hot brew, which she called "uisce beatha", and an assortment of china. Before she had time to deposit her load, Magheen spoke, "Oh, Moll, Uncle said we may have a fine ball for my birthday."

"Well, of course he did. You didn't expect anything else, did you?" She winked at Magheen, gave a little bow to Tom O'Connor, and seated herself at the end of the table, allowing Magheen to serve the dessert.

After dinner, Magheen and her uncle went to his reading room to draw up a guest list, for the invitations would have to be sent immediately and Sean, the yard man, would have to set out as soon as possible to deliver them. As the list was compiled, there were certain people whom her uncle wished to include, especially his good friend, Liam O'Sullivan, a physician from the town of Sligo. Then there were the Larkins from Ballyburn. They had a daughter who would be about Magheen's age. It might be good for the girl to get to know her, but Magheen should also be introduced to some young men of good families, Tom thought.

When the list was finished, it contained the names of a total of ten of the best families. Some of them, of course, would not be able to attend, others would come, mingle for a few hours merely out of curiosity, and then depart, while close friends would have to be accommodated for a night or two. Magheen spent the rest of the evening writing the invitations, and when they were completed, her uncle signed them.

"Now, my dear, we will consult with our good housekeeper." Tom rose from his favorite chair and waited for Magheen to precede him.

"Moll...! But she's..." Magheen was taken aback. Was her uncle losing his senses?

"Only a servant. Yes, Magheen, she may be a servant, but she's a wise and competent lady. Never be ashamed to seek the advice of those whose judgment you can trust."

Magheen blushed but hid her anger. Her uncle was nearly as bad as Moll when it came to fussing about small things. "Sorry, Uncle."

"No need to be, a gra. You're young and there are things you must still learn, you know. So lead the way, m'Lady." Tom O'Connor gathered up the pile of invitation cards and opened the door, allowing his niece to pass. "Come, my dear, let's adjourn to the kitchen." His step was light. "This is a happy moment, a milestone in my life, too."

"Oh, how exciting!" Magheen looked up into her uncle's face and she knew he would play up the moment to the ultimate. It was not too often that the Master of Inis Fail entered the inner sanctum of his faithful and efficient housekeeper. It would be a memorable occasion for Moll also.

Quickly, Magheen tripped forward. She was about to burst

headlong into the kitchen when her uncle spoke. "Not so fast, young lady. Knock. Moll deserves a little warning. She's not expecting me. Servants should be treated with respect. 'As you would have others do unto you.' You remember, don't you? The old dictum is applicable in every instance." He bowed to her indicating that she should knock.

Magheen was learning a lot this evening, and she realized her uncle was using the opportunity to teach her how to behave toward the servants in a well regulated and orderly household. No doubt she would be mistress of a large estate someday, perhaps one boasting of many servants. She stepped up to the kitchen door, knocked gently, and waited, then called "Moll" as she opened the door slowly. "May we come in? Uncle and I would like to talk to you." Before she entered she turned toward her uncle. He nodded his approval.

Moll didn't answer immediately. They heard a shuffle and a clattering of pots and pans. Tom O'Connor gave Magheen a "you see what I mean" look and then Moll was at the door.

"Why, your Lordship, come in, come in." The middle-aged woman greeted her honored guest, her revered master, with obvious pride and deep respect. "A chair, Mr. O'Connor, Sir. Here, take this one; 'tis the best." She hastily placed the one large arm chair near the fire. "There now, that should be comfortable for your Lordship. Turned out rather chilly, it has tonight, m'Lord." She seated herself opposite him, crossed her hands in her lap and was about to speak when Magheen interrupted.

"Moll..." Magheen, impatient to get to the business on hand, caught her uncle's eye. For a moment she remained open-mouthed, then without uttering another word, closed her lips tight, a little crestfallen.

"Yes, Moll, you were saying?" Tom O'Connor gave his full attention to his housekeeper to her quite evident satisfaction.

Magheen took a stool and placed it near the fire. A little embarrassed, she poked at the turf and decided not to speak again until she was spoken to. Uncle Tom went a little too far at times with his consideration for the servants, she thought and wondered if this trait were unique to him.

"Ahem," Moll cleared her throat. "Well, m'Lord, I was about to ask to what I owe the pleasure of your company? What is it that I can be doin' for you now, Sir?"

"Well, Moll, Magheen and I," he hesitated while Magheen acknowledged his smile, "wish to have your opinion regarding these invitations." He gestured to the pile of cards he still held in his hands. "We need your approval, you know."

"Oh, m'Lord, I'm quite sure if you have decided..." and her rosy face beamed with a rosier hue and her small grey blue eyes sparkled with pride.

"Now, now, Moll, you know I've always considered your good judgment in such matters. A woman's mind, it seems to me, has a way of knowing what's for the best in these affairs."

"Well, puttin' it that way, your Lordship, I'll do m' best an' give you me honest opinion." She squared her shoulders, raised her ample bosom, and adjusted a comb in her thinning, wavy hair.

Tom O'Connor pulled his chair up to the spotless table and placed the cards upon it.

Recognizing her superior position, the honor, and the trust shown her at this most important time in Magheen's life, Moll rolled up her sleeves as she got up. Then pouring some water from a clay pitcher into a wooden bowl, she meticulously washed her hands and carefully dried them in a clean white towel.

She smoothed her apron, caught a stray wisp of grey hair and drew it behind her ear, and finally seated herself at the table.

Magheen watched with some exasperation, then, realizing the importance Moll was giving to the matter, her excitement mounted. It was indeed an auspicious occasion. How could she have overlooked the essential, the most obvious reason for the whole affair? It was not the fact that it would be her sixteenth birthday or an excuse to have a gathering of the prominent families of the province, a celebration for the sake of celebrating. How often had Moll told her, were she listening, that it was high time a good husband be found for her. She would be toasted and feted, evaluated, criticized, and pulled apart. Well, let them. She would show them all that she was second to none in beauty, brains, talents, courage, determination, and resolve.

As the housekeeper seated herself, she spoke: "Wouldn't want any kitchen grease to be gettin' on them grand cards, you know."

Tom O'Connor recognized her careful concern with a nod and as he read off each name, he handed the card face up to her.

Magheen noticed how carefully Moll handled the cards. She examined the writing and when she was sure there was no mistake, she looked at Magheen and complimented her on a job well done. "I'm thinking there isn't another young lady as beautiful, intelligent, and charming as our Magheen in the length and breadth of Ireland," again the pride in her voice and bearing was obvious.

Tom smiled, "Well, let's say 'twould be hard to find one."

"At least I've two on my side and, of course, you're not at all biased," Magheen countered.

The first two or three cards, having passed Moll's critical inspection, were then placed in a second pile.

"Richard Burke, Lord of Mayo!" Moll's chest took on added dimensions. Magheen noted how she pursed her lips with pride. "Sure 'tis said he could buy the crown jewels an' not miss the money."

"Really?" Magheen raised her finely shaped, arched eyebrows and looked for confirmation from her uncle, but he merely smiled a noncommittal smile.

"His Lordship has a fine young son. Ah, I see you have included him in the invitation, Sir." She nodded her approval to O'Connor. "Come from France that lot, about three hundred years ago, an' what they couldn't buy, they took. But we can't be holdin' the sins of the fathers against the children. They've come 'round with time to seein' things our way. Aye, they have indeed. Though I'd prefer a Gaelic Lord for our Magheen here, a rich Sean Ghall wouldn't be turned away, I'm thinkin'."

Tom O'Connor smiled at the good woman's well meaning remarks but held his peace.

Magheen, ever ready with a retort, was about to make known her thoughts on the subject of choosing a husband when her uncle announced the name of the next guest.

When the final card had met with Moll's approval, Magheen could keep her tongue no longer bridled. "Oh, Moll isn't it a grand gathering we'll be having?"

"Aye, I can see we'll need to be gettin' started right away. But before I get side-tracked, there's one or two others you've overlooked, Sir, if you don't mind me sayin' it."

"Oh, indeed no, Moll. I'd appreciate any suggestions."

"Well, Sir, there's your own cousin, O'Connor Don, and, are you aimin' to be in trouble with the O'Neills?"

"Ach, I wasn't thinking of making this such a big affair. Just a few friends from around the area. I'm not so sure I want to part with our Magheen too quickly."

"Amen, to that, Sir, an' you know better, but word gets around and I've a mind folk will look on this affair as Magheen's comin' of age. 'Twould be awful if the wrong impression was given."

"Expect you're right, Moll." Tom O'Connor rested his chin in his left hand as he puzzled over the matter.

Magheen awaited his decision with bated breath. Moll, she realized, was planning festivities the like of which Ballindee had never experienced, at least in her lifetime.

"Magheen, get a few more cards and let's do things right," said her uncle, giving the top of the table a rousing wallop.

Magheen saw the triumphant glint in Moll's eyes as she adjusted another comb in her thinning coils and settled herself more comfortably on her chair. It was perfectly clear to her now that men were less than competent when it came to this sort of thing. She quickly left the kitchen, and as she went to her uncle's room, she reflected on how he had handled everything. Did he really forget to invite his own cousin? Was it an oversight or did he intend to have Moll remind him of so obvious a guest as her own grandfather, the Great Con O'Neill? It would be so like him to have considered such a gesture and she loved him the more for it.

The preparations to be made for such a gathering were so much more than Magheen had envisioned. She had thought about the decorating of the reception room, her new dress, and the food. Pies, puddings, cakes, and tarts would have to be served, accompanied by gallons of mead, ale, and wine. But she had scarcely an idea of the help needed to service so many people, the amount of food to feed those who had to come a long way and stay overnight, and all the other incidentals.

"My goodness! I could never have imagined that my birthday festivities would mean so much work for everyone," she confided to Moll.

"Oh, it's time we had a little excitement in an' around Ballindee.

Sure, in the great houses of 'The Pale' they'd think nothin' at all of an affair like this. Dining at the big houses, joining in the dancing that follows, an' attending the musical evenings, that's all them fine young ladies think about, and they're expected to attend several such events each season." Moll gave a quick nod, screwed up her thin lips and lifted her sandy eyebrows to assure Magheen that she knew exactly what she was talking about.

"My, I just can't imagine having four or five new gowns every year."

"Well, some o' them grand ladies do...aye, an' more. But you'll be findin' them things out for yourself soon enough, I'll be bound. Come help now, I need to get these curtains hung."

Moll, aided by two women from the village, had scrubbed and polished the house from "stem to stern". After the velvet window hangings were beaten and brushed, they were rehung. The delicate lace inner curtains washed, starched, and ironed, looked like new. As the last curtain was hung, Moll panted, "There, thank the Lord, that's done."

With the housework out of the way, Moll devoted the next week to cooking. The final week was given over to cleaning and polishing crystal and china. Finally, last minute touches were given to the furniture; fresh floral arrangements were set in place and all was ready.

Magheen was in a frenzy of excitement and anticipation. She went from one room to another checking to see that nothing was forgotten for the comfort of those who would be spending the night. She inspected the reception hall and feasted her eyes on the miracles Moll had performed, and at that moment she realized more than ever before how much love nestled in the "old" woman's heart for her. "The creature, she must be exhausted," she said as she passed along the aisle between the large banquet table and the mullioned windows that commanded such an exquisite view of the wild Atlantic. She noted the extras that Moll had added to the room, little hand embroidered pieces lending new richness and color to the old chairs, a bow, a flounce to wall hangings, a cheerful silk runner for the sideboard. When did she have the time for all this? She marveled and wiped away a tear.

Returning to her own room, she looked again for the umpteenth time at her gown now hanging beautifully pressed on the door of her armoire. She was proud that she had been able to help with the making of it. A pale lavender velvet, soft as down, light as a feather, the material was specially imported from Paris. The tight-fitting bodice, peaked and slightly gathered at the waist, was sewn with pearls, the full slashed sleeves held in place by satin ribbons of a darker violet hue. Underneath it, she would wear her first fathingale. The hoop support, introduced into England by Catherine of Aragon, first wife of Henry VIII, had become very popular. The three petticoats which lay carefully across the back of a chair were trimmed with lace and tiny pink rosettes. A pair of pink slippers complimented the outfit. Magheen couldn't wait for the next day. She had to show it to her uncle.

"My word! What have we here?" He got up from his desk. "Magheen, you look dazzling! Ah, if I were but twenty years younger!" He placed a tender kiss on her burning cheek.

"Thank you, Uncle. Thank you so much for making all this possible."

"I'm very happy to be able to do it for you, Magheen, love. Now let me see you walk the whole length of the room," Tom O'Connor said as he brushed a tear from his cheek. His little niece had grown into a beauty. How proud her mother would have been to see her, as he did now, in all her loveliness.

"You are a pearl of great beauty, my dear. I have not seen such charm, such elegance and grace, even in the great homes of England and France. You will steal all hearts." And all at once he was afraid, for such beauty could be dangerous to herself as well as to others.

"Oh, Uncle, you're teasing me." Her flashing white teeth rivaled the tiny pearls on her gown as her shapely red lips parted in an enchanting smile.

"No, indeed, my dear. Only I would have you use your great gifts wisely." Inwardly he prayed it would be so.

"Oh, Uncle." Magheen threw her arms around his neck and kissed him again and again. "Thank you for all you have done for me during my whole life. At this moment you have made me the happiest girl in the whole world."

"It has given me great pleasure to have done so. May you live many years to enjoy this gown and hundreds like it."

Magheen left her uncle with a heart flowing over with love and gratitude. She knew she would never forget this wonderful moment. Now, all was ready, the guests would start arriving the next day, and she could hardly wait.

She tossed and turned in a fitful sleep that night. Never in her whole life had she been the center of so much attention and tomorrow would be her day, her's and her's alone. She would be feted and toasted and she would know what it felt like to be a real princess. Maybe even a queen!

Five

The day dawned in a glorious display of summer's finest. Magheen got up and went to her window, pulling aside the heavy coverings. Over against the sea, a delicate mist was still clinging to the fringes of the white capped waves. The sun, caught in this lingering embrace, showered amethyst, pearl, silver, and rose gems along the amorous trail. The dew lay so heavy on the fields that they glittered like cloths of silver, while beneath in the short meadow grasses she could see that the yellow buttercups and golden hearted daisies were already wide awake. What a racket the crows were making in the hedgerow yonder, probably fighting over their morning meal. She opened the window, the tang in the air was strong and fresh. It would be a beautiful day.

She turned from contemplating the beauties of nature and caught a glimpse of herself in the mirror as she slipped into her white underskirt. A pretty face, she took hold of her long golden curls and wondered how she should wear her hair. It was always escaping in rebellious strands and wisps, no matter how she tried to tame it. Perhaps she should comb it to one side in a bundle of ringlets and then tie it with a bow. No, she tried piling it on top of her head. Again, the silken tresses refused to be bound and tumbled to her shoulders, then to her waist. "Perhaps, if I had a jeweled frame like the ladies my uncle described, this hair of mine would stay in place. Oh, well, I'm not going to let this mess spoil my day. I'm sure Moll will help me later on."

She finished dressing, donning a simple skirt of pale blue, gathered at the waist, and a light blue, loose-fitting bodice.

As the day wore on, the guests started to arrive. First came the physician, Liam O'Sullivan, his wife, and eldest son, Donald. The older folk were soon absorbed in lengthy conversation, leaving the young people to entertain themselves. It had been a long time since they had seen each other.

Donald was a shy young man of about twenty, his manner appeared stiff and rather haughty. But Magheen refrained from judging him too hastily. Perhaps his deportment was due to the fact that he had but lately returned from Spain, where he had been studying for several years. No doubt it would take time for him to readjust to the customs and habits of his native land. He was not an unattractive youth, with large hazel eyes, a straight, well-shaped nose, a strong chin and jaw, and a head of dark brown wavy hair. Small ruffs of Spanish lace adorned his manly neck and wrists, and a doublet of rich brocade was tailored to his slim figure. The black silk stockings she thought looked elegant. His hands were pale and delicate and the nails well manicured, showing refinement. He wore black leather shoes, no doubt of Spanish design, narrow and slit. For a while she did her best to entertain the young man, but she was inwardly relieved when the arrival of other guests demanded her attention.

"By your leave, Mr. O'Sullivan. I must attend..." she glanced in the direction of the group gathering in the entrance.

"Certainly," he said as he arose and bowed as Magheen withdrew. He was seemingly listless, detached, uninterested and would remain so for the better part of the evening as it turned out.

The dinner bell rang at seven sharp. The great reception room had been decorated with huge bouquets of fresh fern, red roses, and snowy white lilies, while forget-me-nots blended with delicate lily of the valley to form a very attractive centerpiece. Brightly burning candles spluttered in the huge candelabra, casting rosy shadows on the cream walls. In the hearth, the peat fire danced in brilliant, happy shades of red and purple. The vibrant tones of the harp mingled with the lively chatter and happy laughter filled the house. Magheen awaited her uncle's signal with a pounding heart and a flutter of excitement...her moment...her hour had come.

Magheen entered the room in regal fashion, escorted by her uncle. A hush descended on the guests, the harp fell silent. Proud and handsome, attired in traditional Gaelic dress black satin tight-fitting trews, a fine white linen shirt with sleeves wide and pleated and edged with delicate lace, he didn't wear a cloak, but on his left shoulder the emeralds in the Tara brooch glistened in the changing lights. Tom O'Connor bore himself as the prince he was. He led her to the place of honor at the head of the table and as he seated Magheen, her eyes fell on the red velvet box resting on the dinner plate. She took it up with trembling hands and opening it, a gasp of disbelief escaped her.

"What...what is this? Is this for me?" she asked as she looked up into the proud, loving eyes of her uncle.

"It was your mother's. She would have wished you to have it today. Allow me." He picked up the elegant necklace of rubies and fastened them around Magheen's slender throat. It was too much for the highly strung, sensitive girl. Overcome with emotion, two large tears welled up in the corners of her eyes, her throat restricted as she bent her head and tried to whisper: "Uncle Tom, you are so...so very...good to me."

O'Connor walked quickly to the other end of the table and raising his glass, said, "Ladies and gentlemen, a toast to my beautiful niece. May she always remain as beautiful as she is tonight. May her years be filled with health, happiness, and fulfillment." He saw that she had regained her composure.

The spell was broken. Words of admiration arose from all quarters. Magheen looked radiant in her new gown. The rubies sparkled against her creamy skin and vied with the crimson that suffused her burning cheeks. All eyes were upon her. Magheen was ecstatic; her every wish had been fulfilled and for this night, at least, she was a real princess!

The meal was served as platters of roast beef, pork, and lamb, surrounded by choice fresh vegetables, were passed around. Hot oatmeal breads, as well as rolls of rye, wheat, and barley, were hurried from the ovens of Moll Flynn's kitchen to the table. French and Spanish wines and Irish mead sparkled in the heavy crystal decanters. It was a veritable feast for eye and palate. Side dishes of freshly picked watercresses, mushrooms, leaks, celery, and radishes were garnished with nuts and a variety of fruits. The long sideboard flanking the wall was heavy with pies, jellies, pastries, fruit cakes, sponge cakes, trifles, puddings, and tarts. Moll knew how to entertain the high and mighty and she would make sure that the whole countryside was aware that Tom O'Connor's table was second to none.

Magheen's grandfather, now known as The Earl of Tyrone, was unable to attend. Having submitted to Henry VIII in 1542, he was harried on all sides, by his own who mocked him for compromising, and by his so-called allies, the Sasanach, whose only aim was to seize his land and exterminate his people. But to show that he had not forgotten her, he sent a diamond pendant with an enclosed note which read: "Learn from the mistakes of your forebears."

As the guests settled into the delectable business of satisfying goodly appetites, lengthy conversations and humorous repartee gave way to monosyllables and head nodding. To Tom, who sat opposite Magheen at the other end of the long oaken table, the part of the congenial, eloquent host came naturally. On his right sat O'Malley from neighboring Murrisk and his beautiful wife, Margaret, while on his left-hand side the older members of the Burke family were seated. Tom, never at a loss for stimulating topics of conversation, kept everyone entertained. At one point in the course of the meal, it seemed that all ears were straining to catch the remarks and banter from that part of the table.

The Rory O'Connors, descendants of the Kings of Connaught and the distant relatives of Tom, were seated opposite the O'Sullivans about midway down the table.

"Proper gentle folk they be. Come from Felem O'Conor's line. No bad blood in that lot," was Moll's comment to Magheen the day before when they were deciding on the seating arrangements.

Eveleen, at fourteen the eldest daughter of Rory, sat beside her father. Magheen noted with a little twinge of jealousy that Eveleen was not without charm. Large blue eyes fringed with heavy dusky lashes cast coy glances across the table at the handsome Richard Burke.

"Richard's a good catch," Moll's words came to Magheen's mind as she looked at Richard Burke. Then as she watched, Magheen could tell, with some satisfaction, that Richard was not really interested in her dark cousin. Aoife Larkin was the one to watch. That dazzling damsel could very well steal the show from Magheen, herself, if she weren't on top of things. It seemed the whole center of the table, made up mostly of young people, was hanging on her every word. Yes, Aoife was the young woman to watch and besides, if she were making a play for Richard Burke, Magheen had decided that Aoife had several advantages. She was at least eighteen, a mature woman in Richard's eyes. From snatches of conversation Magheen had gathered that Aoife had been educated in France and had been introduced into "society" at the Marques de Grandville's chateau just outside Paris—a sophisticated mademoiselle from all accounts.

Magheen bit her lower lip, lifted her chin, and her voice. She wasn't going to allow Aoife to monopolize Richard Burke.

"My dear Aoife, I'm sure Mr. Burke knows all about Paris. Every young man has been to the French capital." Magheen's eyes caught Donald O'Sullivan's. "Why, Mr. O'Sullivan here has just returned from Spain, but I think all these gentlemen must find Ireland more interesting at the moment. Am I not correct, Mr. Burke?" Magheen had thrown down the gauntlet. Would Richard take up the challenge and fly to her defense? Would he, the most eligible bachelor in all Connaught, acknowledge her, Magheen Ni Neill, for what she really was, a real princess superior to all others in the room.

"Ah, our lovely hostess honors me." He arose, lifted his glass, and made a gracious bow towards Magheen. Then, all eyes watching, he seated himself again with a flourish and continued to speak: "Ireland is a marvelous country for those who, shall I say, can afford it." He glanced around the table. A few heads nodded in agreement, but the older folks had turned their attention to each other, ignoring the brash youth.

Magheen never knew whether or not she had awakened Richard's interest at that moment or whether he was merely slighting her, but she did realize she could not impress him by embarrassing Aoife, no matter how slyly she did it. Had he really divined her intentions, had her approach been too obvious? A delicate blush rose to her cheeks. As she tried to appear involved in the conversation in her immediate presence, she noticed Donald O'Sullivan's eyes were riveted upon her. He had been watching her intently all evening. Did he, too, see through her little ploy? She lowered her eyes, but almost immediately her defiant nature surfaced. Oh, what of it. Who cares anyway, she thought. I'll do what I have to do. Yes, I'll do whatever I have to do to achieve my own end, and she held her head high, a flash of contempt in her lustrous brown eyes.

The ball that followed climaxed a perfect day. Magheen and her uncle led the first dance of the evening, and to the silver strains of the harp they introduced the stately measures of the pavane to some of their guests. There was loud, enthusiastic applause and Magheen noticed Richard appeared impressed, if condescendingly, by her accomplishments. Still, he made no attempt to engage her in conversation nor did he offer to dance with her.

It was well into the evening before Donald O'Sullivan again found an opportunity to speak to her. By that time, he had overcome his inhibitions; the good Spanish wine had loosed his tongue and freed a much more attractive character.

"Magheen, I pray you, may I have a word with you?" Donald's voice was soft, appealing, his eyes were warm and inviting, and his smile attractive, especially when his strong lips parted to reveal milk-white teeth.

"Why, of course, Mr. O'Sullivan."

He drew her aside. For a moment he gazed into her beautiful eyes, scarcely cloaking his ardent longings. The creamy skin was tightly drawn over her high cheek bones, flushed from the excitement of the evening. The color of her cheeks emphasized the shapely face, but now Donald's gaze was riveted on the mouth. Yes, he concluded, it was the mouth that had bewitched him the first moment he saw her. Perfectly shaped with a delicate upper lip, the lower one was full and sensuous. What untold delight for the man who would be privileged to steal a kiss, he thought. He hesitated and then, taking her hand, he bent low, Spanish style, and lightly kissed the tips of her fingers. Raising his dusky head, he whispered, "Magheen, I'm falling in love with you."

Magheen blushed and withdrew a little.

"Nay, don't leave. I've been watching you all evening, your loveliness surpasses anything I've seen in Paris, Madrid, none can compare with such radiant beauty."

"Mr. O'Sullivan, you do me honor, but your feelings toward

me, albeit sincere I'm sure, have I confess, been too...," she hesitated.

"Magheen, my dear, perhaps I have been too hasty. Nevertheless, I do assure you of the sincerity of my feelings. Perhaps if I were to ask your uncle's permission to call on you."

She again hesitated. No man had ever spoken so boldly to her before and, although she did not dislike this ardent youth who stood before her, she was not prepared to accede to his wishes. She, Magheen, was an independent spirit and would decide who would be an acceptable suitor.

"I thank you for your compliments. I am honored that you should consider me so highly as to wish to further our acquaintance, but at the present time I desire to retain my freedom, Sir."

Taken aback by her forthright declaration and obviously crestfallen, Donald, nonetheless, was in admiration of her outspoken reply and her firm determination to be her own person. He recognized the fire that burned within and could not help contrasting her with the young women of her rank in Spain, so submissive, self-effacing and eager to please. It was quite obvious that Magheen could not begin to comprehend such subservience.

"I respect your honesty. If I cannot at this time have the privilege of becoming better acquainted, I beg you, allow me to admire you from afar."

Magheen's musical laugh rang out: "Mr. O'Sullivan, I am afraid I can do very little to control your thoughts or actions from afar, but at the moment I would suggest we join the dance. We begin to attract attention; I care not for gossip."

Donald, though disappointed, resolved to be patient. Proudly he led her back to the dancing and only grudgingly shared her company with the other guests for the remainder of the evening. He was hopelessly and passionately captivated by this utterly enchanting and exquisite creature and knew that his heart was forever enslaved.

Magheen made several attempts to inveigle Richard Burke, short of asking him to escort her onto the floor, but to no avail. She noticed he had danced constantly with Aoife, avoiding everyone else. When finally he did approach her, obviously at the behest of his father, she felt intimidated and not at all herself.

Richard seemed taller than she had calculated now that she stood beside him. He was almost too muscular to be considered genteel. He had large, clear blue eyes which he could easily conceal behind long, fair lashes. Magheen couldn't be sure whether he was laughing at her or whether he was trying to fathom the inner deeper recesses of her mind. A straight nose and clean-cut features gave him a boyish look for all of his twenty-three years, and she felt the strength in his hand as he guided her through the intricacies of an Irish eight-handed reel. There was more to Richard Burke than his riches, she concluded, and she was determined to find a way to get to know him. Better still, she'd find a way to make him realize that she was really the "gem" he was seeking.

Magheen would never forget her sixteenth birthday, a real princess she was and had been treated accordingly; acknowledged as such by the most powerful and influential in the area. Before she retired for the night, she again sought a quiet moment with her uncle.

"Uncle Tom, no words will ever express how much I appreciate all you have done for me. No girl was ever so blessed as I am to have you and Moll."

"My dear, I am the happiest man in the world. You have made this one of the most memorable days in my life. Thank you so much." He kissed her warm brow before saying good night.

Magheen lay awake for hours; sleep eluded her. She allowed her imagination free reign. Her thoughts lingered on Donald. She was flattered by his attentions. Was she really that pretty? After all, he was a man of the world, had travelled, and seen many beautiful faces in France or Spain. He had said as much, yet he thought she outshone them all. What was it he had seen in her? She arose, lit a taper, and holding it close to her still burning cheeks, examined her face in the mirror.

"Mmm…got nice eyes. Yes, I'll grant you that." She looked at her nose but made no comment. It was slender, straight, and delicately flared. Her lips showed up glossy and red as ripe cherries in the flickering light. "Could be some handsome swain would want to steal a kiss or two," and she smiled at her own impertinence.

She placed the sputtering taper in a wall bracket, stepped back a pace, and raised her head to catch the dancing light as it played with the gold in her hair. Her ample linen nightdress was ill-suited to display the womanly figure that had been admired throughout the evening. She pulled the silken ribbon so carefully tied earlier. The outline of her young breasts was barely visible in the dim light. She lit another candle and as it hissed and sputtered into life, she raised her hands to her shoulders and drew the soft folds apart, then emboldened by the beauty that was displayed before her, she allowed the garment to fall to her feet.

"Oh, yes. I am beautiful!" she exclaimed softly and remembered the story of Helen of Troy, the face that launched a thousand ships. "You may not cause a war, Magheen Ni Neill, but...wait a year or two." She smiled at her reflection.

Six

"Ah ha! I have it," exclaimed Magheen to herself as she lay in bed a few mornings after all the house guests had departed.

Her thoughts were focused entirely on the Burke family. She had hoped for an opportunity to speak to Richard Burke before he left, but, unfortunately his family and the Larkins departed at the same time, and Magheen was determined not to give Aoife the satisfaction of suspecting that she was even remotely interested in Richard. She had tarried with some other guests, a little apart, then as the Burkes were about to leave, she noticed that Richard Senior took her uncle's hands in both of his. Clasping them tightly, she heard him say, "A cara dilis, I won't leave till you promise me you'll come spend a few days with me soon. The fishing is superb on the lake and the hunting...ah, but you don't care for that. I wager I can still tempt you to a game of chess, though. What say you?"

"Richard, 'tis right kind of you to ask. Now, you know I'm not one to gad about, but your suggestion is tempting. I've had a mind to visit Cong Abbey for a long while, I don't mind telling you. Maybe I could kill two birds with one stone," he said with a twinkle in his blue eyes.

"As you will, Tom. As you will. You might even persuade me to go to the Abbey with you." He laughed and laid his hand on Tom's shoulder. "Well, I'll be expecting you. Aye, and bring young Magheen along, too."

At that point, Richard drew closer to Tom O'Connor and whispered something in his ear. Both men smiled and parted.

Lying now in bed, with the early morning sunbeams dancing

through the mullioned windows and across the polished floor until they pivoted and careened about the long mirror, Magheen relived the scene. She had an invitation to visit Cashel-Corrib, the ancestral home of the Burke family. If she could only persuade her uncle to accept, she could then put her little plan into operation.

The Burke family was Sean Ghall. Had she forgotten *her* roots, true Gael, and her grandfather's words: "You will marry a Gaelic prince" rang through her head. Her ambitions, to wrest her beloved land from the foreigner and to achieve a name that would live forever in the hearts and minds of her people, would be better served by strengthening ties with the old families, those who had for centuries proved themselves great and powerful, like the O'Flahertys, the O'Malleys, the O'Sullivans. "But times are changing," she said quietly. "Those older and wiser than I have had to recognize that. Even grandfather has had to abandon the old ways, acknowledging Henry as his supreme lord and renouncing his ancient and honored position as The O'Neill for a new meaningless title, Earl of Tyrone...whew...disgusting...."

Were the Sean Ghall any worse? She remembered the Geraldines—The Houses of Kildare and Desmond. How many of their lives had been sacrificed, how many imprisoned and tortured because they refused to submit to English laws—renounce religion, language, customs, marriage with Gaelic families, fostering sons in Gaelic houses. How did her grandfather compare? He had saved his life...but at what price? Magheen continued to ponder. O'Neill was an old man now, wiley and astute, yes; he had kept his lands, he had protected his people. Mayhap...there was more to his behavior than was commonly acknowledged.

Again her thoughts returned to Richard. The Burkes were rich. Wealth spoke, an important, in fact, essential ingredient in the struggle to achieve power and prestige. If Aoife Larkin had wormed her way into Richard's good graces, if not into his heart, then she could certainly do no less. What would a creature like Aoife do with such great wealth? A brainless, though supposedly educated girl, obviously possessing little self-respect or character. She would be content to hover in the shadows or slink in menial fashion behind her would-be lord, anticipating his smallest needs, acceding to his every wish and fawning on him in slavish obedience. Richard, on the other hand, she had noticed, paid little attention to Aoife, scarcely aware of her existence except as an avid listener. So full of his own importance and bent on impressing others was he, that there was neither time nor space for anyone or anything else. "Conceited...a braggart, a bombast, brash," she spat out each word with determination and disdain.

Getting out of bed, she wasn't as convinced as she had been some fifteen minutes earlier that her plans to conquer Richard would succeed. But it took only one look at herself in the mirror for her confidence in her own inner worth and her obvious beauty to return. Perhaps all was not lost as far as Richard was concerned. He was still young and, given the opportunity, she felt she could handle his re-education.

"Even a stubborn mule or a wild hawk is not completely intractable," she mumbled. "Mayhap it's not all his fault. As the first-born and heir apparent he has been, without doubt, over indulged, pampered."

And the thoughts of what she would be able to do with his vast resources and how much she could accomplish from a position of wealth and power again held sway in her mind and she reasoned that such considerations were far more important than an overbearing, self-centered husband. It never occurred to her that someone as selfish as Richard might not be too eager to part with or share some of his wealth even for, what she considered, patriotic reasons.

She had heard that Richard was a fine sportsman, had a stable of thoroughbreds, and was considered one of the best falconers in the country. She had never competed, but she felt that in both sports she was equal if not superior to most. She was determined she would soon find out. Color mounted to her cheeks as Magheen thought of young Richard. He offered a challenge. She liked the idea, an opportunity to demonstrate her own abilities and to "open" Richard's eyes.

Until now, when suddenly she seemed all grown up, Magheen had not seriously considered marriage. She knew it must come someday, but not until the festivities for her sixteenth birthday had she ever given it much more than a passing reflection. She recalled her grandfather's words again. "Choose a husband from the Gael."

Why had the old man been so emphatic? Were not the Sean Ghall more Irish than the Irish themselves? she asked herself. Upon further consideration, she assured herself that what she intended to do would turn out for the best. She had her pride, however; she would not throw herself at Richard's feet. She was no Aoife. Riches or no, she would not forget who she was and that there wasn't a Sean Ghall family in the country that had a history and a lineage as ancient as her own.

Magheen paid more attention to her dress and to her appearance in the days that followed. After carefully bathing in rosewater, she went to her armoire to select a gown. Her wardrobe was scant and didn't consist of the latest fashions. She concluded that a visit to the Burke estate would most certainly require a few changes of dress. She reached in and pulled out her favorite summer skirt. Why, even that looked a rag! How could she ask for more clothes when her uncle had so recently paid a huge sum for her gorgeous birthday gown? She'd have to talk to Moll. Somehow, Magheen felt the good woman would have a solution to the problem.

She dressed in a bright blue, tight-fitting bodice and a full linen skirt of a deeper hue. Then, she drew back her hair with two small combs and secured it behind in a loose fall of golden ringlets which reached to her waist, a shower of radiant beauty. Putting on her house slippers, she descended to the breakfast room.

"Good morning, Uncle."

Tom O'Connor looked up from a manuscript. "Good morning, my dear. You look as fresh and lovely as a May flower. And I can see you have new fire in those charming eyes."

"Arrah, Uncle, I don't know how you ever escaped. A handsome man with such honeyed words early in the morning."

Tom laughed, "I'm better off, I'm thinking. 'No sense borrowin' trouble,' as they say."

Magheen wasn't too sure. He had so much to give. He had buried his head again in his manuscript and soon became absorbed in meditative perusal of the Greek work.

She ate in silence for a few moments, wondering how best to approach the subject of a trip to Cashel-Corrib. Then lifting her hand to her lips she cleared her throat "A...ahem...How's it coming, Uncle?"

"Eh? Oh, this." He nodded towards his work. "Can't say I'm making much progress. This one's particularly difficult to translate."

"What you need is a change." Magheen seized the moment. "Why don't you decide to accept Richard Burke's invitation? It would be nice for you to see some new places and besides, I know how much you've wanted, for a long time, to visit Cong Abbey."

"Maybe you're right, at that. I'll give it some thought. You'd like to accompany me, no doubt?" He looked at her with raised eyes and bent head.

Magheen nodded. "I'd like that very much."

"Then why give the matter any more thought. Let's set the date and send word to our gracious hosts."

Magheen was ecstatic. "Oh, Uncle, you're an angel!"

"I'm not sure that's the correct appellation, my dear." Tom smiled at his niece. "But better that than the opposite."

"Uncle, you've always been my angel." She got up from the table and stood beside him a moment, looking down with pride and admiration in her eyes. Then she bent and placed a kiss on his upturned cheek.

"Well now, where were we? Oh, yes. About to set a date we were for our little trip. A fortnight from today? Could you be ready by then, do you think?" Her uncle smiled one of those teasing smiles he used when he was in a particularly good humor.

"I'm sure I'll be ready by then, Uncle. But there are a few things I ought to talk over with Moll, first."

"Then let me know this evening. I'll make inquiries in the village. Perhaps someone going south could deliver a message for us." With that, Tom got up from the table. "I'm off for my morning stroll. See you later, my dear."

Magheen was in a frenzy of excitement. She barely picked at her food, having swallowed only a few mouthfuls of bread and a half-slice of bacon, she summarily descended on Mrs. O'Flynn. All her uncle's careful coaching regarding the treatment of his worthy servant had been forgotten in the tizzy and flurry of the moment. She burst into the kitchen. "Oh, Moll, Moll, I'll give you three guesses."

"What now?" Moll stoked the fireplace and swung the kettle

over the flames. "Must be that uncle of yours is spoilin' you again. A new pony?"

"Wrong." Magheen skipped around the table and came within a few inches of Moll's plump right elbow, giving it a little squeeze. "Give you a clue 'cause I know you'll never guess," she teased.

"Arrah, go on with you. Think I've got nothin' else to do but play with you this hour o' the morning. Shoo, out of my way with you." She picked up her apron in the old familiar way and shook it at Magheen.

"Oh, you're an old spoil sport." Magheen puckered her lips and pulled a pouting face, just as when a small child she demanded her own way.

Moll, who had begun to sweep the floor, stopped with one hand on her hip, the other supporting the long handled broom, her face a mixture of anxiety and amusement. "Come now, it can't be that bad!"

"Oh, you've gone an' spoiled it all." Magheen pretended to be hurt.

"What do you expect of an old woman at this time o' day? I'm not sixteen you know." Moll laid the broom against the wall and sat on the nearest stool. "Well now, it can't be another new dress?"

"Mmm...could be partly right," said Magheen, puckering her pretty lips.

"Ach, I give up. My old head has ne'er a thought in it before I got something in my stomach."

"Then I'll tell you. We're off to Cashel-Corrib!"

Moll's mouth dropped open and her grey-blue eyes grew wide, showing so much white Magheen was reminded of young spring onions. After a moment of silence she found her tongue. "Is it joking you are? Trying to fool old Moll?"

"An' why would I be doing such a thing? Don't you know Richard Burke asked uncle to visit him?"

"Sure, sure, but I...."

Magheen hurried to throw her arms around old Moll's neck. "Isn't it wonderful? Oh, I'm so excited, I can hardly stand it." Then she straightened up and grew serious. "But you know something, I'll be needing some clothes. What am I to do? I can't ask Uncle to spend more money at this time!"

"One thing at a time, girl. I'm flabbergasted. Things happening too fast around here these days. Here, finish the floor and let me think."

Magheen took the broom without objecting and made short work of what Moll considered a twice daily necessity. Then she seated herself beside the housekeeper and with patience, a virtue she badly needed to cultivate, waited for a solution to her difficulties.

"You'll certainly need some changes. Can't have you going to such a fine establishment as Cashel-Corrib in a few rags." Moll screwed up her face.

It must help her thinking process, Magheen thought.

"Your uncle's gone for his walk, I suppose?"

"Yes, he left just before I came in here."

"Then, let's get the breakfast things cleared away and we'll take a look in your armoire. Maybe some things there that, with a little flounce or some new lace, could be made to look halfway decent."

Magheen and Moll spent several hours going through the wardrobe. Articles no longer fit to wear were promptly discarded and those having hope of redemption were set to one side, while her good dresses were carefully replaced in the armoire.

"A little tuck here and a flounce there will give this one a new look. Now let me see." Moll rubbed her chin. "Two weeks. We can do a lot of damage in that time." Her eyes twinkled with merriment and the wrinkles around her mouth almost disappeared as she smiled, anticipating the pleasure of outfitting "her child".

Magheen smiled also. Moll's brains were working. Everything would be fine. Then, as if she had completely dismissed the whole project, Moll said, "It's time I pay that sister of mine a visit."

Magheen's mouth dropped open. Was she mistaken? Surely Moll wouldn't desert her now, the old woman was losing her head completely.

Moll saw Magheen's anxiety. "Oh, quit your fretting. You'll be old before you're twenty. Now don't you know it's a way for me to be doing a wee bit of shopping in Ballina. I've kept a little money from the allowance, and I have a little extra that I saved for emergencies. This is certainly an emergency! So, I think we can be sending you off in right proper style."

By this time, the tears were flowing fast. "What…what can…I say. No girl could ask for a better mother." Magheen had hit the right cord.

"There, there, child. Old Moll will see you lack for nothing. Not as long as there's breath in this old body o' mine, you know that, don't you. Eh?"

"Yes…of course. But I don't want you spending your own money on me."

"Who says I'm spending my own money?"

"I thought…"

Moll interrupted. "'Tis too much thinking you're doing. 'Tis bad for you. Now if you'll be helping me a wee bit in the kitchen, I'll prepare enough to last the both of you for a day or two, and tomorrow bright and early, I'll be off to see my sister."

With that Moll gave Magheen a big hug. "Come, young lady, we've a lot of work to do."

Seven

All nature was determined to celebrate this special occasion. The sun shimmering in an almost cloudless sky lent warmth and additional brilliance to land and sea, giving the lie to the yardman, Sean, who earlier had predicted rain.

"A red sky in the morning's a shepherd's warning" was his greeting to Moll when he entered the kitchen ready to load the carriage.

"Arrah, go on with you, haven't you anything better to say? Don't go spoilin' it all for them now," she answered. "'Twill be a fine day, I tell you."

As the horses plodded up a steep hill, Magheen put her head out of the window. Every sense was pleasantly and powerfully assaulted. Honeysuckle and wild roses drenched the air with delicate perfumes, and from the sea came the tang of kelp. The lark had left the meadow and soaring aloft, challenged the warbling of blackbird and thrush. The gulls and terns offered uninterrupted accompaniment to the intermittent chirrups from the hedgerows. Gorse in golden clumps, daisies and buttercups in extravagant perfusion, clouds of Peacock and Red Admiral butterflies hanging low to the ground, and tumbling happy streams of crystal water were displayed before them. She was alive to everything.

"Oh, Uncle, it's all so lovely." Her beautiful eyes fairly danced in her head as she spoke.

"Aye, my love. 'Tis an exceptionally beautiful day and the countryside is at its best." He looked from one side to the other admiringly. "So old and yet eternally young, this land of ours." She did not respond and he allowed his thoughts, for some time, to carry him to other more peaceful times. At length he sighed...a little sigh.

"You feel it too?" Magheen had withdrawn from her place at the window and now rested her back against the well-worn black leather upholstery, lost in contemplation of the mysteries of life and nature. Her uncle's sigh had aroused her.

"There's a strange enchantment, a mystical hold on this land. I feel that a soul dwells deep within. Ireland has a life of her own and none will ever rob her of it. She belongs to the ages past as she does to future, yet unborn, generations."

"Well spoken. Yes, I too feel the spirit of this great land... strong, vital, unconquerable."

It was late afternoon when they stopped at Mulrany. While Sean saw to the horses, Magheen and her uncle stepped into the local inn for some refreshments. As they entered, the occupants grew silent, eyeing them suspiciously, waiting for some sign—a signal imperceptible yet perceived. No word was spoken, yet the visitors' identity was known within seconds of their entering. Conversation resumed and the newcomers were left to enjoy a modicum of privacy.

Magheen overheard the comments as she sampled the mutton stew. There was talk of crops and weather interspersed with local scandals, and there was mention of fighting and rebellion. Times were unsettled. There was a restlessness in the country, a feeling of uneasiness. She heard the rumors of destructive forces at work in Munster; 'twas said that the whole province was laid waste, from Waterford to Kerry, and in every county there had been burning and complete devastation. England had spared nothing to rid itself forever of the accursed Gael. In their gathering places, around the peat fires, in small cabins, before the blazing hearths, and in the great halls of the chieftains and lords, the comments were the same. It was time the country's leaders organized. It was time for all Irishmen to make a stand against the cold-blooded atrocities of these murdering barbarians.

Sean joined Magheen and her uncle in the cosy inn about ten minutes later and soon made short work of the mutton soup, the platter of fresh mackerel, and the fine oatmeal bread that Tom

O'Connor had ordered for him. The meal was finished with mugs of buttermilk.

An hour later the trio were on their way again. Eleven miles or so of rough road separated them from the big and important town of Westport. The carriage waved in and out between the monochromatic, low lying, drystone walls and there were rocks everywhere. Clew Bay, itself, was dotted with a seemingly endless assortment of rocks and boulders.

"What on earth?" Magheen asked, seeing the unique landscape for the first time.

Her uncle smiled. "When God made the world, my dear, he had a lot of useless stones left over, so he thought the best place for them was right here in Clew Bay."

"Oh, Uncle!" she said as she smiled at his fanciful explanation.

"Well, it makes for a good story. I should imagine it's just part of natural erosion, or maybe volcanic activity long ages past."

They arrived in Westport late in the evening and were so tired that they decided to go straight to bed after supper. The town was still asleep the following morning when they left, promising themselves to shop on the way back.

A short distance outside Westport they came into a region of lakes, undulating land where sparkling, gurgling streamlets surprised the newcomer, for they seemed to appear in the most unexpected places. Approaching the village of Partree, the scenery became even more spectacular, as on one side of the carriage lay Lough Carra and on the other Lough Mask.

"What beauty!" cried Magheen, obviously enthralled by so much loveliness.

As far as the eye could see, the waters of Lough Mask spread southward crystal clear, sparkling in the golden glow of the afternoon sun. The placid surface was disturbed only by playful trout and fat-bellied salmon. Plovers, wild ducks, and a couple of grey herons gathered close to the water's edge; the latter dipping long necks into the shallows in search of dinner. On the west the Partry Mountains seemed to rise out of the lake itself, protecting the gentle waters from the western breezes. Tranquility and a quiet contentment bathed the entire scene.

The travelers could not afford to tarry longer. With a "Gee

up, there" and a light jerk on the reins, the carriage headed south into the Plain of Moytura.

"What are they?" Magheen pointed to a grouping of stones.

"Cairns, marking the graves of those who died in prehistoric conflicts. The Dedanaans, who came from Greece, and the Firbolgs fought for possession of this area. You remember, my dear, these were the peoples who inhabited our country long before the Celts conquered them."

"It's quite obvious why so many would wish to own this spot," Magheen remarked as they neared the end of their long journey.

Lough Corrib lay before them in all its glory. Magheen gasped, "It can't be real; it's got to be a fairyland."

"The Lake of a Hundred Islands, it's called."

"Words are inadequate! It's too beautiful," was all she could say.

"Yes, I know what you mean. God has surely given our people a beautiful land, an' sure, he knew the Celt had the soul to appreciate such things." Tom contemplated the scene a while and the artist in him exulted. "Look, see over there, it's barely visible among the trees. That's Cashel-Corrib, the stone tower on the Corrib. But it's more than a stone tower now, I tell you. Well, we'll just about make it before dusk."

It was still light when the carriage reached the gates. The sun takes a long time to set in Connemara on summer nights. The lough was now a pool of gold reflecting the afterglow. The trees had donned a dazzling garb of russet hues and towering in the background, the mountains, clothed in a shadowy mantle of blue, contrasted boldly with the crimsons in the slashed and bleeding sky.

The carriage slowed down considerably before drawing to its final halt because Sean, the fortunate driver for the occasion, was not oblivious to his new surroundings either.

Stately did not do the dwelling justice, yet to call it grandiose, one would lie. It was a structure of no mean dimensions and had at one time, it was plain to see, boasted of a tower. That portion of the building now rested beneath a cape of ivy and wild woodbine, no doubt a haunt for fairy folk on summer evenings such as this.

Sean jumped down from his perch and hastened to open the carriage door. "We're here, Sir," he announced.

"Right you are, Sean. An' a very good job you've done, man.

No need to tell you, I suppose, to take good care of the animals. We'll be needing them on the way back, you know," and he laid a hand on Sean's shoulder.

"Leave everything to me, Sir. Have no fear, Sean Murphy's not one to be sleepin' on the job."

"That's the man. Knew I could depend on you," Tom answered before he turned to assist Magheen from the carriage and up the stone steps to the large entrance.

"Welcome, Sir, m'Lady." The servant bowed and stood back to allow them to enter.

The entrance hall was large and spacious, surrounded by a gallery on the upper floor. Huge chandeliers hung from the beamed ceiling and cast shadows on the Celtic designs in the tapestries and floor rugs. Several pieces of furniture, chairs, potted plants, and a large oak table were arranged tastefully around the periphery. There was a spaciousness about the place. Magheen was impressed.

Before the visitors could speculate on what was behind the large oak doors on both sides of the entrance hall, the jolly resonant voice of Richard Burke greeted them from the second floor. "Cead mile failte, a chairde dilse." How proudly he rolled the customary Irish welcome.

Moll was right, as usual, the Sean Ghall had indeed learned the Gaelic ways and were proud to display their knowledge.

When Richard Burke appeared around the curve of the stairs, Tom and Magheen were a little taken aback to see the Lord of Cashel-Corrib wearing traditional Irish dress. A loose milk-white linen gown reaching below the knees was gathered at the waist with a golden sash, on his right shoulder an enormous gold Tara brooch studded with emeralds, rubies, and diamonds held the end of a rich, red velvet cloak. He wore black silken hose and black kid leather shoes.

"As you can see, I've dressed to honor this occasion," he said and bowed. "So you've come all the way from Ballindee today? You do me great honor, Tom, Magheen." Again he bowed slightly to each in turn. "Had you a good trip?"

"Indeed, we had. A very pleasant one, didn't we, love?" Tom addressed Magheen as he answered Burke and she nodded her assent.

"Well, you'll be wanting a wee rest and a change, no doubt, before you meet the family at dinner." Burke turned to his butler. "Brian, show his Lordship and the Lady Magheen to their rooms, if you please."

"Yes, Sir. Certainly, Sir."

Magheen felt a surge of pride. She had been addressed as "Lady". As she and her uncle were escorted to their respective bedrooms, her thoughts were with Richard; she was busy planning. She was here in Cashel-Corrib with one aim and she mustn't allow anything else to divert her from her purpose.

After freshening up, she chose a brand new gown, one Moll had managed somehow to make for her in those few short days of hustle and bustle before they left Ballindee. It was a pea green silk, cut daringly low in front, Magheen thought. But Moll, who knew all about these things, insisted that she was now a young woman of high society and according to the fashions of the day, a discrete display of her charms was appropriate. The bodice was tightly fitted to her shapely body, the skirt very full, the underdress, a darker shade of green made of the new light-weight taffeta, gave form to the outer garment. A mauve velvet ribbon was woven into the neck line, into the sleeves above the elbows, and around the skirt in several places. Magheen pondered whether or not she ought to wear her farthingale then she finally decided against it, a bit too formal for the first evening.

She looked at herself in the enormous bronze mirror and twirled to get the full effect of the lavish skirt. "Mmm...it's just beautiful. Bless old Moll, whatever would I do without her." She was satisfied she really did look elegant in her new gown. With both hands, she scooped up her hair and piled it on top of her head. Yes, she thought, with her hair up and held in place with the two new mother of pearl combs, she could pass for a young woman of seventeen or even eighteen!

The family had already assembled in the great hall when Magheen and her uncle were announced. A fire burned in the enormous grate at the other end of the hall and before its blazing peat flames, two massive wolf hounds were stretched, enjoying the warmth. There was a spicy aroma of homemade mead and cider and a lavish display of cut roses in the center of the table. White linen table clothes and monogrammed silverware, obviously French, and glistening crystal decanters and goblets, lent an air of festivity and opulence.

Richard, clad as he had been earlier, came forward, his arms extended. "Cead mile failte." He then introduced each member of his large family. All were lavish with their compliments, making Tom O'Connor proud of his niece.

A quick glance around the family gathering caused Magheen some consternation. Young Richard was nowhere to be seen. Was all her plotting and planning for nought?

After a few words of welcome from each of the five sons and four daughters present, Richard Burke escorted his stately wife, Maeve, to her place at the end of the long table. Then he stepped up to Magheen and guided her to a place one removed from the lady of the house. No sooner was Magheen seated than she realized that a young man had quickly assumed a standing position behind the vacant chair to her left. Dare she hope? It would be unpardonable to steal an upward glance. The female members having been seated, the young men of the family assumed standing positions around the table.

"In nomine Patris et Filii et Spiritus Sancti, Amen...." The Latin rendition of the grace before meals rolled off the tongue, the host demonstrating once again his total commitment to the Irish ways. Fluency in both languages, Gaelic and Latin, separated the Gaelic Irish and the Sean Ghall from other English intruders.

It was only when the blessing of God was called down upon his family, his household, his food, and his country, not forgetting an extra invocation for his guests, that the noble Sean Ghall seated himself, followed by his fine sons. But before anyone spoke, the master of Cashel-Corrib again raised his voice.

"Since my eldest son seems to be making it a habit lately of being late for dinner, perhaps he can make amends by leading us in a toast to our honored guests."

"My pleasure, Father." The response was quick and confident.

Magheen's heart missed a beat. Richard! Richard was actually sitting at her left-hand side. Mother of God, if her heart didn't stop pounding like a bodhran he'd surely hear it when he reseated himself.

Raising his glass, Richard spoke in an evenly modulated voice. "Slainte, to our most honored and distinguished guests. To the noble Lord of Ballindee and to the elegant Lady Magheen."

There was a clinking of glasses and unanimous approval from all at the table. Then in a rising crescendo, Richard continued: "And to the household of the great Burke family, Slainte, to the fair and gracious Chatelaine, and to the Lord of Cashel-Corrib."

"Well spoken," a small voice piped up from under Magheen's right elbow. It was Micaleen, the youngest son of Richard and Maeve Burke, who promptly added for Magheen's benefit, "I'm going to be six tomorrow."

"You are! Well, happy birthday, young man," said Magheen.

Everyone laughed and general chatter began all around the table, but it was obvious that the guests were the topic of conversation.

It was some time before Richard actually spoke directly to Magheen. Seated so close to his mother, he naturally allowed her to begin and then direct the conversation.

Just before the dessert was served, when most stomachs were already full, there was a lull in the chatter. It was then that Richard turned and looking straight into Magheen's eyes, addressed her. "So you'll be staying with us for a few days. You must make time to ride with me."

Did she detect a hint of arrogance in his voice? Magheen wondered.

"S'pose he wants to show off his falcons again." Micaleen sounded bored at the idea.

Magheen glanced at the child but immediately returned her attention to Richard. "You follow the hawks? How exciting!"

Richard's face lit up. "You interested in falconry?"

"But of course!" she answered enthusiastically.

"Most ladies don't like to follow the hawks. That's what Richard says," Micaleen's voice interrupted again.

"Oh, shush, Micaleen. You talk too much. And besides, Magheen isn't like most ladies," insisted his oldest brother.

Magheen wondered what he meant by that statement and again was aware of the inflections in his sonorous voice, but she was determined to stick to her course.

"How about tomorrow? Do you think you'd like to..." he was obviously anxious.

"Richard! The young woman has only arrived. Give her a day at least to settle in." The Lady Maeve laid a hand on Richard's arm as if to restrain his rather impulsive nature.

"Oh, 'tis quite all right, m'Lady, I'm used to such things. If Richard would like to show me his birds, I'll be happy to accompany him," Magheen said reassuringly.

"Good. 'Tis settled then. We'll ride tomorrow morning at nine." With that matter taken care of, Richard presently forgot Magheen and she was forced to converse for a while with Micaleen.

After dinner, the family adjourned to the adjoining room and broke into little groups more or less according to ages. Kathleen, a little younger than Magheen, joined her soon after she left the table.

Kathleen was a slight, rather small girl for her age. She had her mother's delicate frame, grey-blue eyes well spaced above high cheek bones, a small, slightly turned-up nose, and too large a mouth that Magheen thought made her a rather plain girl. But if Kathleen's features were not particularly attractive, her posture and dress lacked nothing. She wore a beautiful gown of pink satin with inserts of rose velvet. A single rosette of the same hue caught above her right ear was the only adornment to her long brown tresses. On her creamy throat rested a small tear-shaped diamond which was suspended from a slender gold chain.

"I've been looking forward to your visit. Papa told me all about your coming of age celebration. I won't have mine for another two whole years. I hope you will be able to attend." Kathleen was excited.

"Oh, I'd love to," Magheen said, but she was only half listening as Kathleen rambled on. From time to time, her eyes sought Richard's restless figure, but she was unable to catch his attention or engage him in conversation for the rest of the evening.

Meantime, Kathleen chattered on. "Magheen, Micaleen told me that Richard intends to whisk you away in the morning, to go falconing with him." She drew closer and lowered her voice, "Don't let Richard make a fool of you, Magheen. I know I shouldn't say bad things about my own brother, but he makes me so angry at times. Says I'm too young to go out hunting with him. Only wants older women to accompany him. Can't be responsible for children. All he thinks of is his old birds. Papa says he believes Richard's brain has about the same amount of grey matter as his peregrine. He lives with his birds for days at a time, talks of nothing else when he's at home. Mama, too, thinks he's bird crazy."

"Doesn't he have any friends?" asked Magheen, somewhat bewildered by this unexpected disclosure.

"Not many. He's not especially popular with the ladies; changes his mind too often."

"Then he doesn't have one special sweetheart?" Magheen had not anticipated further competition. She had calculated the odds of wrestling with Aoife's hold on Richard, but the man she now perceived was already a rake, a libertine....What if this Richard, for all his wealth and illustrious name, were no more than...? She shuddered.

Kathleen prattled on, oblivious to Magheen's musings, glad to have someone near her own age to whom she could talk.

"Papa would like Richard to settle down, you know. That's the only reason Papa ever attends the parties and soirees given by the local gentry...." Kathleen quickly drew in her breath and placed her hand over her mouth. Her eyes fairly bulged in their sockets so shocked was she by her own blunder. A moment's silence followed. Then Kathleen, becoming aware that what she had said did not seem to affect Magheen, continued to elaborate.

"It's not like as if we lived in a populous area, Papa says, where Richard would have his choice of many young women."

Magheen was becoming embarrassed by Kathleen's obvious indiscretions, but her curiosity was aroused. She was, in fact, fascinated. Despite her better judgment, she was anxious to hear all she could about Richard Burke. Every little bit of knowledge was as extra ammunition, strengthening her own position against the time when she would have to do battle alone.

"So you think your papa is eager to find a wife for your brother, Richard?"

"Oh, yes, indeed. He's twenty-three, you know. Will be twenty-four in October," Kathleen again grew confidential. Drawing closer to Magheen, she whispered: "Papa has given him six months to find a suitable bride for himself. If he fails in that time, Papa will decide."

"Putting a little pressure on him, eh?" responded Magheen carelessly, smiling at her new friend.

"I suppose. But you know, he's lucky. Most men are," confided Kathleen.

"Why so?" asked Magheen.

"They get to choose whomever they like." Kathleen looked downcast as if a great burden were weighing on her slender shoulders.

"Most women do, too. At least here in Ireland, we can be thankful for that," Magheen said reassuringly and raised her proud head defiantly.

"I won't. Papa and Mama said they already know who my husband will be, and the worst part is they won't even tell me." She pursed her thin lips. "I only hope he's not like my brother, Richard."

"Tut, tut, I'm sure he's not as bad as you think, I mean Richard." Magheen tried to soothe the girl, who looked as if she might burst into tears at any moment. Inwardly, she did not envy Kathleen's situation, and told herself she would never marry anyone who was not of her own choosing.

At this point, The Lady Maeve came toward them from the opposite side of the large, luxuriously furnished room into which the family had gradually drifted after dinner. Magheen had hoped to learn more from her loquacious new friend regarding the opinion in which she, herself, was held by this family of wealth and position. But then the thought occurred to her that the very fact that she was at that moment in their ancestral home in Cashel-Corrib, was sufficient evidence that she was at least under consideration.

"You two seem to have become friends, or is Kathleen boring you? She can be a chatterbox, I'm afraid." Maeve gave her eldest daughter an indulgent smile.

"Oh, Mama! You always say that. Magheen and I have been having so much fun."

"I'm glad to see you two young ladies enjoy each other's company." Lady Maeve looked for confirmation from Magheen, who smiled and answered, "Kathleen is a very interesting conversationalist." She could say that much without blushing.

"That's such a nice way of putting it, Magheen. But come; it grows late. Young ladies need their beauty sleep, especially those who so rashly commit themselves to early morning hunting ventures." Lady Maeve cast a mischievous glance in her direction.

Magheen merely smiled and followed her hostess. Having bid everyone goodnight, she was glad of the opportunity to be alone, especially since she knew she would not get a chance to talk to Richard again that evening.

* * * *

The early morning was a peerless overture to what Magheen hoped would be a flawless day. She awoke with the birds; the great household was still asleep. She quickly got out of bed and tiptoed to the large window. "How beautiful!" she whispered to herself, gazing in wonderment on the spectacular view before her. From her third-story window high above the world, she could see for miles in several directions. The Cashel-Corrib estate and all the lands of the Burke family lay on the east side of the great Corrib Lake. Sweeping lawns and well-trimmed flower beds stretched from the gravel driveway that skirted the great stone mansion to the green rushes hemming the dark blue waters of the Corrib. Beyond, in O'Flaherty country, the verdant undulating pasture lands were dotted with sheep, and further still, the hauntingly beautiful hills of Connemara were slowly divesting themselves of their misty mantles.

A slight shuffling noise from the rooms above alerted Magheen to the fact that the servants were astir. She'd probably have an hour or more before the family arose for breakfast, so why not avail of the time to do a little exploring by herself?

Magheen quickly washed in cold water in the porcelain basin. The young maid assigned to take care of her would undoubtedly bring her hot water later, but she didn't want to wait around that long. Hastily, she dressed in a light summer gown, tied her hair loosely behind with a ribbon, and covered her shoulders with a small knitted shawl. She decided against her sandals; the early hour and the dew-drenched grass made them most impractical.

Slipping noiselessly down the sweeping stairway, she soon reached the entrance hall where she stopped for a moment to enjoy a tapestry depicting Diana as goddess of the chase. "Mayhap the goddess is on my side?" Magheen addressed the painting. "Diana the huntress! Is meeting you first thing this morning a good omen?" Then she whispered, "Let's hope so."

A door squeaked on its hinges. She didn't really want to have to talk to anyone at that moment. Instinctively, she darted behind a huge fern and waited for the intruder to go about his business. As soon as the receding figure had reached the front door, Magheen decided to take a peek. "Oh, ho! Richard!" she gasped.

Young Richard was decked out in knee-high boots and black trews. A dark leather jerkin covered his white linen shirt. An early riser, had he changed his mind? Was he taking off? Perhaps he hadn't really intended to go hunting with her after all. She remembered what Kathleen had said the evening before. "Richard only wants older ladies to accompany him." Why did he ask her then?

Quickly she crossed the highly polished marble floor and slipped through the great front doors. If Richard were taking off for the day she wanted to know now, not be surprised and embarrassed before all at the breakfast table when the butler announced that Master Richard had decided to go to....

Richard had already made strides across the gravel expanse that separated the house from the lawn and was heading toward the left wing.

Magheen allowed him to get to the corner before she decided to follow. When she reached the corner of the house, Richard was opening a door close to the stables. Well, if he was going for a morning canter she might as well go along, she thought. Why not? As she started forward the door closed behind him. Oh, ho, so much for that idea; she was, by this time, standing right outside. Should she wait? But as the minutes passed and Richard did not reappear, she began to think that perhaps there was a back door and that he had chosen to leave that way.

"Easy, easy lass." Richard's voice was soft and tender on the other side of the door.

Magheen held her breath. He was still there. Why had he closed the door? Then suddenly it dawned on her, he was talking to his falcons. Of course, he'd have to keep the door closed else the birds would escape. What to do now? If she called to him she might frighten the birds. She waited. She could possibly stand there for the next hour or more. Nothing remained but to revert to her original intention and take her walk. She turned and was about to leave when the door opened.

"Magheen! You're out early! Were you waiting for me?" Richard asked with a cynical grin on his boyish face.

"Well, yes and no. I woke up early and thought I might take advantage of the beautiful morning." She was watching his reaction carefully.

"'Twill be a grand day to hunt. I'm glad you're here. Can show you my prize collection if you like. Save time later." As he spoke he again opened the door without waiting for Magheen's reply. "You must be very quiet, you know."

"Yes." Magheen barely mouthed the word as she slipped into the dark room behind him. She was painfully aware that one thought and only one occupied his mind.

"Stay there, and don't move. Aileen isn't accustomed to strangers. Not many ever come in here. In a moment or two she'll see you and grow used to you."

As Magheen's eyes grew accustomed to the dim light, she realized there was more than one room; there were, in fact, several. Richard was talking to a beautiful peregrine falcon, obviously his pride and joy, which was perched on a low wooden rung in the far corner of the room, her head covered with a black hood. He removed the bird from her perch onto his gloved hand. Slowly, he took off the hood by loosening the leather thongs that kept it in place. The hawk's eyes were on Magheen at once and for a moment, she thought that the fierce hind talons would find their way onto her scantily clad arms.

"If your falcon is being temperamental this morning, perhaps we had better call the whole thing off," Magheen counseled and then remembered she intended to feign ignorance of the sport.

"Oh, she's like all women, she has her days," Richard responded stroking the bird. "But she'll succumb to a man's touch.... See!" He continued to stroke the bird very gently, talking in a monotone the while. "A typical female, you are. Aye, I know my women."

The bird's ruffled feathers settled into place as Richard kept talking to the falcon. Then flexing her hind talons, she settled peacefully and confidently on his leather gloved hand, as he began again to stroke the peregrine with his forefinger, preening her shining plumage.

Magheen watched the black-circled eyes, eyes whose acute vision gave hawks such an advantage. She was well aware of their tremendous gifts and thought of her own, Maeve.

"We'll take her out after breakfast as we planned."

"I'd like that," was all she dare say.

Richard turned to replace the bird on its perch.

"She's beautiful," said Magheen.

"She's that and more. You've never seen such a beautiful hawk, I know. I'll show you the others later. I've got to go now. See you at breakfast."

Before she knew what was happening, Magheen was ushered out again into the morning sunshine. She turned to say something but found that Richard had already put half the yard between them.

"Well...of all...He's a conceited wretch. Just wait, Mr. Know-it-all!" and she stomped off in the opposite direction. Somehow, Richard had a way of spoiling an otherwise perfectly lovely hour.

Eight

Magheen's temper had cooled down when she returned to the house after a brisk walk. She had just time to wash and dress for breakfast. Still determined to see if there weren't some way of reaching Richard Burke, although this latest experience with him had not given her much encouragement, she planned accordingly.

Her confidence was at a low ebb and her anger at the boiling point when she left him in the yard or, rather, when he left her. Anyway she looked at it, they had gotten off to a bad start. Perhaps, after all, it was all her fault; he hadn't bargained on entertaining her so early in the morning. She had, in fact, walked in on him unexpectedly. He had probably several chores to do and many things on his mind, so she couldn't blame him for his offensive behavior. A man of many talents, he was just too busy at that hour. He'd give her his full attention later and then they'd be able to come to an understanding. She'd charm him as she obviously had charmed his father. Richard, too, would see her for what she really was, a young woman of beauty, intelligence, and, like himself, talented.

After breakfast, Richard escorted Magheen from the house to the back garden by way of the servant's entrance. "It's a short cut," he said curtly.

She didn't comment but she soon realized that Richard was hardly aware of her. His mind was elsewhere so she followed without speaking until they reached the garden.

It was even more beautiful than it had been earlier. The sky was crystal clear and only the faintest breeze coming from the lake rustled the leaves of beeches and willows.

"A good omen, look at that sky!" exclaimed Magheen.

"My Aileen will enjoy herself today," was Richard's response.

"I'm sure she will. I know if I..."

"Shh...." said Richard as they had arrived at the falcons' house. "I'll go in. You wait here."

Magheen nodded. Having raised her own birds, she knew they were easily frightened, but she thought Richard's manners boorish, treating her like—like a child. "Yes, a petulant small child!" she whispered furiously to herself.

Richard reappeared carrying the hooded falcon, the leather jesses wound through his fingers. He paid no attention whatsoever to Magheen, but headed toward the hilly area behind the castle. Magheen quickly and quietly followed a few paces behind, mentally trying to excuse Richard's bad manners by telling herself that he had to give his whole attention to the hawk, and, of course, silence from her at this point was critical. They reached a high spot. Magheen stayed at a distance.

Aileen was a big bird, almost as long as Richard's forearm, with blue-black feathers above, white below, and crosswise bars of grey. She was obviously a hawk possessing great strength.

Richard talked constantly to his Aileen as gently he removed the hood. For a few seconds she preened and fussed, but soon settled down quietly on the leather glove. Presently, he undid the jesses. The great bird remained on the gloved hand a second or so, moving slightly, balancing, then effortlessly she spread her mighty wings and rose swiftly into the air.

At first, she did not climb very high; she hovered, as if deciding what to do, then circled the castle and its surroundings. Finally, using all the power of her mighty wings, she made her ascent, climbing up....up.

Magheen strained to see, placing her hand above her eyes to shield them from the bright sun. As she watched, the bird became a mere speck and then vanished from sight, lost in the blue beyond.

"Look.... Look below!" cried Richard. His voice clearly told of his excitement and his features showed animation, the likes of which Magheen did not think him capable. "See how the birds rise! The sparrows, the blackbirds, even the crows. If they know what's good for them, they'll seek cover."

Magheen watched, caught up in the excitement of the moment. How often had she experienced this same exhilaration on the hills above Inis Fail. The atmosphere had become tense, as if every living thing sensed danger.

"You know she's the swiftest thing on this earth." Richard was still watching the sky as he spoke. "No one knows for sure, but it's said that when she stoops, she reaches speeds of well over a hundred miles an hour."

"She will come back?" Magheen, feigning ignorance, still wasn't having much luck gaining Richard Burke's attention.

Richard's glance told her she was a fool. "Are you serious?" Then recollecting that she was a mere girl, a child at that, he again turned his gaze to the heavens. For a moment he was silent, intent, searching the cloudless blue.

"Yes, she'll come back. She's tame. She knows her home. She knows where she's well treated. It's true, falcons don't take kindly to the captive life, that is, unless they're reared to it as this one has been. She's an eyas falcon. Found her when I was hunting several years ago. Almost dead when I got her, but I took good care of her, fed her, watched her like a new born babe for days. Then, one day, she was well and strong and had confidence in herself, in her own power. She was alive. I knew I had to tame her then or lose her. Started by teaching her who was boss by making her eat what came from my hand. I sat up with her night and day, talked to her to keep her awake until finally, I got her to eat. Then I followed her routine of waking and sleeping, all the while allowing her only to eat from my hand. We became friends and I knew I had her forever."

"A lot of hard work," Magheen interjected.

"Hard work! More like fighting a battle, but once I'd gained her confidence, she took to the jesses, the swivel, and the leash as if they were second nature." There was pride in his voice, arrogance in his stance.

Magheen was hesitant to ask the use of the swivel. But Richard was talking to her! "The swivel....what?...."

He gave her a quick contemptuous glance but continued. "The swivel allows the bird to move with ease on her block, or on the perch without getting tangled."

"I see." Magheen tried to appear as if she were a novice in the art.

The peregrine was soaring now within sight and they could see the great span of her wings as she glided and dipped, feigned stoops, and played, truly enjoying her freedom.

"What a sight! She has eaten well this morning so she has no need of food. Now she flies for the love of flying, for the joy of feeling free, but always she'll come back to me." Again his haughty bearing was too obvious. He had barely finished speaking when the hawk came sweeping across the sky straight for his outstretched arm. As soon as she had settled down, he placed the hood on her head once more.

"Do you always keep the hood on her when you carry her from one place to another?" Again Magheen tried to engage him in conversation.

"Yes, it calms her. She doesn't seem to care about anything when she can't see." He laughed, a sarcastic laugh. "Might be a good way to tame a woman, eh? Anyway, one day, I plan to carry her about without her hood. She's a well mannered bird. She'll respond to me."

Magheen could see the flush of excitement mount to Richard's cheeks as he anticipated accomplishing the ultimate with his toy.

"Then, I'll know I have complete mastery over her while at the same time she'll think she's completely free. That's the real kind, the only kind, of love worth having between man and animal, between man and woman. And there isn't a woman on this earth who'd give me that kind of love. So to hell with all of them. I'll stick to the hawks and be done with it."

The words fell like hail stones on summer flowers and for a moment Magheen faltered then she faced him squarely. "So you think love means power, dominion over another creature?"

"I wouldn't put it that way. I see the creature's love of his master through loyalty and obedience."

"That seems a one-sided arrangement. How is *your* love for the creature shown?"

"I feed her, look after her. What more does she need?" Then turning his undivided attention to Aileen he spoke, "You're the prettiest girl in all Ireland, the only female I care for." He turned to

Magheen. "I'm a discriminating man," he said as he stroked the bird's breast. He noted Magheen's reaction. "If you don't like my honesty, you're free to leave. I'm up to your little games, you see."

Magheen had taken enough. "Insufferable!" She turned swiftly and walked away, the hem of her flowing skirt swishing against the long grasses. Her slight, agile body was rigid, her anger and scorn barely contained. She no longer was able to stop the tears that began to slip down her face, but her pride prevented her from brushing them away. She walked with deliberate step and head held high. Her unseeing eyes looking straight ahead, she made her way toward the lake.

The clear waters made little ripples over the grey pebbles and tiny minnows flipped in and out among the slender reeds, but Magheen paid no attention. Her head had started to throb. She clenched her fists. Richard Burke was scum, a louse, and like all loathsome vermin should be exterminated. She turned away from the water's edge to tell him what she thought about him, but Richard was no where to be seen.

"Insufferable! He's a cad...left me to return to the house alone."

He knew how to heap insult on injury. Well, she wasn't finished with him. He wouldn't dismiss Magheen Ni Neill from his presence as if she were a scullery maid. She was determined not to give Richard Burke the satisfaction of knowing her true feelings. If she had her games, as he called them, so had he and she intended to beat him at his.

For the next two days Magheen did not see Richard. She, her uncle, and several other members of the Burke family spent the time visiting friends. So when, without any mention of their previous meeting, Richard again asked her to accompany him and his Aileen, Magheen felt this was her opportunity to chop him down to size.

She had been rebuffed, ignored, humiliated, and insulted by Richard Burke. She had walked away from him deeply hurt and now, despite his unpardonable conduct toward her, he had completely neglected any attempt to apologize. On the contrary, he had the gall to ask her to attend him at the stables behind the castle the following morning at ten o'clock. What reason could he have, other than to insult her again, to put her in her place. Had he no feelings whatsoever where she was concerned, or was this part of his game?

Magheen pondered these questions through many sleepless hours until light finally began to dawn. But, of course. Of course! What else but a game! He as much as told her, had she been listening. He would train his women as he did his hawks. "Well, how gallant! He thinks he can treat me as his birds! So, he *is* interested, but only on *his* terms. She turned and pushed her head hard against the pillow. Having answered her own questions to her complete satisfaction, Magheen decided she had everything under control.

It had not rained all week, not even a dribble to dampen the ivy on the old tower or kiss the heather on the hills where Richard had planned to go as soon as Magheen joined him.

They met at the appointed hour. She looked as fresh as the morning itself, a youthful glow shone from her creamy skin and her eyes were bright with excitement, or was it mischief?

"All ready?"

"Yes, I see you're punctual." He looked at his time piece, then returned it to an inner pouch. "I'll get Aileen."

Returning with the hooded bird, he said, "We'll go into the hills. She hasn't eaten."

He mounted and turned his horse. Magheen followed and they rode in silence for some time. As they ascended the southeast side of the hills, Magheen was able to appreciate the magnificent view. Away to the north, Lough Mask sparkled like an amethyst set in an emerald bed. To the south, Lough Corrib lay still, a cool blue-green opal surrounded by sparkles of bright color. They climbed higher and came to a flat spot where Richard dismounted.

"This is it. Now we'll see the greatest sight in all the world." He was excited. Carefully and slowly he removed the hood and then gently released the jesses from his fingers. Aileen hesitated only a moment, then, as she had done on the previous occasion, the great hawk rose in the glory of her strength and power and was soon lost in the great wide spaces above.

"Today she'll kill. But, she's particular; she'll not choose the grouse in her immediate view nor will she pick the weaklings of the bunch. No, ma'am, only the strong, the leader of the covey for her."

"Ah ha!" Magheen's eyes lit up. She might learn from this creature. "Choosy, isn't she?"

"Indeed she is. Watch now."

Magheen squinted as she tried to follow the black spot diving from the sky. There was a brief glimpse of her upside down, her deadly talons stretched. Then she righted herself, opened her wings wide and canted to control her speed.

"She's missed," Magheen hissed.

Richard didn't answer.

Then Aileen was again in pursuit, above this time she took careful aim and stooped, like a flying arrow, with wings half closed the talons struck and the grouse dropped from the sky to be instantly followed by the hawk.

Richard was wild with excitement. "She's a queen!"

"Will she eat now?" Magheen again pretended ignorance of the sport.

"She'll clean and eat...then play awhile...and when she's good and tired she'll come back again to me."

"Then this would be a good time for us to eat also?" Magheen suggested.

"Aye. Let's find a nice spot to sit down. I'll get the lunch basket."

Magheen hardly knew what to say. Was he beginning to thaw out, starting to show a human side?

They ate chicken and fresh bread and washed it all down with a flagon of ale.

"There's nothing like a ride to sharpen the appetite," said Richard, stretching out on the sweet scented mosses. His head was half hidden by the yellow gorse and a clump of purple heather. He closed his eyes.

Magheen moved closer. "You know, Richard, you have talents." She would pander to his pride.

"Talents? Who, me? Sure." He opened his eyes and looked at the sky.

"You do. I mean it. You've done so much training that hawk. It takes patience, perseverance, dedication, aye, and goodness knows how many skills to teach and train a wild creature like Aileen. I think you...you perhaps have underestimated yourself, haven't given yourself the credit that's your due." Magheen knew Richard was listening to her every word, even though he didn't give her any further indication that such was the case.

"One day all this will be yours. If you can do so much with one small bird, think what you might do with Cashel-Corrib."

Richard raised himself and rested his head on his right hand. He looked at Magheen intently. "You don't give up easily, Magheen."

For a moment Magheen saw a spark of fire spring to life in his grey eyes, then just as quickly die.

Richard shrugged. "I live only for today. The future...it means nothing to me. At times I think I have none...but it doesn't worry me. I think only of today, this hour, this minute."

She had struck a resonant chord. Should she continue to play it? She hesitated. Then, as if by some involuntary reflex, she stretched out her hand and jerked Richard's arm from under his head. He fell back upon the soft heather and the next instant Magheen bent over him while her lips found his.

His response was automatic at first, then Magheen felt his body relax and his kiss answered hers. She was beginning to think she had conquered the unconquerable, but no sooner had the thought entered her head than Richard broke from her grasp. He pushed her back in the heather and stood up, then with legs astride a clump of gorse, head held high, and eyes frenzied with contempt, he looked down on her.

She shuddered.

He enjoyed seeing her fear and for what seemed an eternity he held her in a hypnotic stare. Then his pent-up anger exploded. "Slut, don't you know I loath the touch of...."

He broke off as Magheen raised her hands to her ears. She had had enough. In those few seconds she knew. She understood all. A chasm had opened between them that was abysmal and she saw hate and cruelty in his eyes.

The cry of the hawk distracted Richard.

"She's coming! My queen is coming back to me." His whole appearance had changed.

Magheen waited only a moment then arose and walked slowly, deliberately away from Richard as the great bird landed on his outstretched arm. She started to run. She must get away.

"Aye! Where do you think you're going?" The sudden harshness in her master's voice frightened the falcon. She rose into the air, her jesses trailing.

Frantically, Richard tried to regain composure. He called gently to Aileen. The bird hesitated then again swooped in the direction of her master, but the jesses became entangled in a nearby tree. Before Richard could reach the spot, the bird had choked to death.

For one brief moment, Richard stood looking at his treasure as she dangled upside down from the twisted limb. Then he turned to look for Magheen. "You bloody bitch," he growled through clenched teeth.

Before Magheen knew what had happened, Richard Burke had covered the distance between them. He grabbed her dainty bodice with both hands and ripped it to the waist, saying, "You've been asking for this."

In the struggle which ensued, Magheen was jolted from nothingness to vivid awareness. A hawk with bloody flaying wings...A man bird clawing at her loins. Contorted bodies mocking as they dangled upside-down from knotted thongs appeared and disappeared. Aoife Larkin! Richard Burke! Faces, faces. Hoarse voices crying in the wind. A sad refrain:

> The princess killed, killed, killed.
> A hawk upon her grave.
> Her blood they spilled, spilled, spilled,
> The hawk to save.

* * * *

Magheen opened her eyes to the gentle rain that had begun to fall. For a moment, she didn't know where she was or what had happened to her. She sat up.

"My God!"

There was no one around. She got up with difficulty and slowly made her way to a nearby stream. There on her knees, the proud Magheen tried to cleanse her creamy skin of a crimson crust.

Her anger had gone. She saw life for what it was: prey and predator, the weak, the strong.

She had been a child.
Now, she was a woman.

Nine

Tom O'Connor endured the formalities and the endless round of comings and goings at Cashel-Corrib for the first few days with grace and patience, but as the week drew to a close, he was anxious to be away from it all. He had hoped that Magheen and Richard might become friends; an alliance with the Burke family would have made his responsibilities to his niece so much easier and assured her of a gracious lifestyle, if a hectic one. But, as the days passed, he noticed her interest in Richard had waned and when she quietly asked one evening when they would be returning home to Ballindee, he was both relieved and happy to set a time. It was obvious, he concluded, that Magheen, like himself, did not feel comfortable in Cashel-Corrib and for that he couldn't blame her. As for a prospective husband, the matter could wait. She was still young. She had a year or two to make up her mind and in the meantime, he would make further inquiries. Someone accustomed to a less ostentatious style of living would be, he felt sure, more in keeping with her tastes. So they left the Burke castle to Magheen's relief and her uncle's delight a day before they had intended.

The journey home was uneventful. They stopped at Westport to buy a gift of perfumed soaps for Moll, but did not delay further as both were anxious to get to Inis Fail as quickly as possible.

In the days that followed, Magheen made a desperate effort to forget Cashel-Corrib and the whole horrible experience she had known. She was unable to confide in anyone, so for a month she agonized over the possibility of public dishonor. As time passed and the realization of what might happen to her took on larger proportions, she decided to confide in Moll but, fortunately, nature came to her rescue and she resolutely hid her shame deep in her heart. Gradually the physical hurt healed but a mental wound remained festering.

She had been taught a cruel lesson and was determined that for the rest of her life she would never again allow a person of the opposite sex take advantage of her. She recalled her narrow escape at the hands of the young Bill Jenkins, realizing her forethought on that occasion had given her the upper hand and consequently saved her life. Instinctively, she knew to be wary of the sly, conniving lower classes, but for the subtle intrigues and callous machinations in the homes of the rich, she was totally unprepared. Henceforth, she promised herself, she would never again trust any stranger be he king or knave. She would be armed at all times and, to this end, she fashioned a sheath for her knife and carried it beneath her skirt.

She had always spent long hours away from the house accompanied by Leprechaun, her mare, so Moll didn't detect any real change. Eventually, Magheen came to grips with her tempestuous feelings, comparing herself to the little village of Ballindee which had suffered a similar fate. An innocent people had known humiliation, rape, and even murder. Her home, her land, her people...perhaps she too was destined, she reasoned, to suffer like indignities.

As she thought on these things, she grew to admire the indomitable strength of the villagers. She learned from watching them how to cope with fear and uncertainty. She observed their dogged determination and, for the first time, appreciated their fortitude in the face of almost insurmountable obstacles. There was no time in Ballindee for anyone to feel sorry for himself. Life was tough, and if one were to survive one had to be tough too. Thus, she concluded her sufferings were insignificant compared with what the villagers had endured, and she asked herself, could she, Magheen Ni Neil, be less courageous, less determined, less steadfast?

She was well aware that at her age young women of her class had to think seriously of a suitable husband. If she were unable to choose for herself, the choice would inevitably be made for her. But Magheen was not the usual docile female who waited to be told what to do by the male in the family, or who allowed others to run her life. Always independent and free spirited, she also had learned from recent experiences. She would marry when she decided to do so and she let it be known that she would marry only the man of her own choosing.

The first awakenings of puberty had evoked vivid pictures of tall, dark, handsome noblemen. A prince of the realm mounted on a silver charger, arrayed in the finest ermine cloak flying in the breeze, plumed hat and velvet breeches, would alight beneath her window. He had heard of her beauty even in his faraway province and would have none other to wed. They would fall in love with each other at first sight and, despite the protestation of her uncle and Moll that as yet the lovely Magheen was far too young, she was spirited away by the gallant prince and taken to his castle home.

Looking at her beautiful body, she couldn't help those feelings, those raw tuggings that left her limp, and no matter how hard she tried to keep them under control, she wanted, needed to be loved. A smoldering fire deep within yearned to be free, to leap into a devouring flame, igniting all those buried passions. She thought she could have loved Richard Burke, have helped him to build a stronghold that would have been a bulwark against the advance of the Sasanach into Connaught. In time, the lands of her uncle would be hers. A marriage with Richard would have extended the Burke territory to the north. A truce with The O'Malley to the west and The O'Flaherty in the south would have made Connaught impregnable. But, her temper flared. Amadan—he hadn't the wit to see the sense of it. Then recollecting the cruel streak in the Burke heir, she felt consoled for that she would have no part in his life. He might crawl on his knees to her; she would never consider a union with him. The painful experience had taught her that a handsome face did not guarantee a keen mind nor was a keen intellect insurance against crude manners and boorish behavior. A good education was often lost or wasted on a proud and dissipated character.

Magheen was, therefore, determined to take her time and exhaust every means in her power to ascertain the character and background of any suitor that might be presented to her.

She was used to hiding her feelings, this had been instilled at an early age. People of breeding controlled their emotions. Consequently, she bore sufferings, physical and mental, stoically and in secret.

Outwardly she kept her calm, happy disposition and as the months passed, her self-control grew stronger like the walls of a stout medieval fortress or the rocks that protected her western home. If she were to take a position of importance, if she were to leave her marks on the pages of history, she knew it would not be without pain, sacrifice, even blood. So she considered this time of suffering one of trial and training. She kept her secret hidden deep in her heart. Her uncle suspected nothing other than the fact that she had no interest in Richard Burke as a prospective husband. Moll, if she did observe a change, attributed it to maturity. Magheen was, after all, in her seventeenth year.

* * * *

The men of Ballindee had been training regularly for several months, ever since the day the hated English, under Captain Hawks, had raped the village. They had formed their own small unit. The anticipation of French help raised their spirits and most believed that a great French army would land on their shores, join their forces, and together rid the country forever of the Sasanach. But the rank and file were not without skeptics.

"Arrah, them Frenchies 'ill never set foot on our soil," the voice of Dugan rang out.

"You're damn right, man. We've never got help from any o' them foreign countries that's ever amounted to much," said Owen O'Grady.

"A great lot o' talkin' an' promisin' but hell all when it comes to action," Seamus Murphy answered.

"We've got to look out for ourselves," Dugan again spoke.

Tom O'Connor listened to the comments and tried to reassure his men but he, too, had no real faith in obtaining help from abroad.

One evening when he returned home rather later than usual, a concerned Magheen asked, "Has there been a sighting?"

"Unfortunately, no. I'm afraid our hopes will be dashed as before. Support too late, always too late."

"So you don't expect the French to come through?"

"It's hard to say, but one thing I do know, we'll have to be ready to go it alone, to defend ourselves, to fight for what is ours whether the French come or not."

Magheen could not stand idly by while the men prepared. Her uncle doubted the French would help, so she must do as he suggested...go it alone. She organized the women and children; they would fight if necessary. Just as she had armed herself before meeting with Lieutenant Jenkins, henceforth no woman in Ballindee would leave home without being armed. The children were taught to hide in hallows and caves. Food and other supplies were stockpiled in secret places throughout the countryside.

As Ballindee prepared, so did the rest of the country. A revolt expected to be the greatest of the century would shock the Sasanach and hasten the day when Gerald of The House of Kildare would be among them. He, who in the service of the Knights of Malta had fought the Turks, would once again give the country a king. Ireland would be free to conduct her own affairs, to follow her own customs, speak her own language, foster her own literature, art, and music. Irish ambassadors came and went from the lands of the Gael and the Sean-Ghall to the French king, and the Irish monks and friars carried the fiery cry of revolt throughout the land. But, as always, the English were well informed and believed there would be a general uprising as soon as Gerald Fitzgerald and the French made their appearance on Irish soil. They planned accordingly.

Time passed. No French help! No Fitzgerald!

Magheen became more involved in the life of the village, and activities in preparation for battle ultimately led to those that flourished in peacetime. She taught the children the rudiments of reading and writing and told them the stories she had learned from her uncle of Ireland's glorious past: tales of Cuchulain and Finn and the great Epic of the Ferian cycle, which declared Ireland's literary tradition to be older and more sophisticated than any of its earliest European counterparts, apart from Graeco-Roman. Thus occupied, her emotional wounds healed. She was in no hurry to marry, however, but she did spend some time on her trousseau. She knew she would have to choose a husband someday so she would be ready and prepared for that also.

One evening, while she was sewing the lining of a fur cloak, she raised her eyes and looked out her window. A few sheep, fat from the lush summer grasses, browsed lazily on a rise of ground to the left. Beyond, the sea had a tawny look. A little curragh bobbed upon the kelp strewn waters. It all looked so peaceful now, but she knew how quickly that could change. Those calm waters and that tranquil honey drenched sky might, at this very moment, be scheming to unleash vengeance on the unsuspecting. And just as scheming and cruel as the elements, were the treacherous actions of the Sasanach. Magheen knew they were, even as she thought, planning and plotting the destruction of her country.

She threw down her work. Something more had to be done. She went to look for her uncle. As usual, she found him pouring over an old manuscript. She had just seated herself, intending to discuss her thoughts, when Moll knocked on the door.

"Excuse me, Sir, a messenger just arrived." She handed him a large envelope. "He's awaiting your reply."

"Please see he gets something to eat, Moll. Ah, it's from my good friend, Liam O'Sullivan."

The housekeeper withdrew as Tom opened the envelope. It contained two letters.

"This is for you, my dear."

"I wonder what he can have to say to me!" Magheen scanned the contents.

Avonmore House
The Strand, Sligo.
Sept. 17, 1544

My dear Magheen,

I take this opportunity to write to you knowing that my father intends to invite your uncle for a few days visit. The town of Sligo will hold its annual country fair on Sept. 25. It's a big event here and I know you would enjoy it.

I hope you and your uncle can join us for this occasion. It would give me great pleasure to show you lovely Sligo.

Yours respectfully,
Donald J. O'Sullivan

"This is from Donald, Uncle."

"Does he ask if you will make the trip also?"

"Yes, but I don't understand. In these times?"

"It does seem odd. Perhaps my good friend needs me. We should accept. It will be risky, but Liam would not ask us to undertake this journey if he didn't think it important."

Magheen wasn't sure she wanted to renew her acquaintance with Donald, but she saw her uncle thought the journey necessary and besides, she had never seen Sligo.

"When do you wish to leave?" Magheen asked.

"The journey will take at least three days. A night in Ballina, one in Cloonacool, and if we're lucky we should make Sligo the following day. We should leave Monday. I'll write a note now to Liam."

Despite the fact that Magheen was not too enthusiastic about the prospects of spending several days in the company of Donald, she did enjoy the excitement of going on a journey and of seeing new places.

The coach was made ready and Sean, all decked out in his best, again took the reins. It was a typical Autumn morning...dull.

"At least it's not raining," said Tom as he stepped into the coach.

"Giddy-up!" Sean jerked the reins, gave a flick of the whip, and they were off. They started at a quick pace and maintained it for quite some time.

After they had left O'Connor lands behind, they took the road to the east. It lay winding before them past the thatched white cottages of Bangor and Bellacorick. Tom knew the country well; he had often visited these villages and towns in his youth, thinking nothing of an eight-mile hike or a twelve-mile ride on a summer afternoon.

Magheen leaned back against the soft, if worn, upholstery determined to enjoy the journey which turned out to be uneventful until they reached Ballina late in the day. Tom put his head out of the window as they drew near the town and spoke to Sean. "I'd like to purchase a few small gifts, Sean, before we look for rooms."

Magheen bought a couple of things for Moll. The old lady had a weakness for perfumed soap, so when she found a purple bar labeled Spring Violets, she knew she had the perfect gift. Since there was no inn, they had to content themselves with a room in a farm house just beyond the town. Sean slept in the barn.

The following morning they started out early. They reached the village of Bunnyconnellan, a tiny spot for all the letters in its name, in good time but they were detained there half an hour while Sean took care of a loose horseshoe. Then on they went through the pass in the Slieve Gumph mountains to the town of Cloonacool.

It was difficult finding lodging there. Eventually, they were directed to a small inn at the other side of the village, a place called The Sparrows Nest. Dingy, smelling of onions and fish, there were only two rooms available, so Tom O'Connor decided to share his with Sean, leaving Magheen the privacy of the other. After a hasty freshening-up, they were served broth by the red-faced, pock-marked innkeeper in a dimly lit room within spitting distance of the open hearth and its display of iron pots. While they sipped the hot soup and ate the homemade bread plastered with butter, they planned the next day.

To the weary travelers, sleep came easily. Even Magheen found that she could not long hold onto the thoughts which came and went in her drowsy mind. One moment Richard Burke stood before her, arrogant and proud, then galloped off over the hills with his Aileen. The next instant, she saw Donald gazing at her with loved-filled eyes, his outstretched arms inviting her into his embrace, while she saw herself running from him along the seashore, a stormy rugged seashore. Suddenly, she felt the waters engulfing her, and the words, help! help! resounded in the vacuum in which she floated.

She opened her eyes, a streak of light under the skirts of receding night was visible in the sky. It must be approaching 6 o'clock, she thought. Then, the memory of her dreams returned. One's mind did play tricks. Strange that she should dream of drowning, so vivid the experience that she could have sworn she felt the waters, actually endured the horrible sensation of choking and being suffocated. Then a noise in the next room and she knew her uncle was up.

"It was only a dream and one doesn't believe in dreams, no matter what the gypsy fortune tellers claim," she murmured, turning her attention to other things.

Wide awake by this time, she got out of bed and went to the

small barred window which looked out on the sleeping village. Only one chimney showed a thick, curling column of smoke.

"One early riser anyway," Magheen whispered to a busy spider as he emerged from his home in the top left corner of the recessed window in search of breakfast. Then she realized she was hungry herself. "Time to get a move on, young woman," she said as she turned her back on the waking world of Cloonacool to take care of her toilet. Washing in cold water wasn't her favorite way to start off the day, but she knew she was darn lucky to get any water at all in such a godforsaken place.

The sounds of pots and pans from somewhere below told her that others were making ready for the new day also. When she descended the rickety stairs some fifteen minutes later, she saw her uncle and Sean already seated. They were obviously discussing the upcoming journey.

"Yerrah, 'twill be an easy day, yer Lordship. We'll make Sligo in good time."

"I'd like to make it well before sundown," Tom said emphatically.

"That we'll do, Sir. Indeed we will. Ah, here's the little lady, herself. Mornin', Magheen."

"Good morning, Uncle." Magheen addressed her uncle and nodded. "Sean."

"Morning, love; did you sleep well?"

"Like a wee leprechaun after his night's work," she smiled at them.

"We'll be off as soon as you're ready."

"It seems Uncle's anxious to reach Sligo before dusk," Magheen said to Sean, teasing her uncle.

"I've no mind to spend another night in one of these flea bags, and Sean here isn't the most congenial companion to sleep with." There was a twinkle in her uncle's eyes.

"Does he snore?" Magheen asked.

"Snore! Did you say snore? Aach, 'tis a wonder he didn't blow the roof off."

Sean winked at Magheen. "I'll not be telling any stories on your good uncle this morning, but I'll get my own back one o' these days," he said as he stood up from the table. "I'll be off now to see to the horses."

Magheen and her uncle resumed their places in the well used

carriage and were once again bouncing over the dusty road that zigzagged its way past Coolaney, Coolooney, and Ballysodare.

Sligo was reached early that evening, as Sean had promised. Approaching the town, the great Benbulben, Table Mountain, dominated the landscape.

"What an interesting shape that mountain has!" Magheen said.

"It has a distinctive appearance, but more interesting to me and to most Irishmen, I may add, is the legendary love story of Diarmuid and Graine."

"So this is the place!" Magheen was excited.

> "There is one
> For sight of whom I'd gladly spare
> All! All the shining, golden world
> Though such a bargain be unfair.

"Graine's words to Fionn spoken from a heart broken with grief and sorrow. Am I not right?"

"Yes, love," answered Tom. "Do you remember the story?"

"Most of it. Princess Graine had fled with her lover, Diarmuid, rather than be wed to the aged Fionn. They travelled the length of Ireland trying to hide from the great general and leader of the Fianna. Eventually, Diarmuid was killed in a boar hunt. I think it was sad and unfair what happened to Graine."

"Why so, a gra?"

"Because she had to marry Fionn even though she didn't love him, and also because his son, Oisin, and grandson, Oscar, didn't seem to have any sympathy for her. It was Oisin who stood up at the banquet given to celebrate the wedding and cried against the fickle woman saying, 'I trust my father will keep her fast from this time onward.' I don't think she was fickle. If her lover was dead, she didn't have much choice, did she? But I love the story all the same and Graine's song to Diarmuid.

> "Sleep, my love, a little sleep
> There is no fear abroad to keep
> You from me, who owns my heart—
> Oh, my love; my Diarmuid.

"Who'd separate my love and I
Must separate the sun and sky;
Must part my body and my soul,
Oh, soldier from the bright lake shore."

Her uncle joined her in the last lines of the poem.

"A beautiful poem surely, Magheen. I'm glad you know it so well. Any way you look at it, it's a sad story no doubt," he said.

"It seems to me more sad things have happened around Benbulben than anywhere else I know."

"You might say that, I suppose. Benbulben's past history would seem to give that impression. I've walked its table-like surface in the quiet of the evening, imagining the many battles fought at its base so long ago. It's easy to hear the shouts of warring men, the clash of arms, and the neighing of frightened horses on that deserted spot. First, the Norsemen came plundering and destroying and carrying off all that was valuable, including our women." Tom smiled at his niece.

"And with the coming of the Normans about three hundred years ago, more slaughter and plunder," added Magheen.

"Yes, it does seem that everyone wants a slice of dear old Ireland. There won't be much left if we ever get it back again."

"Oh, don't say that, Uncle. Ireland will one day be a free and proud land again." And in her heart she vowed to play her part to make it so.

Ten

The sun was about to dip behind some low lying clouds when they reached the O'Sullivan home. A large house it was, standing facing Sligo Bay with an excellent view of the coast. From its vantage point, about a quarter of a mile back from the road, it also was an ideal refuge for foreign visitors. A graceful avenue of willows led to the house and beyond the seemingly calm waters of the bay was the hilly arm of land that supported Benbulben.

Gracious hosts, the O'Sullivans wined and dined their guests. Donald's mother, a frail and pale-faced lady dressed in black, wished to engage Magheen in conversation while the men chatted.

"So this is your first visit to Sligo."

"It is that, and delighted I am to have the opportunity to see this fair town."

Donald seized the opportunity. "An' right happy I'll be to do the honors."

He had been rather reticent. His eyes alone spoke, softly with warmth, a strange blend of curiosity and longing, planning a thousand little schemes to ensnare the lovely Magheen. A throbbing pulse ruddied his sallow cheeks and clammied his palms.

"And how have you been spending your time, Donald?" Her voice was magic to his already bewitched senses.

"My dear...I've...I've been trying to follow in my father's footsteps," he said, casting a glance at his parent.

"An' a good job he's doing, too," the proud reply immediately resounded. "Sure, 'tis a fine thing entirely when a man can depend on his son to carry on where he leaves off." With that, O'Sullivan reached for the crystal carafe and poured Tom another glass.

After they had satisfied healthy appetites, Liam drew his chair close to the hearth and invited all to gather around. He waited a few minutes.

"Your presence here this evening gives me great pleasure. Would that pleasure were the sole reason for the visit, but matters of a weightier nature have been communicated to me which I felt you should be advised of without delay." Liam cleared his throat and continued, "We are expecting an important visitor from abroad and, if you get my meaning," he looked behind him to see that the serving girl was not present, "his advent will guarantee that our cherished hopes and expectations have not been for naught."

"At last!" Magheen exclaimed.

Liam put his finger to his lips. "But I must warn you, there are rumors that spies abound in the city; be on your guard. As soon as our visitor arrives, a chairde dilse, you'll be the first to know," and he placed his hand on Tom's shoulder.

"Then the time is come." Tom didn't look at his friend as he spoke but into the purple flames of the turf fire. "May God be merciful to our people in the rough days ahead."

"Amen," Liam answered as he got up for the carafe. "Ladies, a little wine?" Tom, alone, accepted.

Donald took the opportunity to draw his chair close to Magheen. "We're living in trying times. God alone knows what the coming weeks will bring. We must snatch at pleasure's brief moment. I've planned many exciting things for us to do." He searched her eyes hoping, anticipating.

"You're so kind," she heard herself say and she felt drawn to him in spite of herself.

While the older folk discussed further the implications of the good news and the bad, Donald plied Magheen with questions about her visit to Cashel-Corrib.

She briefly described the journey and spoke kindly of the Burke family without mentioning Richard, which was duly noted by Donald.

The next morning the fairgrounds opened early and Magheen and Donald were among the first arrivals. There was much to delight the ears and gladden the eye, much to charm the heart and weaken the will. On raised platforms, brightly garbed dancers were already tapping out jigs, and from a distant corner, the sound of bagpipes tuning clashed with rippling arpeggios of practicing harpists.

"Oh, look! Donald, look at those jugglers, they're fantastic! Why, that fellow must have a dozen painted balls going at once. How on earth can he do it?"

"He's good, probably been at it since he learned to walk."

They moved on. Strong odors of boiling cornbeef and cabbage, of frying pork sausage, roasting lamb, and sizzling nuts mingled with the kelp laden breezes. A group of children, munching acorns and laughing uproariously, were watching a puppet show.

"You know, I think the horse racing is the best. Let's go see." Donald took Magheen's hand and led her to the race track, where the second race was in progress.

Young men and women were clapping their hands and hollering, "Come on, come on" to their favorite horses.

"Get a move on, Sally Gap," shouted a man standing close by.

"Let's see what you can really do, Colleen Dun," another voice yelled.

"I'd like to put a groat on the favorite for the next race." Magheen was caught up in the frenzy and her beautiful eyes shone with excitement.

Donald longed to take her in his arms there and then, but he had to content himself with a little squeeze of her hand.

"Wait here, I'll go get some slips."

Donald scarce had left when Magheen noticed a figure, robed as a monk with a cowl pulled close to the face, make his way among the vendors. It wasn't the appearance of the cleric at the feis that seemed odd, but the manner in which he conducted himself. Why didn't he mingle? Why was his cowl so carefully drawn?

By now he was within easy distance; she would confront this fraud—a spy no doubt. About to ask for a blessing, she looked into the steely grey eyes and a cold shiver ran through her. The blood drained from her trembling limbs. Hawks! With mouth open, she just managed to hold the word before it sounded. She turned to go, but in an instant felt her wrist in an iron grip.

"Not so fast, young lady. Not so fast," he hissed. Then, noticing people were eyeing them suspiciously, he released her hand and raised his in blessing while between clenched teeth he snarled, "You're not as innocent as you appear. I'll be watching. Have a nice visit, my child," he raised his voice as she turned her back.

"Watch him, he's a spy," she whispered to a group of young men as she slipped past them. Soon lost in the crowd, she made her way to a booth festooned with brightly colored ribbons where a small boy was playing with a hoop. Approaching him, she held up a penny. "I'll give you this if you'll find someone for me!"

"Sure, Lady, it'll be a pleasure." He bowed from the waist and then presented a smiling rosy face, eager blue eyes.

"Go to the ticket booth, find a young man named Donald and bring him here. Go, go quickly before he leaves that spot."

"Ah!" The child's expression changed. "Is he your lover?" he asked, anticipating the reply.

"My what?"

"You know, your sweetheart?"

"You rascal. Go at once." Magheen bent to administer a playful tap on his behind as he ran off, his dirty bare feet scarcely touching the ground.

"You don't look well," Donald said anxiously when he saw her.

As they walked toward the race track, Magheen told Donald of her meeting with Captain Hawks, the very same who had ravished Ballindee was now in Sligo parading as a monk.

"Father's right, they're everywhere, the city's crawling with Sasanach. We heard of the atrocities." He paused, trying to decide what to do. "The devil take them." Donald was agitated.

Magheen, calm, with an air of cool determination said, "We're not going to allow Captain Hawks to spoil our day."

The race began. The favorite, Mocushla, a spirited filly from the stables of the Kildare country, was marked number three and was in the lead.

"What a beauty! She's got to win, she's just got to. Come on, Mocushla, come on, girl." Magheen was on her toes, eager, anxious. "Oh, Donald, she's falling behind."

"No, she's coming on again," Donald replied. "Watch, I bet

she takes the lead as she rounds the bend." Donald was, however, paying more attention to Magheen than to the race. The excitement had heightened the blush in her cheeks. He was captivated by her glistening teeth, her ruby lips. She was so beautiful. Looking deep into her sultry brown eyes as she turned to speak, he interrupted her. "No wonder the bloody English won't leave us alone."

"What are you talking about?" she asked, surprised.

"About you. Oh, Magheen, Magheen, you've enslaved me entirely."

"About me!" She threw back her head and laughed and then deliberately turned her attention to the race. Mocushla was nearing the finish line; Magheen tensed. "She's won! Mocushla has won!" she cried and grasped Donald's arm.

"What...what did you say?" Donald asked.

"Didn't you watch the race? Donald, she's won!"

"Oh, of course, the race, I got distracted for a moment."

Magheen slipped her hand into Donald's and looked into his face. "'Tis you who are the strange one entirely, Donald O'Sullivan."

He thought he could see love in her beautiful eyes and for a moment he was puzzled by her seemingly mercurial nature. At one moment almost cold, certainly indifferent, and the next, so full of concern. Dare he hope? He raised her hand to his lips and savored the softness of her silken skin.

"Oh, Donald, you're impossible. Come, let's go for our winnings," she said with a forced gaiety.

Five to one! Magheen had now five extra bright groats to spend.

Donald tried his skill at pitching horse shoes, but it wasn't his sport. They watched a puppet show and laughed heartily at the antics of the marionettes. As they were about to leave, they stopped at a jewelry stall. "Look, Donald! Isn't that an unusual ring?"

"Unusual and very beautiful. It's called a Claddagh ring, first appeared in the little fishing village of Claddagh, just outside the city of Galway."

"Do you know what it symbolizes?" she asked, picking up a gold one.

"Yes, indeed I do. The crown symbolizes loyalty, the hands are clasped in everlasting friendship, and the heart, of course, represents true love. Would you like it?"

"I'd love it."

"Then 'tis yours."

Donald purchased the ring and placed it upon Magheen's finger saying: "I hope when you look at this you'll sometimes think of me, my beautiful Magheen." He raised his eyes to search the deep, dark pools that were studying his face. "It most certainly represents the feelings I have for you."

Magheen, forgetting where she was, reached up on tiptoes, took Donald's face between her hands, and lightly kissed his smiling lips.

"Thank you, my dear, dear Donald. I'll always cherish this beautiful ring."

Before they left for home, they were prevailed upon by an old gypsy to have their fortunes told. She took Magheen's hand and looked at it long and hard.

"You will travel far, my dear. You will cross the seas. I see a dark stranger in your future. A foreigner."

Then a gasp of surprise escaped her. She hesitated. "You will have suffering...but, yes, you will find true love." The gypsy would say no more to Magheen. She turned quickly to Donald.

"And you, Sir, what about you? Sure you have a secret desire and a wish to know its outcome, Sir?"

"I think not, at least not at the moment. Thank you. Come, Magheen, it's getting late."

The gypsy's somber tones put a second damper on Magheen's spirits. "What can she mean?"

"Oh, pay no attention to the old hag. She's a fine one with words."

But Magheen was not one to take things lightly.

The merrymaking continued for the next two days. Donald and Magheen went back, but somehow there wasn't the same enthusiasm and spontaneity since the meeting with Captain Hawks.

As they strolled home just before nightfall on their final evening together, Donald invited her to walk along the strand to watch the moon rise on the dark waters.

"This is a beautiful town. I'm so glad I came, Donald! You've been an excellent companion. I would..."

"Magheen, there's something I must say to you," said Donald interrupting her.

"Oh," she looked at him almost surprised. He had acted in such a gentlemanly manner, gone out of his way to give her a good time, was he going to spoil the whole thing now by asking her to marry him?

"Magheen, I haven't changed my mind about you." He took her hand and raised it to his lips.

"Magheen, you've stolen my heart completely," a slight break in his voice, he waited, motionless yet expectant, his heart pounding, his eyes riveted on her upturned face.

"Donald," the music of her voice thrilled. "Donald, I've enjoyed your company. I've really loved every minute we've spent together. You've been..."

"Oh, Magheen, don't say anymore. The words I wish to hear are not in your heart...not yet. But, I'll not cease to hope." Again he kissed her fingertips and pressed her hand to his heart before he released it.

"We'd better return. The folks are expecting us for dinner this evening and Mother has planned a real treat."

The dinner was a banquet. The smoked salmon was followed by platters of pork chops, lamb, and tender veal. Silver bowls of parsnips, turnips, and green beans covered in a white parsley sauce were offered by the servants to each in turn. Several varieties of breads were daintily arranged in little straw baskets. A glorious feast of desserts stood waiting on the sideboard.

Liam O'Sullivan raised his glass. "Health and happiness to our dear guests."

"And to you, likewise, Slainte to our generous hosts." Tom O'Connor's smile held warmth and gratitude.

"This has been one of the most wonderful times in my whole life." Magheen looked at Donald. "I'm really sorry it all has to come to an end so soon."

"Well, now that you know where we live, maybe you'll come more often. You'll surely be most welcome, my dear." Mrs. O'Sullivan looked with affection at Magheen. She knew something of her son's feelings and wished with all her heart that his love might be requited.

Eleven

During the winter months, the letters to and from Sligo came and went on a regular basis. As the breath of spring came to warm the land and scattered the fragrant perfumes of a multitude of tender blooms, Tom O'Connor noted a change in Magheen's feelings toward Donald O'Sullivan. She spoke of their visit to Sligo, it seemed to Tom, with a warmth and enthusiasm he had not heard before.

"You know, Uncle, I think our visit to Sligo was one of the nicest times we ever had. I really can't remember a better time in my life."

"I'm happy to know that you enjoyed your stay with the O'Sullivan family."

Having thought about it for some time, Tom suggested that the family might be asked to pay them a visit. Tom O'Connor felt sure that Liam O'Sullivan would welcome the chance to take a few days break, and the opportunity of paying court to Magheen, he knew, would not be lost on Donald.

* * * *

Hearing the sound of the carriage drawing up to the front entrance, Magheen quickly adjusted the clasp in her hair. A stray strand insisted upon escaping. She caught it, pressed it into place, and quickly left the room. Then, as she heard the joyous greetings in the entry hall, she paused a moment on the stairs. She realized her pulse was throbbing. A little tremble of excitement ran through her body. What was the matter with her? Why was she affected so? Was she, deep down, really in love with Donald O'Sullivan? She tried to compose herself. It would not do to give herself away, if indeed, she could trust these feelings. She had better suppress them until a more suitable time and place, until she had a more reasonable understanding of their meaning.

When Magheen descended the stairs, all conversation ceased. She was a vision of delight. Dressed in a rose colored gown, she was, in Donald's word, "More bewitching than the fairest summer rose." A full skirt, gathered at the waist into a tight fitting bodice, was so designed as to show her shapely figure to full advantage. The low cut neckline was trimmed with delicate lace, and upon her breast she wore a small gold Tara broach. Her silken hair hung in thick coils about her shoulders, framing her oval face. The excitement of the occasion had heightened the color in her usually rosy cheeks, and her beautiful eyes glowed. Donald stepped forward and, as she reached the last step, Magheen offered her hand.

"Welcome to Ballindee, Donald."

Donald took her slim fingers in his firm grasp and before he pressed them to his lips, his eyes held hers for a brief moment. Magheen was aware of the burning love in those clear, honest eyes. A sudden rush of blood to her cheeks caused Magheen momentary embarrassment, but she quickly regained her composure.

"How nice to see you all again." She disengaged herself from Donald and went forward to greet his parents.

The days that followed allowed the young people ample opportunity to be reacquainted. Magheen found that the better she knew Donald the more interested she was in him as a person. She really looked forward to the walks, the rides, and the musical moments they shared.

Donald was a real gentleman. Had he no faults? A man could be too perfect. Then she remembered their first meeting. On that occasion he seemed aloof, distant. She had even been glad of the opportunity to escape from his company then. What had changed him? She became increasingly curious about this seeming change in his character.

"Donald," she said determined to fathom the mystery. "Donald, there is something I'd like to ask you."

"Ask, my dear. I'm all ears to your sweet voice," Donald replied.

"I'm curious as to your seeming change of character. The first time we met I saw that you were rather reticent. In fact, I found it quite difficult to hold a conversation with you."

Donald threw back his head and laughed. A deep baritone laugh, hearty, gay.

"Oh, Magheen, you're a cautious one. I can see I shall have to bridle my moods or else be accountable for the many inconsistencies of my intemperate nature."

"Arrah, Donald, you're teasing me. I really want to know you. Your colorful personality is intriguing."

"Oh, ho...o, so I've a colorful personality now, have I, indeed. Well, I'll tell you, queen of my heart, your wondrous beauty left me dumbfounded, and this time I'm not teasing. You stole my heart the very first moment I laid eyes on you, Magheen Ni Neill."

Could she believe him or would time reveal some hidden flaw? Magheen resolved to beware.

The two took advantage of the fine weather to go for a canter on the final evening of his visit. As they made their way home, Magheen decided to stop off near the cliffs. They dismounted and stood some time looking down at the churning waters in silence.

"Donald, I know that you love me very much, so in all fairness to you, I must tell you about the terrible incident which took place here two years ago last October."

Donald looked at her, but his eyes only spoke of love.

"You remember Captain Hawks and that party of English soldiers who were dispatched to patrol the coast?"

"Yes, we had our fill of them in Sligo also, don't forget."

"True, well, you know the details of the murders in the village. God knows what else might have happened had it not been for Uncle Tom's quick thinking. Anyway, I knew he had to know why that detachment of soldiers was in this area." Magheen paused.

Donald noticed that the color had drained from her face and there were tears in the corners of her beautiful eyes.

"Are you ill, dearest?"

"Oh, Donald, it was awful. The very thought of it...."

"You don't have to recount the gruesome details, Magheen." He thought she was referring to the deaths of the O'Reilly family.

"Oh, yes, Donald, I have. You see, if we are to become closer than friends, I want you to know me as I really am."

"Magheen, anything you could tell me would make no difference to my love for you." Donald was puzzled. "How can I get you to understand that?" He moved closer to her and put his arms around her waist.

She faced him, looking straight into his honest hazel eyes. "Donald, I killed a man."

Donald flinched, but he did not loosen his hold on her. "You what?" After his initial shock, Donald continued, "I'm sure you must have had a very good reason."

"At the time, I thought I had."

Magheen then told him the details of that terrible day. She was sorry her victim had been the young Lieutenant Jenkins. Yet, on the other hand, her anger and hatred of all Englishmen justified, in her mind, any means to gain her end.

"Donald, I would do it again. I know I would."

"Magheen, what you have told me in no way lessens my respect or admiration for you. On the contrary, I see before me a woman who is brave, courageous, and ready even to sacrifice her own life for the sake of her country. Magheen, darling, think no more about it. You did what you had to do."

"Donald, I was hoping you would see it that way. Thank you."

Donald drew near. He took her hand and kissed it lightly. She turned to look at him. Her luminous eyes seemed the most ravishingly beautiful he had ever seen. He took her into his arms. Magheen trembled ever so slightly, but she did not resist.

"Magheen." He drew her close. He saw her close her eyes. Then closing his own he gently touched the lips he had waited so long to claim. "Magheen, precious pearl, jewel beyond compare." He ached for her, but he did not want to frighten her. "Oh, Magheen, tell me you love me just a little."

"You know I do, Donald. I not only love you, but I've learned to respect and admire you also. You have so many fine qualities, Donald. You are truly a very special person."

"Magheen, I've waited so long to hear you say those blessed words. You are young. I will be patient. I will not ask more at this time." Again he took her in his arms. This time his passion aroused, he lingered to relish the sweet freshness of her honeyed mouth. She responded. The moment was pure delight. Magheen's first kiss!

"Oh, Donald. I do love you," she murmured.

"Magheen. I will make you happy someday. I will spend my every waking hour for you and you alone, my eternal love."

They walked home hand in hand, the horses trailing leisurely behind them. The unspeakable joy of first love was all around them. It was contagious. The older folk caught the infection. The evening that ensued was a veritable triumph. Moll's culinary accomplishments filled the house with delicious aromas and, when it came time for the tasting of the fruits of her labors, the guests had quite exhausted their knowledge of superlatives before the dessert was served.

A round or two of backgammon was played by Magheen and Donald, while the older folk engaged in a card game. The evening hours soon took wing and as the guests were eager to set out with the first light of the morning, they retired a little earlier than usual.

Magheen stepped into the library for a few minutes before she went to her own room.

"Uncle, I know you're concerned about my future happiness. I, too, have been giving the matter much consideration. I would like to wait another six months or so before I commit myself, but as of this evening my heart belongs to Donald O'Sullivan."

"Magheen!" Her uncle came toward her. "This news calls for a celebration. Perhaps we should ask our guests to postpone their departure and announce the joyous news tomorrow?"

"I prefer to wait. Donald and I have talked it over and he agrees that I'm still quite young. So, Uncle, if you don't mind, I'd like to keep the matter within the family, at least for the present."

"As you wish, my dear, as you wish. I'm very happy for you. I think Donald will make you a fine husband. Donald's father and mother will certainly be delighted. They think the world of you, Magheen."

"I know that, Uncle. They are such wonderful people."

"Now I can die in peace, knowing that you will be cherished and cared for as long as you live."

"Oh, Uncle, I don't want to hear you talk of dying. You're a young man and have many years still ahead of you."

"You've certainly added at least ten years to my life this evening. Why, I feel like dancing a jig." Tom O'Connor started to hum a rollicking tune to accompany his exaggerated step dancing. Then he caught Magheen and twirled her around the room.

"Ach, I'll have to start practicing my steps if I'm to dance at your wedding, girl. I'm as rusty as an old iron pot."

"Indeed, Uncle, you could dance the legs off many a man half your age."

Tom paused to catch his breath.

"We'll give you six months, young lady. Remember it takes time to prepare for a wedding. Not like a birthday fete you know."

Magheen laughed. "Yes, Uncle, I promise to give you plenty of time to invite all your friends." She then kissed him and said, "Good night."

"Good night, my dear."

The mention of the words six months brought back memories. Richard Burke's father had given him an ultimatum—"six months or else."

Those days seemed so long ago now. Magheen had heard bits and snatches of gossip in the intervening months. It seemed that, after only six months of married life, Aoife Larkin Burke had become so infuriated with her irresponsible, half-crazed husband that she took off, one fine day, home to her mama. How the difficulties between husband and wife were eventually resolved one can only speculate, but resolved they were somehow, for a year later a son was born and thereafter Aoife stayed put. The arrangement did not, however, change Richard's lifestyle.

As Magheen remembered, she felt her blood boil. "That despicable creature. I'll show him. The day will come."

It was at that moment that she realized her life was not going as she had planned.

Her hopes and ambitions seemed to have no bearing on reality. What of the works and the achievements she envisioned? Where were the high places and the positions of eminence for which she knew she was destined? No mighty ruler had knelt at her feet offering to make her queen of his realm. No lord had come begging her hand. Were her dreams, her presentiments regarding her future only so many figments of her imagination?"

Magheen tried in the ensuing weeks to resign herself to what she considered an inferior station in life. She tried to adjust her standards and expectations. Up to this point she had thought that the only way to fulfill her destiny and carry on the traditions of The O'Neill, striving to rid Ireland of the foreign invader, was to achieve power, wealth, position, and influence.

Being the granddaughter of Con O'Neill she had a duty, she felt, to an old and honored family, one of the greatest in all Ireland, the descendant of the ancient Ardis.

Magheen knew that the great man had in his old age submitted to the English Henry VIII, renounced his title of The O'Neill, and accepted the title Earl of Tyrone instead.

Three years before, in October, 1542, he, the last of the great princes of Ireland to submit to England, had gone to Greenwich, and in the presence of Henry VIII and his court, humbled himself and became the subject of the foreign king.

As a result, English law and customs would, in time, replace Irish customs and the Brehon Laws. The Church in Ireland was to be renounced, the monasteries closed, and their treasures plundered or confiscated for the Crown. The English language would replace the older Irish tongue.

It was obviously up to the younger generation to carry on the fight. Thus, Magheen, fired with patriotic enthusiasm, recalled the bravery and courage of Silken Thomas son of the Earl of Kildare. This young man had dared to lead a rebellion against the English. The result of his forceful but short-lived revolt was that Thomas and five of his uncles were taken to the Tower of London, where they were hung, drawn, and quartered.

As Magheen thought about young Thomas, old ambitions and aspirations tugged at her heart and mind. Was she making a mistake? If she married Donald, she would have to forget forever the destiny to which she felt called. The role she was born to fulfill, for which she had been preparing for so many years, would have to be abandoned. She was confused.

The months had slipped away. She would have to make up her mind. There was only one month left before she was to be married.

As she undressed, she looked at herself in the mirror. "You

will soon be a married woman, Magheen Ni Neill." She paused, then continued to address her image. "The question is, will Donald O'Sullivan be your husband?"

Part II

Twelve

For sixty years, under four kings, the French frequently crossed the Alps into Italy, the pretext being that they had some claims on the Duchy of Milan and the Kingdom of Naples. Out of these Italian campaigns came the wars, many and varied, which plagued Europe for so long.

Francis I, who reigned from 1515–1547, did not care much for the English Henry VIII, and, for that matter, he did not like his archrival, Charles V, any better. Most of Francis's showy reign was taken up with ambitious campaigns against this rival, Charles V, Emperor of the Holy Roman Empire. In his constant wars, Francis grudgingly sought the aid of Henry VIII of England, and indeed, actually met with him in 1520 on the field of the Cloth of Gold in France. But Henry did not trust Francis and so decided to ally himself with Charles. The battles continued until 1525, when Francis was taken prisoner at Pavia and kept captive by Charles for more than a year.

Sometime after his release, Francis had a brilliant plan, one which would set up a power favorable to France. This plan was to bring about the marriage of Gerald Fitzgerald of Ireland with Mary, Queen of Scots, who was heir to the thrones of England and Scotland. The alliance would unify the three countries, Scotland, England, and Ireland, assuring Francis of strong support from the north.

During 1544, the armies of Francis I and Charles V were encamped near the French-Italian border. Inside the vast royal tent embroidered with fleur-de-lys, where the mud was, as elsewhere, ankle deep, Francis I listened in consternation to Count Etienne de Marnay. The Count had just ridden from the front lines and the report was not good. He had seen disaster before. He had served his Sire well in many campaigns in the past twenty years. At fifty, he was considered an old man, but he stood tall and the good looks of his youth had not completely vanished: a determined jaw, a drooping mustache, a straight nose, and flashing black eyes. Neither years nor fatigue seemed to have affected his mind. Count de Marnay did not mince his words; he had seen too much of war to be enamored of it.

"Sire," he said. "It's hopeless! Food supplies are desperately low, and our wagons are stuck in the mud several miles away. The men are hungry and are beginning to quarrel among themselves. A few more days of this weather and they will revolt." De Marnay removed the steel camail which covered his head and shoulders and ran his fingers through his greying locks.

The King walked back and forth, nervous, alarmed. "Damn this detestable weather!"

De Marnay tried to get the King's attention. "You must decide, Sire."

Francis was getting tired of the seemingly endless struggle. He had no stomach for defeat at this point in his life. Better try to make a truce while there was still time. Perhaps that was all he had, time.

"Curse to hell this Charles. He has long evaded my sword, but, by God, he'll feel it yet." The King tried to appear resolute.

On the opposite bank of the river, the forces of Charles V were in much the same condition. Emperor of the Holy Roman Empire and King of Spain, Charles was the elder son of the Emperor Maximilian and Joanna, daughter of Ferdinand and Isabella of Spain. He inherited the Netherlands, and in 1516, he became King of Spain by right of his mother. With that crown, he obtained possession of Italy. In 1519, he inherited the Austrian dutchies from his grandfather and, as ruler of this immense realm, he was chosen Emperor, the most powerful man in Europe.

An equerry raised the flap of an elaborate tent pitched high on a hill overlooking the battlefield. The rain still fell in torrents.

"I long for the defeat of the King of France." The Emperor sat in council with several of his advisors. "And," he went on, "I am present here today to see an end to this troublemaker. Nay, I'll reward the man who dispatches the French hog with a purse of gold. This bastard has been a thorn in my side far too long."

Charles brought his large fist crashing down on the table at which he was seated. His shield, his helmet, and his sword lay within reach. He ordered that the men be given a jigger of brandy. In the wretched conditions in which they found themselves, the men of the Imperial Army were underfed, cold, and drenched to the skin. It was impossible for them to give their best under such circumstances. As in the French camp, squabbles were frequent among the rank and file, for the men were overly tired and ready to return to their homes. It had been many, many months since any of them had had any domestic comforts.

The Emperor, in agreement with his military advisors, decided to attack the French at dawn the following morning. To that end, he ordered his officers to round up all the able-bodied men and give them an extra ration of food. With a concentration of his most powerful forces in strategic positions, Charles felt he could carry the day and so bring an end to this otherwise futile struggle.

Across the river, young Hugo, Viscount de Breville, was restless. He had turned in soon after he and the other officers had been dismissed from the Royal tent, and did not look forward to the next day's stand. It would be a bloody affair at best. Though he did not lack for courage, he could not quite get used to the wanton waste of human life, the destruction of homes, the raping and pillaging of tiny hamlets and villages.

Hugo had not seen a lot of action, yet the past few months had emblazoned the scene of the battlefield on his mind: the long, weary hours of waiting as the nights dragged on, the fitful sleep, the anxious watching; and, as a weak sun crept over the soft, wet earth, the dun battle lines showed faintly at first.

Then the command "Fire" sounded weak, even hollow, in the morning air, he remembered. And, as the hours wore on, the barrage worsened and the first line of advancing men fell. Others hurried to take their places until the lines became moving zigzags. All semblance of order was lost as the men engaged in scattered skirmishes. The dead and dying, friend and foe, lay mangled, disemboweled, or decapitated in grotesque poses; the dead released from their sufferings, the dying seeking such comfort.

Hugo, still pondering, recalled that as the long hours dragged on, the able-bodied were ordered to retreat or advance, to take or retake the dark bloodied ground they had so lately traversed. And, while the carnage continued unabated, the utter futility of the battle with its anguish and pain burned deeper into his mind.

"Oh, God. Why? The poor, ignorant soldier, why should he suffer so? He doesn't really know who the enemy is."

Hugo continued for some time to brood on the injustices of life in general and his own in particular. Then, realizing that the morning's light had a way of creeping into his tent all too quickly, he decided there was nothing he could do to rectify the world's many problems, not to mention his own, and that it was high time he had some sleep.

He has been born into a family who for generations had ties with the royal houses of France. His great-grandfather served under the Valois, who ruled France from 1328–1498. Henre de Breville distinguished himself on the battlefield in 1464 and was awarded by Louis XI the title of Viscount and given a stately home near Chantilly on the Oise River. His son, Roland, continued to follow in his father's footsteps and not only maintained the family property, but added to the house and annexed several smaller parcels of land. In turn, Roland's second son, Victor, father of Hugo, established himself and his young bride in the Chateau de Breville shortly after the tragic death of his older brother Roland II. The throne of France was held by the Valois-Orleans branch and Louis XII was King at the time.

From Louis XII, the throne passed to his cousin, The Count of Argouleme, who as Francis I was the reigning monarch when Hugo was born in 1526.

The country around Chantilly was peaceful, at least for the children. It was true that Hugo's father was far away fighting with the King, but for him, his two brothers and little sister, childhood was a joyous time. There were the long summer days spent fishing in the Oise. What fun they had jumping from rock to rock where the water was shallow. Mama had forbidden it; she was so afraid that someone would get carried away with the current. But then

Mama was a woman, and women didn't understand a man's world or how brave men had to be. When a boy grew up, he was expected to fight for his King, for his country, and for the protection of the women and children. Hugo, though he didn't like to disobey his mother, felt he had to prepare for this future life by doing brave things as a little boy.

"Look, look how I can balance!" Hugo had managed to make his way across a relatively shallow part of the river by hopping from one large rock to another. He was now perched in a rather precarious position with only room enough for one foot. The next rock was quite some distance away. With outstretched arms and leg, he shouted to his brother, Victor, and his baby sister, Valerie, who were sitting on the bank watching him. Within seconds, Hugo's attention was diverted by a huge frog, which had leaped out of the water and now sat on the stone onto which he wanted to jump. It blew its chin into a huge bubble, so big that Hugo thought it must surely burst. At that moment, he lost his footing and down he went into the chilly waters, gurgling and splashing about.

"Oh, help, help," shouted his brother.

"Hep, hep," cried little Valerie.

A fisherman close by heard the commotion and ran to see what was happening. He laughed as he saw Hugo splashing about in a foot of water. "You're a fine fish," he said as he grabbed the boy by his breeches.

A mortified Hugo was deposited on the bank, dripping and gasping for breath.

"Mama said not to go next to the river. You'll catch it now, Hugo," his brother teased.

"Don't you dare tell," warned Hugo.

"What'll you give me if I don't tell?"

"I'll give you my white rabbit, honest I will."

"Oh, very well."

"What you give me, Ugo?"

Hugo lifted his little sister into his arms. "You love your big brother, I know you won't tell." He kissed her.

"What you give me," Valerie pleaded.

"Something you'll really like."

"What, what, Ugo?"

"How would you like to have two of my new colored chalks?"

"Oh, I love you, Ugo."

The children played together for sometime longer. Hugo's clothes soon dried in the warm air. Hungry at last, the boys raced each other home, Hugo losing the race as he had stopped to give his little sister a piggy back.

He put her down in the entrance hall and whispered, "Remember our secret; you promised."

"I'm not going to tell." Her voice carried into the reception hall.

Mama was soon standing at the door and Valerie instantly ran to her and exclaimed: "I got a secret, Mama." The Viscountess bent to her youngest child. "Ugo fell into the river, but I'm not going to tell."

Hugo waited. He knew what it felt like to be a criminal.

"Hugo, is this true?" Across his mother's pretty face worried lines appeared and her beautiful eyes darkened with fear.

"Yes, Mama."

"Hugo, you know what Mama has said. Why do you disobey?"

Hugo looked straight into his mother's sad eyes. "I want to be brave, Mama, that's all. I'm sorry to have made you sad."

"Come, my son," the Viscountess drew her eldest son to her. "You'll have time enough to be brave when you're a man. Right now, I want to be sure my little boy will grow up to be a man."

"Yes, Mama."

When Hugo grew older, he was sent to a nearby monastery to continue his education. There he excelled in his studies. A very bright student, he quickly mastered several languages, as well as the martial arts, particularly fencing. Nor were the fine arts neglected in those religious schools.

It was understood that when his studies were completed, Hugo would join his father's regiment. He would serve under him until he gained experience and was capable of commanding his own battalion. So it was that in the spring of 1544, when he was barely eighteen, Hugo found himself at the front among the veterans of many wars and in the company of hundreds of raw recruits like himself.

Hugo had slept fitfully during the night. It was cold and damp in the tent, but at least he had a dry spot under his head. So many of his comrades were left to their own resources and, when unable to secure the relative comfort and protection of a clump of trees, had no alternative but to lie down in the open fields. Drenched through, they shivered all night. Poor sick men, most of them would not have a chance in the coming battle.

Hugo's young alert body was easily able to adjust to the duties assigned him. Awaking early on that final morning of what would be the last campaign of Francis I, he left his tent and went to a vantage point to observe the enemy camp. Scarcely had he taken his position when a young runner informed him that a movement was observed along the enemy line.

Could it be that Charles V had decided to make a surprise attack? As quickly as the idea crossed his mind, Hugo ran for his horse. He rode in the direction of the King's tent, alerting all officers on his way. The camp was quickly aroused.

The King, having spent the night in council and prayer, had determined that the best course of action was to make peace with his long-time enemy.

Hugo entered the King's presence. "Your Majesty, there is no time to be lost. The enemy appears to be preparing for a surprise attack."

"Tell me, de Breville, what gives you that idea?"

"Your Majesty, I have just this moment come from the front lines, where I was on duty, and it appears that the enemy is placing troops in position."

The King realized that if he were to save his own life he must act at once. He commended young de Breville for his alertness and presence of mind and looked a moment at the stately bearing, at the clear, honest black eyes before he spoke.

"Hugo, Viscount de Breville, I entrust you with the destiny of your King and country. Here, take this flag and carry it, if necessary, even to the very tent of Charles. I request a conference."

Hugo bowed and without another word left the tent and rode straight for the enemy lines.

By day's end, a permanent truce had been negotiated and a grateful King had rewarded the brave young de Breville with the title of Count, amid the acclaim of his peers. His father, suffering from battle wounds, seemed to gain strength from the honors accorded his son. However, the older man did not long survive his many ordeals and shortly after they had returned to their chateau in Chantilly, he died. Count Hugo was now the head of the family and, as such, was expected to take a wife and carry on the family tradition.

Thirteen

It was late Autumn in the year 1544. The countryside around Dijon was drab. The trees had been stripped of their multicolored gowns and their naked limbs impatiently awaited the first, soft, white mantle of winter. Animals, large and small, huddled together in groups, close to barns and houses, seeking warmth and protection against the chilly winds that swept through the Loire Valley from the Jura Mountains. The peasants, with hurried steps and muffled faces, headed for home hoping to gain shelter before the storm broke. Meanwhile, the carriages of the rich hastened to the nearby chateau. The occupants in the luxurious interiors were unmindful of the hardships without. More bent on extravagant pleasures, they had little thought for anything else.

The ball was splendid. The rooms were crowded with elegant ladies and distinguished gentlemen. Yvonne, the youngest daughter of the house, was pouring forth a torrent of song from her swanlike throat and the guests were really listening.

Henri Rene Albert Charles de Lamadon, Comte de Mount Rogue, was resplendent in his field marshal's uniform as he played host to his distinguished guests. It was an affair of which he was proud, and worthy of the noble cause for which it was held, the return of the troops and the end of the long years of struggle with Charles V.

The singing ended and the dancing began. A rustle of skirts, a flurry of dainty slippered feet, and the dancers were lined up ready to enjoy the latest rage, the pavane.

The Count had returned from a recent visit to friends in Dijon.

While he was there, he had attended the spectacular festivities, held at the Burgundian Court, consisting of a series of banquets and balls. The highlight of the festivities was kept strictly secret until toward the end of the celebrating period. At that time, the privileged guests were ushered into the main hall of the castle, ablaze with the lights of innumerable candles and torches. It looked fabulous. Liveried servants stood waiting, their dress of grey and black frieze cloth contrasted with the gay, bright velvets, satins, and brocades worn by the guests.

Several stages had been erected and, before the meals were served, those present were entertained by sideshows. Models of famous cathedrals, of palaces complete with miniature figures, were on display. Clockwork animals prowled through delicately designed forests and jungles, and tableaux of live people portrayed biblical scenes or well known works of art. One exhibit or performance followed another: jugglers, acrobats, and even a falcon hunt with living birds. During the banquet, the food was lowered from the ceiling. Finally, the grand ball concluded the entire affair.

De Lamadon, Comte de Mount Rogue, was so excited about this new diversion that he introduced the idea to Chartres when he returned to his home. Although not quite as elaborate and spectacular as the banquet presented by the House of Burgundy, Henri Rene Albert Charles de Lamadon's display and feast caused quite a stir.

Count Hugo de Breville remained aloof. He was seated in an alcove absorbed in his own thoughts. It had been several months now since he had returned from the front. It was refreshing to be able to plan his day and arrange his own affairs. But even as he was growing accustomed to his new freedom, there were already rumors that the King was contemplating an attack on England. A man ought to do his duty to God, King, and country, but a man also needed a rest. He needed to be able to enjoy life, to read, to hunt, to plan his future....

Hugo, at nineteen, was still very young to have had so many responsibilities thrust upon him. He had been betrothed from childhood to the Lady Charlotte, eldest daughter of the Marquis de Saint Jacques, and although they had seen each other several times in the course of their lives, Hugo was not in a hurry to enter the holy state of matrimony. A devout Catholic, he had been educated by the monks at Cluny and had, on occasion, contemplated entering the monastery and dedicating himself to the religious life. A gentleman of refined tastes, he abhorred the atrocities of the battlefield. But what else could a nobleman do? Besides, his father and his grandfather before him had been soldiers, proving themselves worthy in that profession. As he pondered, his mind turned to the gentle countryside near Angers: the seemingly endless stretches of neatly tilled land, the fruit orchards, the rich earth, and the chateau where Charlotte awaited him.

Charlotte de Vertielle was a pretty little thing. Already seventeen, she felt old and abandoned, her younger sister, Odette, having been married off earlier in the year.

Hugo could not attend the wedding, unable to leave the battlefield and the fighting. The fighting...how many sleepless nights he had had during that time. Then he remembered that it was the thought of Charlotte that buoyed him up. How wonderful it would be when, at last, he could go to her, have his own home, his family. It was time for him to take her as his bride. He had delayed long enough. And Charlotte? What had she endured during all this time, particularly since her younger sister already was married. He could imagine the taunts and jests of her peers.

"Not yet married, Charlotte, why, you'll die an old maid."

"That fiance of yours is a sly one. When did you hear from him? No doubt he has known several young women by now."

Hugo bestirred himself. Why had he not acted? He was now free to do so. Although he did not seem particularly drawn to her, Charlotte was a product of her time and class. A sophisticated young woman, her talents were directed to the management of servants, the running of a large estate, and while she waited her future husband, her days were spent with making and remaking gowns or other items for personal and household use. She attended the many balls and dinners given by the local gentry. And, of course, there was the Annual Grand Ball and the Royal Festivities in Paris, which were always eagerly anticipated.

As Hugo thought of these things, he decided it was high time to make his appearance at the chateau and formally declare his intentions. He withdrew a locket from his pocket, a small gold case, which held a portrait of his bride to be. Gazing on it, he realized as if for the first time that Charlotte was a young lady of exceptional charm. An aristocratic face, well poised, with a small, straight nose, and pretty, full lips; her high cheek bones were clearly outlined under her olive complexion. But there was a coldness in her large hazel eyes. Hugo wondered what lay behind the high forehead, which was surrounded by dusky ringlets falling in neat clusters over her slender shoulders. Again his attention returned to the eyes, deep set, but.... Perhaps that was the reason. Did he really know Charlotte? She had never crossed him, never hinted that she might have any other thought than to please him. Come to think of it, their conversations were usually superficial and pertained only to matters of the moment, trivia, nothing of consequence. Was she capable of deeper thought? Or was she destined to be an ornament rather than a companion?

"Come now, Count, such serious contemplation of a lady can only cause you problems." Then in a whisper intended only for Hugo's ear, Count Charles de Lamadon continued, "All of which, of course, can be quickly alleviated at Madam Flores." With this remark, de Lamadon's infectious bass laugh caused those in the immediate vicinity to turn their attention to the pair.

"Let's share the joke, Cheri."

"Ah ha! You two, what fair lady's reputation is in question? Do share your secrets with the rest of us," cried the Countess of Clermont.

Before Hugo had time to return the locket to his pocket, she had deftly snatched it from his grasp. "Ah, so...this is the lady, quite lovely. Who is she?" By this time, several other ladies had gathered round the Countess.

Hugo never did care for the woman. In his estimation, she was trouble! Always happened to be in the right place at the wrong time, whenever there was a dram of gossip or a gallon of scandal to be brewed.

The Countess regarded Hugo with suspicion. A man of his physique: tall, impressive, with almost perfect classic features, black velvet eyes, a sensitive Greek nose, and full, well-shaped lips, no wonder she could never understand why he was not more popular with the ladies and particularly herself. Goodness knows, it wasn't for the want of trying on her part.

"Come, come, monsieur, admit we've found you out."

The Comte sized up the situation and thought the whole idea very amusing, especially since Hugo bore the brunt of it.

Hugo was embarrassed and quite at a loss as to how to extricate himself from the web the Countess had skillfully spun about him. His first thought was to retrieve the locket. He stood up and cast a glance around the group of ladies closest to him and was about to speak when a throaty voice interrupted him.

"Mes dames, you do Monsieur Le Comte a great disfavor. This is no common strumpet but the picture of the worthy gentleman's fiancée, Charlotte de Vertille."

A hush descended on the little group and the owner of the husky tones stepped forward. It was the Princess Louisa, first cousin to the King of France. The ladies curtsied as the Princess handed Hugo l'objet si precieux, then she offered him her own arm, leading him toward the music and the dance.

"Your Royal Highness, how can I possibly thank you?"

"If you really want to know, I suggest you stop moping and find some way to make a very lonely young woman in the Angers countryside an honorable one."

"You're perfectly right, Your Highness."

"Of course I'm right."

Guiding the glittering princess about the ballroom, Hugo became the talk of the evening. His composure, his handsome manly bearing drew the attention of all.

"You won't be left alone again this evening, mon cher, I can see there are many young women eager to take my place." The princess smiled, "And what's more, I'm afraid I'll have to give them the opportunity, not as young as I used to be. These affairs quite tire me out."

"Would you like to be seated, Your Royal Highness?"

"I think perhaps I'd better."

Hugo led the princess to a chair and then brought her a cool drink.

"Thank you and now, young man, remember what I said. Do not waste your time in pondering the image when you can make love to the original."

Those within earshot caught the final words. Cautious glances were cast and casual remarks were audible, but no one dared to voice his innermost thoughts.

Fourteen

The journey from Chartres to Angers was an uneventful one, except for the fact that, at Montoire, the inn was dirty and the food cold. Hugo had shopped in Chartres before he left, buying a few little trinkets: some fine perfume, a box of bonbons, and a spring parasol for his fiancee.

The arrival of Hugo at the chateau caused quite a stir, particularly when he insisted on talking to Charlotte's father, the Count de Verteille, before he would consider seeing her. The interview was brief but satisfactory and soon the whole household was thrown into utter chaos.

Celeste, one of the parlor maids, overheard the Count saying, "I'm proud to have you for a son-in-law, my boy," as he accompanied Hugo from his study to Charlotte's apartments. "You say three weeks?" He paused. "Not much time, eh?"

"Two weddings in one year! This house can hardly stand it," Claudette, the cook, said, wiping the perspiration from her upper lip. The kitchen was oppressively hot and the thought of all the extra cooking caused her temperature and her temper to rise.

"Oh, I think it's high time the Lady Charlotte got her man. She's done nothing but feel sorry for herself ever since her sister, Odette, got married," answered Celeste as she was about to return to her duties.

"Celeste, watch your tongue, girl. Remember your position." Having dismissed Celeste, Claudette tried to gather her own thoughts. "Now, where was I?.... Oh, yes...so much work. Can't be done.... For the life of me, I can't see how everything can get done.

She did say three weeks? Maybe she meant three months. Young people nowadays...."

None of the kitchen maids interrupted. They merely cast side glances at one another and were inwardly delighted with the prospects of another festive occasion. Before Hugo had a chance to even propose to Charlotte, the whole household was privy to the news.

* * * *

The wedding was a quiet one. Only two hundred guests, including family, were invited. Charlotte had wished it. The grounds around the chateau were festooned with garlands of fresh flowers, as was the entire chateau. A magnificent sight!

The ceremony was performed by his Lordship, the Bishop of Angers, in the beautiful old church which had been erected several centuries before at great cost to the townsfolk. The stained glass windows cast a glow of iridescent light, lending an ethereal air to the scene. It was a hot, sultry afternoon and the many lighted tapers in the nave and sanctuary seemed to consume the last breath of air as the Bishop moved with slow, shuffling steps.

The wedding gown was a work of art. The satin bodice was embroidered with pearls and diamonds and the full skirt was trimmed with Brittany lace. A delicately blended spray of lily of the valley and tiny blue forget-me-nots adorned the curve of Charlotte's white bosom. Her long train was borne by two small pages dressed in white military outfits decorated with red and gold braid trimmings. On her dusky curls lay a diadem encrusted with sapphires and diamonds.

Hugo's aristocratic deportment was enhanced by the colorful officer's uniform of black, white, and gold. As he took Charlotte's trembling hand to guide her up the white marble steps to the high altar, he whispered, "I love you, Charlotte. You are the most beautiful woman in the world."

Charlotte, indeed, looked radiant; excitement had brought a faint blush to her usually sallow cheeks. Looking into her dark hazel eyes, Hugo knew no onyx ever displayed such brilliant and varied colors. Framed by long, curving lashes, they seemed to sparkle and glisten with a concentrated radiance. As he continued to gaze at his young bride, her frail body trembled.

"Are you all right, my dear?" he asked anxiously.

Little beads of opal formed at the corners of her eyes, quivered an instant, and then ran down her cheeks. Hugo raised a gloved finger and gently stroked the dampness. "Are you ill, Charlotte?" he repeated.

"Just a little frightened," she whispered.

Hugo smiled and squeezed her hand. "No need to be afraid, my love. I'm here to protect you."

The Bishop cleared his throat. "In nomine Patris et Filii et Spiritus Sancti. Dearly beloved, we are gathered here today in the sight of God to..." He droned on.

Hugo pressed Charlotte's fingers again before she joined her hands in prayer and placed them on the prie-dieu in front of her. As she did so, she swayed. And as her eyes closed, she saw the face of her mother. An agonizing face whose purple lips seemed to call to her. "Ah!" A little gasp escaped and just before she slipped sideways, Hugo's strong arm was around her waist.

There was a murmur from the crowd. The Bishop stopped, his arm raised in a blessing, his mouth wide open. Someone had the presence of mind to grab the cruet of water from the altar and a few drops were forced between Charlotte's clenched teeth.

After some anxious moments, the ceremony continued. The Bishop, however, a very old man, completely lost his place. He fumbled, skipped several passages, and thoroughly confused the young altar servers while a junior cleric tried to fill in the awkward gaps. Eventually, the service was brought to a rather abrupt conclusion. The Bishop was escorted to a side altar allowing Hugo and Charlotte to exit down the main aisle to the entrance door.

Cheers broke out as the young couple left the church. The air was permeated with the sweet smells of orange blossoms and roses as people vied with one another in casting handfuls of petals at the open carriage. The church bells pealed above the noise and little children in treble voices sang out their joy of the occasion.

In the banquet hall, the courses which followed each other seemed endless. Wines of the best vintage filled and refilled the crystal goblets. There was toasting and speeches and finally, Hugo rose to reply to them. As he stood, he caught Charlotte's gaze for a split second. Those eyes...why did they affect him so? He noticed they had lost their brilliance, the radiance he had seen earlier. She was probably overwrought, a few days rest would revive her vitality, he thought.

Hugo and Charlotte spent the next two weeks in a lovely villa in the country. A wedding present from her father, the house and lands were pleasantly situated among rolling hills. There, they would have a chance to get to know each other better.

Charlotte was born in 1527 and was baptized Marie Therese Charlotte. Her mother, a pretty girl of sixteen, had great difficulty with the birth of her first child. Shortly after delivering the baby girl, as she lay weak and exhausted, her husband came into the room. He was a man of about forty, a crude, overbearing person. His watery grey eyes showed that he had not had much sleep. He had returned to the chateau late the night before in expectation of the birth of his son.

"So you give me a little bitch," he shouted. "Don't ever let me see the brat. You know I need a son and heir." He strode from the room, banging the door behind him.

Countess de Verteille allowed two tiny tears to escape; they rolled down her tired face, and she didn't even try to wipe them away as she set her pretty lips and forever closed the door of her young heart.

Charlotte did not see much of her father as she was growing up. On the rare occasions when her papa was home, he was hurtful and abusive to her and her mama. When she was very small, she had seen her pretty mama quickly wipe away a tear or two, but as she got older, she noticed that Mama pretended not to hear Papa's bad words. Papa, she learned, was always away on important business in a town called Paris where he had to attend the King. Then Charlotte's little sister was born and her lovely mama got very sick. She remembered hearing her cry out, "Cruel men, they kill, kill." Then, all she remembered was that someone took her and her baby sister to another house. After a while, she came back to kiss Mama good-bye.

When they had covered her mama's face with a cloth, they placed her in a box. She heard them hammer the lid on, but she didn't cry. It was cold and she was afraid. Her papa and some other men carried the box to the cold little house where her grandparents were waiting for God to tell them to come to Heaven. Her mama would have to wait there too.

Charlotte and Hugo had been together for more than a week and had not as yet consummated their marriage. At night, as they lay together, he would stretch forth his hand to caress her but, beneath his touch, he could feel her body instinctively resist and repulse him. At first, he thought it was her youth and inexperience. He did not wish to force himself upon her. On their wedding night, after she had repulsed him, he got up, lit a taper, and then sat on the side of the bed for a long time with his head in his hands. Finally, he left the room and didn't see Charlotte again until the next morning.

At breakfast he inquired if she slept well. Charlotte responded in the affirmative and settled into a hearty breakfast. Once their eyes met across the table and once again, he thought he detected an icy flash.

The passage of time did not change things; the barrier between them was always there. Finally, he came to the conclusion that she wasn't in love with him.

"Darling," he spoke gently to her at breakfast after several days had elapsed. "Do you not love me?"

Charlotte gave a little start, then hesitated before she answered.

"I'm sorry you think that way, my dear." The same glint of steel was apparent in her hazel eyes. "You must know that you were the most eligible bachelor in the whole of France. The real truth of the matter is that I loved you from the first moment I saw you, and that was ten long years ago. The fact that I cannot make love to you has nothing to do with my feelings for you. Perhaps, because you are still practically a stranger to me has some bearing on the matter. Dear Hugo, I'm sure in time our lovemaking will be as perfect as the other aspects of our lives together."

Hugo finished his breakfast, wiped his mouth with a silken serviette and pressed Charlotte's finger tips to his lips. "My darling, forgive me, I should have been more sensitive to your needs."

Charlotte considered she had been completely honest, so immediately proceeded to dismiss the whole matter from her mind.

Hugo, on the other hand, considered the subject carefully. He tried with gentleness and warmth to show Charlotte how deeply he loved her.

One night shortly before their prearranged visit to Chantilly, he entertained some of the local gentry. Whether the reason for his heavy drinking was to drown his frustrations or merely to play his part as an affluent host, he ordered the keeper of the cellar to produce large quantities of the best wines.

It was late when Hugo finally went to bed. Not fully in control of himself, he was, nevertheless, in a jovial, carefree mood and hummed to himself as he removed his clothes; black velvet doublet and silk hose were tossed in a heap on the floor. He pulled at the buttons of his white satin shirt as the small candle sputtered and threw a golden sheen across Charlotte's face.

He was captivated as he looked down at her. "My darling, let me show you how much I love you," he whispered as he got into bed, blowing the candle out. Without pulling the covers over his naked body, he took her face between his soft, warm fingers.

An irresistible feeling of pleasure coursed through her slight frame as he gently pressed his fingers outlining the curves of her face. Then realizing that her body was responding to his advances, Charlotte checked herself and stiffened slightly.

Hugo, gripped by an intense desire to possess his wife, sought her pretty lips in the dark and as his mouth covered hers, Charlotte could resist no longer. She gasped as his hand traced rivulets of fire down her back. She pressed closer and drew his head to the softness of her full shapely breasts.

But again her mind took control. She cried silently at her inability to curb the responses of her flesh. What had she been taught by the good Abbe-Pierre? Pious women didn't have such feelings!

The sensations were heightened when his mouth passionately lingered on her throat, then moved slowly, deliberately to the curve of her breast. Finally, the touch of his tongue on her taut, extended nipples drew a moment of bittersweet, unexpected pleasure from her. With the slight relaxing of her frame, Hugo took advantage. A few seconds later, a little scream escaped Charlotte and for one rapturous moment she was one with Hugo. Then she lay alone, weak and spent. Tears of shame and feelings of having been violated overwhelmed her. She felt soiled. The innocence of yesterday was no more!

Charlotte was angry when she at last recovered her composure. She had not expected to experience pain. Brought up by nursemaids and tutors, Charlotte knew little about the intimacies of the marriage bed. She had heard her mother's cries as she lay dying. "Men are all alike. Only for one thing do they need a woman. Use them merely to satisfy their carnal desires."

"My dearest one," Hugo spoke softly. "I'm sorry if I caused you pain, but what has happened between us tonight is most natural. The first time is the hardest, you'll see."

Charlotte had made up her mind that there would be no repeating the experience. Natural or not, she was not going to allow any man to send her to an early grave. She wiped the tears from her eyes and turned her back to Hugo. Not wishing to make matters worse, Hugo contented himself with kissing the nape of her neck and settled down to the sleep of the fulfilled, if not contented, husband.

The icy glint became a permanent part of Charlotte's expression in the days that followed. Hugo became moody, then abrupt; eventually, a feeling of guilt took hold of him. The hours of leisure he once longed for now seemed to pall. He found himself longing to be rid of the oppressiveness of his present existence and ached for the company of men.

Then one morning a messenger arrived and Hugo learned that he was required to attend the King within the week.

He spent the last days of his freedom setting his affairs in order. Arrangements had to be made for removing the entire household from Anger to Chantilly before the cold weather set in. Charlotte could not be left alone in the villa. He was now head of the de Breville family, and it was understood that he would be the lord and ruler of the chateau on the Olse, where he would eventually bring his new bride to live.

Busy from dawn to dusk, he saw little of Charlotte in those final days, while Charlotte, for her part, seemed herself again, but she kept her distance being quite formal in her parting kiss. Yet, as soon as Hugo had ridden out of sight of the chateau, she raced up to her room, flung herself on her bed and sobbed uncontrollably. "I'll never see him again, I won't go to Chantilly."

Hugo, feeling the eagerness with which his faithful mount took to the road and the sting of the morning air against his cheek, grew high spirited. He dug his heels into the horse, "Let's go, Gypsy." He was happy to be free but wondered what weighty matters had obliged the King to summon him so urgently to Versailles.

Fifteen

The days passed and the weeks turned into months and Charlotte became aware of the changes that were occurring to her body. Fear gripped her heart; she became morose and sullen. She scarcely left her room. Although the de Breville family welcomed her with open arms, Charlotte never could feel at home in the strange surroundings.

The chateau at Chantille was an old, rambling affair and its closeness to the river gave it a damp, musty smell. Charlotte sorely missed her quarters in the chateau in Angers where she had accumulated a lifetime of treasures: her doll's house, the old mechanical clock that hung near her bed given to her by dear grandpapa, and, above all, the lute which was her mother's and on which she learned to play so well. Even the bed in her new home seemed cold and hard. So many strange faces, she needed someone in whom she could confide, someone to love her, to hold her close.

Her younger sister came to visit her shortly before the Christmas celebrations, bringing her little son. But Charlotte had grown listless and showed no interest. As her time drew near, she daily became more languid. She was often heard sobbing. At night, as she drifted in and out of fitful sleep, she could be heard calling for her husband.

"Hugo, oh, Hugo, I loved you so much." And at other times, "Cruel, selfish men, they hurt, they don't care."

Hugo's mother, the Viscountess Colette de Breville, was very worried about her new daughter-in-law. She sent for the best physicians. They assured her that everything was normal. The Countess was very young and this being her first child...but the Viscountess was not assured.

"My dear Charlotte, what can I do to help you?" She tried to place her arm around Charlotte's shoulder but was repulsed.

"Hugo, Hugo, oh, where is he? I hate him!...I hate him," cried Charlotte.

"Now I'm sure you don't mean that. Hugo loves you so much. He would be here with you, were he not on an important mission for His Majesty. Come Charlotte, eat a little. It will help you gain strength. When the baby comes you will be so happy, you'll forget this uncomfortable time."

"Oh, how I wish I had never seen him! I'll never forgive God for making me a woman. Now I know what my mother felt. She told me of the insensitivity of men. My poor mother, dear, delicate mother, so young, so pretty...."

"Rest, my dear, your mother did not mean all she said when she lay weak and dying. She was young, perhaps frightened at the prospects of death, but you are strong and need not fear."

"I wish I could believe that," Charlotte whispered, then her ramblings continued. Interspersed with her ravings about Hugo, she voiced negative sentiments about her father, for his neglect of her and her sister in those lonely years after her mother's death had left its mark. As she thought about him, she realized she never really knew him. He had wanted a son and heir and had blamed his wife for the first disappointment. But when the second child came, causing the untimely death of its young mother, and it too turned out to be a female, the Count found no end of excuses to absent himself from his home and his two small daughters.

"Why does Papa go away again? I want Papa to stay here with me." Charlotte raised herself, stretched out her arms as would a small child pleading for its parent not to abandon her and cried, "Papa, Papa!" It was a pitiful scene. Then she broke into convulsive sobs, as no doubt she had done in her early childhood. Pathetic to listen to were the babblings that followed. "Liffle Dette is crying. She want Mama. Papa bad. He go fa' fa' 'way."

It was not too difficult to fathom the pent-up emotions, the bitter, deep-rooted feelings that had stifled Charlotte's mind and heart. She had never known real love. Her tutors had spoken of her as being a docile child, but one given to bouts of depression. Had it not been for Charlotte's nurse, who had been her mother's before her, it is doubtful whether the child would have survived.

It seemed now, in her extreme anguish, that all these childhood feelings and deprivations returned to plague her. She had barely found what might, in time, have proved to be the only real love in her life, when cruel fate stretched forth its ugly hand and snatched all.

At five o'clock on Saturday morning, the first Saturday of the New Year, 1545, dawn was breaking in the somber hues of drab grey mists. The temperature had begun to drop quickly; cold drafts crept in and around the chateau. Charlotte had been in labor since midnight. Large beads of perspiration formed on her forehead and on her upper lip.

The physicians in attendance shook their heads. "If only she would relax; she continues to fight against nature," they murmured. "As long as she persists in rejecting this child, we can do nothing."

As Charlotte raised her voice in a wild, terrified scream, the wind wailed in long, low moans. Then gathering strength, it howled around every corner and furiously fought its way through cracks and holes until the candles and tapers in their sconces spumed, sputtered, and died. Then the rain came, at first in giant drops, whipped by the driving winds, it broke into a fury and flung itself in a tempestuous, unrelenting downpour against the window panes.

Charlotte shivered as if the fury without, having penetrated the depths of the chateau, had entered the very marrow of her bones. The lady-in-waiting drew the covers more closely around her mistress. "There, there, my Lady, 'twon't be long now."

The hours passed slowly, so slowly for poor, suffering Charlotte. But no less so for all who stood by watching the young life ebbing away. As the storm gathered momentum, it appeared that the tortures wracked on Charlotte's delicate frame also grew in intensity. How long could she endure such agony?

Forty-eight hours and as yet the baby had not been delivered. The doctors not only feared for Charlotte's life but for the infant as well. They consulted together. She was fast failing now; her strength was spent. Even as they hesitated and fumbled, not daring to interfere with the workings of nature or the will of God, Charlotte gave vent to one last pitiful cry and then surrendered. Pale and exhausted, she looked around one last time. And those close by heard the words "They kill...kill...kill." Then her head slipped to one side and she was gone.

The baby boy that was born was beautiful of limb and comely of face, but he scarcely had time to open his eyes when he, too, joined his mother.

The little one was wrapped in a white linen sheet and placed on his mother's breast. Both were finally laid to rest in the family cemetery.

There was no way to inform Hugo. "Whereabouts unknown," was the reply from his commanding officer.

PART III

Sixteen

It was a blustery evening in the Spring of 1545 when tired, wet, and mud flecked, a horseman approached Ormond Castle, the family estates of the Butlers, occupying large areas southwest of The Pale. The castle commanded a view of the Suir River and was a large, symmetrical structure with a gabled roof line. Inserted in the stone facade were grand mullioned windows. An imposing building by any standard, it was particularly so to a visitor from the more remote regions of the country.

The rider had ridden hard. As he reached the castle, he reined in his horse and, readjusting his weary body to the stirrupless saddle, he gave the sweaty neck of his faithful friend a few pats before he dismounted.

His mission was a very important one. The Butlers, like many Norman families, had lived in Ireland for several hundred years but, unlike most of those same families, the Butlers had not formed close alliances with the Gael. The House of Ormond was, in fact, separated from the Gaelicism influence for nearly two hundred years. Its wards, when minors, were reared and trained in England as Englishmen. Their policies and outlook, therefore, were anti-Irish.

The old line of the House of Ormond expired with Thomas, the seventh Earl, in 1515. The younger branch, the Butlers of Polestown, had deputized for the Earl Thomas, who lived in England. This office was formally conveyed by deed to Edmund Mac Richard of Polestown, to his son James, and to his grandson, Piers. This Butler family, in defiance of the Statute of Kilkenny, married Irish wives. The marriage between James Butler and Sabina Kavanagh was for a long time a celebrated law case. It was their son, Piers Roe, who became Earl of Ormond on the death of Thomas, the seventh Earl. Piers Butler had stood in high favor with the Crown, but his son James decided to take a firm stand. He had married a daughter of James, eleventh Earl of Desmond, thus uniting two of the great houses of the South. This union, Butler hoped, would one day make him ruler of most of Southern Ireland. He had but to bide his time and eliminate his opponent, the Earl of Kildare.

The castle door was opened by a venerable looking man named Liam, who performed the duties of butler and valet to his Lordship, the Earl. His livery of scarlet, donned only on special occasions, and the sounds of much chatter coming from inside, surprised the young courier. He drew back and hesitated to address the man who eyed him intently. Liam sized up the situation and motioned for the stranger to be quiet. He checked to see that all was clear in the entrance hall, and bade him follow. When he was safely behind the closed doors of the Earl's personal reading room, Liam addressed his guest.

"I gather you have urgent business with his Lordship. May I enquire about your name an' from whence you're coming, Sir?"

Phelam O'Neill, although not easily disconcerted, was guarded in his answer. "I am a servant from The O'Neill household and bear a message which I must deliver personally to the Earl of Ormond."

"It will be difficult for his Lordship to be leaving his guests at this moment, but I will see what I can do," responded Liam. "In the meantime, I gather that you have ridden hard today. You will, doubtless, be needing food an' drink for yourself an' your horse. Please make yourself comfortable. I'll see to these things myself. His Lordship would wish it."

So saying, the old man was about to leave, but abruptly turned in his tracks. "Do not be alarmed, I intend to lock the door behind when I leave. A mere precautionary measure, my good Sir."

Phelam was about to make a run for it but Liam's kindly face was his reassurance that he meant no harm. Still, when he heard the key turn in the door, Phelam O'Neill had other thoughts. Was it a trap? It was difficult to know friend from foe, even in the camp of those who were known to be loyal.

Although Lady Eleanor Fitzgerald, of the House of Desmond, had done a superb job gaining the friendship of most of the leading families, there was still a feeling of uncertainty where the Butlers were concerned. With the alliance of this large and influential family, most of Ireland could again be united. A nation speaking its own language, cultivating its own literature, observing its own laws and customs, and practicing its own centuries-old religion, was the objective. Through marriage, kinship, and fosterage a bond would be formed that would cement the nation once and for all. To help further this plan, Phelam O'Neill had ridden from the far north, from the territory of The O'Neills, with the proposal that the oldest son of the Earl of Ormond be joined in marriage with Magheen Ni Neill, granddaughter of Con O'Neill. This union would extend the influence and bind together the great houses of the North and South, thus preparing the way for the implementation of the plans so long brewing between France and Ireland. In a few short months, the stage would be set for the return from France of Gerald of Kildare who would immediately be acknowledged as King of all Ireland.

Phelam, exhausted, had slumped into a kind of reverie, but his dreams were quickly shattered when he heard the door being unlocked. A tall man in the prime of his life entered. A striking figure in any dress, he was particularly so in the outfit he had chosen for that evening's entertaining. He wore fashionable satin trews and to Phelam's discerning eye, they were cut from a particularly rich material with gold embossed threads on a black background. Over a loose fitting silk shirt of olive green, His Lordship had donned a black velvet doublet fastened with gold buttons. Black leather shoes completed the dress.

Phelam arose to greet his host. James Butler's steely grey-blue eyes scrutinized his guest. "My man Liam has told me that you have business of great import."

"My Lord, I'm honored," responded Phelam, "but before I lay before you the plans with which my father has entrusted me, I should introduce myself. Sir, I am Phelam O'Neill, son of Con O'Neill, bastard according to some, but none the less, a son of the great man."

"It is a great pleasure, Sir, to make your acquaintance and may I extend a traditional Irish welcome to you. Cead mile failte."

The two men extended their right arms, as was the Irish custom, their hands falling heavily on each others shoulders represented the force of sincerity which each had for the other. Then they embraced and continued to speak in Gaelic.

"We of The House of Ormond have made strides in acquiring the language. I am ashamed that my forebears took so long to become more Irish than the Irish themselves."

His sense of humor put Phelam at ease, "Better late than never, Sir."

Liam returned with a large silver platter bearing generous portions of beef and pork. A tankard of ale and a bowl of vegetables accompanied the meats, which were all steaming hot and a welcome sight to Phelam.

"We can talk as you eat. No doubt, after a short rest, you'll want to be on your way again, Phelam."

Phelam, true to the tradition of his clan, was not at a loss for words. He painted a vivid picture of the general feelings of the Princes of the North. He spoke of their unrest and their dissatisfaction with the English policy. O'Neill had had enough of the Sasanach. He had gone out of his way to placate the English monarch, even going so far as to renounce his birthright, The O'Neill, for the empty title of Earl of Tyrone. He was now ashamed of himself. He was hopeful that his sons would regain the greatness that once was his. He had no quarrel with the Princes and Lords of the South. It was time they all unite in the face of such a persistent and insidious foe.

"'They rape the land, burn our forests, and plunder our homes,' cried The O'Neill to his assembled warriors not five days gone," Phelan related. "The man still has fire in his soul. He abhors the desecration of the countryside." Again Phelam quoted O'Neill's words. "'With the loss of our trees comes the loss of our advantage over the Sasanach. Our men will have naught but stumps to hide behind while our enemy reaps huge profits in the wine countries of Madera and Canaries where this valuable resource is reduced to casks and barrels'"

James Butler listened, he was very interested. He, himself, had been considering the possibility of a united Ireland ever since the last visit of the Earl of Desmond.

"Aye, Phelam, the old man is right. The time is come for us to band together to drive our common foe into the Irish Sea or to Hell, whichever."

Phelam came to the point. "An alliance between the House of Butler and that of O'Neill would be a first step."

The Earl nodded his assent. "Yes, why not?" It would not be the first time the Butlers joined in marriage with the Gael despite the English law which forbade such unions, the Earl thought.

"Con O'Neill offers the hand of Magheen, daughter of Brian O'Neill, to Dermud, son of the great Earl of Ormond," Phelam announced in a formal, well-articulated manner.

The Earl thought on it a while.

"This Magheen is, I presume, the young woman who is even now living at the home of Tom O'Connor. Aye, I've heard that she is a spirited lass and well read."

"She's that and more, Your Grace. She speaks several languages and is known and loved for her patriotic ideals. Her love of Ireland is second to none."

"Well, Phelam, I think we should not delay in this matter." The Earl offered his hand to young O'Neill. "The sooner this union takes place, the better. The details of the official wedding can be worked out later but for the present, only the immediate family and the most trustworthy of our friends should know of the negotiations. There are informers and spies throughout the land only too eager to profit from this kind of information."

The law would be broken once again by the Butler family. But James Butler was determined to ally himself with the powerful houses in the country at this crucial time. A strong Ireland would be a formidable foe. Henry would think twice before attacking.

"If the young lady is agreeable, it would be wise to have this marriage consummated before the Christmas season begins. I bid you God's speed."

"Very well, Your Lordship, I'll be most happy to convey your wishes to Magheen."

On his homeward journey, Phelam was to convey the news to the trusted clans of the West. Two days hard riding and Phelam was across the River Shannon and heading north on the western bank into O'Kelly territory, rich flat land now proud and swelling with life, new and vigorous. Herds of cattle with round, hard bellies and sheep, nearing maturity, there were a plenty. There would be no empty stomach in O'Kelly country come winter.

At dusk on the third day, Phelam crossed into the lands of O'Connor Don. O'Connor was not always friendly to the O'Neills, but Phelam had to take that chance. He was reckoning on the intelligence of O'Connor. A true Irish warrior and fiercely patriotic, Phelam was sure O'Connor could set aside personal enmities for the greater good of the country at large, but he would have to be handled diplomatically.

For this particular task, Phelam was a logical choice. His personality was such that he easily made friends, and his open, honest approach instinctively won confidence even where one could least expect it. A handsome young man with bright blue-grey eyes and a head of auburn, wavy hair, Phelam had a strong, straight nose and sensitive, full lips. He was of medium build, with firm, sinewy limbs, and was fleet of foot. Many a lass had known his passion but none, as yet, had gained his love.

On entering the main hall of Clonalis Castle, Phelam was greeted by O'Connor Don.

"Well, indeed, and to what do we owe this honor now? So you're Phelam, son of the great Con O'Neill. Well, well, well...and what would The O'Neill be wantin' from an O'Connor? It can't be that he seeks another young wench for his bed. 'Tis said he's bedded every lass from Lough Foyle to Lough Neagh."

O'Connor threw back his shaggy head in a boisterous roar. "But come, lad, we won't hold it against ye. Sorry's the man that can't handle a few wenches, especially the plump ones, eh? Ha...Ha..." With that, he spat in the fireplace and beckoned to Phelam to be seated on the stone bench across from him. Phelam disliked the man he now confronted. A bear of a man, his jet black hair covered his barrel chest and arms and grew in tangled masses on his square jaws blending with the flying locks that fell on his broad shoulders. His large brown eyes peered through the flames at Phelam, and he waited for the younger man to speak.

"Sir, I know full well that you have never had much love or respect for my father, but you're no fool. You're fully aware of what the chieftains of the North and South are planning. It's my mission to secure the loyalty and commitment of the House of O'Connor Don.

"Spoken like a true Gael. I like your brashness, lad. So ye would have the clan of O'Connor Don join yer ranks?"

"Aye, I'd say 'twere better to have an O'Connor with you than against you," retorted Phelam.

O'Connor saw the sport of it and chuckled. "Well, lad, there's nothing I'd like better. Ye can count on the support of O'Connor Don."

They conversed for an hour or more. O'Connor's keen and cunning mind, working in circuitous paths, tried to trip Phelam but, eventually, he was convinced of his sincerity and was won over by the youth's candor and straightforward manner.

"We'll make our plans later, but for now I'd like ye to meet my family." So saying, he rose and conducted Phelam to the west wing of the castle, the quarters occupied by his immediate family consisting of his wife, Nora, his five daughters, and three sons.

As O'Connor led Phelam through his home, he proudly pointed out the fine furniture, the paintings, but above all, the beautiful manuscripts he had managed to collect over the years. Honored for his service to Spain, the great man had received the title of Don from the Spanish King.

O'Connor's children ranged in ages from three to seventeen. It was supper time and Phelam was asked to partake of the evening meal. He was seated next to O'Connor at the large dining table and opposite to the eldest daughter, Deirdre. At first sight of this beautiful young woman of fifteen summers, Phelam was transfixed. He had never before seen so much grace and beauty in one so young.

"Slainte maith." O'Connor raised a goblet of ale and drank to the health of his guest.

The bluest of blue eyes, limpid as a clear spring pool, gazed at him from the protection of black velvet drooping lashes. A delicate nose, a rose-bud mouth, and the fairest of Irish skin contrasted with glossy, blue-black tresses that fell in rippling waves to a slender waist. This was the vision that held him spellbound. A glorious smile illuminated the perfect face as Deirdre realized the effect she was having on the stranger.

O'Connor made as if to clear his throat. He repeated the toast. "Slainte maith."

Phelam blushed, hastily took hold of his goblet and raised it to return the toast in his native tongue. As he seated himself, and again glanced across the table at Deirdre, the words of an old poem came to his mind.

> "My heart is turning in me,
> Yet I must go my way;
> My love remains behind me—
> If I could only stay."

"But, by all that's holy, I swear I'll return for you one day," he mumbled under his breath.

"Eh, what's that ye say, Sir?" interjected O'Connor.

"Oh, nothing, Sir, forgive me, I was distracted."

"Aye, so I see," chuckled O'Connor.

During the course of the meal, Phelam became acquainted with the lovely Deirdre. This exquisite creature grew more fascinating as the evening progressed.

His eyes moved from the perfect face to the elegant, stately neck, to the full, firm breasts that were barely visible under the low-cut bodice. Her voice was sweet as the minstrel's harp and, as she engaged in lively conversation with her parents as well as himself, he observed her wit and vivacity. Phelam was hopelessly in love before the evening ended and it was time for him to retire to his chamber to rest.

O'Connor was well aware of the situation. He had admired the deportment of the young man from their initial meeting and considered that an alliance with an O'Neill might indeed prove to be a step in the right direction, even for him. As O'Connor was escorting Phelam to his room, he decided to try to probe O'Neill's inner thoughts.

"Well, Phelam my lad, 'tis ye that have the glad eye for the pretty girls. I couldn't help noticing how well my darlin' Deirdre and yerself got along at supper. Now, lad, I'll have ye be telling me what yer intentions are. Ye won't mind me saying it, but I care not to have a chip o' the auld block casting eyes at my daughter."

Phelam was taken aback. He had, as yet, not really had time to evaluate his feelings; he only knew that his heart told him he must see Deirdre again.

"Sir, you do me honor to compare me with the great Con O'Neill. My father has been, and still is, a man of many and varied passions. His eye for feminine beauty has not been his greatest virtue nor his greatest vice. Yet, I claim none of my father's qualities as I claim none of his vices. 'Tis said I favor my mother, daughter of O'Roark. I am an honorable man, Sir, and would ask your permission to see your daughter again. I will be journeying to the House of Tom O'Connor, your cousin, tomorrow, but before the week is spent I should again see the fair land of your clan. I dare, then, to request an interview with your lovely daughter upon my return."

"Well spoken. I admire a man who knows his own mind. Your request is granted, but I'll warn ye, Deirdre is not a lass that's easily pleased."

O'Connor's hearty roar filled the spaces in the narrow hall that separated the sleeping quarters of the family from the house servants. This familiarity between master and servant was a trait which clearly marked the Irish Lords from their English counterparts. It was the custom in the Irish households for the Lord and Master to eat and sit with his servants and, in fact, to treat them as he would his own family.

Phelam's heart beat high as he bade farewell to O'Connor Don the following morning. And a fair morning it was too, with the sun rising all red and gold among the mists that stood over against the dense, deep, purplish-brown bogs laced with glittering water. And stark against the morning sky, the thorn trees, twisted and bent, were silhouetted. The April winds drove dappled clouds across the heavens, casting dark shadows or brightening the surface waters of limpid lakes. Sparkling streams sang a gurgling tune and in the distance one could view the veiling and unveiling of drowsy hills. Phelam watched as the grey of the craggy rocks across the vale were enveloped in shadow one instant and the next the furze blossoms clinging to their feet were ablaze with light. And, over all, the spectrum of the rainbow's arch was poised. The air vibrated with a flight of passing swallows, while down below a tiny cottage chimney puffed to life a blue-grey streak that whirled and danced for one brief moment, then was no more.

"Ah, but 'tis grand entirely! 'Tis a land worth fighting for, boy!"

Phelam caught the reins, climbed into the saddle, put spurs to his spirited gelding and headed west. He would reach Ballina by sundown the following day and, if all went well, the home of Tom O'Connor and Magheen the day after.

Seventeen

The journey through Mayo was a rough one. The roads, where there were any, were in very poor shape, and the early spring rains had not improved them. The terrain was barren and bleak, large stretches of rock and slate, sparsely covered with clumps of lichen and moss, became more familiar as he neared the coast. This was a desert land, a vast waste of scrub, gorse, and tufts of heather. Yet, there was a lovely mystic charm in it. The air was sweet with the fresh salt tang of the ocean, and only the cry of the curlew or the song of the lark broke the silence.

Phelam stopped beside a streamlet towards noon. He would refresh both his horse and himself with the clear, cool waters. Slender willows bowed to kiss the ferns that lined the water's edge and the odor of spring filled his nostrils. He stretched out on a moss-covered flag and decided to take a short rest. Gazing up at the sky, he watched the woolly clouds form a hundred patterns as they glided across an azure background. The quiet, the warmth, and the smell of the soft moss beneath him invited sleep. He had not given himself much of that luxury since he had left Butler territory, but now, at last, he accepted the gift.

The soprano voice of a shepherd lad, ringing true and pure in the afternoon air, awoke Phelam. He leaped to his feet to realize, as he scanned the sky, that he had slept for at least three hours. He retrieved his grazing horse, which had wandered some distance, and immediately mounted. When the child drew near, Phelam inquired as to the whereabouts of the town of Ballindee.

"Oh! 'Tis a long, long way yet, Sir. Ye'll not be gettin' there 'till the stars are high and the moon is sittin' on her side. But keep yer horse with his face to the sea an' ye'll reach the village before the wee folk leave their hidin' places."

Phelam flung a coin to the upturned hand and dug his heels into his mount. It was, as the lad predicted, well into the evening when Phelam rode up to the main entrance of Tom O'Connor's home.

A hearty welcome was accorded him and a splendid meal was served by Mrs. O'Flynn. Magheen had already retired for the evening, but, on learning that an important guest had arrived, got dressed and descended to join her uncle. As soon as she learned that a marriage between herself and Dermud Butler was proposed, she drew herself up to her full height, raised her head, and stoutly declared, "I'll not be wed to any that is not of my choosing be he king or knave."

Magheen was well educated. She knew the Brehon Laws, whose traditions had been preserved despite the pressure to eradicate them. English law might force her to marry against her will but Irish law viewed her as a superior being. She had to be "wooed and courted" before marriage; she was free to show her disapproval of any suitor be he king, chieftain, or scholar. She also knew that according to Irish laws a marriage was a contract between equals. She would never be the property of her husband nor would what she possessed in money or lands before marriage ever be his. So Magheen stood her ground.

"Magheen, darling," her uncle spoke kindly but forcefully. "You know I wouldn't have you do anything you do not want to do. But I would have you consider this matter very carefully, that's all. This proposal of marriage may have excellent prospects. It certainly would mean that you would be married into the most prominent Sean Ghall family in the land, and it also means that you, Magheen Ni Neill, would be contributing to the unification of our country. This marriage, my dear, is more than a union between man and woman, it's a political alliance of great import. You, it seems, have been chosen to play a very important role in the history of our times. Not only the present, but future generations of Irish men and women will stand in judgment of your actions."

Magheen was silent, weighing the pros and cons, calculating, evaluating. Then, in a whisper, she pronounced the name, "Mairgret of Offaly."

"What was that you said, a gra?"

"I was thinking of my namesake, Uncle. Perhaps, like her, I'm destined to live in the memory of my people." As if understanding for the first time what her uncle was really saying, Magheen's pulse quickened. She could feel the pounding of her heart. Her dreams, her aspirations, her lifelong hopes.... Were they now within her grasp? She had only to say yes, and all would be as she had envisioned. She knew, she always knew, she was destined for greatness!

Her uncle's voice recalled her to reality. "The life of those called to rule is not always peaceful or easy. You will, no doubt, have to sacrifice much. You must ask yourself, are you ready to shoulder great responsibilities?"

Again Magheen was silent.

Meantime, Phelan continued to give the details for the proposed union.

Magheen heard none of them. Her mind was a whirlwind of thoughts and images. It was too much to grasp. One moment she was the fiancée of a country doctor, the next, she was to wed the Earl of Ormand's son. She had just recently accustomed herself to the fact that she was to spend her life in the small town of Sligo; now she would have to attend State dinners and balls, host receptions and banquets. She would have to bid farewell to the security and assurance of a loving husband, for Donald would be that and more. She would have to give up a peaceful home and embrace... the unknown. She smiled to herself. The unknown! She didn't even know this Dermud, this proposed husband! For a moment, the image of Richard Burke flashed through her mind.

"No! No, I can't," she cried.

"What, what are you saying? Do you reject all without further thought?" her Uncle Tom asked incredulously.

"No, Uncle, I was thinking of something else, that's all. But, surely it's not unreasonable to want more information. I can't marry someone I don't know."

"Not unreasonable at all. You'll have all the information you wish," answered Tom as he looked for concurrence from Phelam.

Phelam nodded and added, "Indeed, I'll only be too happy to tell you all I can."

Magheen, ever practical, proceeded to ask questions.

"I want to know, first of all, what kind of man this...this Dermud is? I want to know the color of his skin, his age, his character, his talents, his accomplishments. And, most of all, I want to know Dermud Butler's weaknesses."

Tom O'Connor rubbed his chin and tried to suppress the smile that had spread across his face.

"Well, now, I'd say these are fair questions, aye, indeed."

Phelam did his best to reassure her that the young man who was proposed as her husband was indeed worthy of her. He painted a picture such that all the waking moments of Magheen's life for the next few weeks were filled with visions of the tall, handsome youth whose manners and charm were second to none in the whole Province of Munster.

Her uncle reassured her that the decision was entirely up to her; whether or not her grandfather had decided upon the matter was beside the point.

"Take your time, child. Think about it." He turned to Phelam. "When is her answer required?"

Phelam hesitated a moment, not wanting to acknowledge that the matter, according to The O'Neill had, in fact, been settled.

"Well, as you said, Tom, it's a weighty matter." He looked at Magheen, in his mind trying to decide what course to take.

"Do you think you could give me an answer in a couple of days, my dear?"

Magheen glanced at Uncle. He appeared to be waiting with some concern for her answer.

"Well," she hesitated, "I suppose..." Realizing at that moment that she was probably being evaluated by her other uncle, Phelam, she gave a decided, "Yes, I'll give you my answer in two days."

Phelam relaxed visibly and Tom went to the sideboard to offer a toast of Spanish wine all around.

While they sipped the wine, the conversation turned to things of lesser import.

Magheen soon excused herself, saying that the events of the past few hours had been more than enough for one night. She knew she would get little or no sleep that night and probably very little for many nights to come.

As the hours slipped slowly by, Magheen's thoughts battled with images of the prince who awaited her in the Southlands and the ardent youth who loved her so much in the North. How could she turn her back on Donald? Why! She was practically engaged to him. What would she say to him? "Donald I'm sorry, you see I just found out that Dermud Butler..." It was a terrible mess. It would break Donald's heart. He had waited so long. And besides, she had just begun to love him.

"Oh, Lord," Magheen sighed and turned on her other side. "Better forget all and try and get some sleep." But no sooner had she settled down when the conflicting thoughts started the fight again.

The initial excitement caused by the unexpected announcement and all it entailed had given way to grim reality. Magheen began to realize that as the wife of Dermud Butler, the challenges, the responsibilities, and the expectations would be enormous. Could she handle all that such a life would demand? The questions asked by her uncle were valid. Perhaps she really was asking too much of herself....

By daybreak her old self-confidence had returned. The awareness of her own noble lineage, the fine education her uncle had given her, and the conviction conceived at an early age and carefully nurtured over the years that she, Magheen Ni Neill, was destined for great things had won out. This was the opportunity for which she was waiting. Her calling was to be one of heroism, generosity, even sacrifice. Yes, Magheen was convinced, after two days and nights of pondering, of weighing the pros and cons in the balance, that she had a God-given duty to her country and her family to accept the hand of Dermud Butler in marriage.

Then, no sooner had she made up her mind when thoughts of Richard Burke caused her to shudder. Oh, God, what if Dermud should turn out to be another Richard! Nobody would ever know. Just as nobody knew the devil that lay behind the smiling, boyish face of Burke, so it might be with Butler. A handsome youth with a cruel heart. She had to find out. She just couldn't walk blindly into a life worse than death. So she decided she would accept the hand of Dermud Butler on one condition, a visit to the Butler Castle must be arranged for her uncle and herself as soon as possible.

Phelam O'Neill seemed satisfied with Magheen's conditional answer, and promised to have a letter to her within a fortnight. Tom O'Connor, too, was satisfied. She knew what she was doing, he felt sure. He was proud for himself and his niece. "Sure, 'tis a glorious day for Ireland," he murmured.

As the days passed, Magheen pondered the turn of events. Her preconceived ideas regarding the advantages that wealth and position would give her again came to the fore. Her ambition for power, for fame, albeit philanthropic in nature, and for prestige grew with each passing day. The dreams of youth were reborn to live now in a new and suddenly attainable dimension.

What would she not do as the wife of Dermud Butler! To what heights would she not rise as Lady Mairgret of the House of Ormond! She would glow as the brightest star in the firmament. Her light would shine not only in her own country and among her own people, but its diffused rays would filter far and wide, even to the ends of the earth. Magheen's name would be a household word long after her earthly existence had ceased to be.

In moments when the vindictive side of her character was dominant, Magheen gloated. She was really going to enjoy the advantage her future position would give her over Aoife and Richard Burke. She had promised herself on that horrible day, now so long ago, that a day would come when she would make Richard Burke pay for every insult, hurt, pain, and humiliation that he had caused her.

But there were more pressing things to think about at the moment. For one, there was the situation with Donald O'Sullivan. She hated the thought of having to inflict pain on Donald. He had proved to be a perfect gentleman. Life with him would have been serene, peaceful, happy. To break up with him now on the eve of their wedding was...was asking so much.

In the end, her uncle came to her assistance. "Do you think Donald O'Sullivan less heroic than Magheen Ni Neill?" he asked her.

"Of course not."

"Then we need say no more about this matter except that we'll both pay the O'Sullivan family a visit in the next week or two."

Tom O'Connor inwardly marvelled at Magheen's strength. He did not doubt her love for Donald. He, himself, had played a part in fostering that love, a foolish move in the light of present events. He even questioned his wisdom regarding the visit to Sligo and his plan to lay the matter squarely before Donald and the O'Sullivan family. Yet, he could think of no other way, no other honorable way.

He also had a duty to Magheen and would stand by her decision, and support her in this difficult matter. It was only right. He had been too hasty with regard to Donald. But what was a man to do? He had acted, he told himself, for Magheen's best interests. Tom O'Connor felt old. He sighed. "In matters of the heart," he mumbled to himself, "it's always better not to interfere."

Magheen had decided that it should be she and no other who would break the news to Donald. Accordingly, they undertook the journey to Sligo.

That June was a delightful time to travel in Ireland. The country roads wound in and out among verdant fields, and the ditches were covered with foxglove while the air was sweet as a baby's breath.

Magheen's heart was heavy, however, despite the beauty around her.

"Are you quite sure, Magheen, my dear, that you want to undertake this painful duty alone?"

"Yes, Uncle, I think it the only honorable thing to do. After all, Donald and I love and respect each other. It would be shameful and unfeeling of me to allow him to learn the news from anyone else."

"It's noble of you, my dear. I hope you can continue to be good friends."

Magheen and her uncle arrived in Sligo late in the evening. After dinner, the two young people took themselves off to a little arbor at the end of the garden. The fading light filtering through the climbing roses formed an aureole about her golden curls. A faint tantalizing odor of lavender floated about her warm body as her great sad eyes held Donald's. She could only guess at the effect her closeness and beauty was having on him when she saw the love deep in his eyes. For a few tense seconds they sat in silence.

Then Magheen spoke, "Donald...Donald. I have something

very difficult to say. I need your help, It's not easy for me, as it will not be for you, to accept what I have to tell you."

"Magheen, are you ill?" Donald was aware that the color had left her face. "The evening air may be too cool for you, darling."

"No, Donald. I'm quite all right. But my heart is breaking."

"Magheen. What...?"

Magheen placed her finger on Donald's lips. "Shhh, my dear, let me...Donald, we can never be man and wife."

"Magheen, what are you saying?"

Magheen quickly outlined the events that had taken place during the previous weeks. Donald listened, at first incredulously. It was a prank. Would Magheen tease him in this way? Play with his emotions? Surely she would not torment him in this fashion.

He interrupted her. "Magheen, you do not love me then? Have you never loved me? You allowed me to hope." He bit his lower lip; his cheeks burned with the angry flush of his first reaction.

"Donald, don't. Don't make it any harder. The real truth is, darling, I would have liked to have had your child," she whispered. "A son bearing your likeness." Donald took her in his arms. His anger turned to grief. His eyes filled with tears. He choked as he tried to hide his emotions.

"Magheen, that is the nicest thing you could have said to me. God knows how I have longed to possess you ever since the very first time I set eyes on you. Was I merely reaching for the stars?" He sobbed.

"Donald, you will always be my star, my true guiding light. Being with you, knowing you, has enriched my life, given it a meaning hitherto undreamt of."

Magheen looked at Donald's unhappy face. Then they clung to each other for some minutes, each trying to gain a grain of comfort from the closeness.

The stars had scattered their first grains of dust and the moon had grown full when they, at last, entered the house.

* * * *

The following morning after breakfast, Donald and Magheen were discretely left alone. Neither of them had slept well the night before. A palpable gloom had descended on the usually lighthearted household. Magheen looked tired, her eyes were swollen and the tip of her nose red.

"Donald, we have not spoken of the years that lie ahead. Now that our plans have been completely altered, what will you do?"

"I've hardly had time to give much thought to it, Magheen. I suppose I'm still dazed, shocked. All my plans were centered around you, even now, you are my only concern. I can only think of you and hope that your future will be a happy one."

"You have always been selfless, Donald. Perhaps...dare I say it? Had you not been so considerate, so concerned for my feelings, who knows? Perhaps if you had been a less patient man, a more domineering man, we might today be man and wife and no one else could have claimed my hand."

Magheen was clearly beside herself, hardly knowing what she said.

"Oh, Magheen, don't. Don't make our parting more unbearable. You forget your own forceful nature. You would not be pressed. You would not be hurried. You, alone, delayed the time of our union." The torture that racked his heart was visible in his eyes and voice while Magheen's own emotions were apparent in the tears that welled up and then freely dropped from her heavy lashes.

"You're right. I'd forgotten. It was I who decided, Donald." She fell silent again for a moment. "Perhaps I shouldn't have come."

"Magheen, I thank you, thank you from the bottom of my heart for coming. I know that the journey was an inconvenience and this meeting a most difficult one. But, I would surely have died had I heard the news from someone other than yourself."

Magheen could not control her tears.

"My heart is breaking at this moment, but it grieves me even more to see your tears. Since fate, in the guise of duty to our country, has asked this sacrifice of us, we must be brave. God has other plans for us. We must bow to His will. Come, my dear, there are some hours left before you leave. See, the sun is breaking through and beckons us. Dry your beautiful eyes, my love. Let's walk by the shore together once more," he said.

"Oh, Donald, you're the brave one. At this moment I thank you for having enough courage for both of us."

So Magheen and Donald parted. The young love in their hearts, still vibrant and strong, made their last farewells sheer torture.

Donald appeared strong, but for several weeks his behavior was such that his father suggested he take a trip.

"Do you good, Son. Go look up your old friends in sunny Spain. Get away and enjoy the company of some of your schoolmates. You know how insistent the Valdez family has been that you spend some time at their estate in Malaga."

"Father, that is considerate of you. I have hardly earned a vacation such as you propose, but I agree with you, I need to get away for a while."

So Donald journeyed to Spain late in that summer of 1545. Nor did he return for several months. He eventually married Ramona Valdez and settled into an old rambling estate in the south of Spain. In time, Donald became the proud father of three sons and a pretty daughter. He was admired and respected as a fine physician. Although he and Magheen never met again, his letters to Ireland often mentioned her name. He was aware of the political scene in his native land. He used his influence on more than one occasion to get aid for the "rebels" in their fight for freedom. Donald took his family to Sligo to see the old folks several times when his children were young, but after his mother died he did not care to return to his home. He lived to see his grandchildren become prominent citizens in his adopted country.

Magheen's days of freedom, the carefree life she had known since first she came to Ballindee, were now swiftly drawing to a close. She had things to do before she could take her place at the head of a large household and at the side of a very important man. As the summer wore on, she was caught up in the excitement of preparations for the great day, and this despite the fact that she didn't get the opportunity to make the journey to Butler Territory prior to her wedding. Times were uncertain. Secrecy regarding this union had to be maintained until it was a fait accompli.

Her trousseau had to be chosen and made. Her uncle was insistent that she have the very best. Irish linen was prized the world over, and Magheen would have several gowns of the most delicately woven types.

"If Queen Clemence of Hungary could send for 'Irish silk' for her wardrobe," O'Connor announced one day, "then the loveliest queen of them all must certainly have as much."

It seemed the old man would spend his last penny to see that Magheen lacked for nothing. The best of Irish friezes and serges were purchased. Several mantles of fur and wool also were added to her wardrobe. As Irish leather goods were high fashion, Moll was given free rein to choose the finest. Thus, the pleasant summer days passed and Inis Fail was a beehive of activity.

And, in the little village of Ballindee, the folks whispered. In each heart there was a new song and fresh hope, and everyone knew of the great event that was soon to take place, yet, not a soul knew when the knowing of it was not to be known.

Eighteen

St. Malo, in the north of France, was built at the mouth of the Rance River. It appeared to float on the water like a mirage, a fantasy isle of glistening ramparts. But stark reality was quickly thrust on the traveller as he entered the island stronghold and perceived the granite bulwarks that had protected this seaport for over three hundred years.

In 1545, St. Malo was a thriving cosmopolitan town. Merchants came from many parts of northern Europe to sell their wares at this center of commerce. Ireland had a particularly large trade with this port known as the "City of Corsairs".

This ancient town of twisting, cobbled streets and tightly packed buildings was a hub of activity on the morning of August 28th when the *Orleans* and the *Bordeau* lay at anchor in the waters of her sheltered harbor. Whiffs of tangy air swept across the decks.

The captains were at the helms shouting orders to the first mates. It was time to weigh anchor. The sails were hoisted as both ships glided from the calm waters that protected St. Malo's fleets into the choppy seas of the English Channel. The ships hugged the coast for several miles before heading north. In the morning light, the emerald coast of France bade farewell. Further on, cliffs, sheer and massive, plunged into the sea where exploding pillars of spray crashed and careened in a frenzied death dance. The air was soft. A gentle, misty, melancholy light bathed the coast as the last stretches of land faded out of sight.

"No turnin' back now," said one of the sailors.

"Ah, 'twill be a short run, I'll be bound. Not much food taken aboard this time," said a second.

"Must be Ireland or Scotland."

"Why do you say that?" asked the second sailor.

"More pikes and swords than wine in her hold," answered his friend.

"Ah ha, a bloody business then, it is, mate?"

"Hope we don't get caught up in it. Have no stomach for the battles of foreign kings. Now, I'm not sayin' I don't like a good fight. But, if I've got to die, I'd like to know what I'm dying for."

"I can't agree with you more, Francois."

The *Orleans* and the *Bordeau* had been fitted during the preceding weeks for an important trip. The bilges were laden with barrels of the best French wines. There were crates and boxes of expensive velvets and laces, silver platters and goblets made of porcelain. The pikes and spears, hundreds of them, were stacked aft.

The men who were chosen to man the vessels were no ordinary sailors. No, indeed, they were a picked group and they were aware that the mission was an important one. Each man had to be self-sufficient and capable of undertaking practically every task: mending a sail, making a rudder, cooking, splicing, even forging metal parts. A ship at sea was an isolated world, and in order for it to survive, it depended on the complete cooperation of each and every member of the crew.

Jean Paul Le Doux was Captain of the *Orleans*, a man of experience, he had spent twenty-five years on the decks and in the cramped quarters below them. He started out as a young boy of ten, doing odd jobs and running errands for the captain. Then, through hard work and ingenuity, he had fought his way step by step up the ladder until finally, he was given command of the *Orleans*. He was, at this time, a well-seasoned, reliable sailor, a fair man and well-liked by most. The men who worked with him depended on his skill and judgment to get them through. Le Doux had never married, although his manly bearing and weather-beaten features were not unattractive to the women who served in the taverns and inns near the waterfront. He had long ago decided that his responsibilities lay with his vessel and crew. And now, at the height of his career, he had been singled out by his King and entrusted with a mission both sensitive and secret. Le Doux, thus honored, was determined to prove himself worthy of the trust placed in him.

The members of the crew were veterans of many voyages and were loyal to their Captain. The only newcomer was Pierre, a youth of fourteen who had run away from home. Pierre had proved that he had both brawn and brain in the two weeks prior to sailing. He was fleet of foot and nimble on the masts. Le Doux had decided that the youth would be of value to him.

The men had their appointed tasks to complete, and since they knew each other, it did not take long for a regular routine to be established. And so the crew and the vessel were in working order when Hugo, Count de Breville, introduced himself to the Captain.

"Hugo de Breville reporting for duty, Sir."

"An honor, Sir, to have you aboard."

"Thank you, Captain Le Doux. In view of the nature of our mission, I think it would be wise to keep my identity confidential."

"As you wish, Sir."

Hugo settled into his quarters and familiarized himself with as many aspects of the ship's daily routine as he thought would be beneficial in the days ahead. He did not think it beneath him to undertake the menial tasks performed by the common sailor in the course of each day. In fact, Hugo's training as a soldier had taught him many valuable lessons that could be applied equally to life on board the *Orleans.* He soon made friends with many of the men and, in particular, with young Pierre. It was not unusual for a ship to carry soldiers in such perilous times, and especially when travelling the seas around England, the enemy of France, for so many generations.

"Bon jour, Monsieur." Pierre's voice sounded thin above the splashing of the waves and the blustering squalls. The hustle and bustle of the other sailors as they went about their morning chores added to the general din.

"Bon jour, Pierre. How are you this fair day?"

"Fine, fine, Sir."

Pierre then drew close, as if to impart some very secretive piece of information.

"In truth, Sir, my stomach tells me I'm not so fine, but I can't let anyone know about it. I'd be the laughing stock of the ship, Sir, that I would."

Hugo nodded. "Tell you the truth, I feel just as bad."

"Don't worry, Sir, no one 'ill ever pry it loose from me. Your secret's safe," whispered the boy.

"We'll shake on it then." So saying, Hugo extended his hand and the boy eagerly grasped it. Hugo winked at the lad, so young and anxious to make friends. It was such a thoroughly new experience for both that they naturally became friends. As the days passed and the struggles of man against the sea became so strenuous that even some of the seasoned deckhands were squeamish, their friendship grew. Together, they learned their way around the one hundred-fifty-ton vessel. It had no proper castle up forward, merely a raised quarterdeck. The main mast was made of one piece and was higher than the ship was long. Words such as bowsprit, ratlines, and gunports became familiar terms.

It was their second day at sea. The Captain spoke to Hugo. "How are the old sea legs, Sir?"

"Have kept me upright so far, Captain," Hugo answered.

"Life aboard ship is anything but comfortable, I'm afraid."

"Life on the battlefield is no luxury either. But tell me, Sir, have we sprung a leak?" Hugo was concerned. As the ship heaved, the bilge water could be heard sloshing below.

"These wooden ships leak quite a bit, but pay no heed, she's safe enough." The Captain smiled.

As the days passed, the bilge water became the happy refuge for the seaman's inevitable companion, the cockroach. As the men threw most of their slops into the bilge, the stench that arose from that quarter became more intolerable with time.

Hugo did not complain. He had learned to endure hardships, yet he did concede that the food the soldiers ate was, by and large, far better than the fare set before the sailors.

The only means of cooking was on an open firebox provided with a back to screen it from the wind. Hot food was the first comfort to be sacrificed with the onset of bad weather, so Hugo soon became tired of beef and pork pickled in brine. Sometimes they ate dried or salt fish with dried peas and beans. The basic meal was a kind of stew, a meal which could be readied without waste. The foul taste of the water had only to be covered. Water was always a problem. Stored in oaken casks, within a few weeks it could be drunk only out of dire necessity. Large quantities of wines were carried to supplement the water, so no one complained. Bread took the form of pancakes, but in time, it too became stale and moldy and riddled with weevils.

No sleeping place was provided for able seamen or soldiers. The men slept where they could, upon a straw-stuffed palliasse, covered by their day clothes. Bunks were available for the pilot, master comptroller, and a visitor or two. The captain had a snug stateroom and the officers a general cabin. These quarters were provided aft between the main and poop decks. Like most ships, the decks of the *Orleans* were arched so that they had considerable camber and the only flat place was the main hatch amidship. This was a favorite sleeping spot. The few hammocks noticeable on board were fashioned after those discovered among the Indians by men on the Columbus voyages.

"Landsend, ahoy!" shouted the watch.

There was a scurry of excitement on board. It had been easy going so far. Three days of sailing found the wind and sea on the stern giving the caravels a regular lift and roll, the motion that sea legs take in their stride. Landsend, the most southerly tip of the English coast, was bathed in the golden glow of the evening sun, and as the men watched the receding peninsula, the sun was swallowed up in the vast bubbling caldron of the Atlantic. On the fourth day, the sails were filled with a brisk breeze and by mid-day the Irish coast was sighted.

The *Bordeaux* , obeying orders, was to lay out of sight of the mainland until dusk. Then, by the fading light, she would cautiously edge her way toward the shore and the Bay of Courtmacsherry. There, the lighted faggots would signal the exact location for the rendezvous. The crew of the *Orleans* bade their companions "God speed."

"Courage mes amis!" shouted the Captain of the *Orleans*. "Pour la belle France et pour L'Irlande! Adieu, adieu."

The *Orleans* hugged the coast of Kerry as it changed course and prepared for its journey north to the lands of the O'Neills. By midnight, the winds had risen considerably and the *Orleans* began to take on water. The Captain did not pay too much attention to this late summer squall.

"It's nothing, 'twill blow itself out in an hour or so," he assured the men.

Hugo was managing quite well, despite the fact that he was not able to keep much food down. By the time the *Orleans* had reached Clare, the winds had definitely changed. A steady gale was now in progress. The seas were running in swells of ten to twenty feet high and the decks of the *Orleans* were constantly pounded. The vessel, tossed by the battering force, scarcely made any progress. As night fell, the Captain would have pulled into the safety of an inlet or cove, but none was visible. Only the black, hard face of the formidable Cliffs of Moher, with the treacherous outcropping of jagged rocks and reefs, confronted them through the driving rain and the flying spray.

"Good God! What are our chances of weathering this storm?" Hugo asked a sailor.

"I've seen 'em worse, Sir." He looked around for some rope. "Best bind yourself to yon mast, Sir. If this gale don't blow herself out soon she'll blow us all to kingdom come."

Hugo did not take the advice. He calculated that the small craft could not long sustain the onslaught and that the mast would be first to go. He sought instead some more insignificant structure, an empty water cask positioned in the stern on the poop deck. This cask was securely lashed under the coop of the counter. Taking up his position, he muttered a hurried prayer to God, and thought that all was finished. "Great God Almighty protect us all."

As a nauseous feeling swept over him, he instinctively tightened his grasp on the barrel and closed his eyes. He would wait for the hungry sea to eat him up as the storm continued to gather momentum. Although Hugo could not see them, the waves, curling up in volutes, were supplanting each other, then mingling and climbing in leapfrog fashion one over the other. Between the waves, the hollows deepened with each towering upward surge. The *Orleans* was now flying before the wind faster and faster. In fact, the gale, the sea, the *Orleans*, and the clouds, all possessed by the same diabolic frenzy, were driven in the same direction. Enveloped in foam from each subsiding wave, the deck was impassable.

Toward the early hours of the morning of the fifth day, there was a change in the direction of the wind but the torrential rains and the mountainous waves continued unabated. Truly, this was the roughest and wildest seaboard of western Europe. Hour after hour, the now exhausted and hungry men battled to keep the vessel afloat. Below deck, casks of wine had been ripped apart. Silk and porcelain pieces were scattered in disarray among the splintered and broken crates and barrels. Chaos reigned supreme.

For the next twelve hours, the storm raged on continuously. The driving fury of the gale hurled the vessel before it and drove it north at a dizzy speed. As dark of day turned to blacker night, the *Orleans* was listing badly. She was taking on water at such a pace that it was impossible for the dazed and struggling crew to cope with the situation. The Captain could no longer control the limping craft. A shudder went through her. From below him, Hugo heard a prolonged grating noise as the hull scraped against a rocky reef. His breath came in short fast quips. His heart seemed to leave his chest and pounded in his throat. As the thunder rumbled off in the distance, a new sound reached his ears, a long, tearing sound followed by a violent crash. He held his breath as the deck shuddered and shook. The foremast had gone. It had fallen across the deck and crashed through the bulwarks.

Hugo felt alone, terribly alone. Still clinging to the barrel, he sought with clouded eyes the faces of the men he had learned to admire, but none could he see. He felt the skin of his cheeks burn and with every passing moment his breath grew shorter. Slowly his strength was ebbing. How long could he endure the onslaught? His blanched lips uttered a desperate cry, "My God, my God, why have you forsaken me?"

A shudder, a grinding wrenching, and the *Orleans* was torn in two. No human sound escaped the doomed craft. As if in total subjection to the wiles of an avenging God, the tiny ship spilt out its entrails, its life blood in the ultimate sacrifice, on that briny, aqueous altar.

Blackness...only blackness. He was sinking into the dark depths of the sea. There was water in his eyes, his nose, his mouth. His hair and beard were frosted with salt. He kicked out with his legs, clawed with his hands, but the pounding waves battled against him. Eventually he was swept onwards toward the rocks. Frantic, he lifted his head and, with a burst of energy, leaped upward. The cold air rushed into his lungs. He tried to open his eyes. Again, only blackness met his blurred gaze. The rain beat down upon his head. Then a tremendous wave roared out of the belly of the ocean and tossed him floundering onto a flat ledge of rock.

Nineteen

The late summer of 1545 had been unusually hot. August began with a period of several scorchers. A little reprieve came mid-month and the thirsty land eagerly soaked up the deluge that finally broke loose. Then, toward the end of the month, the summer sun was back and it beat down from an almost cloudless sky. Little streamlets that usually danced and splashed lost their vitality and barely made their way over the pebbles.

"We've got to have rain soon or the crops are finished this year," declared Rory O'Doyle.

"Aye, can't remember weather like this since I was a boy, an' that's going on seventy year." Mike O'Flaherty spat on the dry ground as he withdrew a straw-colored stalk from between his broken front teeth. He glanced cautiously about, shuffled a little closer to his young friend, Rory, and, in whispered tones inquired: "Tell me, what's with the lads? Are they really preparing to leave soon?"

"Whist Mike, for God's sake. You know well they are, but we can't tell the women folk, at least, not yet."

"Can't be too careful, Rory, I know that. As the sayin' goes...tell a woman..." Mike cackled.

"I'll let you know as soon as things get lively. In the meantime, keep your mouth shut, man."

"Aye, I'll do that. No need to say any more." The old man ran his sleeve across his tanned brow to wipe away the drops of moisture which had gathered above his bushy eyebrows. He groped for his black thorn, which lay against the stone wall and haltingly made his way to the cover of his low thatched home nearby. Inside, his wife, Bridie, had the turf fire well stacked and the black kettle steaming with vegetable soup. A delicious aroma of freshly-baked oatmeal bread filled the air as she raised the cover of the pot hanging over the red embers. A puff of smoke escaped into the room as the door opened and old Mike entered.

"What's kept you at all, at all?" his wife inquired.

"Oh, nothin', nothin'. Had a few words with young Rory. Not much goin' on."

"Nothing going on! Well now, isn't that strange. I've heard the young lads are planning to be moving out in a day or so. Going to join up with O'Connor Don, I believe is what was said." She looked at her husband as she drawled the words, trying to catch him in a slip.

"Well now, you heard wrong. And who would be telling you such stories?"

"Oh, I have my sources." She knew she had him trapped.

"Well, I'll be jiggered, it's a strange thing indeed. A man can scarce have an idea in his head when lo and behold, every woman in the neighborhood is talkin' about it. I swear the devil himself will be fooled by a woman." He laughed.

"Ah, go on with ye. It's just the way God made us. Women are smarter, that's all." She had the last word for a while.

Eventually, the banter back and forth would commence again and Bridie would know all that there was to be known about the local goings on.

As the day wore on, the animals about the small house became restless. The birds fought with each other for better shelter among the trees, and even the crickets at the hearth grew louder. Dark, ominous clouds crept stealthily across the trailing crimson skirts of the evening sun. The air hung heavy with the pungent smell of kelp.

"It's coming, I feel it in my bones. All hell will let loose before the night is out." Mike fumbled as he slowly raised himself from the settle.

"Better get the goat tied up, Mike. I'll be bringing in the clothes now, an' some more turf; could turn mighty cold when that storm breaks." Bridie made her way to the door.

As the village folk of Ballindee prepared for the worst,

Magheen, who had just returned from a canter, made sure that Leprachaun, her old sorrel mare, was well watered and fed. She secured the latch on the stable door and headed for the house. A gust of cold air from the sea swirled in eddies, forming a little cloud of dust in the path before her. She shivered slightly as the cool breeze penetrated her light gown. Then, turning to face the sea, she watched as the mounting white caps battled and jostled each other in an attempt to scale the highest outcroppings of the jagged rocks. As far as she could see, the broad Atlantic was one boiling cauldron.

"How beautiful! How exciting! I can't wait for the storm. I want to be part of it. If only I were a sprite and could wing my way into the very center of it." Magheen allowed her thoughts to carry her away. She twirled and raised her arms to the sky.

"You best be getting inside, young lady."

Magheen was rudely awakened from her reverie by Sean, the yard man.

"I think it's wonderful! Look, Sean! Look! The lightning has started way out where the water and the sky are one. It's a fairy-land for sure."

"Aye, an' ye know what mischief the wee folk can do. I've heard of many a one that's been struck dead by those wild sparks and lights."

"I don't believe it, Sean. It's too, too beautiful and wonderful to be harmful." Reluctantly, Magheen turned toward the house as the first large drops of the summer storm splashed with a hollow thud on the parched earth.

"Oh, well, I'll have more time to work on my trousseau, maybe." She really didn't like the idea of sewing on such a night. There was frenzy in the air and she wanted to be part of it, cause a disturbance…something.

Moll heard her enter. "Magheen, that you?"

"Yes, it's going to rain." She hurried toward the kitchen. "Do you have enough turf in? I think we're in for a long night of it." She was eager to return outside. There was magic in the air. She didn't want to miss the excitement of it.

"Oh, yes, there's plenty o' turf, but I've run clean out of milk. I made some pancakes for this afternoon and used up my last jug."

"I'll take Leprachaun and fetch some from Eileen Dugan. She's bound to have some left since this morning."

"Would you, darlin'? Don't tarry now. 'Twill be pouring cats an' dogs very soon by the looks of it." Moll glanced out the window as she spoke.

Magheen fetched her cloak and was on her way. As she rode over the rough path that ran along the edge of the barley field in the direction of the Dugan farm, she planned what she would do for the remainder of the evening.

"It's going to be an exciting night, Leprachaun. Yes, it has all the appearance of it, my pretty." The horse didn't seem to be in the least interested. Magheen looked at the sky. The black clouds were chasing each other in from the sea and the rain had become a steady stream. It beat against her bare shins and ran in little streams down into her sandals. She dug her heels into Leprachaun's sides.

"Come on, old girl, we've got to get moving. You don't want me to drown, do you?"

When Magheen reached home, she quickly got out of her wet clothes and made herself comfortable in a loose robe. Her uncle had lately acquired a bundle of old manuscripts and she was anxious to get her hands on them. She would sit by the window and make use of whatever daylight was left to read, while at the same time she could keep an eye on the progress of the storm.

Her uncle was standing looking at the rain as it beat against the window panes. It had been nearly two weeks since the last shower had watered the soil. He turned as Magheen entered the room.

"Looks like we're in for a big one, Uncle!"

"'Tis badly needed. Everything has been so dry. Well, my dear, what would you like to do this evening?"

"That's partly why I'm here, Uncle. I'd like to read the old manuscripts you got a while back, if I may?"

"Certainly, my dear, just be careful. They are in a pretty poor condition." Tom opened a drawer in his desk and withdrew a packet. He carefully unbound it and, one by one, separated several of the fragile parchments from the stack.

"How wonderful, Uncle! This is quite a haul!"

"I'm lucky to have got these. They are very valuable."

Magheen picked up a leaf. A poem by Prince Alfred of

Northumbria was beautifully transcribed on the dark paper.

> I travelled its fruitful provinces around
> And in every one I found
> Alike in church and palace hall
> Abundant apparel and food for all.
> Gold and silver I found in money;
> Plenty of wheat and plenty of honey;
> I found God's people rich in pity,
> Found many a feast, and many a city.
> I also found in Armagh the splendid,
> Meekness, wisdom, and prudence blended,
> Fasting as Christ hath recommended,
> And noble counsellors untranscended.
> I found in each great church moreo'er,
> Whether on island or on shore,
> Piety learning, fond affection,
> Holy welcome and kind protection....

"'Tis beautiful, Uncle. It proves there was a time when our enemies really appreciated what we here in Ireland had to offer."

"Yes, that was the era when scholars came from every country of Europe to be educated in this land. But, unfortunately that time is no more."

Magheen picked up another loose page. Glancing through it, she learned that the Irish monks had introduced rhyme into European verse. These educators wrote and taught in Latin, but because they were influenced by the poetry of their own language, they naturally infused this concept into the Latin tongue. As she read, she also found that the Irish had always been passionately devoted to music and their performers had reached standards of proficiency which astonished visitors.

"I didn't know that," she murmured, half to herself.

"What didn't you know?" her uncle asked.

"That the musicians of this country were responsible for introducing harmony and polyphony into European music. It says here that both ideas were unknown and that plain chant alone existed before the coming of the Irish musicians."

"There have been many contributions of great value made by our countrymen in all ages to all parts of the world. I'm not surprised to learn this." Her uncle knew so many things about Ireland. He reminded her then of the unique contribution of Irish art to western Europe and of its influence on Carolingian art.

Magheen had listened to stories like these all her life. Her long winter evenings had been spent curled up before the peat fire at her uncle's feet. She had become fluent in English and French. She had learned mathematics, history, music, and poetry.

"I'd like to take some of these to my room, I'll be very careful. If this storm turns out to be anything like I think it will, it should be fantastic to watch. I don't want to miss the fireworks."

"Fine, enjoy yourself."

Magheen eagerly picked a handful of loose sheets. "Thanks, Uncle. See you at dinner."

Magheen decided to stop by the kitchen for an apple or two, to make a perfect evening. As Magheen entered the warm, sweet-smelling domain of Moll O'Flynn, she asked, "Any apples left?"

"I think I can find one or two." Moll went into the pantry. The stone shelves still held the dregs from last year's pickings.

A spicy smell escaped into the kitchen, reminding Magheen that the time was not far off when once again the rich harvest would be in full swing. That was not only the busiest time of the whole year, but also great fun. The best part came when all the thrashing was done. Then everyone in the village took the day off. There was feasting, games, and, in the evening, a barn dance. The newly made cider was lavishly ladled out into large wooden mugs. Dozens of homemade apple pies were devoured by the insatiable merrymakers. Moll was kept busy from morning until night cooking and supervising the extra help. The house never smelled so good, delicious odors reaching into every corner. One awoke in the morning to sniff the aromas of fried bacon and fresh pork sausage challenging the residue of fragrant cinnamon, nutmeg, and ginger from the evening before. As the day wore on, these odors were replaced by others of a more heady nature, boiled or roasted meats, and large cauldrons of vegetables bubbling or simmering over the open fire. It was the custom for the whole village to gather at Inis Fail for the Harvest Feast.

"Here you are. They'll be the last now of the old batch."

"Thank you. Just wanted to munch on something while I read these. This is part of the manuscript Uncle got a few weeks ago and I can't wait to get to it."

"Off with ye then and don't bother me again tonight. I've enough to do, God knows. Shoo..." Moll took her apron and fluttered it at Magheen as she often did when she was a little girl.

"All right, all right. I'm gone." She turned on her heels and sped up the stairs to her room to the seat, her favorite one, on the wide window sill. Magheen bit into a rosy apple. Not bad, she thought, for an old one. But her mouth watered for the really juicy ones as her mind again turned to Moll.

How much she had learned from the kindly old lady. She had spent hours watching her bake. She learned how to make butter and many varieties of cheese. She helped crush the apples for the cider and gathered the honey for the mead. The curing of the great cuts of pork, the pickling of beef, the smoking of salmon, trout, and mackerel, all had become second nature to her.

It was at Moll O'Flynn's knee that Magheen had had her first lesson in reciting the Lord's prayer. This good woman had taught, too, by her example. How often had Magheen heard her late at night whisper a prayer as she lay on her little fireside bed.

It was a well run, orderly home, if not a pretentious one, and Moll saw to it that none of the essentials of life were missing for "her" family. Indeed, it was well known among the villagers that if someone went without at Inis Fail it would be Moll O'Flynn.

After supper, the storm had risen to a furious gale. The rain fell so fast that the roads, hardened by the long dry spell, became veritable rivers of mud. The thunder and lightning kept up a continuous barrage all through the evening until it seemed that the earth's foundations were shaken to their very depths.

Tom O'Connor had dismissed the hired men early.

"No night for man or beast to be abroad," he said to Rory as he bade him good night. Then he lit a good fire in his library where he intended to spend several hours with his manuscripts.

"And may God Almighty protect all those at sea," exclaimed Moll as she bolted and barred the shutters against the gale.

"Amen," answered Tom.

"And may God and His Holy Mother protect all here, too," she concluded as she closed the door to the library. She then took herself off to her own quarters to settle down for the night.

Magheen had watched the storm grow from faint rumblings far out on the western horizon, until, like a giant octopus, it inched its way slowly toward the coast, little by little, spreading out its inky tentacles and enveloping all in a mighty embrace of complete blackness. At regular intervals, flashes of forked lightning burst in jagged flares across the dark face of the western sky.

To be a part of it all! To be one with the great drama enfolding before her was, to Magheen, an ecstatic experience. She stood spellbound at the spectacle, her eyes and ears exquisitely sensitive to every sight and sound. The wind, it seemed, had shifted direction. It now blew from the southwest. In sudden gusts and blustering squalls, the great chorus of the elements was bracing for the grand finale.

A sudden hush, a pause...a momentary lull...then a piercing sound reached Magheen's ears. She sprung to life, flung wide the shutters and listened intently. Again it arose, like the keen of the banshee, fierce, blood curdling, as if from the bowels of the sea. Magheen's breathing seemed to stop for a moment. Magh-e-e-n, Magh-e-e-n, Magh-e-e-n. Her name! Was she dreaming? Was the wind playing tricks on her? Had the wee folk indeed possessed her? She roused herself. What nonsense.

She, an educated, sensible girl, she told herself, must not start imagining things. There was a reasonable answer to everything and, as her uncle had often told her, if she did not know, it was her business to find out. She got up.

The wind had whipped itself into gale-like furies again, but the rain seemed to have done its worst. She reached for her shawl, stuck her feet into her leather sandals and raced down the stairs to the library. It was late, but a dim streak of light was visible from under the door. Her uncle was still up. Thank God. He would know what to do.

As she reached the door, she caught herself just in time. What if he had dozed off? A sudden entry might give him a shock. She knocked, then entered. Sure enough, his head had fallen forward, and the assuring sound of a quiet snore told her that the storm had brought rest to at least one soul on the wild western seaboard. She roused him.

"Uncle! Uncle! Wake up! We've got to get down to the strand."

"Magheen, is it crazy you are? What in the name of God would we be doing on the strand in this weather and at this hour of the night?"

"Oh, Uncle, I'm sure something has happened. I heard...." Magheen had no time to finish. A loud rapping at the door and the excited exclamations of several men from the village brought her and her uncle to undo the huge wooden bolts quickly.

"What in thunderation is going on? By all the powers that be, have you all gone mad?"

The men waited respectfully for Tom O'Connor to finish.

"Sir," young Seamus MacMahon spoke up, "a terrible thing has happened."

"What? What? Explain yourself, man."

Liam Larkin stepped forward. "Sir, what he means to say is, well, there's a ship floundering; we've seen it. An' the sea's awful. It's impossible to do anything without more help."

"Well, don't stand there. Round up the rest of the lads and let's go."

"Uncle!" cried Magheen, and with that she sped out into the night and headed for the cliffs and the path she knew so well, which led to the strand and the thundering breakers below.

Twenty

Padraig O'Toole bent his back to the wind. His strong, ruddy, weather-beaten face, topped by a red thatch of tight curls and the merriest of clear blue eyes, gave him a roguish look. He had broad, sloping shoulders and long arms, a fisherman's body bent to the oars. His trews were made of coarse homespun wool, greyish in color, and over them he wore a wide-sleeved saffron linen shirt which reached to his lower thighs.

He was brave as the next man and skilled at his trade. And he was the best man in Ballindee at handling the tiny skiffs called curraghs. This was no small honor in a village where every man was a master in the very same art.

But Padraig had another skill, one which earned him a very different reputation, one which he didn't really deserve—"The Butcher of Ballindee."

It had been out of the sheer goodness of his heart that one evening on his way home from the sea, he stopped to assist Sheila Dwyer. The young girl of about twelve was sobbing her eyes out and holding her hand over her mouth as she sat on the stone wall near Padraig's stone cabin.

"An' what in the world ails you, Sheila? Such woeful sorrow. Has someone died belonging to you?" he asked.

"Sure, 'tis myself that's dyin'," she answered.

"Dyin' is it you are? How so?"

"'Tis my mouth. It hurts something fierce. I can't go...on...like this."

"Well," said Padraig, "there's no earthly use in your sitting here cryin'. Come home with me. My mother's a fair hand with the herbs. Maybe she'll have something for you."

At the cabin, Padraig's mother took one look at Sheila's mouth and said, "'Tis that back tooth." She then nodded to Padraig who moved toward the door.

"Now, I'll get you a nice drink. It'll help the pain." She stroked Sheila's fair hair and walked to a shelf of earthenware jars. She quickly mixed several herbs in a pot of water and put them to simmer.

Sheila had stopped crying, her interest peaked by the activities.

"Now sip this, a gra." Kate O'Toole handed her a mug of warm red liquid.

Soon Sheila grew drowsy. Kate motioned to Padraig, "I want you to do it."

His eyes opened wide but he didn't say anything.

"Now open your mouth, Sheila, I want to rub something on that tooth. It will help."

The child did as she was told.

Kate quickly massaged her gum with a resin-like substance. A moment later, Padraig, pincers in hand, extracted his first tooth.

The word spread and Padraig quickly became the acknowledged tooth physician of the area.

But misfortune comes to most sooner or later. To Padraig it came in the form of Miles O'Keefe, a burly farmer from Ballina.

Miles had long been plagued with bad teeth. Unable to obtain satisfaction from his local physician, he turned in desperation to Padraig.

At first all went well. One tooth came clean on the second try. It was when Padraig tried to pull a stubborn molar that O'Keefe's jawbone broke.

"Glory be to God! Sure 'tis a bloody butcher ye are, Padraig O'Toole!" With that O'Keefe jumped up, threw down the towel he had in his hands, and took off as fast as he could.

It was an unfortunate accident and the news of it spread quickly and widely.

Padraig's friends made light of the whole affair, but he was hurt personally and financially. Still, it wasn't like Padraig O'Toole to be cowed for long.

"Arrah, let 'em say what they like. Sure it doesn't matter a damn. 'Twon't change how the people of Ballindee think about me an' that's all I care."

Tom O'Connor recognized a native intelligence in Padraig that others of his class didn't possess. He encouraged and fostered the young boy's love of learning. As soon as he had mastered the art of reading, Tom loaned him books and manuscripts from his own library. He helped him gain a rudimentary knowledge of French, Latin, and English. Who could tell, perhaps one day Padraig would like to travel, expand his fishing trade to foreign parts. There was a big demand for Irish fish and other goods on the continent. The O'Flahertys and the O'Malleys to the south had become wealthy by trading with Spain and Portugal.

So Padraig's evenings were spent studying. What had been denied him as a result of the plunder, first of the Vikings and then the English, he sought at Tom O'Connor's feet.

There was no greater pleasure in life for him than to spend an evening at Inis Fail in the company of this learned man. There he would discuss the discoveries he had made during his previous hours of reading, the wonders that this mighty universe had to offer.

"No one can ever know enough and surely no one life is long enough to learn all there is to know," he often said.

Padraig and his mother also prepared for the expected storm on that September evening in 1545. It was late when he finished his work and almost dark when he got home.

The weather had grown worse. Most of the men from the village who had been out to sea that morning had returned early. They had recognized the signs. None were foolish enough to be caught in the Atlantic in the face of an upcoming gale. They considered themselves fortunate for the warning. It wasn't often that mother nature was as kind, to which every family in the village could attest. But today, all the curraghs were safely beached. Away from the pounding surf in Muire Cave they lay, their black bottoms up.

"Will you be eating now, Son?" Padraig's mother turned from the open hearth, a wooden spoon in her hand as he seated himself.

"Aye, Mother, I'll be taking a bite."

She placed a bowl of steaming potatoes and a platter of fish on the table.

Padraig ate in silence for a few minutes. Then suddenly, he jumped up and went outside again. He walked to the back of the house and climbed the hill where he could get a better view of the misty coastline. He thought he had seen what might have been a sail far out to sea earlier in the evening. He wasn't sure. So he had to make certain before the last light left the sky. The waves looked mountainous as his eyes scanned the now almost invisible horizon. From time to time a flash of lightning lit up the vast expanse for a few brief seconds. But the towering waves out to sea and the endless spray against the shore dimmed the visibility until it was impossible to detect anything.

Padraig decided to return to the comfort of his home for the evening. As he descended the hill, his keen sense of hearing detected what he thought might be the sound of cannon. It could not be the dreaded Sasanach. There were no soldiers or guns in that part of the country now, thank God. Then, again, the sound came. It was clearer this time. Nor did it come from the land. No, it most certainly came from the west, the open sea.

Padraig knew what he had to do. His long legs lengthened their strides and within half an hour he had rounded up six men who were willing to risk their own lives to go to the aid of the distressed ship. Quickly the long curragh, Padraig's pride and joy, was carried to the water's edge. By this time, some women folk had reached the rocks that protected the hinterland from the angry waters. As they stood huddled together, their long black cloaks wrapped about them, they voiced their concern.

"Mother o' God! They don't stand a chance in them terrible waters," cried Eileen Dugan.

"It's a fool's errand. They'll no come back any last one of them," wailed Katie Byrne.

"I'll tell you one thing, if any man has a chance against them seas, it's Padraig and my Owney," Rosie O'Grady's voice sounded confident.

"Only God, His blessed Mother, and our own dear St. Patrick can protect us all this awful night," Molly O'Toole was telling her beads as she peered through the blackness in the direction of the small group of brave men who were desperately trying to launch the fragile craft.

For men of lesser skill and courage, the project would have been sheer suicide. For men of Padraig's breed, it was a matter of their Christian duty. The frail craft, made of lath and light cloth, was used by all the fishermen of the western seaboard.

After several attempts to launch the boat had failed, the near exhausted men made one last desperate effort, clearing by inches the nearest rock. Once afloat, the crew worked as one man. They glided over the towering waves. Padraig, his face set and determined, was the guiding mind. Soon the men were soaked through and through with their own sweat, while the rain, the spray, and the churning waters drenched them further.

Making headway was painfully slow. It seemed hours before the curragh finally drew close enough for them to realize that there was no hope for any survivors. Even as they watched, the last vestiges of debris were being swallowed up in the frenzy that boiled all around them. Disheartened because their efforts had been futile, they caught the next wave but it rode them toward the rocks. Then, with the agility and alacrity of a Bengalese tiger, they spun the craft towards the open sea to avoid instant destruction on the jagged crags that raced to meet them. It was during that split second that Padraig's keen eye caught sight of the limp body which had been gathered up by the waves and dashed onto the very ledge he had so deftly managed to avoid. A wild cry escaped him. Again the frail bark spun and lunged towards what must be inevitable doom. But, with hair-raising accuracy and split-second calculating, Padraig swung his huge body onto the slab. The curragh again spun and, from the force of Padraig's catapulting, took on a large quantity of water.

Desperately, the men fought for control. Tom Dugan was now lead man and he knew instinctively what he had to do. Seizing a coil of rope, he hurled it with all his force towards Padraig. The first attempt failed as Padraig, blinded by the driving surf, was unable to grasp it before it was washed back into the sea. A second attempt was all that Padraig needed. He quickly secured the rope around himself and the unconscious man, then waited for the right moment. As the breakers receded, he gathered the man in his powerful arms and sought the higher ground. He half carried, half dragged the seemingly lifeless form to the leeward side of the rocks, where the curragh was able to approach in the relatively calmer swells.

Triumphantly, the exhausted men propelled their fragile craft in the direction of the huge bonfire which had been hastily kindled. After what seemed an interminable period, they at last heard the acclaim of their fellow villagers as eagerly they waited, waist deep in the churning waters, to grasp the speeding craft as it neared the shallows.

Magheen reached the shore as the curragh was dragged onto the wet sand. Gently, they lifted the body of a man from the belly of the boat. They laid him on the damp ground. Magheen was on her knees immediately. She scanned the pale features, then noticed the ripped boot. Blood was congealed around the ankle and shin of his left leg. She placed her head against his heart. "Yes, praise be to God. There's still life in him," she said. Quickly she loosed her long cloak and placed it beside his body.

"Carry him to the house," she ordered.

Twenty-One

The hot weather had definitely left the west. September had begun with a heat wave, but after the storm, blustering winds and the never ending drizzle that so often clings to the western coast persisted. They came, however, from the south so there was a softness in them which gave new life to the ferns and wild flowers.

The Frenchman was gradually regaining his health. Tom O'Conner had deduced from the tattered clothes and boots that their shipwrecked guest was an officer of the highest rank in the French army. As yet, he had spoken only a few incoherent words but the accent proved Tom correct.

Although he bore his sufferings well, he seemed at times to be in great pain. Tom, assisted by Moll and Magheen, had worked miracles locating and setting the broken bones in his leg. He had sewn up several lacerations and thoroughly cleansed the more superficial wounds. This done, nature was allowed to take its course. In the meantime, Magheen attended to his every need.

After three days the man opened his eyes, looked about, and tried to sit up.

"Where am I...Mon Dieu!...je ne comprends pas..." He ran his hand down his leg.

Magheen answered him in his own tongue, which seemed to give him some comfort, and told him how he came to be in Inis Fail. Finally, she told him her name.

"Ma...gheen...Magheen...beautiful." He smiled and relaxed.

"Perhaps you'll be good enough to tell me your name, Sir?"

"Oh, I beg your pardon, Mademoiselle, I forget my manners.

I'm Hugo, Hugo de Breville from Chantilly, in the north of France, at your service." Then he laughed, realizing his present condition. "I'm afraid it will be some time before I can be of any service to you, Mademoiselle."

Magheen noticed the warmth in his dark eyes. His laugh was hearty and had a musical ring, his teeth were a pearly white. He gently kissed her finger tips as she bade him goodnight.

A warm, happy feeling filled her with a sense of accomplishment...or was there something more? She didn't think so. She had done a good job. Hugo would soon be well and on his way again. Yet her thoughts continued to dwell on him, so handsome, a French nobleman! "You're practically married, young lady," she reminded herself as she undressed for bed.

As the days passed, Magheen found she was greatly attracted to the dark foreigner. His beautiful eyes continually told her how deeply grateful he was for her ministrations. She noted his gentle bearing, his delicate hands, hands not used for manual work. His manners and speech were those of a gentleman. Her conclusions she knew were correct. Although he hadn't said it, she was convinced that she was nursing a prince of the French Royal House.

In due course, Hugo was able to spend a few hours in the open air. He would go for short walks, accompanied by his lovely young companion. With hair and mustache trimmed and decked out in a new outfit, after the fashion of an Irish gentleman, he looked extremely handsome. This outfit of black leather knee-high boots, woolen tight-fitting trews, and a loose sleeved white 'silk' shirt, over which was worn a leather jerkin, Tom had ordered especially for Hugo from Ballina.

"'Tis the fine Irishman you're making, Hugo," Magheen teased first in Gaelic and then in French.

"Go raibh maith agut," he answered with a broad smile as he bowed.

Magheen laughed outright. The broad vowels of the Irish language sounded funny as Hugo pronounced them.

Their laughter mingled with the bleating of roadside sheep as they lazily and reluctantly moved aside to allow the strollers by.

Hugo admired Magheen—an Irish woman of great charm, yet still exhibiting a girlish freshness in her completely uninhibited manner. It was refreshing, this guilelessness, so different from the salons of the French gentry. And her natural beauty, her grace entranced him. He could imagine how all eyes would turn were he to present her in a gown of pearly satin to the King of France.

Nor was he unaware of the effect her closeness was having on him. From the first moment their eyes met, he was conscious of the depths of compassion in those limpid pools. As each new day dawned, Hugo found that he eagerly looked forward to her cheery, "Bon jour, comment allez-vous ce matin, Monsieur?" Her beautiful smile and her happy disposition all charmed him, but he did not like to admit to himself that he was fast falling in love with this captivating and enchanting creature. He thought of his wife, Charlotte. It had been so long now since he had heard from her and it would probably be a great deal longer. Stranded in this isolated place, it might take months to get a way back to France. He wondered how things were at home. But then the music of Magheen's voice bore in upon him. He was again enjoying the magic of her company and the pleasant surroundings.

One afternoon, about a month after the big storm, Hugo and Magheen were, as usual, out for a stroll. The morning had promised rain, for a mist hung low over the sea but, contrary to expectations, toward noon the clouds lifted and the faint rays of the Autumn sun broke through, drenching the surrounding landscape with rainbow hues.

Hugo was feeling better than usual, so they decided to go as far as the strand. He was eager to see the area where, from the rocks, the brave villagers had pulled his half-drowned body to safety.

They reached the level ground and stood a moment to look around. The curraghs were far out to sea; it would be a good day for the fishing. There was no one in sight, only the terns and sea gulls who eyed them suspiciously a second or two and then went about their own business.

They sat upon a rock and watched the breakers crash against the more prominent formations and then spill in splendid splashing sprays into the crevices and crannies at their feet.

"What a wonderful, wild, and majestic coast this is! I grow to love this place more and more each day. Your life here is serene, despite what the English have been trying to do to you."

"Yes, we Irish are proud of our lovely land. I'm glad you like it so." Hugo turned to face Magheen and drew a little closer.

"Magheen," he began as he put his arm around her and held her close. She knew what he intended but didn't resist, not realizing until that moment how deep were her own feelings for him.

As his lips found hers, a wave of intense feeling swept through her whole body. He drew her closer, crushing her breasts against him as his mouth took complete possession of her full lips. Then as he sought to enter, she tasted his tongue and a river of fire shot through her veins, reaching her heart, her breasts, her throat until, with a tingling feeling, it burned her lips. For the moment, she seemed to completely lose her own identity. Her heart was pounding! Or was it the sound of the waves? A voice sounded, the song of the skylark? Or was it a chanson d'amour? Was the ecstasy of taste and the aroma that assaulted her nostrils the tang of the sea, the perfume of wild roses? Or was it Hugo's love that surrounded her, taking possession of her senses? She was speechless, incoherent.

Hugo released her slightly and gazed upon her upturned face.

"Magheen, my darling, you are more beautiful than I have ever imagined a maid could be! I can never rest till you are mine completely!"

With that, Hugo again found her soft fragrant lips and kissed her long and slow, passionate kisses that made Magheen feel she no longer was in control of her own body. What was this thing that was taking away her freedom? She had never known such rapture, had never dreamed such vehement feelings could reside within her.

Oh, God! How easily she could abandon herself to this man. She felt at that moment as if only he lived in her; she wished for no other existence.

Hugo spoke first. "Magheen, you are the most wonderful thing that has ever happened to me! I cannot live without you! I know that now."

Magheen looked at him a long while, then, as a single tear welled up to linger a moment on a silken lash before gently coursing down her soft white skin, she said softly, "Hugo, we must go now."

They spoke little on the homeward trek. As soon as Magheen reached the house, she quickly went to her room. She had had time to compose herself, outwardly at least, but inwardly her emotions and her sensitive spirit were not at peace. She threw herself on her knees beside her bed. She pressed her hands together, her elbows resting on the white counterpane.

"Mother of God, what have I done? Have I betrayed my God, my country, my future husband, and myself? The sin I have committed this day, will it stay with me to haunt me for the rest of my life? Gentle Mother, come to the aid of your child." Tears came fast and furious, and soon Magheen's sobs were uncontrollable. Some time later, when the fountain of her tears was exhausted, she arose from her knees, leaving the bleached quilt a patchwork of wrinkled blotches.

At supper she was not her usual vivacious self, and her uncle inquired about her health. "You don't look well, Magheen dear. Not catching one of those Autumn colds, I hope?"

"Oh, no, Uncle, I'm fine. Just a slight headache, that's all." Fortunately, Magheen's uncle was not a prying man so her response was accepted. He allowed the matter to drop and continued to engage Hugo in conversation.

"And you, Sir, you're looking better these past few days. I gather the soft climate we enjoy in these parts is agreeing with you."

"That, and the excellent care I've been receiving from Mademoiselle Magheen." He glanced at her. Her attitude toward him had changed. He felt guilty as his mind again turned to France and his wife. How could he, a married man, have behaved in such a fashion? He had taken advantage of a sweet, innocent young woman in a moment of weakness. Was that a way to repay the many kindnesses and considerations that had been shown him in this generous household? Magheen had scarcely looked at him during dinner. Had she been crying? Her face showed an unnatural flush, blotchy. He had surely offended her, he concluded.

"You're not yourself either tonight, good Sir. I fear you've met a wee fairy girl. Stolen your heart, has she?" Tom O'Connor laughed.

"Accept my apologies, Sir, but I may have overdone it today. I think I ought to retire early."

Magheen had by this time excused herself and left the room. Hugo, bidding Tom O'Connor good night, arose and left also. He must talk to Magheen before she went to bed.

Magheen was about to undress when she heard a soft rap on her door. She realized at once who it was. Her heart missed a beat as she opened the door. Hugo apologized for disturbing her at such an hour, but he explained that he had to talk to her.

She stood back to allow him to enter and motioned him to take a seat near the window. It was still twilight so she had not, as yet, lit a taper. Hugo hesitated a moment.

Magheen ached for his embrace, but she was resolved to keep him at a distance. Oh, God! How handsome, how desirable. Oh, cruel fate that had brought him to her land, her home, into her heart, the very core of her being, and yet would not allow her to claim him, to possess him, to make him her own. She looked at him in the fading light from under long, silken lashes.

"Magheen, I really meant all I said to you this afternoon. You are more precious to me than all the world. I know also that you are not insensitive to me. I'm sorry if I allowed my feelings for you to be so demonstrative at this point, for I fear I've hurt you and that, I assure you, was not my intention." Hugo knelt at Magheen's feet. He took her small, soft hands in his and, with eyes full of love, gently kissed her fingertips.

Magheen withdrew her hand. She got up, turned her back on him, and walked across the room to the west window. The sun had left the heavens, but in its path a trail of crimson streaks reached to the horizon. A moment of beauty, a scant, fleeting thing. Was this symbolic of her life? Was she to know only a brief hour of true love? Would the real joy, the ecstasy of complete union with the love of her heart never be hers? She turned from the window to face Hugo once more. He had risen but had not moved or spoken. He, too, seemed lost in his own thoughts. Suddenly, impulsively, as if some frantic thing had compelled her, Magheen raced across the room and as Hugo stretched his arms, she flung herself into his embrace. "Oh, Hugo, Hugo, I'm yours to do with as you will. I can't live without you, either."

"Magheen, darling." He held her pressed tightly to his heart for some moments. Then, as if the very closeness of their embrace had shattered her last remaining defenses, Magheen's body went limp. Hugo bore her up and carried her to the bed. He laid her gently on the soft white quilt.

"Magheen, ma petite, are you ill?" How vulnerable she looked.

"Oh, Hugo, Hugo, I think my heart will burst, it's on fire, aflame with love for you. Can't you understand? Can't you see I die, I hunger for your embrace?"

Hugo's manhood was aroused as never before. He would take her now. He bent to savor the burning lips, to caress the lily white throat. She clung to him in wild abandon. He must control himself, take command of the situation.

"Hugo, Hugo, my eternal love," she whispered.

"Magheen, don't, don't. My little one, you do not realize what you are saying." Inwardly, Hugo prayed for strength. He stroked her golden tresses, then gently loosed her hands from about his head. He kissed her fingertips and her fevered brow, whispering, "Magheen, you are overwrought. Rest a while, my little one. Tomorrow things will appear different." Then rising, Hugo left the room quickly.

He was gone before Magheen realized it.

"Oh, God, what have I done? What have I said?" Had she destroyed the only thing of real beauty in her life? Beside herself, she scarcely knew what to do. She, Magheen Ni Neill, proud, haughty, and self-assured had thrown herself at this stranger's feet. Had the lesson of her lost maidenhood not been learned? He had rejected her...just as...another...Richard Burke....

Angrily, she tossed and turned. Sleep, the reward of the just, the innocent of heart, came not to soothe her tortured soul that night. The hours dragged on and on.

The weary minutes, one by one, seemed to chide and mock her in her anguish, as they slowly trudged by into eternity. The searing pain of a guilt-ridden conscience alternated with the boiling anger of her violent emotions. She was betrothed, promised of her own free will to wed, to be the wife of a noble lord within a month. How could she have allowed herself to fall so low? Why, she was no better than the humble, uneducated kitchen maid, who, upon some scant pretext hied it off to the nearest hay loft with the village lads.

Furiously she beat her clenched fists into the down pillow. What a fool she had been. What a cursed, raving-mad fool she was to have offered all, to have thrown herself into the arms of...What did she really know about this man? Had he once, even once, told her of his love?

It was quite clear to her now, as she lay tormented in the darkness. Vividly clear. Hugo de Breville was an adventurer, a man of the world. He took what was there for the taking and went his way with never another thought. He was bound to no one. He had neither home, family, nor country to care about. He was a soldier of fortune. Had he not told her so? He had fought in the battlefields of France and Italy. Even his title he owed to the fact that he had killed. "Le chevalier sans reproche!" she spat the words, mocking.

Why had she, granddaughter of Con O'Neill, The O'Neill, stooped so low? An upstart! She had forgotten her roots. She had again followed the impulses of her heart and had been blinded to the reasonings of her mind. For shame! What would her uncle think of her wanton ways? Had all his teachings, his careful tutoring been for naught.

So distraught was Magheen that when the first shafts of the morning light broke through the low hanging clouds, her pulse was throbbing, and her head ached. She tried to rise but felt faint.

"Oh, God, let me die, now. Take me before I fall any further. I hate him! I loath the very ground he walks on! Unfeeling, insensitive brute. To think that I would have given myself completely to him. I must have been insane, wholly out of my mind."

Again the tears flowed, soaking into the crumpled pillow. "Oh, dear God, what am I to do?"

Golden bands of light shot through the slowly receding clouds. It would soon be day. In the distance a cock crowed. The faint twitter of waking birds was further evidence that the day had begun. Magheen tried to pull herself together. How could she face the household in her present condition?

She got up, and taking a cold face towel held it to her burning cheeks. Several times she splashed the cold water from her basin against her swollen eyes. She had to appear normal at breakfast. She could not allow anyone to guess her sufferings, least of all Hugo. He would never know how much pain he had inflicted. She would show him she didn't give a thought to him or his kind. She clenched her jaws and set her mind to her toilette.

Some hours later when she descended for breakfast, Magheen

was calm and outwardly composed. The only telltale sign of the night's torturous hours was her slightly flushed appearance, which she quickly attributed to the unusually warm weather for that time of year.

"We'll pay for this ere the winter's out, I warrant," said Tom O'Connor.

"Could be," answered Hugo.

"'Twill be good for the grouse hunting anyway. Care to join us, Sir?"

Hugo glanced at Magheen. She sat opposite him but had not addressed him during breakfast. She pretended not to notice the question in his eyes.

"I doubt I would be of much use yet in the chase."

Magheen's eyes betrayed an almost imperceptible hostile retort, the effect of which was not lost on Hugo.

"B...b...b...ut, I thank you all the same, Sir, for...for thinking of me."

As Magheen finished her breakfast, she placed her serviette on the table and got up.

"Please excuse me, Uncle, I have some things to do." She stepped near her uncle, kissed him on the cheek, and then turning to Hugo, curtly said, "Hope you have a good day, Sir," as she left the room.

Hugo did not tarry long at breakfast either. He, too, had had a long night to think. He could not allow their friendship to deteriorate into a squalid feud that might never be set to rights.

He went in search of Magheen. As he left the house, he caught sight of her galloping toward the headland to the west. As her golden hair caught the morning sun, Hugo paused a moment, captivated by the sight. No one would ever tame that free spirit, he thought. No one should ever try. A proud, headstrong young woman, she was still as fragile as the first snowdrops of early spring.

"Oh, Magheen, Magheen, were I but free to love you. To love you as you should be loved."

"Would your Lordship care to have a mount this morning?" The voice that startled Hugo was that of Sean, the yard man.

"Eh? Oh, yes, yes, Sean, I would."

"I'll saddle up the brown mare for you then. Won't be but a second, Sir."

Hugo found Magheen about a half hour later, perched high on a yawning precipice. She saw him coming but did not pay any attention. Neither did she answer him when he called to her from the ledge below. With difficulty, because his leg was not yet fully healed, Hugo made his way to the rocky overhang and sat beside her. She did not speak but gazed out to sea. Hugo did not break the silence either; he waited.

At last Magheen turned her head. In her great sad eyes, Hugo read the words she would not utter but which were burned into her heart.

"Magheen, ma petite, do not cast me out of your life forever. You, who have given *me* life and hope and love. Do not let us quarrel. We can, at least, part as friends." He reached for her hands and looked into her eyes. The blazing anger disturbed him.

Yet, for all her outward hostility, Magheen was only conscious of her own weakness. He had only to touch her fingers and her heart missed a beat. He had not kissed her, yet she could feel the burning heat of his strong lips. She would hate herself if she allowed him to hypnotize her again but she felt powerless in his presence. A moment passed. He still held her hand. A quiver ran through her. He had not tried to kiss her. What was he waiting for? Did he enjoy seeing her thus, waiting, anticipating? How dare he! Damn him!

Magheen, then, summoned up the strength that had, seemingly, forsaken her a moment before. In a fierce whisper, lest the terns and sea gulls hear, she cautioned him. "No, don't, don't you dare!"

In an instant she was galloping along the headland, a wild thing in a wild place.

As Hugo watched her go, his passion for her grew. Every inch of him yearned to possess that fiercely independent, passionate heart. How he could love such a woman. There was fire in her veins. He could stand the tension no longer. Finding his mount, he galloped off in the same direction. He would find her, make love to her, tell her he worshipped her and wished to make her his own.

This time, he found her on the beach. She was digging her feet in the sand, still angry.

He called to her as he approached. "Ma fleur, Magheen, ma petite fleur."

She looked up. She had been hoping he would come.

He dismounted and walked, still slightly limping, toward her.

He looked weak, sad, a stranger in a strange land. Oh, God! How she loved him.

He took her in his arms. She didn't resist. He held her close, so close that she felt as if her breath must cease, her very heart stop. He took her lips and plucked the rich red ripeness from them. He parted, with his exploring tongue, the pearly teeth and savored the freshness of her lovely mouth. Magheen, pliant in his embrace, forgot the tortured hours, the long weary night. In exquisite abandon, she was lost to all save only Hugo.

She was beside herself, almost numb, when Hugo released her. Breathless, she found it difficult to hold her balance. He caught her as she swayed.

"Magheen...Don't ever leave me again." He looked longingly into her eyes. "You're so beautiful."

What was he saying? Was he making fun of her? Had she once again made a fool of herself? She looked at him, straight into his eyes. "Why did you kiss me, now, Hugo?"

He didn't answer straight away, as if he measured well the words he would say. "Magheen, lovely beyond compare. I have tried to tell you that one day I wish to make you mine, only mine."

Again the anger within Magheen's breast flared. Her eyes blazed.

"You're all the same," she screamed. And within, she cried to herself, why can't you say you love me? Why? I'll tell you why, Magheen Ni Neill, because he doesn't know the meaning of the word love. With these thoughts rending her heart in two, Magheen got to her feet, and without looking back, made her way over the rocks to where Leprechaun was grazing. She mounted and galloped off into the quiet countryside.

Hugo remained where he was for some time. He was puzzled by her behavior. What had he said to upset her? Women, he concluded, were unpredictable.

The next few days Hugo spent in solitary walks and much reading. Magheen avoided him and seemed preoccupied with the affairs of the house. She spent more time in her room and only at meal time did she engage in any conversation with Hugo, but all the while she ached for his companionship. Was she being taught another lesson, she asked herself. Would she ever learn?

Hugo's convalescence was drawing to a close. He had decided it was time to be about the business for which he had undertaken the journey to Ireland in the first place. He was feeling fit in mind and body and his leg had grown strong and sound again.

It was a dull afternoon in mid October. The sun, what could be seen of it, was a pale, sickly color. Soon it would go to its watery bed on the rim of the earth. Hugo had left the house in the early afternoon and had taken a brisk walk in the direction of the bogland to the east.

Magheen had seen him go from her bedroom window where she sat sewing. "Oh, Hugo, you have broken my poor heart. It will never be the same again," she sighed. Then, impulsively casting aside the garment she had been working on, she stood up and with determination left the room. She had to find him and make things right again between them. She knew he would be leaving in the next few days. It would not be fitting to allow him to depart without some semblance of a truce between them. Perhaps, he hadn't really meant to hurt her. Maybe she had mistaken his overtures. He was French! Weren't the French known for their amorous ways? "L'amour, toujour l'amour," she murmured.

When she reached the stables, Magheen hesitated a moment before deciding to take Leprachaun, but the mare's welcoming whinney made her mind up for her.

"Well, old girl, you want out, eh? Come, let's see if we can find that handsome Frenchman."

She saw him before he was aware of her. He smiled as she approached. For a moment he was confused. It had been several days since they had been civil to each other. Magheen saw his embarrassment and laughed outright. The ice was broken. Hugo came toward the mare, took hold of the bridle, and assisted her to dismount.

A soft blue mist covered the distant hills and inched its way over the bogland. It would soon settle into a steady drizzle. The narrow road was strewn with the multicolored Autumn leaves. Like small children, Hugo and Magheen kicked the leaves as they walked. He took her hand and pressed it lightly.

"Magheen, it's been torture to have you so near and yet so far. How best to tell you how much I've missed our walks, our conversations, even our silent times together. He looked searchingly into her face. "I have suffered much in mind and heart since you left me alone on the rocks last week."

"Hugo, you have not suffered half as much as I." Magheen looked at him tenderly.

Hugo kissed her fingertips. "Magheen," he whispered.

They stopped beneath an old oak tree. Magheen rested her back against the trunk. Hugo, standing on a little mound of gnarled roots, gazed at her as she looked across the drenched countryside.

"Magheen, you sparkle in all weather. Rain or shine, you're the fairest flower I've ever seen."

"A very pretty speech, Hugo, but please do not tease me," she said as her sad eyes pleaded with him.

"I don't mean to tease you. I only say what's in my heart." Hugo drew closer.

Magheen did not wish to raise the question uppermost in her mind at that moment—Why not tell me that you love me and be done with it? If he did not say the words she wanted so desperately to hear, then why torture her? She tried to find the answer in his deep-set eyes. "Oh, Hugo, Hugo," she sighed.

He held her close and gently kissed the rain drops on her silken cheeks, rain drops that were soon mixed with warm tears. These past weeks she had shed so many.

"Magheen, my lovely Magheen, what have I said to disturb you?"

"Nothing, nothing at all, Hugo," she murmured. But her heart was aching.

He drew her closer for a few minutes and tried to comfort her.

"Let's go, Hugo. It's getting late." Magheen withdrew from his embrace and gathering up the reins, she mounted Leprechaun.

They spoke little on the way home. Hugo made up his mind to leave the following morning.

Magheen tried to be her usual self again. She chatted at dinner, keeping up a conversation with her uncle which included Hugo.

She had given him his last chance; he had failed to tell her of his love. She would not show her feelings again. He was a cad, despite his noble upbringing. It was as well she found out his true worth before she again succumbed to his advances. The great love, the unquenchable fire within her heart that burned for him would henceforth remain hidden. She would never again love with such force or to such unfathomable depths, she told herself. No one else would penetrate so deeply, would enter the inner recesses of her heart. Hugo alone could claim that privilege. For him alone, she knew she would keep those places sacred, closed, barred, even if she never again beheld his handsome face. But what was she thinking of? Did she not loath him for what he had done to her? He had pretended to love her, kissed her, caressed her, called her tender names and then....

The episode was finished. She had to turn her mind to other things; her upcoming marriage to a man she did not even know and the many preparations that had to be made to fit herself for such a life. With time, she would forget Hugo and the whole miserable affair that now tore her apart. These thoughts and a hundred others plagued her.

Later, after the women had retired, Hugo and Tom O'Connor spoke for some time. He thanked his venerable host for his gracious hospitality.

"It's time I were on my way, Sir."

"No hurry, no hurry at all, Sir. You've scarcely got your feet again. Anyway, there won't be a ship to take you back to France from these parts. You'll have to go to Galway or Sligo. But soon enough for that when you're completely recovered."

"I'll go north, Sir. I'll leave by first light." Hugo thanked Tom O'Connor again and then bid him goodnight. He was anxious to talk to Magheen once more before he left her life forever.

Soft, dancing shadows entered and left the room as the setting sun played with the evening clouds. Magheen was seated by the window. She did not rise as he entered in answer to her "Come in."

Hugo went immediately to her side and knelt at her feet. He raised her hand to his lips. "Magheen, you are troubled. I can't leave you so. What is it, my darling?"

Magheen trembled. "I've never felt about anyone the way I

feel about you, but I fear I may have committed some heinous sin in showing my feelings in such an open and brazen way."

"My darling! It's not you who have sinned." Hugo fell silent. A look of anguish furrowed his brow.

She looked deep into his eyes. Was he implying that he might indeed have been a cad! But no such admission escaped his lips. Magheen choked back the disappointment. Here at the eleventh hour he had failed to give her any hope. Why did he bother to come to torment her? Well, she would not give him the satisfaction of knowing that at that moment her heart was breaking. Better terminate this meeting as quickly as possible.

"Hugo, it grows late. If you will take your leave tomorrow you must get as much rest as possible tonight."

"Magheen, you have changed toward me. I can't leave knowing that you are suffering and that I may be the cause."

"Hugo, it is not possible at this time for me to tell you all that burdens my heart. I only know I must forget my own feelings. Before all else, I must consider my country. We live in difficult times. I may be sacrificed..." Magheen stopped. She had already said more than she should. What if Hugo were a spy!

"Magheen, what do you mean? Do not be afraid to speak. I too serve your country. In fact, my sole reason for being here is to assure the Princes of the North, yes, your own kith and kin, that the King of France is willing and eager to assist. So we are on the same side, my Magheen. That is also my reason for wishing to leave as soon as possible. Already my delay here may have jeopardized the plans which have been in the making for so long. Believe me, my darling, I will never forget you, and I pledge here and now that if ever you need help or are in trouble, I will be ready to come to your aid no matter what the difficulty."

Magheen turned her beautiful eyes from him. She could not look on his handsome features again without throwing herself into his arms and begging him never to leave her. She would not sell herself, however. He had not spoken of his love. He had not sworn his undying fidelity. His true feelings for her were hidden... masked...or were nonexistent.

Hugo saw her sufferings, the struggle. He did not wish to prolong the agony. He took her trembling head and gently pressed it with his burning lips. Then he drew from his finger a gold ring bearing his family crest.

"This is a token of my undying loyalty. If ever you return this ring to me I will know you are in trouble and need my help. I will come to you, even from the ends of the earth. Adieu, my lovely Magheen."

"Go with God, my love," Magheen's voice was inaudible.

With that Hugo turned, left the room and Magheen's life.

By sunrise the next morning, Hugo, Count de Breville, was well on his way to the house of the great O'Neill.

Twenty-Two

Hugo spent the next two months negotiating with the chieftains of the North. Eventually gaining the confidence of The O'Neill, he was free to turn his attention to the O'Donnell clan.

The weather was bitterly cold when he set out from Tirowen for O'Donnell Country, Tirconnell. The wind whipped the leafless trees into grotesque shapes, which appeared all the more weird in the eerie half-light. As night descended, a driving sleet caused him so much discomfort that he was forced to dismount. Swollen rivers and streams, and mud thick as dung further hampered his progress.

At the top of a steep incline, he rested against a stone wall and peered into the darkness, hoping to see some sign of shelter for the night. "Surely there must be a cabin somewhere," he murmured. Seeing nothing, he pushed on, then unexpectedly, the fragrance of burning turf filled his nostrils.

"Ah, merci, mon Dieu," he whispered and the thought of a tasty stew drove him in the direction of the smell.

A rather plump woman opened the door and bade him enter. Immediately, he was surrounded by half a dozen rosy-cheeked children.

"Shoo, out of the man's way with you," she said as she lifted her apron to scatter her brood and motioned Hugo to take a place by the hearth.

"Cead mile failte," she said and a warm smile lit up her honest face. "Siobain m'ainm."

Hugo was glad he knew a few words of the Irish language as he thanked her for her hospitality and introduced himself.

The children squatted on reed mats and straw-stuffed pillows, wide-eyed and silent. They had been expecting their father and now wondered who this strange man was who was sitting in his chair. Even the baby sat, thumb in cheek, with great grave blue eyes staring at Hugo.

A huge pot of mutton stew bubbled on the open fire and a freshly baked oatmeal cake browned in a three-legged iron pan. Hugo knew he wouldn't go to sleep hungry. For as he scanned the one-room cabin, he could not but recall what he had heard of Irish hospitality. There were no strangers in this land, only foreigners and they're all Sasanach. Siobain chattered away, half to herself, half to the children, while Hugo warmed and dried himself by the fire. About ten minutes passed, then the door was flung wide and a huge man filled the entrance. With jovial face and cheery salutation, he extended his arms ready to enfold the entire cabin in his embrace. At once, it seemed as if the whole cabin was moving. The bigger children flung themselves against him, the smaller ones clung to his legs, and the baby, trying to crawl, was scooped up and pressed to his great chest. Finally, when he turned to kiss his busy wife, he caught sight of the stranger.

"So, we've a guest for supper?" He introduced himself, "Fiach MacMahon, Sir, you do me honor," he extended his earth-soiled hand.

Hugo tried to answer in the Irish tongue, but failed to find the words. He addressed him in English, "Do you speak the language of the Sasanach?"

"Yes, I know some," Fiach answered.

Siobain ladled the stew into wooden bowls and, for a while, only the slurps of hungry children broke the silence.

After the hot meal, while the little ones were preparing to settle down for the night, Fiach poured pewter tankards of mead for himself and his guest. He stoked the peat and drawing up two stools, invited Hugo to join him.

At first, they spoke in general terms on one topic or another. Finally, Fiach put the question which had been uppermost on his mind, "An' what brings you, Sir, to these parts? An educated man like yourself and French besides is not a common sight hereabouts."

Hugo hesitated.

Fiach noticed. "Sir, you need have no concern in this house. The French are our allies; we have no quarrel with them. I, myself, am a fighting man in O'Donnell's army, ready at a moment's notice to join with your forces when they land on our soil."

Hugo relaxed. He was among friends and, as Fiach told him of his own imprisonment and escape, his admiration for this heroic man grew.

"It was the day we Irish call Little Christmas, January 6. The whole country was celebrating the end of the festive season when my friends and I in Dublin Castle decided the time had come for us to make our escape. 'Twas a night like this, the winds moaning about the Castle, sleet and soggy snow, bitterly cold. Outside the streets were deserted.

"In the guard house, the watch had gathered to keep warm beside a small log fire," he continued. "No need to spend time with the prisoners on a night such as this, they thought. The cells were icy cold and afforded little protection from the chilly drafts that penetrated the chinks and crevices in the damp stone walls. Besides, there was a flagon of ale supplied through the generosity of His Most Gracious Majesty in honor of the Holy Season.

"We waited for the familiar footsteps on the stone stairs which told us 'twas time for our miserable supper of rancid cabbage soup. The guard approached. 'Bloody cold up here tonight,' he mumbled to himself. I remember he had great difficulty keeping his torch lighted and the smell of burning animal fat was nauseous."

Fiach took a drink of mead and continued.

"'Cold, lads?' The guard teased and rattled the keys in the lock.

"'What, cold? We live like kings, don't we, men?' The bass voice of Hugh Flaherty sounded hollow in the great stone cell."

As Fiach continued to tell his story Hugo learned of the cruelties suffered by young Brian Mulligan.

"A lad of only sixteen, a runner for O'Donnell's fighting men, he was captured on his way to warn O'Donnell of a surprise attack. The courageous youth languished for several months before he was dragged from his cell, stripped naked, and tortured while his interrogators laughed at him. They would know the names of all his accomplices. Brian remained stubbornly resolved to die rather than betray his friends. When bribes and threats failed, they flayed his tender flesh till little streamlets of blood coursed down his legs and arms. Still the lad held firm. It was at that point that the newly appointed gaol warden, Philip Jones, decided to take matters into his own hands. As soon as Brian had regained consciousness, he was suspended three feet above the stone floor by manacles attached to his wrists. In that position he remained for two hours till the muscles of his shoulders were knotted. Vivid blue and purple patches were visible all up and down his thin white arms. The warden drew close, so close that Brian could feel the warmth of his clammy flesh and smell his stale breath. He tried to discern how much life was left in the boy.

"He ordered him cut down. Then he commanded his henchmen, two burly cut-throats who had been recruited from the British goals, to pour a mouthful of wine over Brian's parched lips. The shock caused the youth to cry out in agony."

Fiach paused to take another drink and as Hugo sipped his own grog his thoughts returned to Ballindee. He remembered the stories Magheen told him of the atrocities committed there. These English had regard for no one, women, little children, it didn't matter.

Fiach cleared his throat and continued.

"As the lad lay helpless on the cold, hard floor, he felt the force of a heavy boot in his aching ribs. But no abuse could shake his resolve. He would not break faith with his countrymen.

"Exasperated by the strength of character shown by so young a lad, Jones decided on the ultimate. It was known as the Scavenger's Daughter. This, the most excruciating form of torture, was now made ready."

The Scavenger's Daughter was conceived by Leonard Skeffington, the 'noble' English Lieutenant of the Tower of London, and had lately come to be added to the collection of objects assembled in the Castle to inflict pain. It was considered a real improvement on its predecessor, the rack. The main advantage lay in the fact that it was easily transported from one place to another because of its small size. The rack was used to stretch the body, drawing the joints apart, but the Scavenger's Daughter worked in the opposite way. The body was bound into a ball, the lower legs were compressed against the thighs, which, in turn, were placed against the chest and lower body, while the arms were tied tightly to the victim's sides. Finally, the whole body was encased in large iron clamps, and the head was jacked into the body, causing profuse bleeding from nose and ears, and leading eventually to death.

Continuing, Fiach told of the agonizing screams that echoed and reechoed through the Castle, a signal that the young lad's end was near. Then a ghostly silence ensued.

"'Greater love than this no man hath than...' O'Flaherty said as he knelt and praised God for yet another Irish martyr.

"We finished our lukewarm slop and felt a small degree of warmth enter our chilled bodies." Fiach dried a tear with the back of his hand. "The bell sounded. It was time to return to our cell. Sean limped in line behind us. O'Flaherty gave a signal. The old man was quickly dispatched and within minutes we had scaled the granite walls and dropped to the street below.

"We had to get beyond the city limits as quickly as possible. We headed north by way of Drumcondra to Finglass area. Once outside the Pale, we knew we could count on our friends.

"Dawn was breaking. We had but a few miles more to go when suddenly we came face to face with a squad of English soldiers. The early hour and our appearance caused suspicion.

"'Your names? Where are you going, you bastards?' shouted an officer!

"Flaherty was about to answer when I realized that his educated speech would betray him so I struck him one. 'Dun do beal. Pretend to be drunk.'

"'Yer honor,' says I to the sergeant, 'I'm tryin' me level best to get this fella' sobered up. Ye see he spent the night'...I stopped to wink and bow showing my respect, ye know.

"'Enough of yer blabbering. Get him and yourself out of here as fast as you can an' don't let me see you again.'"

Hugo was now confident that he could trust this man with his life. He quickly told him that he needed to get to O'Donnell as soon as possible.

"I'll take you myself, first thing in the morning," Fiach offered. "Now, you'd best get some sleep."

The following morning Fiach accompanied Hugo to within sight of O'Donnell's castle. There he bade farewell and pledged his undying friendship. It would not be so easy to win the trust and cooperation of the great Lord of Tirconnell.

PART IV

Twenty-Three

Although Magheen's days were abundantly filled with the many activities involved in preparing for her wedding day, her nights were troubled. Alone, in those long hours, she sometimes wept silently, and, sometimes in deep anguish, a cry of despair would escape when she thought of Hugo. Oh! How she missed him, his passionate kisses, his hungry embrace. Her whole body ached for his caress. Then, in anguish, she would fling the covers from her bed and cry out, "Fool, you miserable fool, why torment yourself? You know he didn't really love you. He'll never again think of you. Never return...to whom? A courtesan!"

Then to soothe the hurt in an imaginative mind, to cool the burning fever, and to ease the throbbing headache, she would stand by the open window when the moon was high and gaze at his ring. The characters seemed to stand out more clearly in the golden light. Was this also some quirk of her imagination? At the hour when her whole being longed for him, did the brilliant inscription "Semper Fidelis" mock her or were these words of faith glistening in the moonlight meant to give her hope? She didn't know. And so the tears flowed again, big drops falling on the burnished surface.

At other times, when the moon had hidden her face, a straggling traveler might chance to see a sputtering light linger a moment between life and death in the far corner of Inis Fail. At such times Magheen would carefully unfold the hastily written note that Hugo had left before he departed, the note she had found under her door when the first light of dawn had crept through her windows on that cold October morning.

"Oh, Hugo, Hugo!" His name was music to her ears. In her dreams he came to her. In her wishful moments he fulfilled her every desire. He alone could make love; he alone knew how to satisfy her thirsty soul, her hungry body. "Hugo, come back to me. Hugo, I die for you."

But, during the daytime when the romantic vision of Hugo was not so clear, and the stark reality of his seeming insensitivity was vividly before her mind, Magheen would hate the thought of him, would curse the day she met him. He was a fraud unworthy of her thoughts, much less her love. She would brush away the tears that fell all too quickly and bite her lips to keep them in check.

With the coming of winter and the ceaseless activity in preparation for her coming wedding, Magheen had less time to think of Hugo. Although she could never erase the memories completely, she could not dwell on them at length. Too many chores and responsibilities had been thrust upon her and she had to reconcile herself to the fact that she was destined to live with a man whom she had never met.

Magheen was making her wedding gown herself, sewing into it her girlish hopes and the tender, innocent yearnings of her young heart. One evening, while she was working on it, she required the help of Moll to ensure that the length was correct. She slipped into the dress and went to the kitchen. Moll gasped as she entered.

"My! 'Tis the beautiful bride you'll be makin', Magheen, darlin'."

Magheen's spirits were at a low ebb. All morning the grey skies were threatening. Towards noon a driving drizzle gradually gave way to a steady downpour. Dampness in the passageways and a dank musty smell pervaded the whole house, it seemed. Magheen had tried to fight the feelings of depression and loneliness all day, but now with the warmth of the peat fire, the comforting smells of bread and herbs, and the affectionate greeting of her old friend Moll, her last defenses were shattered. She broke down, in spite of herself, in Moll's arms.

"Tis a long time now since you had a good cry, a leana. There...there...you can tell old Moll what's troublin' your pretty head. No sense in keepin' it all locked up inside you, an' have it break your poor wee heart."

Magheen felt better as she poured out all her fears and longings. She told Moll of the great love that had grown up in her heart for Hugo. She spoke of the fears, the apprehensions that had taken hold of her regarding her forthcoming marriage and of her anxiety at having to leave Ballindee and all that she so dearly loved.

"Sure, it's all understandable child. You're still but a slip of a girl. An' so much is expected of you already. But don't you fret, a leana, they'll be loving and kind folks a plenty where you're going. An' I know they'll treat my Magheen like a queen."

Then suddenly changing her tone of voice, "An' if they do otherwise, you let old Moll know. For I'll have you back here afore you can say cock robin."

"Oh, Moll, what would I do without you?" Magheen burst into laughter.

And Magheen and Moll knew at that moment that "her" little girl had left childhood behind forever.

The dress was quickly pinned in place. Moll clasped Magheen to her ample bosom once more, as much for her own sake as for the comfort she hoped Magheen would receive. She stroked the rebellious curls, then bade her hurry and get herself ready for bed, for she would pamper "her" child for the last time. She would find a tasty bite and when she had tucked her in, warm and cozy, she would produce a treat made only for her princess.

"Oh, you're the most wonderful mother a girl ever had!"

Nothing pleased Moll more than to be called mother by the only child for whom she had ever cared.

As soon as Magheen was left alone, her thoughts wandered back over the years of her childhood, the years spent in Ballindee. They had been happy. She remembered her first lessons learned not only at her uncle's knee, but those she had acquired through observation and participating in the natural world around her. She had spent most of her time alone or in the company of her mare, Leprechaun. How she loved to gallop over the boglands. The soft turf underfoot sometimes made the going tough, but it had been such fun to pick her way through the fragrant heather. She relived the feeling of exhilaration when the crisp air brushed her cheeks as she raced across the open fields to the top of the hill where, high above, she commanded a view of the whole countryside. There were days when she had seen all the way to Killybeg in the south, to Bunrose in the north, and to the east, where the green fields dotted with tiny white cabins seemed to reach to the horizon. But when she looked westward, the great Atlantic, mysterious and forbidding, yet living, inviting, stretched on forever.

Now, whenever she looked at it, it seemed to call to her... Magheen, Ma...gheen...Was she dreaming? Ma...gheen...Was it her imagination? Ma...gheen...Could it be? Dare she say his name again? "Hugo," she whispered.

She remembered the night of the storm. She had heard her name above the gale and the roaring sea. He had called her. She knew it.

She sat up in bed. Magheen Ma...gheen. It was the same.

"Oh, God what can I do? He needs me! I know he does." She sank back on her pillow. "This time I can do nothing, absolutely nothing, Hugo. You have called too late."

Would he haunt her thus all her life? She clasped the ring tightly in the little satchel resting on her heart.

The morning of November 10 dawned fair. Magheen had risen early; she stepped to her window. A gentle breeze from the sea glided in and out of the long grasses and reeds that circled the pond at the end of the lawn. A small grey rabbit popped from behind a moss-covered boulder, looked around, then scurried off in the direction of the village. There was far too much activity at the Big House this morning to suit it. The coach was already in the driveway in front of the house. Several large boxes were strapped securely in place.

"Sean, these boxes can go under the seats, and put the small ones on top." Moll, flushed and excited, was supervising the loading process.

"Yes, M'am. Can't help thinkin'...things won't be the same anymore," Sean said glumly.

"Ah, what do you mean by that, Sean?" Moll sounded defensive.

"Sure, without Magheen around here to liven things up, I'm thinkin'..."

"Now keep your thoughts to yourself, man. Don't be making things worse than they are. She's already half sick at having to leave." Moll replaced her handkerchief, sniffed, lifted her long skirts, and re-entered the house.

Magheen moved a little closer to the windows. She noticed that the ivy clinging to the granite stones was displaying the vivid hues of Autumn. The wind played in the leaves, bringing to mind a poem her uncle wrote for her years before. She whispered the words:

"I am the active agile air
That wraps the world around,
And though I'm present everywhere
From lowland bush to mountain bare,
When by my will my mood is fair
I never make a sound.

I march along the mighty hills
I flow across the plain,
I ruffle rivers, ripple rills,
I scatter sparks where fountain spills,
I wave the wheat above the drills,
And lift it up again.

I torture trees, I guide the sail,
I goad the crashing sea—
Tormented, turning green to pale,
To soar and leap to no avail,
To rend the rock and sling the shale
In anger back at me.

I lift the leaf, I strew the straw.
Disturb the quiet room.
Among the ragged eves I gnaw,
I whistle through the fluted flaw,
Not answering to any law
Obey the will of whom?"

Magheen wiped her eyes. "Oh, God!" she cried. "Must I leave it all? Leave him, gentle, kind, he has been more than a father to me—teacher, friend, exemplar, generous to a fault."

Magheen scanned the familiar landscape. She would etch each

detail deeply on her memory. The village in the distance, it looked so small now, but oh, so lovely.

The round tower, in whose shadows and under whose watchful eyes she had played and picnicked, still seemed the same. Like the mighty oaks scattered about its base, it had weathered the onslaught of time, the elements, and the most destructive forces of all, the Sasanach.

On the outskirts of the village stood the small stone church, and nestled in its shelter, the little graveyard lay surrounded by a tumbled down stone wall. Though no one thought to mend the gaps, the graves were carefully tended, and spring and summer saw the wild flowers strewn, in bunches large and small, atop the sagging mounds.

She remembered the happy, smiling face of Father Magher as he greeted his friendly flock. How he liked to tease her when she was little, when first she came to Ballindee.

"So you're one of them foreigners, eh? Ah, no matter, we'll keep you anyway. But on one condition, that you'll give us a wee curl," and Father's merry grey eyes sparkled as he pretended to pluck a golden lock.

The O'Reilly's house, the first to greet the traveler to the little hamlet, now lay deserted, a desolate reminder to all of the fateful day when the Sasanach visited Ballindee.

The forge, the center of activity and a gathering place for young and old, had changed but little since her childhood days. Only a brand new half-door, acquired in recent years, had given it added dignity. The horse trough, old and weather-beaten, was no longer a thing of wonderment. It had been years since she had stood in awe watching the hissing steam rise from its murky depths.

Where had the carefree years of childhood gone? Would she ever be happy again? And the years of her adolescence. How quickly they had sped! Her sixteenth birthday, the festivities, her first beautiful ball dress—she remembered how excited she had been on that occasion. For days before, she had envisioned the celebrations. She imagined herself welcoming the guests; had seen herself preside at the long dining table. Then, when the longed-for day finally came, the reality was so much better than anything she had anticipated. Never would she forget the moment when her uncle led her to the place of honor. How the guests watched spellbound as she was seated and the beautiful ruby necklace was fastened around her neck. She knew at that moment she had come into her own. She was a real princess.

The memories of other events passed through her mind in quick succession, reminders of the painful hours, the tragic days. She recalled the murders in her tiny village of Ballindee. She saw again the surprised horror in the eyes of young Lieutenant Jenkins when her knife met its mark. Her thoughts sped to the Burke estate and the disastrous occurrence that visit had caused. And she blamed herself, for in her eagerness to attain fame and fortune, she had lost what all women prize most.

Her thoughts sped across the sea to Donald. It had been many months now since she had heard from him. He had loved her so much. She might have been his wife...the wife of a small-town physician. He would have tried to make her happy. Would he have succeeded? Deep down Magheen didn't think so. She, Magheen, was destined for greater things.

Then Hugo, handsome, passionate Hugo had come into her life and stolen her heart completely. With him, she could have been happy. He was of noble blood, of that she was certain. As a princess of the Court of Francis I, she would have outshone all others. Had she caught the eye of the French King, himself, she would have used her power to further Ireland's cause with the great monarch. For her beloved country she would not only have exiled herself in France, she would have journeyed throughout Europe. She would have pleaded with the Emperor, laid her cause at the feet of the Pontiff in Rome. By her eloquence and powers of persuasion, she would have bent all ears, turned all hearts to her way of thinking.

Magheen withdrew Hugo's ring from the little satchel near her heart. She examined it, as she had done so often during the weeks that followed his departure. She thought about the inscription, "Semper Fidelis", and knew she would never part with that ring. It would be with her for the rest of her life. If the Sasanach hadn't come to Ireland, things would have been so different. Now all had changed. There was fighting and rumors of uprisings. Life would never be the same again.

Tears streamed down her burning cheeks. Would she ever see

Inis Fail again? Her new home, for all its finery and elegance, could never compare with it. And Ballindee, her village? It was part of her just as the blood coursing through her veins was part of her and without which she would surely die, she thought.

Yes, part of Magheen died when the carriage pulled out of the driveway and through the gateway and over the bumpy, dusty road that travelled like a silver ribbon across the hills towards the East.

Twenty-Four

The coach rumbled on. It had set out five days before, carrying its precious cargo and was now nearing its destination. Magheen grew more excited as the final miles were counted off. Her uncle and Moll accompanied her. It had been a long journey, to be sure, but it was also an adventure, one which Magheen would not soon forget.

The country through which they passed, though not decked in its finest array, was still a vision of loveliness for its robe was of many hues. No wonder, thought Magheen, that the bards had spoken of Ireland as the stately lady "Eirinn" who wore a mantle of emerald green, only now it was flecked with threads of crimson, gold, yellow, and copper.

As they journeyed further south, the lush vegetation, fertile soil, the abundance, and the variety of trees and shrubs impressed her. It was true that Connaught had its own special kind of beauty, stark and wild. This country was lush, soft, seductive.

The ancient Rock of Cashel came into view. Here it was that the Kings of Munster were crowned. The "rock", composed of a limestone outcropping, rose some two hundred feet above the surrounding land, and on it now stood one of the finest ruins of ancient Ireland.

"A MacCarthy fortification, was it not, Uncle?" Magheen asked.

"Yes, m'dear, built in the fourth century. The Kings of Desmond, many of whom were bishops, resided here. Hence the fortified settlements included several churches. After the twelfth century, the buildings were exclusively ecclesiastical and a succession of splendid churches was built here. But as you can see, years of plunder and destruction have left their mark."

"Do you really think we'll ever be free of the Sasanach?"

"Ever is a long time. It's hard to say, but you're even now playing a part in our long struggle."

"'Tis proud I am to be part of it, Uncle."

The snorting horses were straining with the exertion of climbing the hill. The carriage labored to steady itself. With a creaking harness, squeaking and rattling, the rugged frame seemed to remonstrate. The jostling, persistent and unrelenting, was beginning to tell on Moll's usually good temper.

"I hope it's not much further. My poor bones can't support much more o' this."

At last the rise was gained and the archway of trees gave way to open ground. The coach came to a lurching halt.

Magheen slid toward the half-door. She leaned over and looked into the face of a veteran of many battles.

"M'Lady Magheen, I've come to escort you to the castle."

Magheen thanked him and bade him proceed.

The carriage lumbered forward and soon reached the huge iron gates that led to the Ormond Estate. The kern ordered the lodgekeeper to open. Both sides of the great iron gates were slowly pulled back and the carriage started up again. A mile of winding road, lined on both sides by splendid oaks, beech, and spruce led eventually to a medieval castle. Magheen drew in her breath at first sight of the majestic turrets, the imposing entrance portals, the great granite exterior. She trembled a little as the carriage came to a halt right in front of the expansive stone steps that led up to the great doors.

"Uncle, it's a huge place, entirely!"

"Yes, Magheen, but you'll get used to all this and more, my dear."

"I always knew you'd be a great lady some day. My! What things I'll be tellin' them all when I return home," said Moll.

But if Magheen was impressed by what she saw outside the castle, she was completely awed when they entered the great formal hall. From the sparkling black marble floor to the ornately decorated ceiling, the impression was one of opulence. A thick woolen

Celtic carpet woven in a brilliant array of color covered the center and led directly to an expansive stairway. The massive oak bannisters were exquisitely carved and the richness of the dark wood was a sharp contrast to the white walls and ceiling. Tapestries, the like of which Magheen could never have imagined, hung from gold-braided cords while several oil paintings, portraits of three generations of the Butler family, held prominent places. An enormous crystal chandelier hung from the center of the ceiling.

Magheen stood captivated. Her keen eye for beauty appreciated all she saw: the enormous oak chest, the sideboard which supported silver and gold serving plates and trays, crystal bowls, and decanters.

As the three guests were admiring their new surroundings, the Earl of Ormond and his wife came to greet them.

"Cead mile failte," the Earl extended his hand; Lady Eleanor pressed Magheen in a warm embrace. She acknowledged Moll and placed a warm kiss on Tom O'Connor's cheek.

"I hope the journey wasn't too tedious. It's a long way from Ballindee. But now that you're all safe and sound, you'll be needing a rest. We'll show you the rooms we've arranged for you. After a few quiet hours, we'll all meet for supper." Lady Eleanor then led the way as she continued to chat with Magheen. The Earl and Tom O'Connor fell into easy strides behind. Their conversation slowly turned to politics and the growing unrest throughout the country.

Magheen was becoming more excited with each new experience and her eyes lit up when she was shown her room. A picture of pink and blues opened up before her. "How absolutely beautiful!"

"I'm so happy you like it, my dear," said Lady Eleanor. "We had it redone just for you."

"It's just magnificent!"

"Well, my dear, while you are settling in, I'll show Moll to her room. I thought you would like to have her close to you so we have arranged the room next door for your good friend."

"How very thoughtful, so kind. I know my darling Moll will be happy there," said Magheen.

"Happy is it? Well, indeed, I'm sure I've never in me whole life been treated like a queen, but now that I know what it's like, I doubt I'll ever be the same again," answered Moll with a twinkle in her eye.

As soon as the door closed and Magheen was left alone, she was able to examine her new surroundings more carefully. The room was in perfect taste. The highly polished floor had several small carpets. Artistic marvels of entwining white, pink, and red roses. Magheen stooped down to feel the soft texture and ran her fingers over the intricate patterns.

"How lovely! To think that these are now mine, my very own."

A stately dressing table, complete with an oval mirror elaborately adorned with a golden frame, stood against the blue painted wall. Her bed, a canopied glory of 'silk' was so soft and luxurious she knew she could never get used to such grandeur. She seated herself in the blue velvet chair on one side of the bay windows and looked out onto her own private balcony.

As she looked from her beautiful surroundings within to the exquisitely manicured gardens without, the lawns, and the rolling acres beyond them, she could hardly believe that all of this would soon be hers. Away in the distance, a blue mist covered the almost imperceptible hills. The sun had left behind a trail of crimson and scarlet as it moved across the western sky. It was a glorious evening. Serenity and beauty enveloped Magheen. She could be happy here. But deep within a warning voice repeated, glory and pain, pain and glory! Why should she think of such things now? She tried to banish the words from her mind.

She was eager to see the rest of the castle. She wanted to wander through the gardens and even to explore the countryside around it. But there would be plenty of time for that. Yes, she thought, I have the rest of my life.

She reminded herself that she had better prepare for dinner. This would be a very important occasion, her first meeting with the large Butler family and, in particular, her future husband. She wanted to make a good impression.

She chose a soft 'silk' dinner gown of pale blue trimmed with delicate white lace. As she fastened a lace rosebud in her hair, she heard the dinner bell sound and her heart gave a little flutter.

When she answered a knock at her door, she found Moll looking positively regal in her new black dress. Its simple plainness was moderated by white linen cuffs and a large linen collar. Her silky white hair was piled neatly on top of her head. The excitement of the occasion had brought an added blush to her cheeks.

"My, but you look like a duchess!" exclaimed Magheen.

"Ah, go on with you. Indeed 'an 'twould be a long time before I'd look like anything but old Moll Flynn. Now you m'darlin' girl, why, 'tis a beautiful princess I'm seeing. Aye, indeed, an' real proud I am this day to see you where you truly belong."

"Oh, I don't know...it's all so big and grand and wonderful. I'm afraid I'll be lonesome for Ballindee every day of my life."

"Tut, tut, none of that now. You're where God ordained you should be. An' when you meet your handsome young man, you'll soon be forgetting all the rest," assured Moll.

"Never, never! Don't say that, Moll, darling."

"Ah, sure 'tis the truth, but come on with you or we'll be keeping the whole family waiting." So saying, Moll dabbed her eyes with a dainty handkerchief and followed Magheen down the expansive stairway to the large dining room below.

The great double doors were flung wide and Magheen, poised in the entrance, was a vision of loveliness. The Earl stepped forward to escort her to her place. He took her trembling hand in his, placed it on his left arm, while he gently guided her into the room. All eyes were upon her. The men had risen; curious gazes turned to admiration as they perceived the elegant and graceful bearing of their beautiful young guest. James Butler presented Magheen to his son, Dermud, then in turn to each member of the large family. Toasts were made to the bride and groom to be, as shyly the young couple stole furtive glances at each other.

"May you both live to see your children's children," the Earl raised his glass.

"And may they all be as beautiful as their mother and as gallant as their father." The toasting continued. The atmosphere was light and jovial. Magheen had captivated all hearts.

After dinner Dermud and Magheen mingled with the family members for some time before Dermud decided it was appropriate for them to have a few moments to themselves. He escorted her to the library, seated her in the leather chair near the fire, and stood back to take a good look.

After a moment of silent contemplation, in which Dermud gazed in obvious admiration into Magheen's upturned face, he spoke. "Magheen, I am honored that you have consented to be my wife. You are beautiful beyond words of mine to describe. You are charming and intelligent. I count myself an exceptionally blessed man."

Magheen blushed slightly and lowered her lovely eyes. She was about to speak when Dermud drew a leather pouch from an inside pocket of his silken jacket. He quickly loosed the strings. From the red velvet interior he drew a double strand of diamonds. He bent to fasten them around her creamy throat. As he did so, Magheen saw that the chain of diamonds served to hold an exquisite ruby teardrop which now lay nestled in the curve of her breasts.

Magheen rose. "Dermud…it's too much! I'm overwhelmed… what can I say? It's simply magnificent!"

As he closed the clasp, his hands rested on her silky white shoulders. He drew her close and lightly pressed his lips to her lovely mouth. As he released her, Magheen raised eyes full of tenderness and admiration.

"Dermud, thank you. I, too, consider myself very fortunate. I know we were meant for each other and that our future lives together will be"…pain and glory…her head rang. She put her hands to her ears as if to stop the words.

"Are you all right?"

"Yes," her voice was a whisper. Then looking at Dermud, Magheen continued, "I pray that God will guide us in the days ahead."

"We will need your prayers and God's help. You are aware that if our country is to be unified under an Irish ruler, our family must take the initiative."

"Yes, I know."

Again, Dermud kissed her, this time more ardently. But he didn't want to scare her. He drew away thinking it better that they return to the company of the family. By this time all had gathered in the great reception hall. As they walked hand in hand along the passageway, the haunting air of The Coulin floated in rippling waves throughout the castle. The harpist, more skilled than his fellow musicians in other nations, was in residence at the castle. Like all that was truly Gaelic, the harpist came under English edict. Systematically over the years, these musicians who enjoyed a noble prestige next only to the judges, were being eliminated. They were considered seditious and dangerous persons.

* * * *

The wedding ceremony took place in the castle. Magheen was radiant. The Lady Eleanor Butler, herself, came to help with the dressing of the bride. First, came a white chemise edged with lace, then the inner petticoat. Because of Magheen's trim figure, the whale bone corset was set aside. She had never worn one and Lady Eleanor considered it an unnecessary encumbrance on this demanding occasion. Magheen would have plenty of time to get used to stays. The need for them would come soon enough with the child-bearing years, when her young body would lose its youthful shape. A satin petticoat with many flounces and frills of Irish lace came next and over this the Irish lace wedding dress. It was delicately woven with tiny rosettes and cockle shell patterns. Scalloped edges finished off the neckline and the hem.

Holding her long veil in place was a spray of lily-of-the-valley in the form of an exquisitely woven diadem of pearls and emeralds set on a frame of gold.

On her feet she wore white, kid-leather slippers, the toes of which were adorned with tiny clusters of white lace rosettes. And in the center of each rosette a diamond sparkled.

Around her neck, Magheen wore the superb gift her proud husband-to-be had sent to her, a necklace of emeralds surrounded by diamonds set in gold. Magheen had never seen anything so perfect in her whole life. She had not had much time to get to know the young man she was to marry, but what she saw she liked.

The festivities lasted three days. No need now to whisper behind closed doors. To hell with the English; there was nothing now that any of them could do. The marriage had taken place despite their tyrannical laws.

The great hall was generously stocked with delicious foods. The guests were seated at several large tables, magnificently draped with linen cloth, and decorated with delicately wrought filigreed silver centerpieces. A sumptuous display of meats lined the tables. Great silver platters of wild duck, venison, and capon, as well as beef, pork, lamb, and pheasant were placed on sideboards. An assortment of fish also was available. Sweets and jellies, butter, cheeses, and little cakes of wheat, oats, and rye were in abundance. The gille in short tunics of lime green carried dishes of carrots, parsnips, celery, radishes, watercress, mushrooms, and roasted acorns. The extra footmen, hired for the occasion, were kept busy replenishing the silver goblets with a variety of wines: claret, Rhenish, mascadine, and charneco. The clatter of the pewter and silver tableware competed with the lilting banter of the many guests.

The harpist strummed a medley of tuneful melodies. He sat in the place of honor next to the Earl, himself. That was considered his right. He held a unique position; his was a noble profession demanding purity of hand, mouth, and heart.

Each evening after the feasting, a ball was held in the reception hall to which everyone, including the servants, were invited.

Magheen was adapting to her new life and position to the great satisfaction of Lady Eleanor. She was gracious with the guests, a good conversationalist, and an intelligent listener.

For one so young, she carried herself with a grace and elegance rarely seen in the matrons of mighty houses. Nor did her extraordinary beauty go unnoticed.

The flawless creamy skin and the delicate rose that suffused her finely-boned cheeks subtly contrasted. The soft, lustrous brown eyes, truly the windows of her ardent soul, mirrored its depths. Her aristocratic eyebrows, fine and sweeping upwards, proved her breeding and drew attention to the cluster of golden curls that had escaped from beneath the ruby diadem resting on her regal head. The costly gown of pale blue velvet, though simple, was well suited to emphasize the beauty hidden beneath it, while a large ruby teardrop supported on a strand of pearls nestled in the curve of her smooth young breasts.

Magheen was now the most popular topic of conversation at all the supper tables in Ormond territory, usurping the place of honor held so long by topics of the ever-changing political scene which, ultimately, in the larger scheme of things didn't matter in the least, didn't change things at all.

Twenty-Five

Hugo returned home in the early spring of 1545. Several weeks later, he had not as yet grasped the true import of what had happened. His dear wife dead! He had not been given time to get to know her properly, so young, scarcely a woman. Had she a premonition? Did she really know she would die in childbirth, he wondered. She had tried to tell him that she was afraid of...Was that the answer to her initial coldness? Had he, her husband, done this to her? Was he the one who was solely responsible for her premature death? His mind was tormented. He could neither sleep nor eat.

Day after day, Hugo hung about the Chateau, despondent, disconsolate. Each afternoon, in all weather, he would repair to the graveside and stand gazing at the soggy earth in utter abjection. Over and over his eyes scanned the words:

Here lies the earthly remains of
Charlotte Marie de Breville
beloved wife and mother
1527–1545
also
Andre Hugo Charles de Breville
infant son
1545

As the days followed, one on the other, Hugo's health began to fail. He spent more and more time in his room where, lying on his bed, he stared at the canopy, motionless, alone with his misery. At times, he longed for the release of death. But the teachings of his youth were not easily put aside; troubles, afflictions were sent by an omniscient God, one who knew just how much each soul could bear. He must accept his burden and use all adversity for God's eternal glorification and his own salvation. In these hours of despondency, his ardent nature and sensitive conscience plagued him.

Was God punishing him? he asked himself. While he was enjoying the company and the love of a beautiful Irish woman, his own wife was suffering. His thoughts turned to Magheen again. Should he have stifled the passionate feelings that she had aroused in him? In the sight of God he had a wife, and with her, and her alone, carnal love was legitimate. It had been so determined by Holy Mother the Church.

He tossed, unable to find relief for his fevered body, while his agonizing soul gave him no peace. The days slipped into weeks, and Hugo was fast becoming a sick man.

It had been a dismal day in early May, the steady drizzle had continued since late the evening before, and even now, twenty-four hours later, it gave no sign of letting up. Hugo had not left his room since early morning. At breakfast, his mother was quite concerned about him, noting the pallid cheeks.

"Hugo you're ill, I fear. You must see a physician today. I'll send for Monsieur Le Malandain."

"Dear Mama, it's nothing, just a little faintness...it will pass."

"No, my dear, I've been watching you. I've seen you failing day after day. I insist that you see the good doctor without further delay."

"Very well," He hadn't the energy to refuse. "I'll lie down for a while now, if you'll excuse me."

The physician arrived late in the evening. His diagnosis so alarmed the Countess that she cried herself to sleep that night.

Consumption! How could such a dreaded disease have been contracted? Eventually she attributed it to his recent sojourn in Ireland; the terrible ordeals he had been through in the last six months were bound to affect him physically and mentally.

The doctor had given strict orders for him to vacate the north country as soon as possible. He must have a warm, dry climate and plenty of rest in order to regain his health.

Within the week, Hugo and his mother left for the south. In a villa near Avignon, he was to spend the next six months tended by her loving hands.

Slowly, he regained his strength. The grief that was so overwhelming in the spring was now bearable. Magheen, whom he had scarcely learned to love, was becoming a memory, a beautiful, blurred memory. Soon all that remained was a mere veiled shadow of the reality.

With improved health, Hugo was able to attend the religious services in the nearby monastery. His rich baritone voice often blended with those of the chanting monks in the pristine chapel, and, as in his youth, the idea of embracing the religious life again occupied his mind. He felt contentment when he traversed the cool cloisters. When in union with the cowled monks, he raised his voice in prayer, Hugo knew the sweetness of a deep inner peace and closeness with God.

"Yes," he murmured, "I could live a saintly life in such surroundings." But he, unfortunately, also had a duty to his mother and family. He, the eldest son, could not yet relinquish his responsibilities in favor of his younger brother. When Victor had finished his schooling, then and only then, Hugo hoped he would be able to retire to the seclusion of some such establishment.

Then his mind played tricks and he found himself contemplating the old faraway scene, dwelling on each lovely memory: the beach, the honeysuckled hedgerows, the myriad wild flowers, and a hundred singing birds vying with one another in the dew-drenched morning hour. But beyond all this beauty a vision of loveliness appeared and disappeared in the mental pictures his brain conjured up for him. A smiling face, a soft, melodious voice, the limpid depths of warm brown eyes, the finely wrought limbs...a Grecian goddess? No, an Irish princess. Oh, Magheen, Magheen! He ached to hold her, to possess that body so perfectly formed and join his love to hers forever. He recoiled from the thought that even at that moment she might be in the arms of another. He knew something of her passionate nature. She loved him, of that he felt sure.

Had she not intimated, in the rashness of her youth, that she would give herself completely to him. And yet, he wondered, for he knew Magheen would not give easily. But when unleashed, he also knew that her giving would in no way lessen her inward pain. It would be an eruption from the depths of a burning heart. Fiery, spontaneous, uninhibited.... She would hold nothing back.

In his mind's eye, he now consciously held and enjoyed the vision of her loveliness, the curves of her perfectly-shaped body, the full young breasts, the sweet-tasting mouth. This vivid picture brought warmth to the very core of his being. Suddenly, he knew what he had to do. He would write to Magheen, declare his love, and ask her uncle for her hand. And, as soon as he was physically able, he would journey to Ballindee.

But the idea had hardly formed in his mind when he thought of Charlotte. What was he thinking of? His young wife scarcely cold in her grave! Could he be so callous? These were dastardly thoughts! Yet, as he pondered the reality of his position, a new idea struck home. He was free! Utterly free! He was a man unfettered. He could love as he pleased. He had, he knew, been guilty. He had played a dual role—a game. But no more. Now, he could openly declare his love. A suitable time of mourning should be observed, he reflected. That, at least, he did owe Charlotte. On further consideration he realized that it would take time for a letter to reach Ireland, and it would undoubtedly take longer for word to return to him. Yes, he would delay no longer. He would write that very night. His family need not know of his intentions, no reason to divulge his plans to anyone at this time. When Magheen gave her consent it would be time enough to set tongues wagging. The news would enliven the royal salons and the stately halls of the country gentry. What titillating gossip!

Summer was gradually changing her garb in the French countryside. From dappled greens she turned to a wardrobe of shimmering golds, warm russets, and sober browns as Hugo and his mother made their way north.

Having written to Magheen, his mind was at peace and with that came a surge of new vitality to his emotionally drained body. He was eager to resume his responsibilities and to join in the everyday activities of the other members of the family.

The journey, instead of taking ten days, was accomplished in six. Although his mother was tired, she, too, was eager to return home and so was in agreement with the long hours of travelling.

After the initial excitement caused by their return, the household at Chantille settled into the old familiar ways.

France was, for the time being, at peace with her enemies, so Hugo could afford to spend more time on domestic affairs. He enjoyed supervising the outdoor activities and upgrading the living conditions of the local peasantry, particularly those on his own estate.

Then, as the colder weather set in and the King and his court returned to Paris, Hugo found he was drawn to the capital.

Once again a man without attachments, his company was increasingly sought. Despairing matrons hatched schemes to ensnare him. Doddering old nobles promised handsome dowries if only Hugo would relieve them of young daughters or grandchildren.

But Hugo would not be trapped. He had his secret. He would have word from Ireland soon, he hoped.

Twenty-Six

Life in the castle resumed its normal routine after the departure of the many guests. Although Magheen's uncle and Moll stayed on a few extra days, they too passed quickly, and it was with deep emotion that she saw them depart. All at once they seemed to her to have aged. Seen in the light of her new surroundings, the two people she loved most in all the world were mere miniatures of their former selves. Somehow, they appeared to have lost stature, size, and significance. Was she seeing them now as they really were? Where was the buxom woman whose strength and affection had given her security all these years? Only a little old, grey-haired lady with sunken cheeks and stooping shoulders who cried a lot and wouldn't be comforted. And her uncle, the great Lord of Ballindee, was no longer tall and erect. For the first time, she noticed that brown spots spoiled the cream of his shapely hands. At fifty, he was old.

As she watched them depart, her heart tightened and an anxious pain grabbed at her ribs. Would she ever see them again in this world? Before the carriage had rounded the bend in the tree-lined avenue, the tears flowed unabashedly. She left the group, her husband's side, and walked toward the flower gardens. She had to be alone. It was cold and damp, and an air of mold and decay hung over everything… "pain and glory…" again she heard the words. Was this moment part of that pain?

She placed her hand against her heart and felt the pressure of his ring, Hugo's ring, as it nestled in the cleavage of her shapely breasts. As if seeking strength for the days that lay ahead, she clutched it closer. "Hugo, where are you?" she cried. "Why do I need you so?"

Magheen and Dermud had their own quarters and personal servants. By day, their totally different activities kept them busy and apart. She was learning to cope with a large household of servants, learning to supervise the business of running and maintaining a calm and orderly execution of the daily chores, and there were many, from the selection of menus for the family and servants, to the sewing and mending of the many gowns and linens used, the upkeep of supplies, the preparation of invitations to guests, and the usual exchange of visits and receptions. Her days were full but her nights were empty.

Magheen soon found out that Dermud, for all his respect and admiration, was far from a warm and loving husband. It wasn't long till she ached for the tender embrace of Hugo, she yearned for his arms to enfold her. Her body cried for his gentle caresses. How could she control her mind when it flew over the Irish Sea, across the Channel to fair France to the man she could never forget?

If these hours could have been spent in his embrace, what ecstasy! What unspeakable joy would have been hers!

She considered how differently the two men behaved. Dermud made no pretense about wooing her. He took possession of her briskly and seemingly without emotion, as if performing a service, a duty. Thus, Magheen, for her part, could not give herself wholly to him. There was never that wild abandon, that complete freedom and exchange of feelings between them.

How often in frustration did she try to ease her pain in silent tears. The more she thought of Hugo, the more her husband's touch disgusted and repelled her. Night after night, Hugo's image burned deeper and deeper into her mind and heart, and as the tears flowed, she saw only a future without real love stretching before her..."pain and glory." The words mocked her.

To compound her sufferings, she was confused, for despite her seeming love for Hugo, she also harbored feelings of hatred. She heard herself cry out at times, "Cruel, he's a cruel brute." She asked herself over and over how he could have done this to her. He hadn't really loved her. Why did she torment herself? Better far to forget the past. She would never see him again. Then, a second later, she would throw these thoughts from her mind. She knew that with him and only him could she ever know real love. Despite her best efforts, Hugo's image would always remain alive in her heart, and that was the image she worshipped. It was with him she made love when in her husband's arms. It was to him she turned in time of need. Yes, in her heart she lived with him, slept with him, spoke to him, and consulted with him.

Her life with Dermud was a routine of activities, nothing more. She had attained wealth and prestige. She was Lady Butler of the House of Ormond, the most powerful family in Ireland at this time. Her grandfather must certainly be proud of her. She hadn't married a Gaelic prince, it was true, but the next best, a Sean Ghall lord.

As time passed, Magheen turned her attention to other pursuits. Word of her kindnesses and generosity to the poor, the sick, and homeless, particularly those fleeing from the enemy, soon spread far beyond the boundaries of Ormond country. Her dreams of achieving fame, of playing a part in the history-making of her land were becoming a reality.

Her opinion was respected by the Lords and Chieftains who, in increasing numbers and with growing regularity, were gathering at the castle. Her contributions to the lengthy and weighty discussions not only enlivened but often gave new insight.

Tension was mounting. Everyone knew in his heart that the day was not far distant when the smouldering fires of rebellion would erupt into a great conflagration. It was at this point, the late winter of 1546, that an unexpected invitation came from England's Henry VIII.

The climate of unrest throughout Ireland made it necessary at the time for the Butlers and other Sean Ghall families to appear as loyal subjects at Henry's Court. The time was not yet ripe for their dramatic and irrevocable denunciation. For a while longer, James Butler would grudgingly bow his head and bend his knee to the foreign king. He would feign allegiance to the usurper of Irish land and property. But soon, very soon, the Earl of Ormond promised himself this situation would change. Irishmen would be subject to none but a leader of their own choosing. As of old, the Brehon Laws would prevail and this land, his beloved country, would once again stand proud among the free nations of the world.

"By God! I'll lay down my life for the cause," James Butler mumbled to himself as he turned the invitation over in his hands. He decided, without consulting the family, that he, his wife, and his eldest son, Dermud, accompanied by Magheen, would make the journey, and that without further delay.

"Aye," the old Earl muttered, "she should cause a stir. Make for a pretty distraction...an' a wholesome one, I might add, in that den of iniquity." James, thinking of Magheen, pictured the scene. He envisioned the moment when his family would be presented to the King. "The Earl of Ormond, James Butler and the Lady Eleanor Butler. The Earl's son, Dermud, and his wife, the Lady Mairgret." All eyes would be upon them. Magheen would sparkle, dazzle that jaded assemblage. There wouldn't be one, he would wager, who could hold a candle to her. The old man's spirits rose; he would enjoy this journey after all. "Yes, by Jove, we'll show them!"

* * * *

The coachman stood by the open door of the carriage, his face impassive. He held out a gloved hand to assist the Lady Eleanor and then Magheen. The ladies were followed into the carriage by the gentlemen. It was luxurious, all bright and shiny with heavy red satin and velvet upholstery. Magheen sank deep into the plush seats, and couldn't help comparing it with the old black one at home that Sean was so proud to drive. She'd come a long way since those days.

Whitehall was situated to the west, around the bend of the river from the city. The Palace was a great sprawling mass of red brick buildings in the Tudor style. It was a labyrinth of hallways and passages with scores of separate apartments and rooms opening one into another, like a great and complex maze.

This great Palace was the home not only of the Royal Family, but also every court attendant or hanger on who could finagle accommodations there. The buildings perched right on the river bank were so close that at high tide the kitchens were often flooded.

For most of the occupants, privacy was a thing of which to dream. Through the very grounds of the Palace ran the dirty, unpaved, narrow thoroughfare called King Street. Fortunately for the

King, on one side of this street stood the Privy Gardens, retaining some semblance of privacy being protected from the vulgar by a rather high wall. On the other side was that part of the Palace called the Cockpit.

The main hallway of the Court was called the gallery. It consisted of an enormous corridor almost four hundred feet long and fifteen wide lit by scores of candles hissing and dancing from elaborate chandeliers. The walls were hung with tapestries, and here and there a stone statue broke the monotony. Huge baskets of flowers freshened the heavy air.

As they took off over the cobblestone streets towards Whitehall Palace, Magheen took a peek. It was her first glimpse of London in its heady rush at the end of the day. As she drew aside the velvet curtain, it was not yet dark. The narrow street was hemmed in on both sides by long rows of drab houses. Down the center of the street, a wide gutter ran, and it was piled high in places with the filth of many days waste giving off a putrid stench.

"How awful! I thought this was one of the great cities of the world." Magheen turned to her father-in-law.

"That's what they would have you believe. Give me a wee corner of our own garden and they can have the whole bloomin' lot o' this," answered the Earl.

The voices of street urchins aroused Magheen's curiosity. As she again pulled aside the curtain, she saw the dirtiest, most ragged spectacles of humanity she had ever seen in her life. Shrieks of laughter filled the air as these starving, filthy ragamuffins found fun jumping back and forth across an open sewer. Each child was being challenged to greater feats of daring by his companions. Magheen noticed a pool of green scum. Then, drawing nearer, she saw the rotting flesh and animal bones lying beside piles of excrement. "What a place for little children to play!"

The carriage rounded a corner into Chancery Lane and the going was a little smoother. A left turn took them into King Street. Here the crowds jostled in a frenzied attempt to be off the streets before night descended. Street vendors were hastily gathering up the last of their wares.

"Cherries ripe, ripe, I cry," sang out the cockney voice of one grubby lass, as she tried to attract the attention of some passersby.

"Violets, sweet violets, a penny a bunch. Come, Sir, a nosegay for yer lady." The old hag held up the drooping flowers to a young gallant passing near her cart.

Magheen dropped the curtain. She was inclined to agree with her father-in-law. No wonder the Sasanach wanted to have a home in her beautiful country.

Soon they were turning into the Palace yard. This was the moment! This was the hour for which every young woman of noble birth waited. The hour when she would walk into the Palace and be presented to the King.

Magheen's emotions were mixed. In a very short time, she had been propelled into the highest circles of society. It would seem that even her very wildest dreams were coming true. She would meet the King, himself. Exhilarated by the challenge, she began to envision the moment. How should she comport herself? She wanted to capitalize on that moment and gain Henry's attention? Once she had accomplished that, anything was possible. But a part of her mind revolted. Even as she conjectured and planned, as her thoughts projected her into the future and she saw herself consulting with the King, she felt somehow that she was betraying herself. It was preposterous for an Irish princess to demean herself thus. Why should she have to bargain and plead with a foreign king for what was rightfully hers? The English King had come unbidden and unjustly took what he wanted. There had been bloodshed, murder, destruction. She, Magheen, must demand an end to it. Ireland for the Irish, that would be her theme. She would not grovel.

The carriage rolled to a stop. Magheen heard running feet and a commanding voice. The door was opened. Red-liveried servants, bearing flaring flambeaux above their heads, stood in a line leading from the carriage to the great entrance door of the Palace. They wore powdered wigs and wide-brimmed hats, the sides of which were turned up and pinned in place by copper cockades.

The men alighted. The grooms aided the ladies to descend onto the flagstone courtyard. The Earl and Lady Eleanor preceded Magheen and Dermud into the Palace where they were met by a rather rotund footman in red livery. He bowed very correctly before leading them down a long corridor. On one side paintings and tapestries covered the wall, on the other, high mullioned windows allowed the moonlight to challenge the glow of sputtering tapers. Under foot, the rich, red carpet was thick and soft.

As they approached the end of the corridor, two massive wooden doors were opened revealing a vast, elaborately furnished room. Overhead and on either side hundreds of candles flickered and danced and the perfume of a thousand roses filled the air. The effect was awe-inspiring.

"Effective," Magheen remarked.

"It's all part of the formality. The English love ritual." Dermud squeezed Magheen's arm.

About to speak again, Magheen refrained as the sound of music caught her attention.

"Please be seated," the footman said.

For some minutes they waited without speaking. The music of viols floated in waves from a distance.

Eventually the doors on the opposite side of the room were opened and their footman motioned for them to proceed. Another corridor, then finally the highly ornamented door to an antechamber was opened. This room was richly decorated in shades of red and gold, the furniture beautifully carved from cherry wood. The music now was much louder and the sound of laughter and conversation was easily heard.

The footman politely waited a moment, as if allowing the newcomers a chance to catch their breath, before proceeding further. After what he considered a suitable interval, the footman skillfully caught the Earl's attention and silently communicated by means of his raised brows that he needed to know if the party were ready to enter the great ballroom.

The King was seated under a canopy of gold, the most costly material Magheen had ever seen. Looking bored, he was leaning against a gilt throne inlaid with precious stones. The doublet he wore was fashioned in the Swiss style with alternating stripes of white and crimson satin and his scarlet hose, all slashed from the knee upwards, matched the rich doublet. On his head he wore a cap of crimson velvet after the French fashion, the brim was looped all around with braids bearing gold enameled tags. Around his neck was a gold collar, from which hung an oval cut diamond as large as a walnut and from this was suspended an enormous pearl.

Beside the King sat his sixth wife, Catherine Parr. She was extravagantly clothed in a white tissue robe with an overdress of silver brocade. A coronet of rubies lay on her head and a heavy strand of rubies and diamonds on her breast. The twice widowed queen, now in her thirties, couldn't compare with Magheen.

"See how she's decked in borrowed plume," whispered the old Earl to Magheen.

Magheen smiled but did not answer. They were within ear-shot now of the throne and would be next in line for introduction.

In striking contrast to the richly dressed Queen, Magheen wore a simple, pale green silk gown that was molded to her high, full breasts and then fell away. The flowing sleeves of the gown were embroidered in vivid colors displaying the intricacies of elaborate Celtic designs. Her golden hair, braided and held by golden cauls, was looped over her ears. Around her neck she wore a plain gold circlet. There was a faint but very becoming flush to her creamy skin. Her beautiful brown eyes sparkled beneath their dark, sweep-ing lashes.

Before she realized it, she was curtsying to the mighty mon-arch. Although every bone in her proud body rebelled, she had acquiesced to the wishes of her beloved father-in-law only because she felt it might eventually help her, her husband, her people, her country. She held her position. She was not bidden to rise!

The King stirred, then he sat up. Even bent forward a little.

"Ah, a new face! I'd like to see more. Rise, me sweet. Don't be afraid to look at your Sire."

The gawking courtiers and guests surrounding the dais had heard Henry's remarks. Side glances were exchanged, eyebrows raised; some were curious, others ready to cast aspersions.

Magheen arose. She lifted her head slowly and deliberately. As her beautiful eyes looked full upon the King's face, she per-ceived a more than casual interest in his blue eyes. The Queen at his left smiled. Catherine, who had married Henry in 1543, intended to keep her head. She had a reputation for being a pleasant, witty, cultured woman who knew the world and who especially knew Henry and his ways. So the King's interest was aroused. He was happy with this new diversion. The Queen's curiosity was obvi-ous, but no one misunderstood her smiling countenance.

"So you've come from the Emerald Isle, the land of the wee folk, eh? They've sent a charming emissary this time. A fairy princess, I'll be bound. Your Sire is pleased by your beauty, Madam."

"You're over generous, Sir. In my land, I'm only one of many."

"Ah, an' a quick tongue to match your looks. A rare combination."

The King smiled, then nodded. Magheen was dismissed.

Bowing in regal fashion, Magheen did not again curtsy but raised her head and slowly backed a few steps. She caught the twinkle that lit the King's eyes. He hadn't ignored her deliberate faux pas.

There was a murmur of excitement. It arose particularly among the men watching the performance. They could only guess at Henry's thoughts as his gaze followed Magheen.

"Me thinks the King has found a new bedwarmer." The Duke of Suffolk spoke, pretending to cough behind his gloved hand.

"Catherine's smile sits lightly. I'll wager a dagger aggravates her breast," answered his companion, Essex.

"'Pon my word, m'Lord, Her Majesty's well aware that her position is ever tenuous. Were she not such a good nurse and the King's ulcerous leg so painful, our revered Lady might well have gone the same way as...."

"No names, m'Lord."

The conversation was interrupted when the King arose to lead the way to the great dining hall.

Dermud had slipped to Magheen's side and now escorted her to where the Butler party was standing.

"Well done, daughter." James Butler was elated. He felt the shock waves ripple through the pompous, snobbish gathering. Soon, he knew them well, those scheming, conniving, fops, so-called nobles, lately come to wealth and title, yes, soon they would be fawning, hanging on his arm in hope that the Lady Mairgret would grace them with a smile. There was no doubt in their minds about this newcomer. She had aroused the King's interest. It would be beneficial to get to know her.

The thought scarce had entered his head when he perceived m'Lord, The Duke of Brodford, approach, one of the many admirers Magheen would entertain for the rest of the evening. The bored aristocrats that surrounded Henry were suddenly interested, more than willing to oblige the King and further their own ends. They would even have fun with this enchanting creature while doing so.

A fanfare announced the first course of the lavish dinner that followed. A procession of cooks in white aprons and serving lads in royal livery marched between long aisles of tables to the royal dais. Their huge trays were heaped high with suckling pigs, venison, beef, mutton, capons, stuffed duck, chicken, pheasant, lark, and sparrow. Great silver bowls of frumenty and platters of bread followed.

The King chose a large stuffed chicken and, with voracious appetite, tore at the breast with his great chubby fingers.

"There's nothing I like better than a plump juicy breast unless it's a tenderloin." Henry's voice was loud as his eye sought Magheen. For an instant he made contact; then he lolled his great head back and laughed aloud. The nobles near him joined in his merriment.

As soon as the King was served, the dishes were quickly presented to the guests. Young boys, barely able to carry the wine jugs, filled the new Venetian glass goblets. A course of sweetmeats followed. There were dried apples and raisins, comfits and jellies. The last course consisted entirely of confection. Magheen had never seen such pastries before in her life. When she inquired about them, she was told they were the creations of a French chef sent by Francis, himself, as a gesture of goodwill to his new friend, Henry.

At the ball which followed, Magheen was so eagerly sought that neither her husband nor the other members of her family had an opportunity to speak with her.

The King decided to retire shortly after midnight, his leg was giving him trouble. But before he arose to leave, he sent word to the Earl of Ormond that he and his family should attend him in the antechamber.

As the King and Queen left the ballroom and entered the antechamber, the doors were immediately closed. James and Dermud Butler bowed while Magheen and the Lady Eleanor curtsied. The King stood a moment as if making up his mind, then stepping forward, he fixed his gaze on Magheen. "Rise, Lady Mairgret." And when his eyes met hers he continued with a playful glint: "Methinks that even England's might must bow to Ireland's beauty." And so Henry bowed, his crimson cap askew.

Magheen stood before him in silence a moment, then as His Majesty straightened, she spoke: "My Liege, your compliment is most gracious. Ireland accepts it but would remind you that beauty is not her only asset."

"Ha, it's often enough, I'm reminded of that." A frown marked his brow. "Yea, but I'd speak further with ye, m'Lady, Ireland. Anon...."

Then the King offered his hand first to the Lady Eleanor standing a little to his right. She bent low and kissed the heavily ringed fingers. But before the King had time to stretch his hand towards Magheen, she slowly and with great dignity raised her own hand and offered it to the King.

For a split second Henry was taken aback. An audacious gesture! He looked deep into the lustrous brown eyes but saw only innocence. This was disarming, something he couldn't quite put into words. For a moment the licentious old man was moved. It had been a long time, a very long time since he had experienced feelings such as those that now fought for a spot in his depraved heart. Hastily, he brushed the tips of Magheen's fingertips with a kiss. Then turning, he took his departure as quickly as his ulcerous leg would allow.

"Od's blood!" he murmured. To bed such a wench would be a welcome diversion. His old age might yet know some small pleasure, he thought. Henry had a twinkle in his bloodshot eye, and his impaired gait seemed lighter as he made his way to his own sleeping quarters.

Twenty-Seven

The following morning Magheen lay abed much longer than usual. The excitement of the previous evening and the exertions of the strenuous journey left her exhausted. Besides, the Lady Eleanor insisted that she rest. It was unseemly for a woman in her delicate condition to travel at all; but, since that was a fait accompli, she considered it her duty to see that Magheen did not overdo it. Accordingly, she breakfasted in bed, and by the time she had finished her toilette, it was past noon. A light lunch awaited her when she descended to join the family and their hosts, the Duke and Duchess of Harcourt.

"Good afternoon, everyone," Magheen said cheerfully. "I've had enough sleep, thanks to my Lady mother, to last a lifetime." She inclined to the Lady Eleanor as she passed her chair, escorted by her husband. "I'm ready to challenge either lover or foe," she tossed the words lightly as Dermud bent to place a light kiss on her cheek.

"Sure hope I'm not in the latter category," he retorted.

There was general laughter at the remark, to which Magheen immediately responded, "I have it from the highest authority," she winked at her father-in-law seated at the opposite side of the table, "that in the games of love and war, one cannot even trust blood relatives." She tossed her head in a gesture both taunting and haughty and went to kiss the bearded cheek of the old Earl.

He raised his hand and patted Magheen's affectionately. "A young woman with brains as well as beauty. Methinks Harry's no fool. It didn't take him long to draw the right conclusions." Secretly, he now wished the King had never set eyes on Magheen.

"Hark, my dear Dermud, wisdom speaks," Magheen addressed her husband. "Take heed lest Harry choose an Irish lass, a papist wench as his new amour." She raised her head in regal pose and again the sound of laughter enlivened the meal.

"Ah, my dear, I wouldn't wish that fate even on my worst enemy," answered Dermud. "But," he looked around, "let's bridle our tongues. We all know the saying, 'walls have ears'. I'd hate to have to spend more time on English soil than is absolutely necessary."

"Aye, Son, wisely spoken. We forget, at times, how often a careless word has lost a man his head. Better be more circumspect," James Butler nodded.

A moment of silence fell upon the group. Then Magheen, ever vivacious and optimistic but particularly so on this afternoon because of her conquest the previous evening, spoke: "Father, if we may not have our little jokes, we can at least savor our small victories."

"I fear, my dear, even gaining the favor of the King has its dangers," the Earl of Harcourt spoke. "You can't have forgotten," he lowered his voice, "how many of his close friends Harry has sent to their deaths."

"No, indeed, m'Lord. It makes me shudder to even think of it," Magheen quickly changed her tone of voice, "but why talk of dying and death? 'Tis such a beautiful day. We're here in the company of gracious friends and I, for one, have the best family in the world, so I'm not going to allow anything to spoil my happiness." Magheen smiled affectionately across the table at her father-in-law.

"Eh, eh. Did I utter a word of complaint? Anyone hear me say I wasn't enjoying every minute of it?" pleaded James to his amused friends.

"Well," Lady Eleanor wiped her mouth with her serviette, "please excuse us, but the day will be at an end before we know where we are, and I'm determined to see the London shops before dark." So saying she got up.

Magheen hastily swallowed the last mouthful of milk. She, too, touched her lips with the linen serviette, excused herself, and quickly followed her from the room. She donned a plain violet gown of silk, wide lace collar embroidered with golden threads, slashed, puffed sleeves revealing the fineness of the linen underdress, then took her cloak, dark blue velvet, lined with pale blue satin, and draped it over her arm, a precaution against a dismal afternoon.

The Lady Harcourt was in her late fifties but looked remarkably well, her skin clear and smooth and her eyes bright and alert. Smaller than Magheen, her body was slim, compact. Every movement suggested an abundance of controlled energy. Her dress was elegant, fashionable, in keeping with her personality, formal, but in exquisite taste.

The Earl, her husband, on the other hand, was over seventy. Feeble and bent, his powdered wig askew, he walked with the aid of a cane. He was a proud man, who had known both fame and honor in his youth; now, as he neared the end of his long life, his only desire was to be left alone. He shunned the company of the local gentry and spent most of his time in his conservatory, intent on developing a new strain of lily. On this particular morning, he was glad to see the ladies take their leave; he had neglected his work since the arrival of his Irish guests.

The great city of London was a whirlwind of activity. People of all walks of life milled about the dirty streets; a sprinkling of the noble class, richly-dressed ladies accompanied by equally well-attired gentlemen out for a leisurely stroll. And young dandies sauntered by with languid gait and lascivious eye, alert for a slender waist, round, firm breasts, and a face most likely to pleasure them for an hour or two. Businessmen hurried along with an air of having problems of great weight to solve. Soldiers and sailors rubbed shoulders with country squires and their wives. And always and everywhere the unwashed poor: beggars, cripples, and hangers-on.

Magheen noticed young boys wearing flat caps, blue gowns, and breeches of white broadcloth. "What does that dress signify?" she asked, pointing to the youths.

"Oh, they're the apprentices, my dear, become quite numerous. So many new trades cropping up in and around the city. You just can't imagine how the town has grown. No longer able to find m' way around, nothing at all like the old days." The Lady Harcourt was not impressed by progress. Like her husband, a quiet life was much more desirable than this new London, with its throngs, its great recent middle class of yeoman and tradesmen, and the like; it was a world beyond her comprehension.

Magheen noticed the spirit of vitality that was abroad in the city. There was a feeling of exuberance in the air, business was booming.

"They say the influx of precious metals, especially from the Spanish Indies, has given rise to the establishment of many new gold and silversmith businesses. See, there's one! What say you to us taking a look?" asked the Lady Harcourt and, without waiting for a reply, she rapped on the wooden frame of the carriage.

The coachman brought the horses to a halt and stepped down from his high seat. "You wish to stop here, m'Lady?" he asked.

"Yes, we'll take a look in there," she replied, pointing to a small jewelry shop.

The street was lined with small shops of various kinds. Some displayed beautiful woolen articles, brightly colored plaids for shawls and cloaks, and heavy woven fabric for the new-fashioned blankets.

"How lovely!" Magheen drew the attention of her mother-in-law to these colorful materials. "I wonder if those are Irish fabrics?"

"They look like the fine materials that usually come from across the Irish Sea, my dear. But we'll find out."

The ladies soon learned that the splendid woolens were in fact manufactured in England. Magheen clenched her lips and her nails bit into her mittened-clad hands in an attempt to curb her tongue. "They're at it again," she snapped. "Mark my word, they'll ruin our Irish trade yet. Once, we were one of the world's greatest exporters of woolen goods, but these new products from English manufacturers will certainly get preferential treatment. I, for one, won't buy a yard of it, even if it were the last piece in England." Magheen whispered to Lady Eleanor before they both followed their hostess into the jewelers.

The shop bore the name of 'Herr Hans Schmidt' in big letters over the door. The proprietor, a man in his late forties with a round jovial face, was a foreigner lately come to London town. A Fleming, who had had to flee the oppression of the Spanish King, like so many others, he was reshaping the economic life of his adopted country. Lace makers, dyers, brass workers, tapestry weavers, and glass makers, all Flemings, were settling down in their new homes. And, to the great satisfaction of their new sovereign, the English King, were contributing to the growth and prosperity of the nation.

The ladies made some small purchases, earrings for the Lady Eleanor and, for Magheen, a simple gold chain.

Once more out in the noisy street, the voice of an enterprising young apprentice reached their ears. "Ah! My fair and noble dames, what is it ye lack? Fine wrought smocks for yer dimpled children? Perfumed gloves? Lace or edgings? Silk garters? Combs or glasses?"

The Lady Harcourt turned to the lad and smiled. "No, my good lad, we've no need of anything today."

When the youth saw he wasn't having any luck with the ladies, he quickly turned to a richly dressed gentleman whose carriage had just then drawn alongside. "Kind Sir, a perfumed pomander, lace or scented gloves for your dame, or your sweetheart?"

As the ladies were getting into the carriage, Magheen heard a hoarse cry.

"My purse! Od's blood, my purse is gone!" A fat squire shouted and flung up his hands in despair, but the thief, no doubt some half-starved gutter snipe, was long gone. "It's shocking, simply shocking! Crime is rampant in our streets. There was a time when a man would hang for less. Now the pickpockets and scavengers from all over the country are congregating on our very door steps." He was still voicing his anger when the carriage drew away.

Magheen arrived home to find a letter awaiting her. It had been delivered to Harcourt House shortly after the ladies had left on their outing. Addressed to Lady Mairgret Butler, it bore the King's seal.

With trembling fingers, Magheen broke the seal. Inside the envelope, a single sheet of vellum displayed the Royal Coat of Arms. Below, in bold letters, the words: "Your presence is requested in the palace at eight o'clock on Wednesday evening, Henry, Rex."

Magheen looked at the heavy strokes. There was no doubt about it. The signature was his. "The King's!" A note of triumph was evident in her voice.

"Oh, no!" Lady Eleanor cast an anxious glance at her husband.

The Earl seemed pleased and didn't pay any attention to his wife's reaction. "What is it, my dear, an invitation?"

"Yes, yes, indeed, Father." Magheen read the words aloud.

"Then, my dear, the King has really taken a fancy to you. You may yet be able to bend his ear on behalf of our bruised and bleeding land," but behind his remark, the Earl was concerned.

"Father, I pray we do not live to regret this day," Dermud spoke. The blood had left the young man's face; he was visibly shaken.

"We came knowing there was danger. If Magheen, by winning the King's favor, can in any way alleviate the threat of hostility, calm suspicious minds, or silence envious tongues, then I think the risk is worth it." The Earl knew his words did not make an impression on his wife or son. He turned again and addressed Magheen. "But, I warn you, my child, don't be deceived by Henry. He's a crafty old buzzard and nobody's fool. Long years of manipulating, scheming, and double dealing have made him a taskmaster in the art of..." James Butler's voice was a mere whisper, "treachery. Be forewarned, a gra."

"I'll be on my guard, Father. I promise." Magheen arose from her place and quickly moved toward her father-in-law. "Have no fear, dearest Papa, Harry of England may yet be vanquished by a mere maid. If France produced a Joan of Arc, Ireland may one day be proud of Mairgret of Ballindee."

"Not on the same terms, my love, I hope." The old Earl looked at her. There was a deep respect in his grey-blue eyes as he smiled tenderly. "We have enough martyrs in Ireland. But you've got determination and courage as well as beauty, Magheen. If Henry's the man I think he is, he'll at least see that."

"You worry too much, dear Father." Magheen tried to appear unconcerned.

"I've lived longer, consequently have seen more. At my age, I've earned the right to worry. May I see the letter, please?"

"Certainly, Father."

The Earl took the note from her hand and looked at it for a moment. "I see he doesn't command you to appear at the Palace alone; Dermud should, therefore, accompany you."

"Yes, of course," answered Magheen.

"London's a city of crime and violence. You wouldn't be safe to go alone, even to the Palace, my dear."

The next few days were spent in a flurry of excitement and

preparation for what Magheen considered the greatest opportunity of her life.

Noreen, Lady Eleanor's personal maid, came to help Magheen with her toilette on that memorable evening. After she had bathed in rose water, Noreen helped her dress. The girl was meticulous in every detail and knew what an honor it was for her to be given the task of making her young Ladyship ready to appear before the King. She was even more anxious than Magheen that her Ladyship be considered the most beautiful woman that ever graced the English royal Court.

First came a light, cream-colored chemise edged with lace, then the petticoats, three in all, made of fine linen. These were followed by a whalebone corset with busks, and a new farthingale, much more elaborate than the one she had for her fifteenth birthday, was fitted under the voluminous skirt and underdress of pink and burgundy velvet. She chose a tight fitting jacket made of Irish lace, with full sleeves that dipped to a V below the elbow. The bodice of the same burgundy-colored velvet showed up beautifully under the lace jacket.

"I think the pink satin slippers, Noreen."

The slippers were perfect. Trimmed in lace, they each had a little velvet bow of the same rich hue as the gown. Noreen did Magheen's golden hair in a high coif and held it in place with emerald-studded combs. From her pale ear lobes hung two emerald teardrops and around her neck a pendant of diamonds and emeralds.

"M'Lady...?"

Magheen looked at Noreen. "Yes, why not?" The servant handed her a fan of ostrich plumes.

"Well, what do you think, Noreen?"

"Oh, m'Lady, there won't be a livin' creature to compare with ye. But don't you be lettin' that tyrant, Henry, be gettin' any notions about ye, Ma'am. You know what a..."

"Shhh, Noreen, not so loud. We're not in Ireland now. You don't know who might be listening. Remember, we're guests here. The least hint of treason and our dear friends would be in trouble, not to say anything about where we might land up ourselves."

"I'll be careful, real careful, m'Lady. Sure, there's ne'er a one in this place I'd be trustin'."

Magheen's reception at the Palace that evening was a far cry from what it had been the night she was presented to the King. Everything had been prearranged. No sooner had she put her dainty foot in the Palace courtyard than she and Dermud were quickly hurried off to a side entrance. They were met by a footman whom they noticed took great care not to look them full in the face. Upon reaching the King's quarters, they were hastily ushered into the royal presence without any formal announcement. Magheen was more than a little surprised to find the King surrounded by so many members of the court. She had hoped he would be alone, so that she would be able to speak freely.

Henry sat on a raised dais. At his feet, his faithful fool squatted in reverential awe, as he gazed up into his master's face, hanging on every word. The King wore a close-fitting doublet of silver and gold brocade, the sleeves of which were shaped to his ample arms. His hose of green silk and breeches of dark green velvet were fashionably becoming, but Magheen's attention was drawn to the extra large codpiece with its lavish ornamentation. No doubt, Henry in his declining years would have it be known that he was ever vigorous. No fault of his that a legitimate heir and son was not produced; that was plain for all to see. Queen Catherine was seated to one side, engaged in conversation with her ladies-in-waiting.

Magheen's courage seemed to forsake her at that moment; she felt her legs grow weak. All at once, a flush of heat coursed through her body, then as quickly left her with a cold, clammy feeling. Where were all her high and mighty plans now? The thoughts occurred to her that this great hulk of a man had invited her only to make a fool of her before his favorites, before the so-called upper-crust of English society. After all, in his sight, she was only an ignorant Irish coleen. Then she remembered a similar occasion...Her grandfather's castle. The words "You're an O'Neill" seemed to thunder in her head. She felt the eyes of those in the King's immediate circle riveted on her; there was a kind of salacious curiosity concerning the newcomer. Seeing this beautiful young woman, it was difficult not to conjecture.

For a moment, Magheen hesitated, then stepped forward and curtsied.

"Ah, the fairy princess from the Emerald Isle! Come, m'pretty one. Sit here." With his good leg Henry kicked the stool occupied by the court jester, Will Somers. Somers, the only person who could cheer the King, was the very antithesis of Henry, short, lean, and stooping, almost a hunchback; he was always accompanied by his monkey. Wives were changed, courtiers came and went, but Will Somers remained forever in Henry's court.

The King spoke harshly to his fool but Will knew better than to take offense. "Hi thee hence, Knave. Allow the fair lady to come hither." Henry extended his bejeweled hand, and this time Magheen decided to play it safe.

Dermud bowed, kissed the King's hand, and withdrew to the side of the room to watch a game of cards.

"Come, sit here, m' sweetly." Henry indicated the stool at his feet. "I would look upon your pretty face again. 'Pon my soul, its image did scarce leave my mind since first I saw you."

Magheen seated herself as she was bidden. For a moment, nothing was said so she tried to concentrate on the music. Henry, who was very fond of music, kept several groups constantly employed. From the far end of the large room the virginalist, accompanied by a viol, a viola-da-gamba, a flute, a sackbut, and a shawm, played compositions written by the noted composers of the day, Tallis and Fayrfax.

She knew that the King was an excellent musician, that he had composed numerous songs and instrumental works, and played several instruments himself. He was particularly skillful on the Irish harp, a good subject with which to engage the Monarch in conversation, she thought.

"Your Majesty, I've heard that you're a superb musician."

"Ha, ods blood, so they speak some good of me across the Irish Sea."

"Oh, indeed, Sire, much that is kind and good is said of you in Ireland...but...." Dare she?

"But...you hesitate....Would you whisper that some speak ill of their King?" Henry's eyes grew small as he scrutinized Magheen's reaction.

"Nay! Then 'pon my word, 'twould be the first good news from Ireland that I've heard in years. It does my heart good, m'Lady, to learn that my Irish subjects recognize the error of their ways."

"I fear I've conveyed the wrong impression, Sire. 'Tis not with you, m'Liege, that we Irish have any quarrel." Magheen knew better but wished not to offend the King by too blunt an answer.

"What then? For I hear a great tempest blows across your land threatening to engulf the entire isle. I would know the cause of this unrest." Henry's tone had an edge to it.

"The laws. Many laws which the Irish parliament have enacted and are trying to enforce are unjust."

"Unjust! Let it never be said that Henry, King of these isles, is unjust. I am the law, that you must know, m'Lady." His voice rose; heads turned. For a moment Magheen saw fire in his aging eyes; the blood rushed to the roots of his red beard and his great body seemed to swell to even greater proportions. Then as quickly, the crafty Monarch's temper changed, and once again with smiling cheek he spoke to Magheen. "But these are weighty matters, m'Lady Mairgret. Methinks such serious business is best left for men's broader shoulders and subtler minds. 'Twere pity, indeed, for so pretty a head to carry such burdens. Are there no men left in Ireland then that mere maids should play with politics?"

"Sir, you favor me not." Magheen's temper was sparked. "Ireland still bears numerous wise and brave men and her women of equal number are no less so. I'm but one among many who would bend my Sovereign's ear to the plight of our suffering nation." Magheen tried to hide the rebellious feelings that stormed within.

"If Ireland suffers then most surely must her Sovereign know. We will talk anon. For now, let's be merry. I would see you smile, dear Lady."

Henry clapped his hands and immediately the Court Jester summersaulted and landed at his master's feet.

"Fool, play the fool. Blow your bladder, for we would be merry."

Magheen knew she was now dismissed. She arose, curtsied, and backed away. Her bearing, even in the King's presence was aristocratic, regal. She had courage and determination. She had tenacity also. She was not beaten. She was more determined than ever to find a way to reach Henry.

These qualities, when coupled with her extraordinary beauty, would have catapulted her to the fore had she never been presented to the King. But, after her audience with Henry, she became a force to be reckoned with. Henry did not like his authority challenged. He would brook no criticism of his laws, his will. He would keep an eye on this one.

While he watched Magheen, in all her dazzling beauty and grace, float across the room on the arm of her husband, Henry's quick mind pieced together every shred of information he had received from Ireland. He remembered he had heard of the Butler wedding some months previous. Yes....Henry mused, his half-shut eyes continuing to follow Magheen. Then, without shifting his gaze, he called, "m'Lord Surrey."

The most powerful man in the country glided to the King's side. "Yes, Sire."

"You've a subtle mind. Pray tell me from which noble house does the lovely Mairgret Butler hail?"

"Sire. She's an O'Neill. The granddaughter of the Earl of Tyrone."

"Hah! That's it then. Would Con O'Neill play me for a fool? Does he send a wolf in sheep's clothing?"

"The Irish were never known for their loyalty, m'Leige."

"So Butler, the Anglo-Norman Lord, defies his King! He has married with the Gael! Would m'Lord of Ormond then become more Irish than the Irish? I prithee, m'Lord Surrey, look to this matter. I would know the full import of James Butler's associations with his Irish friends and in-laws. I would have this knowledge ere this fox returns to his lair."

"Your loyal hounds will ferret out the information with all speed, m'Leige."

"'Pon m' word, Surrey, you pull a quick quip. See that action matches tongue and who knows what dainty morsel your grateful King may yet serve to tempt your palate." Henry laughed as his friend gave evidence that he understood the implication.

As the King watched Magheen take part in the dancing, some members of the Court gossiped. Conjecturing, taking sides for and against the odds that Henry would or wouldn't. But, when word was noised abroad that the King's interests would best be served by discrediting the Butler family, there was no shortage of ambitious people ready to find fault, to deride, and even to swear under oath to treasonous allegations regarding the Butlers. A slice of Butler land, a castle or two in Ireland, not to mention an additional title, would be reward enough for such expeditious loyal subjects of His gracious and generous Majesty. Conveniently, in the ensuing days, it never occurred to anyone to question the veracity of these trumped-up accusations of the lesser nobles. The fact that some of these same people didn't know or had never before bothered to inquire about the Earl of Ormond and his family didn't enter into the picture. It was sufficient that someone, somehow, had concocted, hatched-up or otherwise contrived a halfway plausible story for the King's Parliament in Dublin to act. The blow would be swift, irrevocable, and mortal.

To say that King Henry was clever, conceited, egotistical, and crafty was to recount only a few of the lusty monarch's traits. For Henry hadn't strutted proud and haughty demonstrating his might before the French King, Francis I, or shown his contempt for the Emperor of the Holy Roman Empire, or so boldly and persistently defied the Vicar of Christ, His Holiness Pope Clement VII, just for the sake of lording it over his tiresome enemies. On the contrary, Henry's motives were much more subtle. His greatest desire was to achieve absolute authority. It was not enough for him to be head of the State, he had taken unto himself the title of spiritual head as well.

And to establish his august and exalted status in the eyes of all, he surrounded himself in lavish, extravagant pageantry. Thus, he impressed those who beheld him. His natural physical build, for in his youth he was tall, erect, and handsome, added a further dimension to this awesome presence. One did not need to meet Henry more than once to be struck by his forceful character and grandiose appearance. Added to his physical attributes were those of a clever, shrewd intelligence. Henry was capable of challenging all and beating them at their own games. He was well read and had a quick, logical mind, all of which only confirmed the illusion of his unlimited potential, his Omnipotence.

Although he was in his declining years when Magheen was presented to the Monarch, still, he did leave an indelible impression on her mind. She realized that like other men, Henry's sensual appetites might be stirred at the sight of a beautiful young woman, yet, unlike other men, Henry knew when and how to use his conquests to his unique advantage. Although Magheen was aware that Henry would have ulterior motives for his actions, her perception of his 'modus operandi' was naive at best.

Magheen had barely left the Palace when Henry summoned his Lord Chancellor, Wriothesley. This gentleman, who had the effrontery to arrest even the Queen and her ladies-in-waiting in the gardens at Whitehall, was well qualified to ferret out any gossip. He would deem it an honor to cast aspersions on the noble house of Ormond and all who had any connections with it.

Henry went to bed satisfied. He would enjoy this game; the fair Magheen...so young, so confident....

Twenty-Eight

Henry limped toward the tall mullioned windows and stood for a moment looking down on the murky waters of the Thames. Slowly, he shifted his gaze and with cloudy eyes scanned the opposite bank. Eventually he focused on a dark cloud in the leaden sky. Was the dismal morning simply reflecting the stygian darkness of a brooding monarch's mind? Henry was indeed troubled.

"A pox on them," he muttered. Would he never be rid of the agitators? Just when he thought he had cleansed the Irish nation of its ulcerous sores, when he felt sure he had eradicated the cause of the distemper, the disloyal and treacherous House of Kildare, he found another festering abrasion, The House of Ormond.

"Christ's blood, I'll have an end of it," he shouted. He turned abruptly. The narrow, stiff, linen ruff irritated his stocky neck and his stomacher was ill-fitting. "I'll hang them all, I swear it." He shuffled towards his tram. He was spending more and more of his time of late confined to that confounded chair.

"Hoby!" The King roared for one of the gentlemen of the Privy Chamber. Sir Philip Hoby came in haste.

"Sire?"

"Send Wriothesly to me at once."

* * * *

The Butler family and their servants were preparing to return home. They had planned to leave early the following morning. The older folk were not really looking forward to the long, tiresome journey, for it would take several days of cross-country travel and then, depending on the weather, the slow sailing ship could take another day before it reached Roslair Harbor in Wexford. The final stretch to their lovely castle home on the Suir River they hoped could be accomplished in one day.

Magheen was rested and ready to make the best of the discomforts that were inevitable. She didn't mind the ruts and holes that jolted the carriage. Long hours on Leprechaun's back had been training enough for the English roads. As she helped Noreen with the packing, her thoughts were on weightier matters. She was disappointed that her sojourn in the English capital and her interview with the King had borne so little fruit. She had been, she felt, dismissed too readily from the royal presence. Had she displeased His Majesty? She hardly thought her personal appearance could have given the vain monarch displeasure. No, he had praised her beauty. Perhaps her words? A little too brash, too outspoken? Considering the time she had at her disposal, she had no choice. There was no guarantee that another invitation would be forthcoming. Disturbed by what she considered had been an unproductive meeting, she decided to request a private audience with the King. Someone had to speak frankly and without further delay about the situation in Ireland.

Considering how she might accomplish such a venture, Magheen was seated on a stool in the embrasure of the great mullioned window of her bedroom when she heard the commotion. As she was about to satisfy her curiosity, Noreen knocked on her door.

"Beggin' ye pardon m'Lady, but...but...b-b."

"What's the matter, Noreen?"

"A highwayman, Mother o' God I'm sure he's robbin' all before him at this very moment."

"You mean to tell me that there's a thief in the house? Gather your senses together, Noreen. How could he have gained entrance? You must be mistaken."

"Oh, no. No mistake. I saw him with my own two eyes. A big man with a black cloak, an' a black mask on his face." She was trembling.

"Well, for one thing, Noreen, highwaymen don't come breaking into houses. The very name should tell you they confine themselves to the roads." Magheen tried to calm her maid, but she couldn't convince her.

"What shall we do? He's locked up with His Lordship."

"Locked up! What do you mean?"

Before Magheen could get any more information, Dermud appeared in the open doorway. He glanced around the room to be sure there was no one else present. Then he quickly told her what had taken place.

'Tis Sir Edward come to tell us to leave without delay...."

Magheen's cheeks lost their delicate coloring. "You mean?"

"Yes, we're in grave danger," he kissed her forehead. "We leave within the hour."

"Oh sweet Jesus! Now, what did I tell ye, m'Lady Magheen. We'll be all killed! We surely will."

"Hush, Noreen." Dermud's words were sharp and immediately had their desired effect.

"So the snake bares his fangs; the chameleon has already changed his colors." Magheen's face registered her disgust and anger.

James Butler had arrived outside the door. His face was drawn and there was a pallid look about his cheeks unlike anything Magheen had ever seen before.

"Are you all right, Father?"

Magheen went to his side and put her arm on his shoulder.

"Ah, I'm just tired, a gra. Tired of all the comings and goings. And a great longing for the peace and serenity of our old home."

"Now, Father, come. No need to be trying to hide the truth from us. Dermud has told us all," answered Magheen.

"Oh, so you know, then." His voice had a hollow ring.

"Perhaps we should leave tonight, Father?" Dermud asked.

The concerned tone caused the older man to raise his head and look his son straight in the eyes. He pondered a moment before answering. "Your suggestion, son, although it would be difficult for your mother and Magheen, is not without merit. We would have the advantage of the night to evade any pursuers. Any edge that we might put between ourselves and, shall we say, the friends of the Crown, would be to our advantage."

"And what of our dear friends, the Earl and Lady Harcourt?

What of their position here?" Magheen asked seething with anger. She had managed to control herself to this point in her concern for their aging hosts.

"I wonder if they would consider leaving with us?" asked Dermud.

"I'll ask," responded his father.

The Earl patted Magheen's hand before turning to leave.

Dermud stepped forward. "Father, why don't you sit down a moment. Here." He offered the shaken old man a chair. "I'll go find His Lordship and...."

"Someone wants to find me? Here I am." The cracked voice of the Earl of Harcourt was heard in the hallway outside.

James Butler did not hear the Earl; he was lost in his own thoughts. "Surely," he asked aloud, "surely Henry doesn't intend to cut us down without a word of warning, without a chance to even hear of what crimes he thinks us guilty?"

"Speak not so lustily, dear Sir." The Earl of Harcourt broke in on James Butler's monologue. "Although I'll wager my fortune, what's left of it, on the loyalty and faithfulness of my household servants, yet one cannot be too cautious."

"Eh? Ah, my good friend. Yes, yes of course, I forget where I am."

"I understand. Believe me, I do understand your apprehension. I wish there was something I could do to assure you. Forgive me, but I overheard your conversation just now. My advice to you is to delay your departure from here no longer than is absolutely necessary. I regret to see you go under such conditions, but I would be no friend of yours if I told you otherwise. As for me, my place is here. I'll not run like a rabbit before the royal hare. Anyway, Harry has no need of me or mine any more. He's already taken all I had of worth. No doubt, he'll leave me my white hairs to carry with me to my grave. But you, m'Lord and your family." He hesitated a moment, looked at Magheen and Dermud, and again directed his words to James. "These young folk, m'Lord, they must be protected." Then the Earl drew near to James and lowered his voice. "I do not wish to alarm the womenfolk, but you must go, my dear, dear friend, as quickly as possible." There was genuine fear in the aging eyes of the old Earl.

James Butler looked at his long-time friend a moment. Magheen saw the moisture gathering in the corners of his eyes. He withdrew a handkerchief, then turned his head and blew his nose. His lips trembled, and as he began to speak there was a quaver in his voice. "'Tis done then.... We'll away within the hour."

The Earl of Harcourt nodded. "I'll see you then within the hour to bid you all Godspeed."

* * * *

The carriage drew up abruptly at the southwest city gate. It was closed.

"Whoa there! Whoa!" shouted Hal.

"W'at 'ave we 'ere? Some fine runaway 'orses, is it?" The guard at the gate stepped from the relative shelter of his lean-to. He looked at the horses appraisingly, spat on the wet cobble stones at his feet, and rolled a clove around in his mouth as he eyed the animals. He spat again and ambled towards the carriage speaking to Hal.

"'Pon me word, them be the finest pair I've laid eyes on today. Bein' as yer in such a 'urry, it occurs to me 'ows ye might 'ave come be them illegal like."

"Of all the nerve!" Hal was incensed.

"Oh, God!" whispered Lady Eleanor. "Is it a ruse? Is the man merely delaying us?"

"Easy, my dear," her husband counseled.

"It's best I speak," said Dermud. "Better to know where we stand."

Magheen, seated beside her husband, swallowed hard. Then a surge of anger filled her breast, stifling her fear, she blurted out, "This is insufferable." Impulsively, she drew aside the leather flaps that protected the occupants from the night air. "What's the matter, Hal? Why are we being delayed? You know we'll not make our destination in time at this rate."

"Well now. So, 'tis gentle folk that bees in a 'igh and mighty 'urry. Beggin' yer pardon an' all, but ain't it some'at late for such fine gentry to be abroad. 'Taint safe fer the likes o' ye." He smiled showing a large gap in the uneven line of his teeth.

Lady Eleanor was petrified. She felt sure they would, at any moment, be surrounded by soldiers and led back in disgrace to the Tower.

Magheen was livid. This fellow was brash. He had no business questioning them....unless....yes, he could have been warned!

The insolent guard drew closer to Magheen. The odors from his dirty clothes and unwashed body were nauseating, revoltingly so. Under his woolen cap, the long, stringy, greasy ends of his salt and pepper hair easily turned the drops of heavy drizzle. Magheen opened her mouth to speak, but he interrupted her.

"My! We do 'ave a beauty 'ere. I say, a real beauty! W'at wouldn't I give to 'ave the likes o' ye, luv, warmin' me bed." Slowly, deliberately, he cleared his throat. Then he spat again. Magheen wasn't squeamish, but this fellow was disgusting.

James Butler could take no more. "Look here, my good man, we have guests awaiting us. I don't want any more of your insolence or His Majesty will hear of this night's rudeness."

At the mention of His Majesty, the man stepped backward. He couldn't risk losing his position.

The Earl saw that his words had their desired effect. "Now let us pass at once and be done with it. Hal, move on."

The guard hesitated. He looked sullenly at the occupants of the carriage and then once more at the horses. "Not so fast, Sir. Bein' as I just got word to be on the lookout for...."

"Aw!" Lady Eleanor gasped. All color left her face. She was near to fainting. Her body went limp against her husband.

"Hal!" The Earl's voice was sharp.

The horses bolted forward. The carriage jolted, almost leaped to catch up. Not a word was spoken till they were well on their way. The experience had drained them of all emotion.

It was the Earl who at length broke the silence. He had been supporting the weight of his wife's body in the circle of his arm ever since she felt faint. Now with the reassurance that they were indeed free and out of the confines of the city, she moved. Her eyes showed appreciation and love as she looked at her husband.

"Feeling better, my love?" James asked. She answered with a nod.

"What a blundering idiot! I wonder what was his game?" Magheen asked.

"I got the feeling he was on the lookout for some stolen horses, or I should say, 'orses," James answered, trying to make light of their situation. With the release of tension all laughed nervously.

The night was cold. A chilly east wind brought with it a stinging bite from the North Sea. For the first hour or two, as the carriage lumbered through sleazy back alleys, squalid side lanes, and the darkest, loneliest roads leading out of the city, it seemed that they had beaten Henry's hounds.

Shortly after midnight and well away from the city limits, the driver, Hal, who was a trusted servant of the Harcourt household, slowed down a pace. It would not do to push the horses too hard.

Dermud peered into the blackness and cocked his ear as he stuck his head out of the carriage. "There's not a soul abroad this foul night but ourselves. We can thank the Lord for the weather; it, by God's help, favors us. He closed the leather flaps against the driving rain and moved back into his seat. The small tallow candle flickered on its unsteady sconce as a cold draft reached inside the protective glass frame.

Dermud ran his hand through his disheveled locks as he looked at his mother's pale, drawn face. Bending forward, he took her hand. Then giving it a little squeeze and smiling into her face he said; "Try not to worry, Mother. God is on our side. We'll be all right, you'll see."

Lady Eleanor's forced smile didn't deceive anyone. "I know, my dear, I know."

"If we travel all night and try to continue into tomorrow, we can make Portsmouth by evening. There's bound to be a ship leaving for some Irish port." Magheen offered what comfort she could.

"Aye, we could even take passage for France or Spain if it comes to that. We've got many friends on the Continent. Try to rest now, Mother," Dermud reassured.

"I'll do that, Son." So saying she closed her eyes, as much to try to convince her children that she trusted their judgment as to be alone with her own thoughts and prayers.

With the Lady Eleanor's fears allayed, tension eased somewhat within the carriage. They had cleverly eluded Henry's spies, and, as far as they could tell there was, at this point at least, no one on their heels.

Magheen felt a queasy feeling in the pit of her stomach, however. Her armpits were wet with perspiration and despite the east wind, which kept the interior of the carriage cold, tiny beads trickled down the shapely cleavage between her breasts. But it was the pain and fury within her heart which caused her the greatest discomfort. She was furious that the family should be treated so ignominiously. Like common criminals they were forced to flee. Even at that moment they were probably being followed. What might happen to them if they were caught; only God knew. She pondered the events of the preceding days. Henry's questions, each nuance, every gesture. They had surely entered a viper's nest; even contemplating the analogy made her shudder.

Then she thought of the inconvenience, the hardships she and her family had undergone to present themselves at the English Court. And now to have to scurry across the country like frightened animals was more than her pride could take. It was monstrous! She felt humiliated. As her anger grew, she tried desperately to keep a calm exterior. She knew it would only upset everyone. She, therefore, kept her thoughts to herself.

The carriage rumbled on, mile after weary mile into the darkness of the night. The Earl was unable to keep his eyes open. Now and then, despite his attempts to stay awake, Magheen noticed how his head would lop forward. When a jolt or a sharp turn in the road would arouse him, he would open his eyes quickly, sit bolt upright and check to see that all was well. The Lady Eleanor, on the other hand, although she had her eyes closed, was wide awake. Each movement of the carriage reverberated in her sensitive frame. It would have been an exhausting journey for her at the best of times. Now, Magheen knew as she looked at her, that every mile and each moment were excruciating pain and agony.

The atmosphere within the carriage was again tense. She could feel Dermud's rigid body beside hers. He, who never said much would, she knew, feel all the more. The responsibility for the family's safety weighed heavily on his slender shoulders.

She studied the fair features of her young husband. In the faint light, he appeared even younger than his twenty years. His black satin jacket, severely cut ,emphasized his slender physique. The small white lace cravat held in place by a golden pin was a close match to the pallor of his skin. His blond hair was drawn back and tied by a black velvet ribbon at the nape of his neck. Reserved, serious, and somewhat aloof with strangers, with his family, he was not quite at home. The long years of separation perhaps, Magheen concluded. With her, a certain delicate formality, an almost timid reverence. She couldn't help comparing him with another....fiery, passionate, warm, unrestrained....the months hadn't cooled her ardent desires; on the contrary, her lonely nights were filled with thoughts of what might have been.

Magheen's thoughts returned to herself. She had hoped to achieve so much but in reality she had accomplished nothing. In her darkest moments she could not have envisioned anything to equal their present plight. Henry was no more than a scheming, cunning tyrant for all his gifts of mind, for all his talents. He had, she had learned to her utter disappointment and chagrin, no feeling, no sympathy at all for Ireland or the Irish. His only interest was to drag whatever he could out of the country, enrich his coffers to pad his pockets, and to pay off some of the stupendous debts with which he had saddled himself and his own country by imposing hardships on her land and its people. Slowly, as Magheen's mind dwelled on these thoughts, she came to the realization that to even consider peaceful methods in dealing with the Sasanach would be futile.

The scudding clouds had, by this time, formed a bank of blackness that hung dense and heavy overhead. The weary eyes of James Butler looked out at the night sky.

"We're in for it!" Dermud voiced his father's thoughts.

James drew his lips together and nodded his head. In his heart he prayed that Dermud might be right. If the cursed weather were indeed with them, then surely God was on their side.

On a lonely side road outside the village of Esher, the Earl ordered the carriage stopped, a short rest for the horses and few minutes for the family members to stretch their legs before the storm unleashed its worst would be a welcome respite.

It was then that Magheen's overstimulated mind and acute sense of hearing made her aware that they were not the only travelers abroad at that late hour. At first, it sounded like a roll of thunder away in the distance. Then, as the minutes passed, the sounds became quite clear and Magheen could detect the galloping hoofs of several horses.

"My God! Horsemen! They're in pursuit, Father!" She ran toward the carriage and Lady Eleanor as they spoke to each other.

James Butler listened. Every nerve tense, his whole body straining; he sought to verify Magheen's words. He looked around.

A short distance further along the road, it appeared as if there might be a large grove of trees.

"Better get the carriage out of sight till these fellows go by, Hal. Quick, quench the lantern and the candle and get us to the shelter of those trees over yonder."

"Oh, James, whatever shall we do? We'll all be killed. I surely don't want to die here in this horrible country." Eleanor's face was drained of all color. In her sad blue eyes could be seen the anguish that gripped her heart. From under her large Spanish hood, a few strands of silver hair always so meticulously groomed, had somehow managed to escape the fine teeth of her ivory combs.

"Now don't you be getting all upset, my love. We'll be all right." James did his best to assure her. He took her cold hands in his and held them to his lips an instant. Their eyes met, and his communicated love and courage.

"My Love, there's more chance you'll die of cold this very minute than anything else. Here, put those icicles into that muff of yours at once." James pulled the fur muff, which had slipped to one side, into position and placed her icy hands within the soft, luxurious folds.

They had reached the trees and pulled well out of sight of the road just as the thundering horses galloped by.

Magheen, tight-lipped, awaited Dermud's return. He had stayed behind near the fork of the road to watch from the shelter of a clump of bushes. As the riders drew near, he saw, without a doubt, that they were picked men of His Majesty's cavalry. He shrank back and crouched low, well-hidden in the thick damp foliage; he could hear his pounding heart. The cold, clammy moisture which soaked his inner garments was not caused by the wet grasses. He had to make certain of the route the horsemen intended to take. Slipping quietly from his hiding place, Dermud ran as quickly as he could along the swampy ditch while keeping to the cover of the overhanging bushes. At the crossroads, he saw the horse soldiers draw up, hesitate for a moment and then, on command, take the road for Portsmouth. Panting, Dermud reached the carriage door. "It seems....they're....headed for Portsmouth."

"Then they're not out for the good of their health," his father answered.

"They're after us and that's for sure."

"Oh, merciful God preserve us," cried Eleanor.

"Well, praise be to God, we've evaded them so far, at any rate," was her husband's retort as he looked at his wife. "Now we'll change our plans, we'll give them the slip once more."

"What do you intend to do, Father?" asked Dermud.

"'Tis for Southampton we'll be making track now. Once we get there, we can make discrete enquiries regarding passage on some ship," answered his father as he turned to his wife and Magheen. He continued, "We'll be all right now. God's merciful. He's saved us this far and He'll be with us to the end." He then kissed both women and helped them settle more comfortably in the drafty carriage.

It turned out to be a most miserable night. The sullen clouds unleashed their pent-up anger shortly after the travelers had again gained the main road. The wind picked up momentum and the rains beat furiously at whatever caught their fancy. Gusts and squalls of even greater intensity punctuated the persistent and continual downpour. Several times the carriage lurched and swayed at dangerous angles, and its occupants, scared, apprehensive, weary from lack of sleep and the exertions of the long, fearful night, were thrown forward or sideways according to the thrust.

Eventually, as the first light of dawn sneaked through sheets of driving rain, the carriage came to the outskirts of the small village of Farndale.

The driver stopped and descended from his place to determine what his passengers wished to do. "Mornin', m'Lord. We be acomin' to Farndale. 'Tis maybe a place to stop for a bite to eat and a rest. Them 'orses be plain tuckered out, m'Lord."

"Yes, yes indeed, Hal, my good man. That's a splendid idea. Just keep your eyes open when we enter the village, you understand?"

"Depend on it, Sir. I care nought for an untimely death either."

Farndale was not an exceptional place, just another country town. Grouped around the village green were the church, dating back to Norman times, a forge of uncertain origin, a conical roofed tavern, and a sleepy, run-down inn. The narrow cobbled streets which led to the green were flanked by wooden shops and the shabby wooden or stone homes of tradesmen, businessmen, and farmers. Across the River Wye by the narrow stone bridge, the stately mansions of the local gentry were carefully situated with ample acreage to ensure privacy.

Hal knocked on the inn door. After several attempts to rouse the innkeeper, he was about to give up when, in desperation, he pounded one last time on the bleached wooden planks.

"Not so loud, not so loud. Forgotten yer manners....'ave ee? W'at be yer business?" The door had been opened slowly by a sleepy, stocky man in a striped night shift and a dirty nightcap.

From within, the stale air escaped and assailed Hal's nostrils. 'Twas no fit place for his gentle passengers, Hal thought. And, then again, maybe just such an unlikely hole in the wall would offer them more protection.

"Speak up, man. I doh want to catch me death o'cold. Is it food or lodgin' yer wantin?"

"Food in a hurry and two fresh horses. Food enough for five people, two ladies and three gentlemen, includin' meself."

"Hah! I'll say nothin' about that last remark. Ye 'ave a mighty tall order for such an' ungodly hour. It ain't a fittin' time to be seekin' vitals," the proprietor answered.

"I've wasted enough time with ye already. Can ye supply our needs or can't ye?" snapped Hal.

"Not so fast." The innkeeper rubbed his eyes with the back of his right hand. "'Tis an unreasonable request at this time o' the mornin', but...." He studied Hal from half-closed eyes. "You say 'tis gentle folk be needin' food an' drink. Eh?"

"Aye, an' they'll pay well."

The proprietor instantly became more interested.

"But they'll not wait forever for yer services."

"We'll have them a fine breakfast in no time. In no time at all." Wide awake now, the innkeeper's shrewd mind was fast calculating the extra profits he might yet squeeze from his unsuspecting genteel guests.

"How soon can we have fresh horses?"

"Oh, I'll have the stable boy look to them immediately. But," he hesitated, "they'll not come cheap."

"They'll be two good horses in exchange. So don't ye go pullin' any fast ones."

"Ain't no under 'and dealin's in this 'ere inn, I'll 'ave ee know."

"Good, that's w'at I likes to 'ear, mate."

With that, the burly fellow turned and made his way into the dim interior of the inn, hollering as he went, to his missus and son.

When finally the greasy breakfast was served by a garrulous, middle-aged woman, the Lady Eleanor was too exhausted to eat much. She had a most frightful headache and wanted only a place to lay her head for just a few hours. "I don't like that woman. She talks too much," she said when they got a moment to themselves.

"I don't like the way she looks at us either. She's snooping. She'd certainly know us again if ever we came this way," said Magheen.

"'Tis best we not delay," said the Earl. "Hal, go check that groom, if you please."

"Aye, m'Lord. I'll skin him alive if he's been loafin'."

Twenty-Nine

They reached Southampton late that night. It had been a hard journey for everybody, but no one complained. They were too grateful to be still safe and together to think of anything else. Stopping in what appeared to be a sequestered alley not too far from the wharf, the Butler family remained quietly in the carriage while Hal went to the docks to make discrete inquiries regarding the destination of vessels leaving on the next tide.

He walked the length of the docks with eyes and ears alert. After several futile attempts on his part to gain information, he eventually learned that the only ship leaving within the next twenty-four hours was a small Dutch trading vessel bound for the port of Amsterdam. Before boarding to make the necessary arrangements with the Captain, Hal decided to take one more look around.

It was very dark. Fortunately, however, the rain had ceased. The strong wind, still blowing from the east, brushed vigorously against the light growth that now covered Hal's sallow face. Pulling his cloak more closely about him, he was about to retrace his steps to the Dutch ship when his sharp ears picked up a few words of conversation which made his heartbeat quicken.

"Sure, I couldn't a done better meself, man. 'Tis grand, grand entirely. Me pretty Kathleen 'ill be charmed."

Hal turned to see two men standing near an assortment of boxes and trunks. One held a woman's shawl, while the other held a lantern raised on high. The man holding the shawl was speaking as he examined it. There was no mistaking that accent. Hal stepped up to them. "Beggin' yer pardon, Sir." He spoke to the man with the shawl. “I couldn’t help overhearing your conversation an’ I gather that you’re Irish.”

“I am indeed, Sir. An’ what is that to you? Kevin O’Grady’s the name.”

“Hal, Hal Hart, Sir.” Hal drew closer. He lowered his voice. “I thought perhaps that you might know whether or not there is a ship bound for Ireland in these waters?”

“Well, now, if it’s Ireland’s green shores you’re wanting to see, sure you’ve come to the right man. Yerrah, isn’t the lovely *Kathleen Mavourneen,* herself, sailing on the next tide.”

Hal’s face lit up. “Oh, am I glad to meet you, Mr. O’Grady. But, tell me where is this vessel docked. I’d like to meet the captain.”

“Well, Mr. Hart, the latter question poses no difficulty at all, for you have the honor, Sir, to be lookin’ at him, but with the former there’s a slight problem.”

“Oh?” Hal’s confusion was obvious. The Irish were impossible. How could any plain-talking Englishman follow their meaning?

“Ye see, it’s like this....”

At this juncture, Kevin O’Grady, Captain of the *Kathleen Mavourneen,* launched into a lengthy and vividly descriptive account of how he had happened on a “spot o’ bad weather.” He concluded his fifth retelling for that day of his extraordinary prowess and his gallant stand in the face of unnatural odds with the words: “An’ the long an’ the short of it, my good friend, is that my queen o’ the seas is in the dry dock for the past four days now.”

Hal’s countenance showed his disappointment.

“I thought perhaps...well, I’ll have to...” Hal soliloquized. He put out his hand as if to bid the Irishman farewell.

“Then you’ve changed yer mind about seein’ Ireland, have ye?”

“Oh, no, no, not at all. It’s just that I had hoped to obtain passage on a ship leavin’ soon...tonight, if possible.”

“An’ sure what have I been tellin’ ye all this time? Haven’t I been informing ye that none other than the be-au-ti-ful *Kathleen Mavourneed*, herself, will be sailin’ at five o’ the clock tomorrow mornin’.”

My God, the Irish were exasperating! Why couldn’t the man have said so initially. It could have saved time and energy, thought Hal.

He relaxed somewhat, but before he spoke he peered into the darkness. There were men coming and going. A drunken sailor was being taken aboard his ship by his less intoxicated comrades. The churly fellow wasn't very cooperative and the operation had all the aspects of being a lengthy one.

Hal's attention returned to his new-found friends. As he was about to speak, he noticed some figures crouching in the shadows. Probably loafers waiting their chance to steal whatever was left unguarded, he thought. He drew nearer to O'Grady, lowering his voice to a whisper. "I'm lookin' for passage for some of your countrymen."

"Ah, sure if it's Irish, they are, they're entirely welcome. But how many are ye talkin' about for the *Kathleen Mavoureen* isn't the *Henry Grace a Dieu* or even *The Mary Rose,* I'll have you be knowing. Although there isn't a finer ship in her class for all that."

"Five, two men, three women," Hal said guardedly.

"Women! Oh, glory be to God! Where in heaven's name would I be puttin' women? Sure...."

"Sh-h-h-h. Ye, don't want them to hear ye' in Whitehall." Hal was alarmed. This Kevin O'Grady would certainly have them all arrested.

At the mention of Whitehall, Kevin's attitude changed. He scrutinized the man in front of him. Hal detected the anxiety. "An' the name of me countrymen?" he inquired.

"Butler...the Earl."

"Aw." The redheaded Irishman scratched his curly brow and raised his eyebrows. For a moment he was silent, then his old confidence returned. "Sir, as I perceive it, that alters the picture entirely. Sure how could I be accommodatin' the likes of them folk on board me little tub?"

"Now, Mr. O'Grady, ye don't understand. Ye may be the means of savin' their lives." There was pleading in Hal's voice.

"What? What's that yer sayin'? Ye mean the Earl...?"

"Sh-h-h-h, if you don't hold yer voice down we'll all end up..." Hal didn't finish his sentence. The dull sound of iron on cobblestones froze the words in his throat.

"My God, man! What is it?" asked O'Grady.

As the horsemen drew near, O'Grady grabbed the shawl from

his mate and thrust it into Hal's hands. He raised his voice.

"Well, I doh know. But if it's the best you've got.... I suppose...."

The soldiers were now but a few feet away. "I'm talkin' to *you.* What's yer name."

"Is it me, you're addressin'?" O'Grady, cool and collected, turned to face the mounted soldier. "Well, now, ye have the honor gentlemen, to be talkin' to none other than the great O'Grady, himself. Kevin O'Grady, to be exact, from the lush green fields of the County Cork." As Kevin introduced himself he bowed low and made a sweeping gesture with his free left hand feigning respect for his superiors. The horse soldier interrupted him. "Hah! Well, Mr. O'Grady, if that's yer name, forget the chatter and state yer business here."

"Well, now, an' isn't it a most peculiar question to be askin' an honest man."

The soldier was about to lose patience but O'Grady sensed it; the quick-witted Corkman lost no time in turning his song and dance to suit the ears of his audience. "But since you, Sir, are also an honest man an' about the business of the law, I'll be for answerin' yer question. Ye see, Sir, I've a mind te buy me a real nice shawleen for the loveliest...."

The soldier perceiving that O'Grady was about to indulge in a lengthy panegyric, no doubt on the incomparable charms and beauty of some Irish colleen, cut him off.

"Then you'll be returnin' to Ireland soon, me good man?" The soldier changed his tone. He might get more information from this bliddering Irish fool if he were less aggressive, he thought.

"Sure an' I will," answered O'Grady.

"An' how do you propose to do that? I don't see any Irish ship in port at this time?" The soldier was watching closely for Kevin's reaction.

"Well, ye see, that's the trouble."

Hal drew in his breath, then gulped. Should he speak up and try to save the day. But before he could open his mouth, O'Grady was spinning another yarn. Hal was simply amazed at the man's eloquence and presence of mind. No wonder his countrymen were having difficulties with the Irish.

"But I thought I might be lucky like, an' find me a place on...."

His interrogator interrupted again. "So ye don't know of a ship leaving for Ireland then?"

"You're a right smart man, that I can see. Sure wouldn't I be on such a ship this very minute instead of standin' here in this miserable cold. No, Sir, you're perfectly right. To my eternal sorrow I have to abide in this foreign land another day an'...."

The soldier was anxious to be on his way. He had wasted enough time with Kevin O'Grady already. Obviously a mercenary returning home after a sojourn in England or on the Continent, not worth bothering with. But before he left he decided to question the other two. "An' you, you're for Ireland too?" he said, addressing Kevin's companion, Colm.

"Aye, that I am, but as me friend was tellin' ye...."

"Yes, yes. I bid ye good night." The soldier could take no more.

"What de ye think of that, man? Not an Irish ship in the blasted port." As soon as the soldier left, O'Grady opened his big mouth and exploded in a riotous laugh. Watching the expression on Hal's face, who was as nervous as a horse facing fire by this time, O'Grady could no longer contain himself. He hadn't had so much excitement since his *Kathleen Mavourneen* was taking the worst of the Irish Sea. "Yerrah, take it easy man, no need to fret."

Hal's hand shook as he handed back the shawl. O'Grady spoke, "Beggin' yer pardon, Mr. Hart, but the English are such bloody fools. Sure it's easy for an Irishman te diddle them right before their very eyes." Then he good-naturedly slapped Hal on the shoulder. "Have the goods here by the fourth watch an' we'll take 'em aboard an' sail away under the very noses o' the Sasanach."

Hal, still not convinced that everything would work out as smoothly as the cocky Irishman envisioned, nevertheless returned with the news that he had indeed secured passage on an Irish ship. He did not give the details. 'Twere best not to tempt fate. And besides, this bloody nerve-wracking business was getting to him. Every extra hour that these Butlers were on English soil meant that much extra time for the authorities to track them down and with them, Hal Hart.

There was still about three hours to wait before boarding the *Kathleen Mavourneen*. So much could happen in that time. He, Hal, had escaped the soldiers once; he might not be so lucky the next time. He crouched in a doorway. In its relative protection, he waited alone with his thoughts, but his guard was up. He was alert to every sound. What he would do in an emergency, he did not know, but at least he wouldn't be caught napping.

To say that the next three hours of waiting were a nightmare to the Butler family would fall far short of the reality. They had chosen the most secluded spot they could find. At the end of an alley where the houses leaned so closely together that it was impossible for any light or air ever to penetrate the filthy blackness, they waited and agonized in silence. The stench was dreadful. The filth and squalor that surrounded them indescribable. Their cramped quarters and the biting cold added to their physical discomfort. But these aggravations could scarcely be compared to their agonies of mind and heart. Petrified with fear and unable to do anything to alleviate their perilous plight, they waited in utter misery as slowly, so very slowly, each minute faded into eternity.

"Hail Mary..." a faint cry escaped the lips of the Lady Eleanor as she told her beads over and over. Magheen's heart went out to her, to have come to this in her later years. This lady of refined tastes and breeding, used to a life of ease and comfort, would be unable to take much more.

Her father-in-law, Magheen imagined as he sat across from her in the darkness, was composed, serene. With his venerable head resting against the upholstery, his eyes closed, she knew he had placed himself in the Hands of God and now awaited, with a peaceful and resigned heart, whatever the heavenly Father had in store for him.

Her husband, Dermud, was not so calm. He, like herself, was very young. He should have, by right, many long years of happiness ahead of him, years in which to see his family, many sons and daughters, grow. Years when he might yet know the meaning and fullness of love.

As if he devined her thoughts, Dermud reached out for her hand. It was cold. "Magheen, my darling...." His words were barely audible.

Magheen stroked his cheek with her free hand. It was damp.

Deep in her heart, she resolved that if they reached home safely she would try to make up to him for the moments they had missed during the past six months. So many opportunities in which to tell him how much he really meant to her. She would try to banish Hugo from her thoughts forever and give herself completely to her gentle husband.

The little serving girl, Noreen, jumped to her feet in terror. A small suppressed cry started up in her throat. Then trembling, she huddled back in the corner where she had remained speechless ever since they had left London the night before. An alley cat had found a mate. Magheen could imagine the girl now, her wild blue eyes darting nervously from side to side. "It's all right," she tried to assure her, "only a cat."

Magheen's active mind knew no rest. The harsh reality of the past twenty-four hours, the realization of what was happening to her and her family was gradually reshaping her thoughts. She felt as if a great tide were sweeping her along in a totally new and unexpected direction. So completely alien to all she had experienced, it seemed that the last terrifying days and this agonizing nocturnal ordeal had utterly transformed her. Some metamorphic process had been at work in those long grueling hours as she fled like a wild thing through the English countryside.

She had come to England hoping to achieve where others had failed. Maybe that was her mistake. Could she really have been so naive? Did she honestly hope to have succeeded where even her own grandfather, Con, had not? How humiliating it must have been for him to surrender his title of The O'Neill for that of Earl of Tyrone, to bow his proud knee to an English monarch. But he had done so only because he had felt he could gain time for himself and some semblance of peace and security for his people.

Magheen saw now that her hopes and aspirations had been nothing more than empty dreams. She had spent so much time and energy in building sand castles. And, like a small child who had labored all day, she was forced to stand by helplessly as the tides of avarice and injustice came crashing in, destroying all.

As Magheen continued to ponder, the servile fear that had at first gripped her heart and held it bound had now given way to anger. She was furious. And, as this inner fire leaped higher exploding into a great conflagration, it enkindled this deep-seated passion that had hitherto lain dormant in Magheen's breast. This living flame, this all consuming vehement inferno devoured every other sensibility in Magheen's soul. She felt she was somehow free, no longer susceptible to mere external forces. She had suddenly and irrevocably been raised above the puerile world and thrust into the realm of the virile. Let England unleash its bloodhounds; let it do its worst. She, Magheen Ni Neill-Butler would fight, would deal the Sasanach back blow for blow. She would fight to the death.

It was in this state of mind that Magheen stepped down from the carriage shortly after the town crier in the distance announced the hour of four o'clock. With head held high in defiance, she aided Noreen along. The poor creature was so terrified she could hardly put one foot in front of the other.

The plan was to get each member of the family safely on board. At the last minute the luggage could be deposited beside the other boxes on the quay and Hal would then be free to drive off as speedily as possible.

They were almost to the end of the alley. A few steps more and they would reach a wide thoroughfare, where they were to split up. Hal would escort Magheen and Nora one way to the ship while the Earl, the countess, and Dermud would go by another route. They awaited Hal's return; he had gone ahead to check things out.

Their bodies pressed close to the black sleeping houses, the Butlers scarcely breathed.

"Pssss...." It was Hal. Gasping, he brought the horrifying news that soldiers had boarded the *Kathleen Mavourneen* shortly after she pulled into the quay wall.

It was all the distraught family needed to hear. Had they come this far only to be caught at the eleventh hour?

Magheen inched her way forward. "I'm going to try," she announced.

"Easy Lass. There has to be a better way," said the Earl.

It was then that Hal produced some old clothes, a cap, and two pairs of men's breeches.

"There has been a change of plans." The servant was obviously embarrassed. He fumbled with the clothes.

"Beggin' yer pardon, m'Lady, but...eh...Mr. O'Grady suggested that one of the women should wear these...He thinks it would be easier for her to come aboard as one of his crew."

"Very well," said Magheen, "I'll don the garb." She immediately took the clothes and drew back into the shelter of the nearest doorway to change.

Hal then turned to face the Earl. "These, m'Lord," Hal hesitated. "'Tis not right...I declare the man's mad!"

"Come, come, Hal. Let me be the judge of that. What does he want?"

"Well, m'Lord, he...he thought perhaps if you...if you would assume the role of a drunken sailor."

"So that's it. If we weren't in such danger, I'd find the part amusing." The Earl chuckled to himself. "A drunken sailor is it? Then a drunken sailor 'twill be." The Earl took the clothes.

"We'll do exactly as Mr. O'Grady suggests. He's our only hope."

The women would go first. The men, keeping close to the buildings, would watch their progress. It was decided that the Lady Eleanor would pretend to be Hal's wife and if stopped he would do all the talking. Their story was that they were seeing their son and daughter off on the Dutch ship.

With palpitating hearts, the four started out. Magheen, determined to face danger with unflinching courage and proud defiance, gripped Noreen's arm firmly. With her own clothes wrapped in a bundle and slung over her shoulder, a knitted woolen cap pulled well down over her hair, she fairly looked the part of a right comely young lad.

They had reached the open area which divided the sleazy waterfront taverns, a run-down inn, and some dilapidated warehouses from the water's edge.

The Lady Eleanor, leaning on Hal's arm, bore up bravely. Only a few more yards to go. They could hear the familiar Irish banter as the men of the *K.M.* went about their chores.

"God grant we make it," Magheen hissed between her clenched teeth.

Noreen's legs grew weaker with every step. Would they ever reach the ship, she wondered. Then just as she was within a few feet of the gangplank, her strength gave out and she crumpled in a heap to the ground, almost pulling Magheen with her.

Kevin O'Grady, watching from the bow, sprang into action. He jumped ashore and in a flash had gathered the inert body of Noreen O'Gorman in his strong arms.

"Let's get ye all below deck fast," he whispered to Magheen as he hurried on board with his burden.

Hal sighed with relief and turned to retrace his steps. It was as they passed beneath the swinging lantern outside the "Dragon's Lair" that he saw them. The same pair that had accosted O'Grady earlier in the evening when he and Hal were talking.

"Christ's blood! We're finished!" He hesitated a moment. Then digging his chin well into his chest and pulling his hat clear over his forehead, he forged ahead. Chances were they hadn't seen him, or, if they had, not recognized him in the dark. He had to get back to warn the men.

Too late! Just as Hal reached the corner, The Earl, hanging on Dermud's arm, staggered out of the dark alley onto the dock.

"Look out!" was all Hal could say as he passed them and went on into the night. He had to steel himself against a building when he rounded the corner. Great beads of perspiration stood on his brow.

"God Almighty! 'Tis asking for trouble to bring the carriage here," he mumbled to the cold wind. Then he had an idea. As he hurried through the night, he decided to station the carriage at a distance and then seek help to carry the trunks to the designated spot.

In the meantime, the Earl and his son were slowly wending their way over the cobblestones. The distance that separated them from the *Kathleen Mavourneen* and their loved ones seemed endless.

Ever watchful, O'Grady saw the Butlers as they approached his ship. But two other pairs of eyes scanning the area were also vigilant.

"Stop!" The word catapulted through the relative quiet.

"Merciful God!" cried Dermud.

"Keep goin', Son. We'll make it."

"Hey, you there, Hogan, McGuire, Murphy. Go help Burke. Seems Sweeney's had one too many again. By all that's good an' holy, I'll have the old codger's wages for this," cried O'Grady.

In a thrice the men swung over the side and onto the pier. As quickly, they surrounded Butler, grabbed him up and pushed Dermud before them across the plank to the deck of the *Kathleen Mavourneed.*

"Cast off." O'Grady's voice rose above the din.

So quickly and efficiently was the maneuver executed that the soldiers were completely taken by surprise and there was naught they could do but stand on the quay and watch the ship glide farther and farther out to sea.

Hal, returning to unload the luggage, sized up the situation and hastily took his departure.

Thirty

Life in the Butler family slowly returned to normal. Time dulled the horrors of their night's journey and the fears of the terrifying ordeal they had experienced.

In Magheen's breast, however, was buried a two-edged sword. It goaded and harried her with savage intensity and ever increasing urgency. Her mind was constantly occupied with thoughts political and seditious. What might Henry not do in Ireland given half a chance? He hadn't hesitated to hound and chase her family and herself from English soil like common criminals. Those whom he had so ostensively courted only a few short hours before, he ignominiously cast aside, and had he managed to capture them would undoubtedly have imprisoned them all in the Tower. Most certainly, she would never again trust such a conniving, loathsome tyrant. Henceforth, she would devote her whole being to thwarting the efforts of the English King to extend his sway throughout the entire land. It would be a bitter fight, of that she was certain, but she would not flinch. She would never again waiver in her determination to be done with English rule. It was now a matter of survival, kill or be killed. She knew what she had to do, and she was determined that her children, her people, her race would survive.

Magheen's basic and instinctive feelings regarding the course her country should take were consistent and inflexible. The methods to be followed and the manner in which to implement them, the overcoming of obstacles along the way, she, as yet, hadn't had time to resolve. She was determined upon one thing, however. She and those who sided with her, would never again seek by peaceful means to rid Ireland of its hated foe. Treachery would be met by treachery, lying and deceit with deception and falsehood. If that was all the enemy understood, then that was the language she, and those who would rally to her cause, would speak. She would beat the Sasanach at their own games.

With the passing of each new day, Magheen contrived, by means foul and fair, to gather the clans of the south into one united body. Many lords and chieftains gladly pledged their support and hailed her brave spirit. Yet few were willing at that hour to risk life and limb. Times were too uncertain. There were uprisings and pitched battles in several areas of the country, but a united stand seemed unattainable. Yet, ever hopeful, Magheen plotted and planned.

So as the days passed into months, Magheen was busy about many things. Her influence outside Ormond territory was great, and the number of those sympathetic to her cause grew. But, despite these time-consuming projects she did not neglect her family duties. She helped The Lady Eleanor with the running of the large household mindful that she would be in charge someday. Then, as her time drew near, she became more occupied with preparations for the expected baby. Her first born would be a son, she was sure.

It was early summer, the loveliest time of the year. All around new life was visible; little lambs frisked in fresh green fields; fledglings perched precariously on slender saplings hourly gained confidence as they tried their wings in their first attempts at flight. A round-bellied robin greedily gobbled up a long, fat worm making its way across the steamy surface of a shower-drenched path, and in the boglands close by baby hares paid little attention to their anxious mothers vainly trying to give their lively offspring first lessons in fending for themselves. The subtle perfume of wild flowers permeated the mists hanging low in the valley. The grass was ankle high and on its waving crest scarlet and yellow butterflies hovered momentarily before chasing each other into the blue. Honeybees hummed a busy song and the air was fresh and clean. It was a glorious day.

Magheen took her morning walk accompanied by Cuchulain, her Irish wolfhound. A splendid animal, gentle, and affectionate, he stood thirty-two inches high. He weighed slightly under one hundred and twenty pounds and his rough short hair was a light fawn color. His coat gleamed in the morning light, a tribute to the constant care of Fiach, the stable boy. The hound always enjoyed the activity of the out-of-doors and this morning raced ahead of Magheen until he lost sight of her; then he would abruptly halt in his tracks to await the reappearance of his mistress. This game he played over and over until at the sound of her voice he would return at once to her side.

"Cu, old boy, what do you think of this morning? Good, eh?"

The great hound raised his intelligent head. With eyes full of warmth and sympathy, he looked lovingly and intently at Magheen. Yes, he knew what she was saying and he agreed wholeheartedly with her.

Now seven months pregnant, too big to sit her horse, she spent much time sewing, knitting, and embroidering for the little one nestling inside her. He was already demanding most of her time and attention.

As her time of confinement drew to a close, she requested the company and care of Moll Flynn. The good woman came with all haste and was again lodged in the room adjoining her beloved Magheen.

It was well that she didn't delay, for the baby came almost three weeks early. Magheen was sure she was going to die. Never used to pain or sickness, this experience was more than she ever imagined. The midwife had come immediately, but there was nothing she could do until the actual moment arrived except place cool compresses on her fevered forehead.

"Now try to relax, m'dear. Its' always harder if you tense up," counseled the woman. "I ought to know, I've gone through the ordeal twelve times."

"I'm trying...." Another sharp contraction caused Magheen to murmur, "Oh, God!" but she would not repeat or display any further signs of weakness.

It was several hours later before the water broke and a little boy was born. A most glorious morning in late July in the year of Our Lord, 1546, heard his cries for the first time.

"He's so beautiful!" declared Moll as she held her "grandchild".

Long and slender, with silken strands of golden hair atop his perfectly formed little head, his eyes were dark, pensive,...her eyes, Moll concluded. Sensitive, long, tapering fingers. Magheen knew he was born to be gifted in the arts. There was nothing Butler about him. If only he'd been Hugo's. Oh, why had she thought of him now? Where was his father?

Dermud had been delayed in Dublin on some business matter, she was told. He would be home presently.

"Oh, it doesn't matter," she told herself. "He's all mine, anyway." She drew her arms more tightly around the little bundle resting on her breast. She intended to keep him close always. No one would ever take him from her. He would never set foot on English soil. No laws made by an English monarch would force Magheen Ni Neil-Butler to send her firstborn to an alien land to be taught to speak a foreign tongue. No edicts issued by a foreign ruler would prevail against her when it was a question of indoctrinating a son of the Houses of O'Neill and Ormond in a false religion, a religion set up by a proud and overbearing monarch such as Henry in defiance of the Vicar of Christ. No commands or orders dictated from across the Irish Sea would force her to deprive her son of what was his birthright...the traditions, the customs, the language, the heritage of a proud and noble Celtic people.

Magheen's son would be educated in his own land and by his own people. All the titles, honors or promises, all the threats of despoilment, displacement or even death would not shake her determination. This was her son, all hers and all Irish.

The little boy was baptized Dermud Thomas Hugh O'Neill-Butler in the parish church three days later amid the gathering of the Clans, the likes of which had not been seen in fifty years.

With the coming of her child, Magheen yearned all the more for the warm embraces of her first love, Hugo. Although his image gradually faded, his memory would never die. Magheen continued to keep his parting gift in a secret place over her heart. It was not only a relic to be cherished, but a lover's gift to be jealously guarded. But deep in her heart she sometimes cursed the day she had met him. His memory would torment her, hound her even to the grave. If he had but told her of his love. If he had once uttered the blessed words, *I love you*, her heart could be at peace. She could weather any storm with the knowledge that her love had been requited. It was the agony of having so freely given the fervor, the fullness of her young heart, of having poured out all her innermost feelings in one spontaneous gesture, and, in her mind, receiving naught, that bruised and crushed the spirit that was Magheen. Yet, she would never allow herself to be defeated.

At times when she looked at her baby boy, she tried to see some likeness to Hugo in him. But soon she would realize that her memory of him, despite how much she had tried to cling to it, or had fought to hold it in her heart, had dimmed with the passing of time.

Dermud and Magheen planned to ask The O'Malley, Prince of Murrisk, living in the far off lands west of the Shannon, if he would be gracious enough to take their precious first born as his foster child. By this means, they would contrive to keep alive the richness that was the Gaelic culture in their family.

Little Dermud was growing more beautiful as each new day dawned. The soft baby quiff gave place to loose golden curls. His large, dark eyes, so like his mother's, verged on violet. A good-tempered child, his dimpled cheeks were ever ready to show his utterly beguiling smile.

Daily the bond between mother and son tightened. Magheen's was the first face he saw each morning and the last every night. She had nursed him for two months, but after that his hearty appetite was not satisfied by his mother's milk.

Two little pearly white teeth broke through when the chubby little chap was six months old to be quickly followed by two more. The infant features were more definite, yet apart from his hair and eyes, no one could definitely say which side of the family he favored. But Magheen knew. "Mama's boy. You're mine, all mine, my pretty one." Then she would hug the precious baby to her breast and lavish kisses on his soft, warm brow. She spent hours on end talking to him in a language she knew he understood. She sang to him and told him stories of the wee folk, beautiful gossamer winged fairies who danced in the moonlight and who liked to play with little ones like himself. Magheen, determined as ever, wasted no time in recounting the legends and folktales so eagerly learned at her uncle's knee. Her baby son would know them all.

As the weather grew warmer, autumn's ripeness burst upon the land, Magheen took her prince for short walks in the garden. He was gaining weight fast, becoming almost too heavy to carry for long periods of time.

"My goodness, but you're a big boy! Mama won't be able to carry you much longer. You're going to have to find your own little feet soon."

Then before the fresh air and the peaceful country sounds lulled him to sleep once more, Magheen would tell him stories about the robins, the wrens, the naughty sparrows, and the greedy cuckoos. He would smell the perfume of cowslips, violets, and lily-of-the-valley, and feel the soft silky petals of the buttercup against his baby cheek. She would point out the animals and sing to him the many nursery rhymes Moll Flynn had crooned into her ear while she was still young enough to appreciate the simple verses.

"Chip, chip little horse
Chip, chip again, Sir.
How many miles to Dublin town?
Three score an' ten, Sir.
Chip, chip my little horse
Chip, chip again, Sir.
Will I get there by candlelight?
Yes, and back again, Sir."

and

"One Monday mornin' I went out
To see where my geese did wander.
The tracks I found upon my ground;
The little red fox's plunder
The screechin' loud did wake me,
From slumber I did shake me,
And I saw the thief, may he come to grief,
For a pauper he will make me.
Hey, run maidrin ruadh
In the foggy Autumn weather;
My geese he's watching to surprise,
With his two little ears together."

It was a joyous happy time for the entire Butler family. Magheen had adapted well to life in the Earl's household and as

Moll had predicted, she was revered and greatly loved by all. Her father-in-law was particularly fond of her, making every excuse to engage her in long conversations. Her knowledge of history was unusually good, and, like all educated people in Ireland, she was fluent in several languages, including Latin. It gave the old man untold pleasure to converse with this charming, spirited young woman.

And so it happened one morning when Magheen and the old Earl were strolling down the long avenue that led to the Butler Castle, that a young horseman approached them. He gave all the appearance of having ridden a goodly distance. His hair was disheveled and perspiration matted the fringes of his beard and mustache.

"Good morning, m'Lady, m'Lord." He raised his cap, bowed slightly and drew in his horse. Having dismounted, he withdrew a package from beneath his cloak.

"This, m'Lord, is for the Lady Magheen Ni Neill. It was sent to O'Connor country sometime ago, but they told me her Ladyship now lives with the Butler family."

Magheen's face blanched. The Earl took the package from the messenger.

"Yes, yes, the lady is here. You have done well, my good man. Go on to the castle and get something to eat. Here, take this for your trouble." The Earl withdrew a gold piece from a silken pouch suspended from his waist.

"Thank you, Sir, thank you kindly."

The man saluted, mounted his horse and continued on toward the castle.

As James Butler handed the packet to Magheen he noticed how her hands trembled. "I hope this isn't bad news. Perhaps you would prefer to be alone?"

A glance of gratitude confirmed the old Earl's intuition. He called to his favorite hound and proceeded to quicken his pace down the driveway.

Magheen fumbled for a few seconds with the crumpled outer covering. Then she ripped it apart. Inside was an elegant envelope on which her name was carefully written. Trembling with excitement and expectation, she broke the seal and withdrew the letter.

Chateau de Breville,
Chantilly, France.
January 21st, 1547

Ma petite fleur, my lovely Magheen,

The long months, nay I count them as years, that have dragged by since I departed from you, have brought me nothing but sadness and grief. I have been, in fact, at death's doors.

I did not tell you of my young wife when I was so madly in love with you. Nor did I know then that I was an expectant father...the father of a son....

Magheen's heart missed a beat as she felt the blood drain from her face. She could scarcely read on; her eyes were clouded by great fountains of water that kept welling up and spilling over, nor would they be restrained. She felt faint. She stepped onto the soft grass by the side of the road and sought the support of a willow tree. There, resting against the rough trunk, she eventually found her handkerchief and dabbed uselessly at her eyes.

So he had written to her. After so many long silent months, he had at last written. For what? To torment her further. To tell her that he had a wife. Even a son. So that was it. She had been right all along. He never did love her. She was just a simple Irish girl. A few days of pleasure. A plaything to wile away the time, yes, the boring hours of his convalescence.

Magheen was about to tear the letter into a hundred scraps and fling them to the wind but curiosity forced her to read on.

....When I returned to France I found that my wife of only nine months was already dead and with her our only son. I could scarcely believe the truth of it. In fact, I was so distraught upon hearing the terrible news that I fell grievously ill and have only lately recovered my health. I was forced, under the doctor's orders, to retire to the South of France and to relinquish all responsibilities.

But, I will not burden you further with my misfortunes. I anxiously await news of you, my dearest one.

If it is, at this time, possible for me to journey again to Ireland that I may behold you face to face, nay even be bold enough to claim you for my own, I could ask no greater joy in heaven or on earth. I swear I will have no other for my bride, if I cannot have you, Magheen.

Respectfully, I await your reply. Let your generous heart be your guide. Do not, I beg you, turn me away. My love for you knows no bounds.

Ever faithfully yours,
Hugo

There was an instant ache in Magheen's heart. She clutched at her breast with her right hand, while she crumpled the crisp vellum with the other.

"Oh, God. Why now? Why has he come back into my life to torture me, to torment me? Too late, too late!"

Then in rage, in a fury of which even Magheen had not known she was capable, she snatched at the letter and ripped it into shreds. A mad frenzy possessed her as she scattered the fragments in a dozen different directions, feeding them to the morning breeze. Then, when the last remaining piece fluttered a few yards and quickly fell to rest on the damp grass, she caught hold of herself and frantically chased after it, attempting to retrieve at least this one last fragment to ease her aching heart. She snatched it up and pressed it to her lips. For a short moment she closed her eyes. He was there again holding her as only he could.

"Oh, God. Heavenly Father, pity your child!"

"Magheen, my dear, are you all right?" It was the voice, the kind voice of James Butler that aroused her.

Try as she might to hide her feelings, it was obvious to His Lordship that Magheen had received a shock. As she did not offer to confide in him, the old man did not pry. "There are times when we must shoulder our troubles alone," he mumbled to himself.

They returned to the castle, each alone with his thoughts. Magheen repaired to her room and there in solitude, she gave vent to her pent-up grief and frustration.

When the fountain of her tears was spent, she stood before

the mirror and acknowledged to herself with swollen eyes and tousled hair that she was still beautiful. The pearly neck sloped gradually to breasts that were fuller now than in those carefree days. But, she was aware that the new life she had nurtured for almost nine months had not altered her girlish figure. A wild and crazy thought entered her mind. She could run away....join Hugo in France! Oh, the thought of it! One night of love! She would meet him in a secluded place. He would be waiting. He would take her hand as he did long ago by the seashore in Ballindee. He would kiss her fingertips and whisper words of love only her ears would hear, those words she so longed to hear! Then he'd look into her eyes and fire the flame within her breast to heights before undreamt of. Then, as the excitement grew, he would claim her lips, explore the length of her slender neck, and she in turn would respond to his advances, her full breasts swelling as he bent to caress the taut nipples with his soft tongue.

A quiver ran through her frame. Magheen's mind and body were aroused. She could feel Hugo's strong but gentle arms around her. She felt the exhilaration of his exploring hand as he sought and found her secret places that ached for his touch. And then the supreme moment when they became one flesh, when she, Magheen Ni Neill, was completely immersed, was swallowed up, lost to all but her only love, her Hugo.

A cry of pain, a shrill wail escaped her, coming from the very depths of her being. The sound penetrated the thick walls and echoed through the hallways of the castle. A servant girl hearing the sound took flight, declaring it was the banshee, blessing herself hurriedly three times as she scurried down the stairs to the comfort of the servant's quarters.

Magheen must have lost consciousness, for it was the bell sounding the Angelus and noon meal that brought her to her senses. She was lying on the floor in front of the large mirror. At first she could not remember how on earth she had come to be in such a position. Then slowly the events of the morning were recalled.

It was clear now to Magheen that she had not only lost her sense of balance but her common sense. She had allowed her imagination to run riot, had given free reign to her heart, and had lost control of her emotions. It was high time for her to face reality. She had a husband, a family, and a country that depended on her. She, Magheen Ni Neill Butler, could not afford the luxury of complete fulfillment, even if only in dreams.

Old Moll's oft repeated quotation rang in her ears. "Greater love than this no man hath, than that a man lay down his life for his friend." Perhaps she was destined to sacrifice the great love of her heart and place it on the altar of immolation, for the sake of her beloved country, to bring peace and happiness to all her suffering brothers and sisters.

These thoughts, at least, gave her courage to persevere, to hold her head high and shoulder the responsibilities that she felt were hers. She had to be strong and brave and resolute. Magheen Ni Neill would not falter. Hers was a proud heritage.

But try as she might, she could not always control her imagination. Dermud was kind, a devoted husband; Magheen knew him also as a reserved, calculating man. Whether he had resolved, after an adolescent infatuation, to bridle his passions and control his nature to the extent that even his lovemaking was predictable, or whether he sensed a reluctance on Magheen's part to abandon herself to him, the result was that her ardent nature was never satisfied, never completely fulfilled.

So from time to time, to ease the gnawing pain in her heart and the unfulfilled ache in her passionate body, Magheen's thoughts turned to Hugo. Strange how the mere thought of him excited her so. Her body tingled all over, her pulse quickened. She longed for his embrace, his passionate kisses, what she knew only he could give her.

Dermud was becoming more preoccupied. A man of fine tastes, he was content to spend most of his time with his books. Little by little, he was relieving his father of the duties and responsibilities of running the very large estate.

The months slipped by. Magheen was expecting her second child. She was, outwardly at least, happy. This one would be a girl. She would name her Moll. There would be plenty of time and many children to name after the members of her husband's family. It was with that thought that Magheen descended the stairs on her way to join the family for breakfast one morning in the spring of '47. She had just reached the entrance hall as Liam opened the door. A very tall man entered and addressed Liam. The old servant was about to show him into the reception room, but he declined the invitation. He could not delay long.

Magheen hastened forward. It was Padraig! The hero of the big storm had come to visit her! She welcomed him with open arms, plying him with questions about her loved ones in Ballindee. Padraig answered the questions as best he could, but seemed embarrassed and disturbed. Fortunately, at that moment the dining room door opened and His Lordship, the Earl, emerged. Magheen introduced Padraig. "Father, this is Padraig O'Toole from Ballindee. I've told you about him many a time."

"Yes, my dear, I remember. Happy to make your acquaintance, Padraig."

"M'Lord." He hesitated, then turned to Magheen. His voice broke as he addressed her.

"Magheen...eh...begging your pardon, Lady Butler, I think you had better sit down."

She looked at him, her beautiful face betrayed the anxiety that had gripped her heart. "What is it, Padraig? Is there something wrong?"

An ominous silence descended.

The three figures seemed to be riveted to the spot, petrified. They daren't look at each other.

Eventually, Magheen cried, "Oh Padraig, it's Uncle.... My Uncle Tom is dead!"

Padraig could only nod his head. Then he turned away to wipe the tears that stained his dust-covered face.

The Earl took Magheen in his arms a moment, then helped her to her room. He knew she would want to be alone.

The details of the death were later related. Tom O'Connor had died in his sleep. Old Moll had found him on the morning of the twelfth of March. She had become worried when he did not appear for breakfast at his usual time and went to investigate, only to find that his gentle soul had departed this life some hours before. The good woman realized that Magheen would not be able to attend the funeral services so she took matters into her own hands.

The inhabitants of Ballindee gathered at Inis Fail to accompany the body to its last resting place. The mist that drenched the sober faces did not hide the teardrops that moistened every eye. Each man, in his own way, felt that he had lost a personal friend as well as a sincere, generous benefactor.

Tom O'Connor was buried in the quiet little church yard that had kept vigil over the village of Ballindee for several hundred years. In the family tomb of white marble, his mortal remains would await the second coming of Christ with many, many generations of O'Connors.

Magheen did not long brood over the passing of her dear uncle; it was the way of all life. His had been a good one; he would receive his rewards. With characteristic selflessness, her first thoughts were for Moll. She would send for her dear friend immediately. Inis Fail could be closed up for a time. She knew her old friend would be happy to be united with her darlin' girl once more.

But Padraig had news of even greater import. From the O'Neills he brought news that Francis I, King of France, had died and was succeeded by Henry II, who had decided that Mary Stuart would marry his son. Ireland and Scotland found themselves mere pawns in the game being played by England and France. But Ireland was still holding her proud head high. The O'Donnells and 15,000 Scot soldiers were keeping the flame of hope alive in the north and in other parts of the country, valiant chieftains and clansmen were taking up the challenge.

Padraig had been dispatched to inform the Butlers that one of the O'Connor clans was even at that moment ravaging the English in Dublin. He had joined the ranks of the O'Donnell several months before when a call went out for volunteers, and it was while on his way to recruit others that he again returned to his native village, there to learn of Tom O'Connor's death.

James Butler was aroused by the news that Padraig and others brought him. It was time to muster the vast resources he had at his disposal, to ally himself with Desmond and carry the banner of freedom to the farthest corners of the country. To this end, couriers were sent to warn the various chieftains and to confirm the conditions of their support. A date was set for the Butler forces to join up with the ranks of those already fighting. A state of tension, apprehension, and suppressed excitement gripped everyone, particularly the womenfolk, for it was they, the women of the country, who suffered most in time of war. They knew not the glories of the battlefield, only the anxious weary hours of more anxious, weary days of waiting. And when the fighting was done, it was then most of all that the women suffered...suffered in mind and body if they were among the lucky ones to witness the return of a wounded husband, father or son. And, if fate were not kind to them, they were left to the lifelong suffering of mourning the lost and the dead. Accompanying their sufferings there was always the awful fear of the enemy's revenge, the fear of the vengeance of conquering armies. For revenge in the hours of triumph was exquisitely severe, and it was the women who paid the price.

Like her countrywomen, Magheen would not shirk the extra work that would be required of her, nor would she be cowered by danger. On the contrary, she wished she could ride with the men. Were it not for her delicate condition, she would have accompanied her husband and his brothers out to the battlefield. Others had done as much. Accounts of Celtic women accompanying their menfolk into battle had come down through the ages. In earlier times, Magheen knew, it had been the accepted thing to do. The Romans had left numerous stories of their encounters with Celtic women warriors.

This was the moment for which Magheen had long waited. For this hour she had been preparing ever since that fateful day when she had so clearly seen the workings of the enemy's mind. For this day her heart had ached. She would at last have her revenge!

It was the eve of their departure. A shroud of thick fog enveloped the area. Within the castle the morale of the men was high, but the womenfolk were vainly trying to hide their anxiety. A messenger arrived shortly after dinner and was quickly ushered into the Earl's presence.

"M'Lord, I bear a letter from His Majesty the King." So saying he handed a large envelope, bearing the Royal seal, to the Earl. James Butler blanched and dismissed the messenger before he retired to his private study. There he stepped close to the crackling log fire as he broke the seal and scanned the content.

Henry VIII, King of England, Scotland, and Wales,
Lord of Ireland
To the Earl of Ormond

Sir:

It has been brought to our attention that you and your followers in Ireland have remained loyal to the Crown during the recent uprisings. To demonstrate our Royal pleasure and to honor your fealty in these perilous times, I, Henry, your Sovereign Lord and King, do invite you and your retinue to attend us within the week at Limehouse in the city of London.

Henry, Rex.
London, January 1547

The Earl's hand shook; a cold sweat broke out on his forehead. He leaned against the mantle piece as if to steady himself. Could this be a plot, another of Henry's ploys? It was true that he, the Earl, and his followers had not joined in the fighting up to that time, but that was only a quirk of fate. Had he known of the intentions of his Gaelic neighbors, and had he been able to round up his men sooner, he too, would be by now fighting their common foe. He would call a meeting and discuss the matter with the different leaders. The Earl was about to step out of his study, when hard on the heels of the first messenger, a second had come. This lad brought the ghastly news of the defeat of the Irish forces and the massacres that followed. It seemed that fate had decided for the Butlers. Time had robbed them of the glory of dying for Ireland on the battlefield; they were hindered from joining their friends in the uprising only because they had not received word in time. Once again the English had poured in men and materials, resulting in the slaughter that followed.

Thirty-One

The women would not make the trip; Lady Eleanor had a bad cold and Magheen was loath to leave her infant son.

The Butler clan had been gathering for several days; uncles, nephews, and cousins, they all came. Eventually, the large party, numbering close to fifty persons, not including servants, would dutifully, if grudgingly and reluctantly, obey the summons of the foreign king.

It was the eve of their departure and a great banquet was in progress; loud and hearty the conversation as local mead and Spanish imports flowed freely. By the blazing hearth, the hounds lay in lazy contentment. O'Flaherty, the harpist, had a flagon of grog within easy reach as he strummed the plaintive strains of 'Oh, Danny Boy'.

Magheen, unquestionably the reigning queen, was dressed in a new gown of palest blue silk. Soft, creamy lace edged the low-cut bodice and emphasized the fullness of her shapely breasts. Gold thread shone in the puffed sleeves and outlined the slashed folds where a darker satin showed through. On her soft, golden hair a diadem of rubies rested and the delicate sheen of her fair throat was accented by a double strand of rubies and diamonds.

"Enough, enough of your sad tones, let's be merry," shouted the Earl to O'Flaherty.

Immediately the harpist plucked a lively tune, a wild passionate song, a throbbing melody that reverberated throughout the great hall like the beating of a mighty heart.

The dancers moved from the shadows of the deeply recessed windows into the light, three young maidens in the first flush of womanhood gliding across the polished wood as gracefully as petals on the breast of a stream. They were tall and slender as a spring sapling, graceful as a willow.

Again the harpist changed the temper of his beat and spun a tale of love to which the dancing feet immediately responded, displaying elaborate steps and patterns to suit the seductive nuances of the Celtic story.

Fascinated, the onlookers watched as the lithe figures spun in wild abandon, allowing their silken veils to float away in billowing clouds revealing cascading tresses of gold, flame, and chestnut.

Soon the entire assemblage became more involved, feet tapping, hands clapping. But within the virile vibrant chests, the hearts of the youth pounded and heated loins throbbed as with the rise and fall of each cadence, the shapely, curvaceous bodies twisted and turned, arched, and relaxed. With the tempo of the music, the dancers invariably kept pace; one moment a rapid movement shot fire and passion into the veins, the next, a leisurely, listless measure caused straining loins to explode.

The eternal love story told, the dance concluded when with outstretched arms, one dancer paused for a brief ecstatic instant before Dermud's stool. Her glistening seductive green eyes fixed upon his smoldering blue ones while with heaving breasts, she tried to lure him to her passionate embrace.

Magheen watched the beautiful creature play with the emotions of her handsome husband. There was no doubt about it, Dermud was intoxicated, bewitched by the green-eyed goddess, and Magheen knew he would make love to her that night and strangely enough, for the first time, she was glad.

"Well, gentlemen, I'll be off to bed. An old man can't take too many late nights and it's a long trip we'll be having in the morning. So goodnight all," said the Earl, rising from his place at the head of the long table.

As he was leaving the dining hall, he signed Magheen to follow. She immediately excused herself and left the room.

Her faithful companion, the hound Cuchulain, as became an aristocrat, merely raised his arrogant head as she passed. He watched her a moment, assessing her intentions, then resumed his wonted posture in front of the blazing hearth.

The harpist continued his rendering of some ancient ballads in the Rinn Ard meter and accompanied himself in the Doh, Re, and Sol Modes; the green-eyed dancer found the company of James Butler, the younger, stimulating, while the rest of the Butler clan, mostly according to age, either retired for the night or continued to converse with kinfolk rarely seen.

"Magheen, darlin', I want a big favor from you," the Earl said when they had seated themselves on the settle that occupied the greater part of one of the alcoves in the entrance hall.

"Name it, dear Father."

The Earl took Magheen's hand and paused a moment, looking into her beautiful face. When at last he spoke, his voice was soft and gentle. "You must be careful, very careful, my dear, while we're away. The Sasanach come as a wolf in sheep's clothing. I know I'm a fine one to talk to you like this when I've done nothing but encourage you in your political enterprises, but I fear now for your safety and that of your son, my precious grandchild."

"Father, what is it? You've never spoken like this before."

"I don't know, Lass. Just promise me you'll be careful."

"I promise."

"If anything should happen to me or the others, it will be up to you to sustain Ormond. For God's sake, don't keep the child here; the sooner you can send him to O'Malley the better."

"What are you saying, Father? You make my blood run cold. Do you know something none of the rest of us know? What is it, Father?"

"I know no more nor less than you, my dear. An old man sometimes talks too much. However, I'm not easy in my mind about this trip."

"Oh, Father, I can't bear to hear you talk like this." Magheen drew the old man to her and pressed his head warmly to her breast as she whispered, "Father, dearest Father, I love you so." The tears flowed freely; Magheen was devastated.

"Come now, Magheen, my dear, it's not like you to take on so," the Earl straightened up assuming a position of strength. "I want to remember you as brave and smiling, proud and defiant." He placed his hand beneath her chin. "Chin up. That's my Magheen."

"You'll take care, won't you?" she tried to smile.

"Of course I will." But as he spoke, she noted how his venerable brow was creased in worried lines. "I'll say goodnight now, a gra." He got up and slowly climbed the stairs to his bedroom.

Magheen didn't return to the hall but made her way to her own room, where she dismissed the maid servant and while taking her place beside her son's cradle said, "Go join the others below, you, too, need a little fun, Eileen." When she was alone, she took the sleeping child in her arms, kissed his golden curls and pressed him to her heart. "Just a few more weeks, my darling. I can't let you go yet. When your papa comes home, we'll both take you to O'Flaherty country. Now sleep well, my prince." She replaced him in the cradle and covered him against the raw night air.

After a hearty breakfast, the men gathered in the large courtyard that separated the back of the castle from the stables. Some were already mounted, their anxious, high-spirited horses prancing in anticipation of the ride, others not yet bridled pawed the ground.

The carriage was ready and awaiting the Earl's arrival. Two of his brothers, both older men, and a distant cousin would accompany him.

Dermud would ride with his brothers James and Sean. Their handsome mounts were ready and stood patiently by as the young men bade their Lady Mother and Magheen farewell, a difficult and heartbreaking parting.

"Hurry back, please, Father," Magheen cried as the coach was about to pull out. The stalwart fisherman from Ballindee sat at the reins. Padraig O'Toole, never a man of many words but one of much feeling, spoke to Magheen as he raised the whip to the two bay mares, "Don't you be frettin' now, m'Lady Magheen. With God's help we'll all be back again in no time at all, at all."

"Go with God, Padraig." Magheen waved, keeping a brave front as the carriage pulled away, turned into the long drive, and became lost to view. Dermud took his baby son in his arms before he mounted. As the moisture gathered in his eyes, he bent his head and buried it in the soft clothing before kissing the warm chubby cheeks and returning him to his mother. He mounted and for an instant longer waited looking down into her upturned face, love and concern in his clear blue eyes. "Take care of yourself, my love. I'll be back as quickly as possible." Then brushing his fair forelock from his pale forehead, he bent his head to the horse's mane and galloped from the yard after the others.

* * * *

The dinner and festivities were scheduled to take place at seven. As the hour approached, the gentlemen of the Butler party bathed and groomed and donned their best attire before presenting themselves at Limehouse.

The Earl looked venerable in his doublet of rich brocade, the ample sleeves were fitted to the wrists in fluted cuffs. A narrow ruff adorned his neck. He wore black silken hose, gold-buckled leather shoes, and at his waist hung a gold-handled sword. His silver locks were drawn back from his broad forehead and fell in loose waves to his shoulders. His neatly-trimmed beard and moustache still showed traces of gold and, although well into his fifties, he was sure of foot and quick-witted.

Dermud caught the eye of many a coy serving wench and many ladies-in-waiting to Queen Catherine made no attempt to hide their admiration when the tall, blue-eyed, blond stranger entered their midst. A veritable hubbub ensued, those who had forgotten or who had missed the Butler's recent visit demanding to know this and that and why this elegant prince of a man was not seen in Court before.

Truly, Dermud was every inch a prince in his velvet doublet of pale blue opened in front to show a cream silk shirt. This undergarment was elaborately embroidered in Celtic designs and instead of the usual jerkin, which was worn over the doublet, the young man proudly wore the traditional Irish cape. Caught at the left shoulder with a gold Tara broach encrusted with diamonds, emeralds, and rubies, the elegant wine-colored mantle of the finest velvet fell behind in loose folds past his slim hips to his shapely legs, then swept up again at the right hip. It was held by yet another splendid Celtic pin. Beneath his long-waisted doublet, his silken breeches, puffed after the fashion of the day, were caught below the knees with garters of gold braid. He wore black silk hose and leather shoes. A small sword with jeweled handle was held in place by a silken sash. He had removed his velvet cap, complete with plume, before he entered the King's presence.

The King was seated on a dais surrounded by the most notable princes of the realm. Rows of tables placed in full view of the King were reserved for the favored guests from Ireland.

The King, as if to impress his subjects from the Emerald Isle, had donned some of his most exquisite apparel. A short collar encircled his gross neck. A doublet of rich red velvet slashed to reveal the gold undershirt embroidered with pearls and rubies was cut to fit closely to his enormous body. Over the doublet he wore an outer garment with exaggerated puffed sleeves. Around the collar and running the full length on either side was a broad strip of ermine. Inserts of gold cloth, generously ornamented with enormous gems, sapphires, rubies, and pearls, added to the magnificence of the King's garb. His Majesty wore silk stockings and his shoes of a gold brocade were cut in the new square-toed fashion. At his waist, a gold sword from which hung a splendid tassel and on his head, and slightly tilted, the latest and very popular flat cap, delicately embellished with gold braid and ostrich plumes.

The tables were well stocked with meats: veal, venison, capon, and wild duck. Waiters served vegetables from large silver bowls, and the wine ran freely.

The meal was well suited to the occasion. Lavish in quality and quantity, it was served with the ceremony worthy of a religious ritual. A procession of servants, headed by the chief steward dressed in sober livery, carried in the many platters and trenchers of silver and gold heaped high with fish, fowls, suckling pigs, whole joints of beef and pork, and mutton which were served with huge bowls of sweet sauces. Great mounds of fruits were set at regular intervals on the carpeted tables in the delft trenchers acquired by Henry a few years before.

"Harry's taste in fruit is as varied as his taste in women," whispered Dermud to his father.

"Aye, 'twould appear so," the Earl chuckled.

Further up the table m'Lord Surrey was passing up a bowl of vegetables. "Our English nature can't live by roots, water herbs, or such beggary baggage," he commented.

"We'll be eating seeds next, I wager. Perhaps we should grow feathers," Lord Harrington on his left quipped in reply.

"Can't say this beer is sitting well upon my stomach," said

James Butler to his son. "Give me one mug o' Irish mead an' they can have their fill of all this damn brew."

"The Dutch grow wealthy on the new-found tastes of their English friends. 'Tis said to be the latest rage and brooks a fair chance of becoming the national drink," said Dermud.

"M'Lord Ormond speaks of our latest pastime." Young Lord Hertford seemed eager to join in the conversation. "'Tis even worse than you think. Can't get a decent flagon of ale in the whole of England now."

"I'll stay with wine. 'Tis the drink o' the gods and it suits me fine," Dermud answered.

In the meantime, the lackeys, huge, burly fellows, filled and refilled the new silver mugs with beer from the old black leather jacks and whatever didn't make its mark was eagerly lapped up by lazy dogs and their whelps lying under the tables.

As the meal progressed, plates of sweet meats seasoned with fruits and flowers, such as primroses and marigolds, were served in the form of pies, pastries, and tarts. These were followed by jellies of many colors, by marchpane which caused no small curiosity, and with conserves of fruits, marmalades, and sundry outlandish confections all seasoned with sugar.

A troupe of musicians entertained at one end of the great hall while the King's buffoon, Will Somers, turned his somersaults and otherwise amused his master, the lords, and the Irish Earls who were seated close to the King.

"The knave cuts a brash pose tonight; I warrant he's had his fill o' grog, eh? What say ye, m'Lord Northumberland?" And as the King spoke, the noise lessened.

"How say you, do the half-wits of Ireland compare, m'Lord?" the King asked the Earl of Ormond.

"Your Majesty must know there are no half-wits in the Green Isle. You, Sire, have seen to that yourself," answered the Earl of Ormond.

"How so, m'Lord?"

A ripple of fear ran through the ranks of the Earl's followers. Was James baiting the King? Butler's voice answered clearly and firmly.

"Sire, only the brave of heart, the quick-witted or the fleet of foot survive Your Majesty's periodic purges. No doubt it is your intent to make of us a nation second to none, only the most gallant live to pass on the strongest traits to their offspring."

There was a moment of silence. The King looked James Butler straight in the eyes, and then he threw his lusty head back on his broad shoulders and laughed, a loud, hearty laugh that filled the great hall.

"Spoken like a true Norman. Take heed ye Saxon swine, the Norman-Gael speaks his mind. Nor does he cower and skulk lest he anger his King. Methinks my interests could be better served had I more outspoken fearless lords at my side rather than the giddy, chattering fools that now surround me, fawning upon me night and day."

A cheer, spontaneous and wild, rose from the Butler followers. The King signaled for Northumberland who immediately arose and went to the King's side.

He bent his head as the King whispered in his ear. A leer spread across Northumberland's face as he stepped from the raised podium and left the hall.

The cheering died down and the King raised his hand to command silence. "M' Lords. We are greatly honored this day by the presence of our Irish cousins. I've sent m' Lord Northumberland to fetch our rarest claret for we must drink to the health and prosperity of our guests only with the very best."

"Hurrah!" Again a chorus of lusty Irish voices filled the hall with exuberant acclaim.

The tumblers were replenished with the ruby wine and the Irish Lords drank and praised the fine quality. Good humor prevailed and the banter went back and forth while the young were loud in their praise of Henry.

The Earl, James, was the first to feel the ill effects as he placed his elbows on the table to support his head. Dermud, beside his father, looked at him anxiously for a moment. "Father, are you ill? What's the matter?"

"I don't know, Son. I've a strange feeling in the pit of my stomach. A burning feeling. And my head...My God! 'Tis on fire."

Dermud arose. "Father, let me help you." He then addressed the King. "Your Majesty, I beg your leave to accompany my father to an adjoining room. I fear he has taken ill and must lie down a spell."

"You have my permission to retire to the antechamber."

Father and son withdrew as best they could. Meantime Dermud, himself, was beginning to feel nauseous and his head was swimming. As he got his father to a couch, he asked, "How are you feeling now, Father?"

"Son, I think they have dealt us death's blow. We've been deceived, walked straight into their traps. We'll never leave this damnable place...we...are...fin...ish...ed."

"Don't, Father, don't say such things." Dermud was on his knees beside his father. "Father, what can we do?" He took the old man's hand in his. "What do you suggest?" Dermud's voice trailed off and his father caught a glimpse of his son sinking to the floor, just as he, James Butler, lost consciousness.

One by one the Irish Lords succumbed, and one by one, their limp bodies were carried out to the antechamber, the great room usually used to accommodate groups or individuals awaiting an audience with the King. There were several large couches in the center of the room and against the wall chairs spaced here and there.

Within the hour, fifty members of the Butler party had sickened. Padraig, who, at the last minute had accompanied the Butler family to the dinner and who had never liked alcoholic beverages had abstained. He was one of the few members of the Irish party to survive the treachery. He bent over the Earl of Ormond and felt his pulse. "M'Lord," Padraig whispered close to the Earl's ear.

The Earl opened his eyes. He tried to formulate a word. "My...sss..."

Padraig repeated the word, "My..."

"Sons...where...are they?"

"Rest, m'Lord," advised Padraig.

"We are done...for. Get...to...hell...out...fast to Ireland...my wife."

"I'll see you safely to your lodging first, m'Lord."

"Go man...go." Beads of perspiration stood on the old man's brow, the exertion of trying to speak had left him exhausted.

Padraig tried to reassure the Earl, but his Lordship was anxious for the safety of his wife, Magheen, and her son. He knew what the enemy was capable of doing; Henry was very efficient. James Butler had been a fool; he had had a presentiment...but, like so many of his countrymen, hope, eternal hope, had blinded his reason. He knew better. He had seen one family after another eliminated. Would the Irish never learn that the Sasanach were not to be trusted. They promised, but failed to keep their word. They made truces and pacts but broke them before the Royal Seal was dry. Now, Henry had struck again. Like sheep they had been led to the slaughter. The Earl groaned while Padraig knelt on one knee beside his couch.

"My sons...my...fine...boys..." The tears flowed freely down the Earl's tired face. "Oh God...Almi...ghty." Again he was silent as his thoughts flew back to his native land. Yes, his family was in danger. The barbarians would come bringing terror and death to the peaceful Suir Valley. Irish blood would flow and the fragrant verdant fields would be washed with crimson streams. And when no living thing, man or beast was left alive, the blackness of the scorched earth and the charred ruins would mark the spot.

Padraig took the Earl to his lodgings and remained with him to the end. A few days of agonizing pain and, eventually, William James Butler joined his sons and the rest of his kin in death. England had triumphed once again; another prominent house had been quickly and effectively eliminated.

Padraig lost no time in returning to Ireland and to the Butler Castle where once more he was the harbinger of devastating news.

"The bastards, the bloody scheming bastards! By God, I'll tear them limb from limb with my bare hands!" Magheen's voice was shrill. "Father was right. He was the only one who really knew them. Yet, he went. Oh, why did he go? Why, why?"

"There was nothing else he could do, Magheen. He was summoned, he had to go."

"No! No. I won't believe that. No Irishman has to obey a foreign power, a tyrant who calls himself a King. May God grant me the strength and the opportunity and one day, I swear, I'll have my revenge."

Padraig had never known such inveterate hatred lay hidden in Magheen's heart. He was aware that she scorned and held in contempt the foreign representatives who strutted impudently about the streets of the capital, that she despised the ignorant boorish men at arms from the highest-ranking officers to the common soldiers. He realized that from her earliest childhood, she had learned that the Sasanach were not to be trusted. He knew she had experienced, first-hand in her youth, the cruelty and barbarous behavior of which the foreigners were capable. But now with the horrific, tragic happenings that had come upon her and her family, the depths of Magheen's hatred were revealed and he was afraid.

Henry was determined to have Ireland. The dreadful price Ireland's sons and daughters would have to pay was of no consequence to him. This Magheen knew and she was equally determined to fight him, to thwart him every step of the way, whatever the cost to herself. Padraig decided his place, henceforth, was at her side.

Left alone, Magheen put her head in her hands and threw herself on her knees. "Almighty God," she cried, "how could you have allowed this to happen? Oh, Father, Father, my fine, generous Father...I should have been with you. They wouldn't dare lay a hand on your dear head if I had been there. Oh, God, help me now in my hour of sorrow." Magheen's fists beat against the hard surface of the settle. "God in heaven, have you completely turned your face from Ireland, from your suffering children? My poor Dermud...I didn't love you as you deserved...but in my heart of hearts I loved you all the same. Yes, believe me, I did. It's too late now, I'll never more see your handsome face, never hear your gentle, considerate words. And your son...oh, God, he'll never know a father! What am I to do? How can I go on?" Magheen slipped to the floor. For a moment, it seemed, she lost track of time and place.

But Magheen could not long allow herself the luxury of quiet mourning. Though crushed with sorrow, she gathered herself together and controlling her emotions, she went to comfort the Lady Eleanor and the other female family members who had lost their loved ones.

In the somber household, Magheen seemed imbued with superhuman energy. She assumed the duties of running the excessively large estate. It had been the Earl's expressed wish, one of his last requests to her, so she took upon herself the many chores that would otherwise have fallen to the Lady Eleanor, and although Moll was invaluable through all those trying days, it was upon Magheen's young shoulders that the final decisions rested.

She was no longer the vibrant, happy young woman of yesterday. Even her countenance seemed to have changed; the young roundness and tenderness had left forever. There was a new maturity about her; she was a woman of purpose and determination. But to those who knew her best, she appeared to have lost some of the old self-confidence and brashness as well. Yes, with the brutal and untimely deaths, the murder of her husband and father-in-law, not only was Magheen's self-assurance shaken, but other facets of her vivacious and outgoing personality also underwent critical and radical transformation.

Few, if any, saw her smile in the days that followed; God knows there was little to smile about. She became absorbed, introspective, preoccupied. Within her heart, she carried a gnawing wound that wouldn't be healed and which ceaselessly sought to be avenged. Her brain throbbed with schemes and plans she knew she would soon execute otherwise her heart would never know peace or solace.

Even in the nursery where her silvery laugh once heralded each new day for her tiny son, where night-time shadows heard her sweet voice sing him lullabies, even in that hallowed sanctuary, Magheen was strangely silent but for one oft-repeated phrase whispered low and clear, "You, they'll never, never lay hands on."

Her appetite almost completely gone, she spent most of her daylight hours occupied with household chores. No one heard her speak, she went about her work tight-lipped and dull-eyed. And when at night her throbbing head found the pillow, it was not to find rest or surcease. Night after night sleep's blessed healing salve soothed not her tired brain, closed not her melancholy brown eyes. Magheen had become, in the words of the household servants, "a walking dead."

Finally, after eight days and nights of sleepless agony, her body could take no more. She sank in a semi stupor to the floor and was forthwith carried to her bed.

It was three days and three nights later before she again opened her eyes in the large feather bed she had shared with Dermud. It felt strangely empty and cold to her dulled and slowly awakening senses. As if in a trance, she at first surveyed her surroundings. Why did she feel so languid, drugged? "Where am I?" she asked in a half-dazed, bewildered voice.

Moll had nodded off. She had sat by the bedside night and day since Magheen had collapsed. But the sound of her beloved "child's" voice brought her to her feet.

"Ah, so you've decided to come back to us. Now take it easy," she cautioned as Magheen tried to rise.

"What day is it?"

"'Tis Tuesday, a gra. But don't be troublin' your head about the day; you'll be wantin' a little soup or something?" Moll coaxed.

"Tuesday...Tuesday? How long have I been asleep?"

"A few days...but you needed every hour of it..." Moll tried to assure her and to herself she whispered, "yes, mo bron." 'Twill break her heart. She can't go on like this. She must give vent to her sorrow, thought the distraught woman, for she knew Magheen had as yet shed no tears. Her great sad eyes were unnaturally cold and hard. It was sheer agony to witness the suffering of her beloved one. What could she do to save her, to keep her sound in mind and body? "If only I could do something," she gasped aloud.

Again, Magheen tried to rise, but she moved as one who was asleep. Then as her bare feet touched the cold ground, she cried out, "Why, oh why?" and sank back onto the bed.

In the days that followed, the torturing questions wound like an endless, poisonous tendril through all her waking hours and at night threatened to squeeze her very life's breath.

As the days lengthened into weeks, Magheen gained little rest and lost much weight. She would awake in a cold sweat from fitful sleep and ghoulish nightmares only to cringe in fear as the shadows of the dead gaunt oak tree outside her window engaged in a dance macabre in the moon-white light. Moll, who stayed close by, was ever at hand to soothe and comfort, but the strain was also telling on her. In anguish, she watched as the beautiful young woman she had once known and loved gradually faded to a shadow of her former self.

Medical help was of no avail. Eventually, Moll, in desperation, took the baby from the arms of his nursemaid and laid him in Magheen's. "There, now you tell your mother you need her," she urged. "She'll listen to no one else."

As if he understood, the little fellow kissed the cold, pale cheek of his mother and cuddled up beside her.

Soon the warmth of his small body seemed to drive the chill from Magheen's. She opened her eyes and looked into the reflection of her own.

"Oh, my baby!" she cried and drew him to her breast.

A few hours later, Moll heard the sobs, and as the tears fell, the pent-up grief and anguish that had gripped Magheen's mind and heart were released.

"Oh, God, I loved him. My dearest Dermud, I did love you."

Thirty-Two

Following the tragic events of the spring of '47, the Butler Castle had become a deserted place. An eerie hush descended on the entire estate; life seemed to have slowed to mere existence. Even the animals were listless. The hounds lay about, caring nothing for their full bowls of food. The servants moved in quiet, careful steps and spoke only in whispers. Some had left their posts, deciding their lives were more valuable than their earnings. Life in the quiet Suir Valley had completely changed.

Magheen arose from her bed, the day after Moll had placed her baby son in her arms, with faltering step but with a strong will and a clear mind.

She was no longer the vibrant, happy young woman of yesterday, that was true, but she had acquired a new maturity and determination. She seemed to have lost the old brashness but acquired a new self-confidence. There was a new purpose, a definite quiet resolve in her deportment and manner. No longer impulsive, unrealistic in her idealism, or given to fanciful dreams of achieving the impossible, she acted now with perspicacity. Every last detail was carefully considered, and every aspect of a project dutifully contemplated before being executed. Once her final decision was reached, she acted upon it and did not look back.

There was, however, an air of frustration about her, born, no doubt, from her inability to change the course of events, to alter the policies and politics that seemed bent on bringing ruin and degradation to her family, her home, and her country. Yet despite this frustration and maybe because of it, she was determined to stand firm in the face of adversity. She would, at all costs, keep a proud exterior, hold her head high and let the enemy see that in spite of his attempts to destroy, to kill and bury the flesh, he could never touch the spirit, her spirit, the spirit of Ireland!

As Magheen reasoned, she knew she had to survive. She had to live, and in order to do so she had to accommodate herself, adapt to a new mode of life, for she reckoned, beyond the shadow of a doubt, that only those who could adapt would survive. In all her days, no matter what the odds, she had never, without good reason, turned away from danger or balked in the face of seeming defeat.

In open and equal combat she could hold her own, where bravery was called for she could be strong, where mental prowess was expected she was second to none, and if sacrifice were demanded, then, surely, she could match any in her unselfish devotion to a noble cause. But the forces which now opposed her were insidious. It was impossible to challenge, to attack or fight a foe that like the proverbial snake struck stealthily, treacherously, deceitfully.

It was all very well in a civilized clime to use diplomacy, to parley and discuss when men of upright character joined kindred spirits and sought by means honorable and fair to amend their differences, but in the hostile environment in which she now found herself, refined and courteous behavior was considered a weakness. Man's baser instincts: brute force, craftiness, and deceit, were the traits she must cultivate; only then could she defend herself against the inveterate, implacable foe called the Sasanach.

Padraig had remained on in the Butler Estate to help the women and oversee the workers. Then, to make sure the vast Ormond territory was well ordered, Magheen had sent him on a trip of several weeks from one end to the other, checking here, advising there. The general populace was aghast at the terrible news he brought of the massacre of the Butler family, and young men all over the south were eager and ready to take up the sword if the Lady Eleanor and the young Lady Magheen Butler should seek revenge. But Padraig assured them that no such thought was entertained by either lady. All they asked was to be left in peace to attend, as best they could, to carrying on for the next generation.

The perfume of June filled the air. Long, bright evenings and sunny, warm days had brought new life to the castle by the River Suir. It was decided that the social life at the castle should resume. Magheen was ready. It was time to dress the crafty lobo that lurked within her in the innocent white fleece of a spring lamb. She had made up her mind to harass the enemy and weaken his defenses by every means in her power.

Invitations were sent to the local gentry. Afternoon gatherings, hunting parties, and gala boating trips on the river became common occurrences on the huge Butler estates. Magheen, it was noised abroad, had become a true Anglo-Norman and Whitehall heard and approved. "The high-spirited filly has been broken to the bit," was the comment.

Magheen appeared gay, lighthearted, and charming, a most gracious hostess, listening dispassionately as her new friends told of surprise raids on English strongholds.

"You can't imagine the destruction that was caused, my dear Lady Mairgret. Not twelve miles from here. Why, the ruffians might be within our very households." Lady Ann Spawling, lately arrived from England, was visibly shaken. She had been warned to expect trouble from the natives. "An unruly people" is what her father had said, and called the whole notion of her going to Ireland "preposterous."

But the young woman would not be dissuaded at the time. Now she was convinced that her father's opinion was, indeed, correct, even though the man had never set foot on Irish soil.

"It's monstrous! This is going too far! I had no notion I was coming to live among barbarians," and her tight ringlets bobbed with each clipped word.

"I quite agree with you, my dear. Our friends in England have no idea what we have to put up with in this backward country." Lady Henrietta Cooke raised her voice. "If this villainy is not suppressed with all speed, we'll all perish. I told Harold several years ago, even before we set foot in this savage land, that he shouldn't even consider the post. But, alas, he was adamant. It was, he said, a way to advance his political career. So what's a woman to do? I declare, I can't see how living in this terrible country can bring us anything but ruination." The florid-faced lady sipped her wine and patted her thin lips with a dainty, lace-fringed handkerchief.

Magheen, presiding at the table, had sat motionless, her head gracefully resting between the thumb and index finger of her left hand, contemplating the scene. As the dialogue concluded, she lowered her hand and with the other took hold of a goblet and mechanically raising it to her lips, she addressed Lord Kingsbury. "I'm so sorry about your prize stallion. How very inconsiderate of those who set fire to your stables." Thus did she seem to commiserate with the local gentry.

He had brilliant dark eyes, alive and full of humor, and as Magheen looked at him he smiled, a most engaging smile that displayed even white teeth. She gasped. Then the solitary word escaped her. "Hugo!"

"I beg your pardon, m'Lady?"

Magheen closed her eyes a second as if to rid herself of the vision. Then recollecting where she was, she hastened to cover up her confusion.

The young man facing her was the Captain in charge of the fort at Dunmore East near the mouth of Waterford Harbor. At twenty-eight, Roland Chadwick was handsome, ambitious, and ruthless; the latter two traits were responsible for his present position.

"Oh, eh. I'm sorry. You reminded me of someone," she answered.

"Ah, I see." He observed her closely. God, she is beautiful! he thought.

But, if young Chadwick was infatuated with Magheen, it was only fair to say that Magheen found she was strangely drawn to the Captain also. The physical likeness to Hugo was remarkable, but even more extraordinary was a similarity of personal traits.

Roland Chadwick was outwardly a gentleman born and bred, his manners were impeccable, his voice soft and refined. Why then had he been sent to command an isolated fort in a small city in Ireland? That was the enigma. There were rumors, of course. Some said that he was the illegitimate son of the Earl of Richmond, others, that he was naught but a rogue who had escaped the hangman's noose, changed his identity, and, having joined the King's army, volunteered for the unwanted post in Ireland. Whatever the truth may have been, it was destined to remain the secret of the young adventurer.

Magheen's emotions were aroused. Seated not far from this handsome young man, her thoughts were no longer under her control; they had taken flight.

Hugo, Hugo. Her heart cried as she looked into those dark eyes. What might her life have been as Hugo's bride? Then as soon as these thoughts had been formulated, others intruded and chased them away. Why do you torment yourself? You know very well, he never loved you, never really loved you enough to....

"I say, Lady Mairgret, don't you agree?" The voice of Lord Kingsbury sounded a long way off.

"Eh? I beg your pardon." Magheen tried to recollect herself. "I'm terribly sorry. I'm afraid I was thinking of...."

"Oh, we all get distracted at times, Ma'am. Think nothing of it, nothing at all," his Lordship interrupted, fussing with his wig. "But as I was saying..." Kingsbury's voice droned on. Magheen's eyes were directed toward him but her thoughts were not with him. She nodded from time to time. The man was obviously in his cups; so he needed no other indication that his words of wisdom were not directed to deaf ears. Only barely conscious of the monologue issuing from somewhere across the table, Magheen allowed herself a luxury she had recently so little time in which to indulge: thoughts of Hugo and perhaps...yes, perhaps the remote possibility that somehow their paths might cross once again.

Hugo had, although belatedly, written declaring his love and his desire to claim her as his own, if she so wished. Now that Dermud had been wrenched from her, there was really no reason why she couldn't, at least, hope.

In her mind, one and only one condition could exist that might prevent this union, her marriage, albeit a political marriage, to Gerald Fitzgerald. Since Mary of Scotland had not become Gerald's wife, she Magheen Ni Neill Butler, could be a likely replacement.

Magheen, though bruised and bleeding in mind and heart, was not beaten. She had fight and determination, and despite all she had undergone, she had a spirit undaunted that would sacrifice, would relinquish all for the supreme good. Even her all-consuming passion, her one and only love, Hugo, she would not hesitate to sacrifice if by her action she could in some small way further the cause, achieve the ultimate, the unity and freedom of Ireland.

As soon as the last guest was ushered from the castle, Magheen became a different person. The light, frivolous air, the mask she had worn during the preceding hours was discarded, and she was once again serious, determined, and purposeful. Retiring to her own quarters, she seated herself at the great oaken desk still stacked and surrounded with the manuscripts and writings of her dead husband. There she outlined and planned the strategies for the next raid.

Later in the evening, when the servants had retired and the castle had settled down for the night, Magheen, accompanied by Padraig, quietly left the sleeping household. Making their way through the woods behind the castle, they eventually came to a sequestered hunting lodge situated about a mile off. There, they held their secret rendezvous with such trusted friends as Taig O'Brien and Rory O'Moore, Con McCarthy and others, and there Magheen's plans were discussed and final details agreed upon.

So it came about that Magheen took to riding abroad by night in the company of these loyal male friends. Disguised as a man, she and her comrades sallied forth on missions so daring and dangerous that even those brave men shuddered when they recounted their covert exploits many years later.

It was toward the end of September in the year 1547, that one such raid was undertaken. The whole month had been unusually wet and cold. Each day it rained and every night an unseasonable wind made every man seek the comfort of his home and fire and every woman the warmth of her husband's bed. But Magheen had lost the latter and had no need of the former, for within her heart there raged a fire so fierce that not even the arctic snows could quench its blaze.

As the day wore on, Magheen grew more agitated; she paced her room several times. This coming night would be a particularly dangerous one. Standing at one of the windows, she did not see the cattle grazing on the lowlands across the river near the bogs, nor did she notice how carefully they treaded the wet ground avoiding, with a knowledge acquired before birth, the tufts of tempting grass that were not grass at all. Her ears were closed to the sounds the winds made, as blowing on the hills they created mournful wailing tones, nor did she hear among the crags and crevices, the Banshee's cry as the servants had. But the one sound she did hear, however, was the beating of her own heart. She tried to calm herself. She had been on raids before, why then was she so concerned about this one? She tried to fathom the cause, but the only logical answer which came to her mind was that she would lead the men that night, and their destination was into the very jaws of death. And, there was a lurking something. Could she? Did she really feel for the young Captain whom she intended to send to his doom?

Captain Chadwick had been smitten by Magheen's beauty from the moment he set eyes on her. As a guest at one of the lavish dinners given at the castle, he swore he would get to know her better, then learning of the death of her husband the information strengthened his resolve. So accordingly, a few days after his visit to the castle, he invited her to the fort that protected the entrance to the port of Waterford. It had been an old Norman castle built sometime in the thirteenth century. Since Henry VIII had taken such an active interest in Ireland, it had been confiscated and turned into a fort with its own compliment of soldiers.

Against the evening sky, the dark rock exterior stood bold and defiant as the sun's rays played hide and seek between the machicolated parapet; they would soon creep to their watery bed, but on this summer evening they would take a long time to fall asleep.

Magheen had made it a rule never to converse on business matters outside the walls of her own quarters at the castle or the hunting lodge, but on this occasion she felt the need to communicate her feelings to Padraig who accompanied her.

"A formidable place, don't you think?"

Padraig looked at her with bent head, indifference in his eyes, and drawled, "You might say that m'Lady."

They had reached the huge iron gates. A guard was slouching on a bench hewn from the stone wall, and as the carriage drew up, he pulled himself together in a halfhearted manner.

"Evenin'," said Padraig as he stepped down.

"Be ye from the Ormond Castle? I've me orders to let ye by." He had somehow managed to pick himself up and without waiting for an answer had proceeded to open the iron gate that led directly into the fort.

Situated on a promontory, the fort was surrounded on three

sides by the sea. Magheen and Padraig took note of every detail; they would compare their observations later.

They were met by Captain Chadwick and his assistant, Lieutenant Charles Leeds. Both men were dressed in their finest black leather jerkins, white linen shirts, and black silk hose.

"Welcome, m'Lady Mairgret." Captain Roland stepped forward to greet Magheen as she alighted from the carriage. "I'm so happy you've consented to honor us with this visit. Allow me to introduce my assistant, Leeds, Lieutenant Charles, m'Lady."

"It's an honor, I'm sure, m'Lady." The young lieutenant was awed by the great beauty of the woman who now stood before him.

"I'm very pleased to meet you, Sir."

Soon the Lieutenant fell behind as his commanding officer led Magheen on a tour of the fort. He accompanied Padraig.

"I'm sure the view from the parapet is breathtaking." Magheen was eager to see the coastline directly below the fort.

"It most certainly is. We'll start there if you like," said her gallant escort.

Nothing of any significance escaped the keen brown eyes of Magheen Ni Neill Butler. Her grandfather would have hailed her as a most valuable spy. She noted well the location of the artillery and when finally she was guided, with much care and concern for her dainty slippered feet, through the dank passages and underground cells of the dungeons, she managed to unlatch a shuttered window at ground level.

Cleverly pretending to be interested in the fantastic display of the spider webs, Magheen raised her parasol. Poking at one of nature's masterpieces she caught the tip of her parasol in the shutter's latch, breaking it off.

"Oh, my! I've gone and wrecked my pretty sunshade, haven't I?" Magheen pulled the most alluring little pout.

"I'm so sorry. I really shouldn't have brought you to such a horrid place, my dear Lady Mairgret." The young captain was sincerely put out about the mishap. The fact that the latch swung loose on the shutter gave him no concern whatsoever.

The dinner that followed could not be considered a feat of the culinary arts, but, nevertheless, it was palatable and, downed by a good vintage wine, it turned out to be satisfactory.

Magheen and the Captain had much to talk about, especially since London and the English countryside were not unknown to both of them.

Being a sensitive host, Roland Chadwick did not refer to the recent tragic deaths which had occurred in the Butler family, but while he entertained this beautiful creature he was acutely aware that she was now a single woman, unattached, a prize worth the effort. It never occurred to him, however, that Magheen might consider herself on a very different plane, a person superior in birth, breeding, and intelligence. On the contrary, Roland Chadwick, being English by birth, thought of himself as a being apart. Like most Englishmen, he was suspicious of foreigners, particularly the Irish and consequently despised them. These sycophantic ideas were second nature to men like Roland, sucked in, they had become part of him with his mother's milk.

So, in fact, he reasoned that he would be actually flattering Magheen, stooping to her Irish'ry and offering her a chance to better herself were she to become the wife of an English gentleman. For the highest praise given to any alien was to say that "he might be taken for an Englishman."

Magheen was dressed, well hell! She did have something on. Captain Roland couldn't tell five minutes after she had left, nor did he care. Silk, satin, straw, it was all the same. But he wouldn't forget her smile. "The smile of an angel, one straight from heaven," he had commented to his Lieutenant.

She didn't smile broadly. All her smile was in her eyes, in her great brown eyes. But there was more to those eyes; her whole soul seemed mirrored in their glowing depths, and there saw innocence, purity, something left over from a time when the world was young, a wonderful simple goodness he did not know still existed.

Magheen's face, every feature, had been etched indelibly into his brain. The brows above those heavenly eyes were arched to perfection. The forehead under the wealth of golden hair was broad and intelligent. The hair, itself, was a mass of fine silk threads all wound in a high, loose coil that somehow failed to confine the corkscrew ends. Her nose, he had observed, was slender, aristocratic, sensitive. The mouth, those luscious lips, fairly begged to be tasted.

From whence came such beauty? Was there no flaw? Roland Chadwick certainly had detected none, for her complexion rivaled, if possible, the perfection of her features, pale, pink-and-white, smooth as the petal of a rose.

God! I'd be the envy of all England were I to ride with her at my side, he thought. Yes, he would allow a suitable time to elapse and then he would venture alone over to the castle. He felt that Magheen was not unmindful of his obvious attractions, but he wasn't too sure how deep her feelings went. Yet, as a soldier, it would be a challenge to woo and win such a lady.

So Roland Chadwick thought as he drifted off into a satisfied, complacent dream world. He had no reason, whatsoever, to think otherwise, for she had left him in high spirits promising to return soon.

"Of course, I'll see you again, Captain. It's been a most enjoyable, a very interesting and informative experience, I assure you."

He remembered every word she had uttered. Her silvery laugh still echoed in the deep recesses of his brain.

"Of course, I'll see you, see you, see you...."

Thirty-Three

Four horses stood saddled and ready in a grove of trees behind the castle. Magheen, dressed in a dark riding costume, came silently from a side door and quickly sought the protection of the laurel hedge that bounded the rose garden. Like the men, she wore a short sword, but in addition, she carried a small knife hidden in the cleavage of her shapely bosom. Before she mounted, she placed a flask in a pouch attached to her saddle.

She stroked her horse and spoke gently. "Not a geek out of you tonight, do you hear?" Then she turned to the men. "Ready?"

Their answers came softly.

"Let's ride in pairs a short distance apart. That way if any of us run into trouble, at least the others will be forewarned."

"Right ye are." Taig answered for himself and Rory.

"Then let's be off and God's speed," she said.

It was a good two-hour ride. The sky was overcast with low-flying dark clouds. No moon lit their path. No light shone from the rude cabins, the stately mansions, or the stalwart castles; the horses and their riders traveled unobserved.

It was well after midnight when they skirted the city of Waterford. All was quiet.

The rhythmic gallop of the horses' hoofs on the soft ground, the beating of her own heart, and in the distance the pounding of the surf upon the lovely rocks were the only sounds Magheen heard.

They approached the fort. It seemed to Magheen that the fortress, where His Majesty's garrison slept uneasily, was shrouded in a thicker blackness, an ominous foreboding pall!

A cold, clutching claw seemed to grip her heart and, in her stomach, Magheen felt a fierce, sharp pang.

They made their way to a sheltered cove about half a mile south of the fort. There they tethered the horses and borrowed a small boat. Padraig at once took the oars and guided the craft in the shallow waters that hugged the sandy estuaries of the area.

As soon as they reached the outcropping of rocks supporting the fort, Padraig pulled the boat into a sheltered inlet close by. It was decided that Padraig would remain with the boat. Quickly and silently, the others leaped ashore and made their way over the rocks in the direction of a subterranean passage leading into the dungeons of the fort. This passage was barred by a heavy door locked on the inside.

Magheen carried a lantern; its small flame was hidden by dark sliding shutters. The men carried the powder kegs, two apiece. They waited apprehensively in the shadows of the wall that surrounded the fort while the soldiers on sentry duty made their way to the other side. Then, with the agility of a squirrel, Taig climbed the rugged precipice that protected the eastern corner of the fort and soon scaled the top.

It took several more anxious moments before he had opened a small, rarely-used side gate to allow Magheen to enter the rather large courtyard. Then he went to join Rory outside at the subterranean entrance.

Magheen slipped easily through the small window she had unlatched the evening before. Unfortunately, as she tried to reach the ground, she lost her foothold and fell forward through the window to the flag floor below.

The drop was nothing, but the fall shook her. She felt a trickle of blood run down her arm, but she could not think of that now, a moment to recover, and then she got to her feet and made her way through the dark passage which led through the dungeons to the door at the other end where her friends awaited her. This door, in turn, gave access onto the beach; by that means she and her collaborators intended to escape when they had accomplished their extremely dangerous task.

Magheen tried the door, first the heavy bolt, it was badly rusted. She managed to pull it from its resting place, a hole chiseled into the wall. Then, as she inched the plank door toward her, its uneven panels sagged badly and rubbed against the stone flags, grating in protest. As she eased the heavy weight onto the rusty iron hinges, the sound echoed through the empty passages behind her.

"Be quick," she whispered to the two men who waited outside.

Taig and Rory slipped into the damp underground passage, each man carrying a keg of gunpowder. Magheen took hold of the lantern.

"We'll leave the door ajar. 'Tis the only way out for us tonight," she cautioned.

They maneuvered to a selected spot and deposited the kegs.

"You damned idiot!" Taig shouted.

"What the hell are ye talkin' about, man?" asked Rory.

"You've put that blasted powder in a pool of water, that's what I'm talkin' about."

"Water! Where's the water?"

"Right there, you amadan!"

"Oh, Christ Almighty. I never saw that damn pool. How the hell did that get there?"

"How de ye think, man? Don't ye know that the sea gets in here betimes. Well, that's the end of that keg."

"We've got three others. Let's get them set up an' get to hell out o' here."

Although Taig and Rory were two brave and patriotic Irishmen, they had their differences; indeed, it was rarely that they saw eye to eye. Magheen would normally not have the pair on the same mission, but on this particular occasion she hadn't been able to summon any others. She had to act quickly; any delay and she might run the risk of finding the window locked and her entrance to the fort barred.

The men set up the fuses while Magheen held the lantern; it took only a few minutes but it seemed like hours. At last the job was done, and it was time to light the fuses and exit the passage as quickly as possible.

Just as the second fuse was lit and the flame had started on its way slowly inch by inch consuming the waxed hemp lead, Magheen raised the lantern on high to light the way for their exit. The three started to leave when out of the darkness jumped Captain Roland and his Lieutenant.

He looked from one to the other. The three intruders, in turn, stared dumbfounded at their unexpected visitors.

Magheen reacted first.

"Who warned you?"

"You'd like to know, m'Lady, wouldn't you?" answered Roland. "Well, I'll not oblige."

He had reached Magheen's side. He stretched out his hand to grab her arm. "Now! Get him," she shouted to Taig.

She had hardly said the words when Taig and Rory hurled themselves on the lieutenant. There was a brief scuffle before the young man's body went limp.

By this time, the Captain had dragged Magheen along the passageway. They had reached a wider section where he thrust her against the wall.

A faint gleam of light from the newly risen moon penetrated the gloom and darkness from the open door at the end of the passage.

Roland Chadwick peered down into Magheen's beautiful face.

"I've longed for this moment since the first time I laid eyes on you. Too bad it's got to be under such dire conditions."

He caught her chin in his left hand as he nailed her to the wall with his strong body and was about to take possession of her trembling lips when Taig grabbed him from behind.

"Run for it, m'Lady!"

Magheen hesitated only a second before darting for the open door.

Behind, she heard the clash of sword on sword, on stone, on steel again, and then....

Magheen froze. "Oh, God! Why had I to see him again?" She had gained the open air. It seemed an eternity before Taig and Rory caught up with her as she made her way toward the beach where Padraig awaited, oars in hand, ready to pull away from the shore.

Only the lapping water with low sounds by the shore and the rhythmic splash of the oars were heard as the tiny skiff pulled out into the harbor. A few moments later the night sky was lit up and the surrounding rocks reverberated, even the waters of the bay seemed to swell, burst, and turn to blood.

"We've done a good night's work, I'd say." Taig rubbed his hands together as he watched the destruction the raging fires were causing.

"Yes," Magheen hissed almost to herself, "we've made them pay." She lowered her head and closed her eyes and her hand brushed her cheek. Rory saw, then looked away.

* * * *

The Butler household was struggling to maintain a semblance of normality. Life had to go on. Baby Dermud had to be cared for and protected. He was the hope of the future, and that was why Magheen had considered parting with her "precious prince" very soon.

"Come to Mama; come, darling." Little Dermud was playing with his puppy but Magheen needed to cuddle her baby. The sorrow, the grief that racked her was more than her young heart could, at times, bear. The toddler waddled toward his mother, and, as she watched him, her eyes glowed with pride. He looked so like his papa now, but he had her brown eyes. "Mama's beautiful baby." She kissed him tenderly. "Oh, God, to think you'll never see your dear papa again." Then she kissed him again and again.

"Papa, Papa, Mama, Mama."

"Come with Mama, we'll go for a walk together." Magheen bundled her son in his winter cloak and pulled a woolen cap over his golden curls, then laced up his little leather boots.

On her way out of the castle, Magheen called to her Irish wolfhound, "Come on, Cuchulain; come on, boy. We're going for a walk."

Her faithful friend was at her side almost instantly, looking into her face with alert, intelligent eyes, she felt the great love this animal had for her.

She left the house by the east door and headed for the open pasture land. These fields lay on a rise of ground that gave a view of the castle and the surrounding country for several miles. It was a fall day in 1547, and there was a crispness in the air. The first of the heavy frosts of winter had touched with tinsel the leafless trees and drooping ferns. A stray rabbit popped up in the path ahead of Magheen. "Look, Dermud, look at the bunny rabbit." The child's eyes opened wide. He quickened his step but the rabbit was gone. He looked at his mother.

"The baby rabbit has gone home to his mama." But the little fellow didn't understand. Soon his attention was captured by a fat worm wriggling its way through the short grass at his feet. He stopped to pick it up. "No, darling, let's see what the birdies have to say." Magheen took the child in her arms. She would have to walk more quickly if she were to keep warm. "Come, love, we'll go to the top of the hill and then we can see all the pretty things."

It was close to noon when they reached the crest of the hill. Magheen stopped to catch her breath and placed little Dermud down, then turned to take a look at the panoramic view below. Shrill cries disturbed the quiet air. She was too far away to see what might be the cause of the noise, but instinctively, fear gripped her heart.

"My God!" She clutched the infant to her and raced toward the castle. As she drew nearer, the stench of burning flesh filled her nostrils. Then she beheld a sight that would remain vivid in her mind till her dying day. The Sasanach! Soldiers! From the rear of the castle two servants came running at breakneck speed; the young women had reached the shrubbery separating the stables from the sweeping lawn, then from behind the hedge a mounted soldier appeared. He swung his sword with such force that all Magheen could see was the stricken forms, as in turn, the women met instantaneous deaths.

Magheen buried her baby's head in her breast and stifled the cry of horror that arose to her lips. "Mother of God! Is there no end to it? What am I to do?" Then realizing her position as Lady Butler, the awareness that she had a responsibility, not just to herself but for the large household, struck her. What would her uncle do were he in such a position? She remembered his calm composure, his self-assurance when the Sasanach came to Ballindee.

"Oh, dear God! Should I face these maniacs, or is it already too late to stop the carnage?" Magheen cried, her eyes searching the heavens.

"Mama, Mama."

Magheen looked at her little son. She had almost forgotten the precious burden pressed against her heart. "Yes, darling. Mama is here..." It was then that Magheen realized where her first duty lay. The child, Dermud's child, the only male Butler had to be saved. Magheen sped from the scene; she would alert the tenants on her way to the village chapel. This structure built on the outskirts of the village of Carrick-on-Suir was comparatively secluded, surrounded by a grove of elm trees. It had a belfry behind the main altar and there the little children, at least, would be safe, she concluded. Reaching the church about thirty minutes later, she was accompanied by half a dozen families composed mostly of women and children. The men, who happened to be near home, gathered what weapons they could lay their hands on. For the most part they were armed only with hay forks and crow bars. They banded together and headed for the castle.

"Kathleen, take care of little Dermud till I return," Magheen spoke to a young girl about twelve or thirteen years old.

"Yer not goin' back to the castle, Lady Magheen, are ye?" a woman asked.

"Yes, I must see to the safety of the Lady Eleanor and...and so many others."

"But, yer Ladyship. Beggin' yer pardon, what can ye do against armed soldiers?" asked another woman.

"I don't know, but I'll find some way. Please watch over my child, if anything should happen to me..." Magheen didn't finish but kissed her infant son. "Come Cuchulain," she called and sped across the fields in the direction of the castle.

Several barns were on fire and the smoke curled up in black clouds as the flames licked the damp outer stone walls. Magheen dashed through the orchard on the east side of the house and entered the castle by way of the conservatory. As yet, that part was untouched. From within, the clash of steel, the din of crashing breaking furniture, and the moanful cries of the wounded and dying contrasted with the eerie silence that hung in the passageway into which she now entered. She pushed on, a few yards farther, at the top of a flight of steps several soldiers were in consultation in the central hallway; it was plain that as long as the soldiers occupied the hall, escape was impossible on that side. Magheen retraced her steps to try another entrance. Out in the open once more, she stopped in her tracks as she witnessed the heroic stand made by one of her tenants against an armed soldier. The man, wielding only a pitch fork, was trying to defend himself. Seizing an opportunity, she picked up a stone, threw it with all her might and struck the soldier full in the face. Blood poured from his nose. The split second was all that was needed. Thrown off guard, the soldier lowered his sword, and in that instant the farmhand lunged forward, driving the three-pronged weapon into the enemy's heart.

Magheen had reached the servant's entrance at the rear of the castle; the door was wide open, the hallway empty. It was rather dark inside, but all the better, she would ascend by the back stairs to the upper story and hopefully gain the quarters of the Lady Eleanor before it was too late. As she reached the landing, Magheen knew her efforts were in vain; a quick glance into the bedroom confirmed her fears. The nude bodies of Lady Eleanor and her personal maid, Noreen, were sprawled across the large bed. Instinctively, Magheen put her hand to her open mouth to suppress the cry of horror that wrestled to escape, then she turned and ran from the room. Half-dazed, she raced through the wide corridors in the direction of her own rooms. Moll, Moll...Her heart kept on repeating, Oh, God, grant that I'm in time to save her. She turned a corner. A few steps in front of her stood a soldier, sword in hand. He had trapped Moll at the end of the hall against the long French windows and as Magheen watched, he drove his bloodied sword into the old woman's side. Mad with rage and bitter hatred, without thinking of her own safety, she leaped at the man. Cuchulain, sensing her intention, also bounded forward. The soldier was taken completely by surprise. The impact of her body and the dog's hurled the man forward against the windows, his sword fell from his grasp as he tried to break his fall, his left hand grabbed at the heavy red velvet drapes and brought them crashing down about his own head. Magheen leaped back just in time while Cuchulain grappled with the struggling figure. She seized the sword and thrust it home before the hated enemy had time to disentangle himself.

Kneeling beside her life-long friend, the only mother she ever knew, "Oh, God! Oh, dear God! How could you let this happen?" she cried.

Moll smiled, a small, weak smile. "Magheen, darlin', go...you can't...mustn't stay here. There's nothin' you can do...go...save yourself."

"I'll go get help. I'll get some of the men to carry you to the church. Many of the tenants are there already." She turned and fled down the back stairs with Cuchulain at her heels.

As she came to the ground floor, a soldier was making his way up the narrow stone stairs. Magheen froze, but Cuchulain never hesitated. He sprang at the man, straight for the jugular and ripped and tore till the opened artery spouted a fountain of blood. Then, as the soldier sank into the pool of his own blood, the great Irish wolfhound crumpled and went down also. Magheen moved toward the dog. He raised his head sensing her presence rather than seeing her; and then for a grief-stricken moment he opened his eyes and for the last time spoke his love.

Bending to caress his noble head, she saw the gaping gash where the sword of the Sasanach had pierced his loving breast.

By the time she reached the yard, the stables were ablaze. The trapped horses shrieked, and she looked about for someone to help her. Not a living soul in sight. Great God, what can I do? She paused beside the stone entrance that led into the orchard. Two soldiers emerged from the back of the castle and ran toward the conservatory.

Could they have seen her? She pressed herself against the cold granite and hardly dared to breathe. Would her heart betray her? Surely the sinister foe would hear the pounding. She heard soldiers panting as they ran past her on the other side of the low stone wall, clearly in pursuit of someone.

She had better quit the spot as quickly as possible; she told herself. Moll was right, there was nothing she could do. Magheen's mind turned to her baby, the only member of her family left alive, and for the first time since she had observed the cruel killings earlier that morning, she felt that she could no longer bear the strain. Sick, sick unto death, she reeled as if awakening from a long agonizing nightmare. Her body trembled convulsively, and every fiber quivered, perspiration oozed from every pore as she mustered the last vestige of her fast ebbing strength for the distance that remained between her and the church. Again the tumultuous pounding of her heart, the thumping beat reverberated in her ears like the hollow thump, thump of an ancient war drum.

How she finally reached the church, she never remembered.

But it was there that Padraig eventually found her, guarding the entrance to the belfry and clutching her baby to her trembling breast.

It was late in the afternoon when Padraig rode into the castle grounds. By that time, the soldiers had done their worst. Bodies were scattered in many directions in hideously contorted postures. The old butler, Liam, his aged head severed from his loyal body, had died, obviously defending the entrance to the only home he had known for over fifty years.

Padraig, horrified, decided to keep to the shelter of the trees on the north side of the castle. His first thought was for Magheen and her little son; perhaps there was still a chance. He circled the house, entered the back and made his way to Magheen's quarters. As he crossed the yard, a young soldier, frenzied by the kill, his right hand and sword dripping with blood, lunged toward him but he sidestepped and managed to trip the man. The soldier was no longer a match for Padraig who used the discarded sword to quickly dispatch his assailant. Now armed, he took care of several others as he fought his way to the north wing. The door was flung wide, but there was no sign of Magheen. Desperately, he raced from room to room till finally, at the end of the hallway, he found old Moll. Slumped against a chair, she was still gasping for breath. Padraig knelt beside her, she who had only kindness and love for all, deserved better than this, he thought. Carefully he took her in his arms...a low moan escaped. She opened her bloodshot eyes and recognizing Padraig, her cold, purple lips moved slightly. He carried her to a bed. Again she tried to focus on Padraig's face, an appealing look, then she tried to say a few words. Padraig bent over the dying woman.

"Magh-e-e.

"Yes, Magheen."

"Chur-ch."

"Magheen has gone to the church. Is that what you want me to know?" inquired Padraig.

Moll relaxed and Padraig knew there was nothing more he could do for her. He hastily kissed the cold forehead, grabbed the sword, and retraced his steps to the back of the castle.

When he reached the yard, the stables were smoldering ruins, flames were leaping from several rooms in the castle. Servants who had been struck down in the final moments of the savage assaults were struggling in agonizing death-throws; others, having fled, had been pursued by horse soldiers, cut down, and hacked to pieces. The carnage was more than Padraig's stomach could take. He braced himself against the gate at the entrance to a rose garden and in long deep heaves, he vomited till his mouth was coated in blood. Dizziness overcame him and a cold sweat bathed his muscular body. He shivered and clung to the supporting wall as the odious, revolting stench of burning human and animal flesh reached his nostrils. The shouting of the frenzied soldiers and the realization that the west wing of the castle was now a blazing inferno, aroused Padraig. Somehow, his numb limbs automatically guided him in the direction of the old church.

As he drew near, he found his path strewn with the dead and dying. Blood still flowed in rivulets and lodged in little pools around the victims. A woman ran from the church, a small child clutched to her breast, her long hair flying in the cold breeze. A husky soldier, his sword drenched to the hilt, was close behind. As he grabbed at her hair, she uttered one long piercing cry...then her head was severed. Still holding the bleeding mass, the enemy kicked the fallen trunk, which even in death refused to part with its precious treasure, and glaring at the pitiful child an instance, he then slashed out and stilled forever the whimpering sound.

Padraig closed his eyes; he didn't want to see anymore. But his mind would not be still, pictures of what must have happened inside the church goaded him to action.

He reached the entrance to the church just as a party of soldiers rode up; torches in hand, they trotted their horses inside. Old Father Ryan, with several older men from the village, strove to hinder their advance, but unarmed, they were no match for the calvary soldiers. Within a few minutes, a bloody orgy ensued; men, women, and helpless little children lay disemboweled.

Padraig managed to hack his way to the entrance of the belfry. Magheen was standing guard at the end of the wooden stairs leading to the tower, her little son clutched to her breast. Her face was frozen in a mask of terror and disbelief. Several other women and children were huddled behind on the steps, above mothers with infants.

"Padraig! Padraig, thank God you've come. I don't know how long more I can protect these babes," she pointed to the petrified children crouched behind her.

The altar linen was set to the torch; the smoke reached the confines of the belfry and soon the uncontrollable coughing alerted one of the soldiers. He dismounted and leaped through the flames licking the altar steps.

"Wat 'ave we 'ere," cried the illiterate veteran of a hundred atrocities. "More Irish beggary...vermin." He brandished his sword about to strike Magheen...

In an instant, Padraig leaped at him. Thrown off balance, he pitched forward, arms splaying and landed with a thud on the stone floor.

"Padraig, look out!" cried Magheen as a second soldier appeared.

Padraig swung around just in time to break the thrust of the crashing sword that would surely have cleft him in twain. But, in her effort to save Padraig, Magheen bore the onslaught of this second butcher. He moved in for the kill, driving his gory blade through the child clinging in terror and bewilderment to her breast. A ghastly shriek pierced the clatter of clanging steel and agonizing wails as Magheen fell to the ground.

As he heard Magheen's scream, Padraig leaped to her defense; his sword found its mark but not before the hated enemy had taken the life of yet another Butler.

"Christ Almighty! They've finished them all off!" was all he could say.

In the momentary lull which ensued, he gathered up mother and child and carried them out of the church. Night had enveloped the countryside in a hellish blackness.

For a moment he hesitated, it wouldn't be long before reinforcements arrived. He must make haste and find a cart; he intended to take Magheen and her baby home to Ballindee.

Thirty-Four

In the anguish and grief of the moment, Padraig assumed that mother and child were dead and fearing the advent of reinforcements bent on total destruction, of executing the scorched earth policy, he had hastily quit the area with his previous burdens.

Doggedly, through sheer willpower, he fought exhaustion, sleep, hunger, and the elements for several hours before he arrived in the village of Bannon where he stopped at a cottage and knocked on the door. A bolt from within was drawn and a burly middle-aged man faced him.

"Glory be to God!" he looked Padraig up and down, horror turning to fear. "Don't ye dare come any further."

In the dim light of the early morning, Padraig saw for the first time what had alarmed the stranger: torn and tattered clothes stiff with mud and blood, a gaping wound in his left arm. He could only guess at how his unkept hair and beard appeared.

"In God's name, let me explain," he begged.

Liam Mooney called his wife, Cait, before he went to help Padraig carry the bodies into the cabin. The infant was immediately wrapped in a sheet and laid on the dresser. As they gently lay Magheen on a straw mattress, she moaned.

"Christ Almighty! She's alive!" cried Liam.

"Alive! My God!" Padraig's mighty frame trembled and cold sweat dripped from his brow.

They carried her close to the hearth. Cait bent to examine the blue-grey body. As she drew the dark crusted bodice aside exposing the ugly wound just over her heart, Magheen again moaned...

weak, faint. Embedded in a congealed mass of blood, Hugo's ring was eventually discovered. Cait handed it to Padraig saying, "You'd best keep this safe…must be of great import to be hid close to her heart.

"We've got to save her," said Cait. As she set to work applying a warming stone to her icy feet and then rubbing her cold hands and arms with heated oil, she slowly coaxed the life back into her limbs. After she had bathed the frail body, she placed a warm towel to the bruised forehead.

As soon as Padraig saw that his precious Magheen was regaining a little color, he slumped to the floor utterly exhausted and in that position slept for the next ten hours.

It was during this period that Magheen lost her second child, a little girl, stillborn.

Five days later, Magheen, though still weak and unable to walk, was transported to Ballindee. Padraig could not rest till he saw her safe in her old home; he was convinced that once there she would quickly regain both health and strength.

But as the weeks passed and she didn't recover as rapidly as she should, Padraig's mother, who was now taking care of her, was most anxious. Then one evening while Padraig was keeping watch by her bedside, and his mother had left to prepare the evening meal, Magheen opened her beautiful eyes and looked around as if for something or someone.

"Can I be getting you something?" Padraig asked anxiously.

"Hugo…where's Hugo?" she asked.

"Hu…ah, yes…of course…You want Hugo?"

"Yes," the word was a whisper.

"Then we'll have to find him, won't we."

It took a week for Padraig to journey to France and several more days to reach Chantille, but he gave himself no rest till he arrived at the chateau. Hugo soon learned all he needed to know. He suggested that Padraig remain in France for a few days to rest while he, himself, would leave within the hour and hopefully obtain passage on one of the many Irish ships that sailed between the two countries.

He docked in Lough Swilly and decided to ride night and day in order to get to Ballindee in the shortest possible time. Padraig had taken care to furnish him with the O'Sullivan address lest he require a night's rest or a change of horses.

By the time Hugo arrived, Magheen had lapsed into a fitful sleep.

"Thank God you've come, Sir." Mrs. O'Toole crossed herself and led him straightway to the bedside.

Hugo's heart missed a beat, and the blood drained from his face as he beheld the shadow of what was once the loveliest maid he had ever seen. He threw himself on his knees beside the bed, thrust his head in his hands and wept bitterly.

"Oh, God, I'm too late. Je suis trop tard."

Several minutes later, he raised his tear-drenched face to look again on his beloved Magheen. With eyes closed, her face resembled an alabaster mask. Her frail body was motionless. He reached for her hand and took it gently between his own, warm and strong.

"Oh, Magheen, Magheen, don't leave me. I'm here. I love you," he spoke between sobs, fearing she didn't hear him.

Magheen remained still, hardly breathing. To reassure himself that her spirit had not already departed, he took her slender wrist between his fingers. The faint pulse was detectable.

Morning was creeping into the cove. Silver shafts of light spilt down through the rain-filled clouds. The honey-colored waves spewed frothing sprays from a jade-dyed sea high onto the creamy strand. Hugo stood at the big recessed window in Magheen's room. All was quiet.

He had not left her side since his arrival three days before and he was dog-tired. He slumped down into Tom O'Connor's leather chair which had been brought from the library for his comfort. Then, a faint low moan, almost an inaudible sound, brought him to his knees beside her bed.

"Darling, Magheen, darling, I'm here. I need you, I love you. Oh, Magheen, don't leave me. Not again," Hugo's pleading was directed half to himself, half to the semiconscious form. He took her cold hand and pressed it to his burning lips.

"Magheen, my darling. Je t'aime, je t'aime," he whispered. "Ma petite fleur."

Slowly Magheen turned her beautiful eyes in the direction of the voice. At first there was no sign of recognition. Then gradually a flicker of understanding appeared, her grasp tightened and a tear arose and glistened a moment in the corner of one eye.

He had come for her at last, her first, her only love! He had uttered the words she had waited so long to hear...blessed words as from afar, coming out of a great void, a place of darkness. Magheen groped for she knew not what, but the voice, the gentle words, "I love you," gave her a new strength, sent a warmth through the cold body that had lain inert for so long. "Beloved, my own. Thank God you've come back to me." Then he buried his head in the quilt and wept.

Patiently, lovingly, Hugo tended Magheen, encouraging her to eat, giving her courage and a feeling of optimism. At first feeding her, then slowly helping her to help herself. Soon she was able to sit up propped by pillows. A new light was apparent in her eyes and her appetite was improving, but the road to complete recovery was painfully slow.

Spring came early to the western lands. Newborn lambs frisked about in stone-fenced meadows, or gamboled over moss-covered rocks to graze on tufted slopes. Daffodils and buttercups made golden patterns in the waving grasses and the air was sweet with the scent of wild flowers, while lark and blackbird vied with each other in full-throated song.

Hugo and Magheen, strolling through the boreens, breathed with satisfaction the clear, warm air and enjoyed the many faces of nature. Slowly but surely the roses reappeared in her lovely cheeks. She was regaining her physical health and strength, but the old lighthearted vivacious Magheen was not yet in evidence.

Toward the end of May, the loveliest time of the year, word went forth. There would be a marriage to which all were invited. The ceremony took place, to the great joy of everyone, in the modest church overlooking the silver Atlantic and the whole village took a holiday to honor the occasion.

Feasting and merrymaking lasted well into the night as Inis Fail rang with laughter and music once again. And when the early hours of the morning came and tired families gradually slipped away leaving Magheen and Hugo all alone, they lay side by side, their forces spent. Then Hugo put his arms around her and drew her close, kissing her the while, and murmured, "We were meant for each other, you and I, my lovely Magheen."

And, in the sweet silence of that summer night, he knew her love again and again with only the crickets and the warm breezes to witness their sweet embraces.

Soon afterward arrangements were made with Padraig and his mother to take care of Inis Fail and so the gentle "giant" of Ballindee lived in quiet enjoyment of the house and lands for many years.

"I will make you happy, Magheen, darling. You will love our home in fair Chantilly."

"I know that, Hugo, my love," she said as she stood watching the lapping waters. Was all great joy born of pain? Her Hugo had come for her, yes, he had come back...but at what a price! She had lost so much, so very much to gain this love, and even as she clung to a faint new hope, she, Magheen Ni Neill, had to sacrifice again!

How could Hugo understand? How could he know the terrible yearnings that fought deep within her soul: the cries of pain and anguish she would hear forever in her heart...the cry of the child of her womb, the cry of her dead husband, the cry of the country of her birth.

Magheen was a true daughter of Ireland. Magheen proud and self-willed; Magheen passionate and wild; Magheen brave, strong, enduring; Magheen always beautiful; Magheen frail, wayward, impulsive; Magheen ever hopeful. She had given all for her country...husband, son, home. Now the final sacrifice was asked...that of country itself. She would leave like so many others to find a temporary abode. She would walk no more on the coral strand; the tang of the gorse and heather would be left far behind; the song of blackbird and thrush would never again thrill her heart.

For a short while she would know peace, security, love, but always hope...for the day would come, would surely come, when her children or her children's children would chase each other over the clean white sands and across the boglands of Ballindee. In Inis Fail or in the tiny thatched cottages by the sea, they would learn to love the language, the customs, and the land that bore Magheen.

A SELECTED BIBLIOGRAPHY

Chamberlin, E.R. *Everyday Life in Renaissance Times*. London: Carousel Books, Cavendish House. 1973.

Dalton, E.A. *History of Ireland*. London: The Gresham Publishing Co. 1912. (MAP of Ireland pg. 432)

Gluyas, Constance. *The King's Brat*. New Jersey: Prentice-Hall, Inc. 1972.

Howarth, D. *The Voyage of the Armada*. New York: Penguin Books Ltd. 1981.

MacManus, Seumas. *The Story of the Irish Race*. Old Greenwich: The Devin-Adair Co. 1979.

McKendrick, M. *Spain*. New York: American Heritage Publishing Co. Inc. 1972.

Moody, T.W. and Martin, F.X. *The Course of Irish History*. Cork: The Mercier Press 1967.

Rook, D. *Run Wild, Run Free*: New York: Scholastic Book Services 1969.

Smith, L.B. *Henry VIII*. Suffolk: The Chaucer Press, Ltd. 1971.